To my mother and grandmothers
and all the women they burned before us

An Introduction

There's no such thing as witches, but there used to be.

It used to be the air was so thick with magic you could taste it on your tongue like ash. Witches lurked in every tangled wood and waited at every midnight-crossroad with sharp-toothed smiles. They conversed with dragons on lonely mountaintops and rode rowan-wood brooms across full moons; they charmed the stars to dance beside them on the solstice and rode to battle with familiars at their heels. It used to be witches were wild as crows and fearless as foxes, because magic blazed bright and the night was theirs.

But then came the plague and the purges. The dragons were slain and the witches were burned and the night belonged to men with torches and crosses.

Witching isn't all gone, of course. My grandmother, Mama Mags, says they can't ever kill magic because it beats like a great red heartbeat on the other side of everything, that if you close your eyes you can feel it thrumming beneath the soles of your feet, *thumpthumpthump*. It's just a lot better-behaved than it used to be.

Most respectable folk can't even light a candle with witching, these days, but us poor folk still dabble here and there. *Witch-blood runs thick in the sewers*, the saying goes. Back home every mama teaches her daughters a few little charms to keep the soup-pot from boiling over or make the peonies bloom out of season. Every daddy teaches his sons how to spell ax-handles against breaking and rooftops against leaking.

Our daddy never taught us shit, except what a fox teaches chickens— how to run, how to tremble, how to outlive the bastard—and our mama died before she could teach us much of anything. But we had Mama

Mags, our mother's mother, and she didn't fool around with soup-pots and flowers.

The preacher back home says it was God's will that purged the witches from the world. He says women are sinful by nature and that magic in their hands turns naturally to rot and ruin, like the first witch Eve who poisoned the Garden and doomed mankind, like her daughters' daughters who poisoned the world with the plague. He says the purges purified the earth and shepherded us into the modern era of Gatling guns and steamboats, and the Indians and Africans ought to be thanking us on their knees for freeing them from their own savage magics.

Mama Mags said that was horseshit, and that wickedness was like beauty: in the eye of the beholder. She said proper witching is just a conversation with that red heartbeat, which only ever takes three things: the will to listen to it, the words to speak with it, and the way to let it into the world. The will, the words, and the way.

She taught us everything important comes in threes: little pigs, billy goats gruff, chances to guess unguessable names. Sisters.

There were three of us Eastwood sisters, me and Agnes and Bella, so maybe they'll tell our story like a witch-tale. *Once upon a time there were three sisters.* Mags would like that, I think—she always said nobody paid enough attention to witch-tales and whatnot, the stories grannies tell their babies, the secret rhymes children chant among themselves, the songs women sing as they work.

Or maybe they won't tell our story at all, because it isn't finished yet. Maybe we're just the very beginning, and all the fuss and mess we made was nothing but the first strike of the flint, the first shower of sparks.

There's still no such thing as witches.

But there will be.

PART ONE

THE
WAYWARD
SISTERS

1

A tangled web she weaves
When she wishes to deceive.

A spell to distract and dismay, requiring cobweb gathered on the
new moon & a pricked finger

Once upon a time there were three sisters.

James Juniper Eastwood was the youngest, with hair as ragged and black as crow feathers. She was the wildest of the three. The canny one, the feral one, the one with torn skirts and scraped knees and a green glitter in her eyes, like summer-light through leaves. She knew where the whip-poor-wills nested and the foxes denned; she could find her way home at midnight on the new moon.

But on the spring equinox of 1893, James Juniper is lost.

She limps off the train with her legs still humming from the rattle and clack of the journey, leaning heavy on her red-cedar staff, and doesn't know which way to turn. Her plan only had two steps—step one, *run*, and step two, *keep running*—and now she's two hundred miles from home with nothing but loose change and witch-ways in her pockets and no place to go.

She sways on the platform, buffeted and jostled by folk who have plenty of someplaces to go. Steam hisses and swirls from the engine, curling catlike around her skirts. Posters and ads flutter on the wall. One of them is a list of New Salem city ordinances and the associated fines for littering, profanity, debauchery, indecency, and vagrancy. One of them shows an irritable-looking Lady Liberty with her fist raised into the air and invites ALL LADIES WHO TIRE OF TYRANNY to attend the New Salem Women's Association rally in St. George's Square at six o'clock on the equinox.

One of them shows Juniper's own face in blurred black and white above the words MISS JAMES JUNIPER EASTWOOD. SEVEN-TEEN YEARS OF AGE, WANTED FOR MURDER & SUS-PECTED WITCHCRAFT.

Hell. They must have found him. She'd thought burning the house would muddy things a little more.

Juniper meets her own eyes on the poster and pulls her cloak's hood a little higher.

Boots ring dully on the platform: a man in a neat black uniform strolls toward her, baton slap-slapping in his palm, eyes narrowed.

Juniper gives him her best wide-eyed smile, hand sweating on her staff. "Morning, mister. I'm headed to..." She needs a purpose, a somewhere-to-be. Her eyes flick to the irritable Lady Liberty poster. "St. George's Square. Could you tell me how to get there?" She squeezes her accent for every country cent it's worth, pooling her vowels like spilled honey.

The officer looks her up and down: hacked-off hair scraping against her jaw, dirt-seamed knuckles, muddy boots. He grunts a mean laugh. "Saints save us, even the hicks want the vote."

Juniper's never thought much about voting or suffrage or women's rights, but his tone makes her chin jerk up. "That a crime?"

It's only after the words come whipping out of her mouth that Juni-per reflects on how unwise it is to antagonize an officer of the law.

Particularly when there is a poster with your face on it directly behind the officer's head.

That temper will get you burnt at the damn stake, Mama Mags used to tell her. *A wise woman keeps her burning on the inside.* But Bella was the wise one, and she left home a long time ago.

Sweat stings Juniper's neck, nettle-sharp. She watches the veins purpling in the officer's throat, sees the silver-shined buttons straining on his chest, and slides her hands into her skirt pockets. Her fingers find a pair of candle-stubs and a pitch pine wand; a horseshoe nail and a silver tangle of cobweb; a pair of snake's teeth she swears she won't use again.

Heat gathers in her palms; words wait in her throat.

Maybe the officer won't recognize her, with her hair cut short and her cloak hood pulled high. Maybe he'll just yell and stomp like a ruffled rooster and let her go. Or maybe he'll haul her into the station and she'll end up swinging from a New Salem scaffold with the witchmark drawn on her chest in clotted ash. Juniper declines to wait and find out.

The will. Heat is already boiling up her wrists, licking like whiskey through her veins.

The words. They singe her tongue as she whispers them into the clatter and noise of the station. "A tangled web she weaves—"

The way. Juniper pricks her thumb on the nail and holds the spiderweb tight.

She feels the magic flick into the world, a cinder spit from some great unseen fire, and the officer claws at his own face. He swears and sputters as if he's stumbled face-first into a cobweb. Passersby are pointing, beginning to laugh.

Juniper slips away while he's still swiping at his eyes. A puff of steam, a passing crowd of railroad workers with their lunch pails swinging at their sides, and she's out the station doors. She runs in her hitching fashion, staff clacking on cobbles.

Growing up, Juniper had imagined New Salem as something like Heaven, if Heaven had trolleys and gas-lamps—bright and clean and rich, far removed from the sin of Old Salem—but now she finds it chilly and colorless, as if all that clean living has leached the shine out of everything. The buildings are all grayish and sober, without so much as a flower-box or calico curtain peeking through the windows. The people are grayish and sober, too, their expressions suggesting each of them is on their way to an urgent but troublesome task, their collars starched and their skirts buttoned tight.

Maybe it's the absence of witching; Mags said magic invited a certain amount of mess, which was why the honeysuckle grew three times as fast around her house and songbirds roosted under her eaves no matter the season. In New Salem—the City Without Sin, where the trolleys run on time and every street wears a Saint's name—the only birds are pigeons and the only green is the faint shine of slime in the gutters.

A trolley jangles past several inches from Juniper's toes and its driver swears at her. Juniper swears back.

She keeps going because there's no place to stop. There are no mossy stumps or blue pine groves; every corner and stoop is filled up with people. Workers and maids, priests and officers, men with pocket-watches and ladies with big hats and children selling buns and newspapers and shriveled-up flowers. Juniper tries asking directions twice but the answers are baffling, riddle-like (follow St. Vincent's to Fourth-and-Winthrop, cross the Thorn, and head straight). Within an hour she's been invited to a boxing match, accosted by a gentleman who wants to discuss the relationship between the equinox and the end-times, and given a map that has nothing marked on it but thirty-nine churches.

Juniper stares down at the map, knotted and foreign and unhelpful, and wants to go the hell home.

Home is twenty-three acres on the west side of the Big Sandy River.

Home is dogwoods blooming like pink-tipped pearls in the deep woods and the sharp smell of spring onions underfoot, the overgrown patch where the old barn burned and the mountainside so green and wet and alive it makes her eyes ache. Home is the place that beats like a second heart behind Juniper's ribs.

Home was her sisters, once. But they left and never came back— never even sent so much as a two-cent postcard—and now neither will Juniper.

Red rage swells in Juniper's chest. She crumples the map in her fist and keeps walking because it's either run or set something on fire, and she already did that.

She walks faster, faster, stumbling a little on her bad leg, shouldering past wide bustles and fashionable half-capes, following nothing but her own heartbeat and perhaps the faintest thread of something else.

She passes apothecaries and grocers and an entire shop just for shoes. Another one for hats, with a window full of faceless heads covered in lace and froth and frippery. A cemetery that sprawls like a separate city behind a high iron fence, its lawn clipped short and its headstones straight as stone soldiers. Juniper's eye is drawn to the blighted, barren witch-yard at its edges, where the ashes of the condemned are salted and spread; nothing grows in the yard but a single hawthorn, knobbled as a knuckle.

She crosses a bridge stretched over a river the color of day-old gravy. The city grows taller and grayer around her, the light swallowed by limestone buildings with domes and columns and men in suits guarding the entrances. Even the trolleys are on their best behavior, gliding past on smooth rails.

The street pours into a broad square. Linden trees line its edges, pruned into unnatural sameness, and people flock around the center.

"—why, we ask, should women wait in the shadows while their fathers and husbands determine our fates? Why should we—we doting mothers, we beloved sisters, we treasured daughters—be barred from that most fundamental of rights: the right to vote?"

The voice is urgent and piercing, rising high above the city rumble. Juniper sees a woman standing in the middle of the square wearing a white-curled wig like some small, unfortunate animal pinned to her head. A bronze Saint George glares down at her and women press near her, waving signs and banners.

Juniper figures she's found St. George's Square and the New Salem Women's Association rally after all.

She's never seen a real live suffragist. In the Sunday cartoons they're drawn scraggle-haired and long-nosed, suspiciously witchy. But these women don't look much like witches. They look more like the models in Ivory soap ads, all puffed and white and fancy. Their dresses are ironed and pleated, their hats feathered, their shoes shined and smart.

They part around Juniper as she shoves forward, looking sideways at the seasick roll of her gait, the Crow County mud still clinging to her hem. She doesn't notice; her eyes are on the strident little woman at the foot of the statue. A badge on her chest reads *Miss Cady Stone, NSWA President*.

"It seems that our elected politicians disagree with the Constitution, which grants us certain inalienable rights. It seems that Mayor Worthington disagrees even with our benevolent God, who created us all equal."

The woman keeps talking, and Juniper keeps listening. She talks about the ballot box and the mayoral election in November and the importance of self-determination. She talks about the olden-times when women were queens and scholars and knights. She talks about justice and equal rights and fair shares.

Juniper doesn't follow all the details—she stopped going to Miss Hurston's one-room schoolhouse at ten because after her sisters left there was no one to make her go—but she understands what

Miss Stone is asking. She's asking: *Aren't you tired yet?* Of being cast down and cast aside? Of making do with crumbs when once we wore crowns?

She's asking: *Aren't you angry yet?*

And oh, Juniper is. At her mama for dying too soon and her daddy for not dying sooner. At her dumbshit cousin for getting the land that should have been hers. At her sisters for leaving and herself for missing them. At the whole Saints-damned world.

Juniper feels like a soldier with a loaded rifle, finally shown something she can shoot. Like a girl with a lit match, finally shown something she can burn.

There are women standing on either side of her, waving signs and filling in all the pauses with *hear-hears*, their faces full of bright hunger. For a second Juniper pretends she's standing shoulder-to-shoulder with her sisters again and she feels the hollowed-out place they left behind them, that emptiness so vast even fury can't quite fill it.

She wonders what they would say if they could see her now. Agnes would worry, always trying to be the mother they didn't have. Bella would ask six dozen questions.

Mags would say: *Girls who go looking for trouble usually find it.*

Her daddy would say: *Don't forget what you are, girl.* Then he would toss her down in the worm-eaten dark and hiss the answer: *Nothing.*

Juniper doesn't realize she's bitten her lip until she tastes blood. She spits and hears a faint hiss as it lands, like grease in a hot pan.

The wind rises.

It rushes through the square, midnight-cool and mischievous, fluttering the pages of Miss Cady Stone's notes. It smells wild and sweet, half-familiar, like Mama Mags's house on the solstice. Like earth and char and old magic. Like the small, feral roses that bloomed in the deep woods.

Miss Stone stops talking. The crowd clutches their hats and cloak-strings, squinting upward. A mousy-looking girl near Juniper fusses with a lacy umbrella, as if she thinks this is a mundane storm that can be taken care of with mundane means. Juniper hears crows and jays calling in the distance, sharp and savage, and knows better.

She whirls, looking for the witch behind the working—

And the world comes unsewn.

2

Sugar and spice
And everything nice.

A spell to soothe a bad temper, requiring a pinch of sugar &
spring sunshine

Agnes Amaranth Eastwood was the middle sister, with hair as
shining and black as a hawk's eye. She was the strongest of the
three. The unflinching one, the steady one, the one that knew how to
work and keep working, tireless as the tide.

But on the spring equinox of 1893, she is weak.

The shift bell rings and Agnes sags against her loom, listening to
the tick and hiss of cooling metal and the rising babble of the mill-girls.
Cotton-dust coats her tongue and gums her eyes; her limbs ache and
rattle, worn out from too many extra shifts in a row.

One of those nasty fevers is spreading through New Salem's dis-
orderly edges, festering in the boarding houses and barrooms of West
Babel, and every third girl is hacking her lungs up in a bed at St. Charity's. Demand is high, too, because one of the other mills caught fire last
week.

Agnes heard women had leapt from the windows, falling to the streets like comets trailing smoke and ash. All week her dreams have been crimson, full of the wet pop of burning flesh, except it's a memory and not a dream at all, and she wakes reaching for her sisters who aren't there.

The other girls are filing out, gossiping and jostling. *You headed to the rally?* A huff of laughter. *I got better ways to waste my time.* Agnes has worked at the Baldwin Brothers Bonded Mill for a handful of years now, but she doesn't know their names.

She used to learn their names. When she first came to New Salem, Agnes had a tendency to collect strays—the too-skinny girls who slept on the boarding-house floor because they couldn't afford beds, the too-quiet girls with bruises around their wrists. Agnes tucked them all under her scrawny wing as if each of them were the sisters she left behind. There was one girl whose hair she brushed every morning before work, thirty strokes, like she used to do for Juniper.

She found work as a night-nurse at the Home for Lost Angels. She spent long shifts soothing babies who couldn't be soothed, loving children she shouldn't love, dreaming about a big house with sunny windows and enough beds for each little Lost Angel. One night she showed up to work to find half her babies had been shipped out west to be adopted by settler families hungry for helping hands.

She stood among the empty beds, hands trembling, remembering what her Mama Mags told her: *Every woman draws a circle around herself. Sometimes she has to be the only thing inside it.*

Agnes quit the orphanage. She told the boarding-house girl to brush her own damn hair and started work at the Baldwin Brothers. She figured you couldn't love a cotton mill.

The bell clangs again and Agnes unpeels her forehead from the loom. The floor boss leers idly as the girls file past, reaching for skirts and blouses with pinching fingers. He doesn't reach for Agnes. On her first shift Mr. Malton had cornered her behind the cotton bales—she was always the pretty one, all shining hair and hips—but Mags taught her granddaughters ways to discourage that kind of horseshit. Since then Mr. Malton saves his leers for other girls.

Agnes watches the new girl flinch as she passes him, her shoulders sloped with shame. She looks away.

The alley air tastes clean and bright after the humid dark of the mill. Agnes turns west up St. Jude's, headed home—well, not home, just the moldy little room she rents in the South Sybil boarding house, which smells like boiled cabbage no matter what she cooks—until she sees the man waiting at the corner.

Hair slicked earnestly to one side, cap clutched in nervous hands. Wholesome good looks, clean fingernails, a weak chin you don't notice at first: Floyd Matthews.

Oh hell. His eyes are pleading at her, his mouth half-open to call her name, but Agnes fixes her gaze on the apron-strings of the woman in front of her and hopes he'll just give up and find some other mill-girl to pine after.

A scuffed boot appears in her path, followed by an outstretched hand. She wishes she didn't remember so precisely how that hand felt against her skin, smooth and soft, unscarred.

"Aggie, love, talk to me." What's so hard about calling a woman by her full name? Why do men always want to give you some smaller, sweeter name than the one your mama gave you?

"I already said my piece, Floyd."

She tries to edge past him but he puts his hands on her shoulders, imploring. "I don't understand! Why would you turn me down? I could take you out of this place"—he waves a soft hand at the dim alleys and sooty brick of the west side—"and make an honest woman out of you. I could give you anything you want!" He sounds bewildered, like his proposal was a mathematical equation and Agnes produced the incorrect response. Like a nice boy told *no* for the first time in his nice life.

She sighs at him, aware that the other girls are pausing on the street, turning to look at them. "You can't give me what I want, Floyd." Agnes doesn't know what she wants, exactly, but it's not Floyd Matthews or his little gold ring.

Floyd gives her a little shake. "But I *love* you!"

Oh, Agnes doubts the hell out of that. He loves pieces of her—the thunder-blue of her eyes, the full moon-glow of her breasts in the dark—but he never even met most of her. If he peeled back her pretty skin he'd find nothing soft or sweet at all, just busted glass and ashes and the desperate, animal will to stay alive.

Agnes removes Floyd's hands from her shoulders, gently. "I'm sorry."

She strides down St. Mary's with his voice rising behind her, pleading, desperate. His pleas curdle into cruelty soon enough. He curses her, calls her a witch and a whore and a hundred other names she learned from her daddy first. She doesn't turn back.

One of the other mill workers, a broad woman with a heavy accent, offers Agnes a nod as she passes and grunts "boys, eh" in the same tone she might say "fleas" or "piss-stains," and Agnes almost smiles at her before she catches herself.

She keeps walking. She dreams as she walks: a home of her own, so big she has extra beds just for guests. She'll write her little sister another letter: *You've got someplace to run, if you want it.* Maybe this time she would answer. Maybe the two of them could be family again.

It's a stupid dream.

Agnes learned young that you have a family right up until you don't. You take care of people right up until you can't, until you have to choose between staying and surviving.

By the time she turns on South Sybil the boarding house is lit up, noisy with the evening talk of working girls and unwed women. Agnes finds her feet carrying her past it, even though her back aches and her stomach is sour and her breasts feel heavy, achy. She winds up Spinner's Row and down St. Lamentation Avenue, leaving the factories and tenements and three dozen languages of West Babel behind her, lured forward by a strange, half-imagined tugging behind her ribs.

She buys a hot pie from a cart. A block later she throws it away, acid in her throat.

She heads uptown without quite admitting it to herself. She crosses the Thorn and the buildings get grander and farther apart, the faded advertisements and tattered playbills replaced by fresh campaign posters: *Clement Hughes for a Safer Salem! Gideon Hill: Our Light Against the Darkness!*

She falls in behind a flock of pinch-lipped women wearing white sashes with CHRISTIAN WOMEN'S UNION embroidered on one side and WOMEN WITHOUT SIN on the other.

Agnes has heard of them. They're always hassling street-witches and trying to save girls from the whorehouse whether or not they want to be saved (they mostly don't). Their leader is named something like Purity or Grace, one of those ladylike virtues. Agnes figures she's the one walking out front—slender, white-gloved, her hair piled up in a perfect Gibson Girl pouf—wearing an expression suggesting she's Joan of Arc's tight-laced sister. Agnes would bet a silver dollar that her maid uses a little witching to keep her gown unwrinkled and her hair neat.

She wonders what Mama Mags would say if she could see them. Juniper would growl. Bella would have her nose in a book.

Agnes doesn't know why she's thinking of her sisters; she hasn't in years, not since the day she drew her circle and left them standing on the outside of it.

The street ends at St. George's Square, framed by City Hall and the College, and the white-sashed ladies begin stamping around the perimeter, chanting Bible verses and scowling at the gathering of suffragists in the center. Agnes should turn around and go back to South Sybil, but she lingers.

A woman in a white wig is speechifying about women's rights and women's votes and women's history, about taking on the mantles of their fore-mothers and marching forward arm in arm.

And Saints save her, Agnes wishes it was real. That she could just wave a sign or shout a slogan and step into a better world, one where she could be more than a daughter or a mother or a wife. Where she could be something instead of nothing.

Don't forget what you are.

But Agnes hasn't believed in witch-tales since she was a little girl.

She is turning away, heading back to the boarding house, when the wind whips her skirts sideways and tugs her hair loose from its braid.

It smells foreign, green, un-city-like. It reminds Agnes of the dark interior of Mama Mags's house, hung with herbs and the bones of small creatures, of wild roses in the woods. The wind pulls at her, searching or asking, and her breasts ache in strange answer. Something wet and greasy dampens her dress-front and drips to the cobbles below. Something the color of bone or pearl.

Or—milk.

Agnes stares at the splattered drops like a woman watching a runaway carriage come hurtling toward her. Dates and numbers skitter behind her eyes as she counts up the days since Floyd lay beside her in the dark, his palm sliding smooth down her belly, laughing. *What's the harm, Aggie?*

No harm at all. For him.

Before Agnes can do more than curse Floyd Matthews and his soft hands six ways to Sunday, heat comes searing up her spine. It licks up her neck, rising like a fever.

Reality splits.

A ragged hole hangs in the air, that wild wind rushing through it. Another sky gleams dark on the other side, like skin glimpsed through torn cloth, and then the hole is growing, tearing wide and letting that other-sky pour through. The evening gray of New Salem is swallowed by star-spattered night.

In that night stands a tower.

Ancient, half-eaten by climbing roses and ivy, taller than the Courthouse or College on either side of the square. Dark, gnarled trees surround it, like the feral cousins of the lindens in their neat rows, and the sky above it fills with the dark tatter of wings.

For a moment the square stands in eerie, brittle silence, mesmerized by the strange stars and circling crows. Agnes pants, her blood still boiling, her heart inexplicably lifting.

Then someone screams. The stillness shatters. The crowd floods toward Agnes in a screeching horde, skirts and hats clutched tight. She braces her shoulders and wraps her arms around her belly, as if she can protect the fragile thing taking root inside her. As if she wants to.

She should turn and follow the crowd, should run from that strange tower and whatever power called it here, but she doesn't. She staggers toward the center of the square instead, following some invisible pull—

And the world mends itself.

3

The wayward sisters, hand in hand,
Burned and bound, our stolen crown,
But what is lost, that can't be found?

Purpose unknown

Beatrice Belladonna Eastwood was the oldest sister, with hair like owl feathers: soft and dark, streaked with early gray. She was the wisest of the three. The quiet one, the listening one, the one who knew the feel of a book's spine in her palm and the weight of words in the air.

But on the spring equinox of 1893, she is a fool.

She sits in the dust-specked light of her little office in the East Wing of the Salem College Library, flipping furtively through a newly donated first-edition copy of the Sisters Grimm's *Children and Household Witch-Tales* (1812). She already knows the stories, knows them so well she dreams in once-upon-a-times and sets of three, but she's never held a first edition in her own two hands. It has a weight to it, as if the Sisters Grimm tucked more than paper and ink inside it.

Beatrice flicks to the last page and pauses. Someone has added a verse at the end of the last tale, hand-lettered and faded.

The wayward sisters, hand in hand,
Burned and bound, our stolen crown,
But what is lost, that can't be found?

There are more lines below these, but they're lost to the blotches and stains of time.

It isn't especially strange to find words written in the back of an old book; Beatrice has been a librarian for five years and has seen much worse, including a patron who used a raw strip of bacon as a bookmark. But it is a little strange that Beatrice recognizes these words, that she and her sisters sang them when they were little girls back in Crow County.

Beatrice always thought it was one of Mama Mags's nonsense-songs, a silly rhyme she made up to keep her granddaughters busy while she plucked rooster feathers or bottled jezebel-root. But here it is, scrawled in an old book of witch-tales.

Beatrice flips several onion-skin pages and finds the title of the last tale printed in scrolling script, surrounded by a dark tangle of ivy: *The Tale of Saint George and the Witches.* It's never been one of her favorites, but she reads it anyway.

It's the usual version: once upon a time there were three wicked witches who loosed a terrible plague on the world. But brave Saint George of Hyll rose against them. He purged witching from the world, leaving nothing but ashes behind him.

Finally only the Maiden, the Mother, and the Crone remained, the last and wickedest of witches. They fled to Avalon and hid in a tall tower, but in the end Saint George burned the Three and their tower with them.

The last page of the story is an engraved illustration of grateful children dancing while the Last Three Witches of the West burned merrily in the background.

Mama Mags used to tell the story different. Beatrice remembers listening to her grandmother's stories as if they were doors to someplace else, someplace better. Later, after she was sent away, she would lie in her narrow cot and re-tell them to herself again and again, rubbing them like lucky pennies between her fingers.

(Sometimes she can still see the walls of her room at St. Hale's: perfect ivory, closing like teeth around her. She keeps such things locked safe inside parentheses, like her mother taught her.)

A raised voice rings from the square through her office window, startling her. She isn't supposed to be dawdling over witch-tales and rhymes; as a junior associate librarian she's supposed to be cataloging and filing and recording, perhaps transcribing the work of true scholars.

Right now there are several hundred pages of illegible handwriting piled on her desk from a professor in the School of History. She's only typed the title page—*The Greater Good: An Ethical Evaluation of the Georgian Inquisition During the Purge*—but she can tell already it's one of those bloodthirsty books that relishes every gory detail of the purges: the beatings and brandings, the metal bridles and hot iron shoes, the women they burned with their babes still held in their arms. It will be popular with the Morality Party types, the saber-rattlers and churchgoers who rather admire the French Empire's bloody campaign against the war-witches of Dahomey, who are eager to see similar measures taken up against the witches of the Navajo and Apache and the stubborn Choctaw still holed up in Mississippi.

Beatrice finds she doesn't have the stomach for it. She knows witching is sinful and dangerous, that it stands in the way of the forward march of progress and industry, et cetera, but she can't help but think of Mags in her little herb-hung house and wonder what the harm is.

She looks again at the words on the last page of the Sisters Grimm. They aren't important. They aren't anything at all, just a little girl's rhyme written in a children's book, a song sung by an old woman in the hills of nowhere in particular. An unfinished verse long forgotten.

But when she looks at them, Beatrice can almost feel her sisters' hands in hers again, can almost smell the mist rising from the valleys back home.

She pulls a notebook from her desk drawer. It's cheaply made—the black dye fading to murky mauve, the pages coming unglued—but it's her most beloved possession.

(It was her very first possession, the first thing she purchased with her own money after she left St. Hale's.)

The notebook is half-filled with witch-tales and nursery rhymes, stolen scraps and idle dreams and anything that catches Beatrice's eye. If she were a scholar she might refer to her notes as research, might imagine it typed and bound on a library shelf, discussed in university halls, but she isn't and it won't be.

Now she copies the verse about wayward sisters into the little black book, beside all the other stories she'll never tell and spells she'll never work.

She hasn't spoken so much as a single charm or cantrip since she left home. But something about the shape of the words on the page, written in her own hand, tempts her tongue. She has a wild impulse to read them aloud—and Beatrice isn't a woman much subject to wild impulses. She learned young what happened when a woman indulges herself, when she tastes fruits forbidden.

(*Don't forget what you are*, her daddy told her, and Beatrice hasn't.)

And yet—Beatrice cracks her office door to check the College halls; she is entirely alone. She swallows. She feels a tugging somewhere in her chest, like a finger hooked around her ribcage.

She whispers the words aloud. *The wayward sisters, hand in hand.*

They roll in her mouth like summer sorghum, hot and sweet. *Burned and bound, our stolen crown.*

Heat slides down her throat, coils in her belly. *But what is lost, that can't be found?*

Beatrice waits, blood simmering.

Nothing happens. Naturally.

Tears—absurd, foolish tears—prick her eyes. Did she expect some grand magical feat? Flights of ravens, flocks of fairies? Magic is a dreary, distasteful thing, more useful for whitening one's socks than for summoning dragons. And even if Beatrice stumbled on an ancient spell, she lacks the witch-blood to wield it. Books and tales are as close as she can come to a place where magic is still real, where women and their words have power.

Beatrice's office feels suddenly cluttered and stuffy. She stands so abruptly her chair screeches across the tile and she fumbles a half-cloak around her shoulders. She strides from her office and clicks down the tidy halls of Salem College, thinking what a fool she was for trying. For hoping.

Mr. Blackwell, the director of Special Collections, blinks up from his desk as she passes. "Evening, Miss Eastwood. In a hurry?" Mr. Blackwell is the reason Beatrice is a junior associate librarian. He hired her with nothing but a diploma from St. Hale's, based purely on their shared weakness for sentimental novels and penny-papers.

Often Beatrice lingers to chat with him about the day's findings and frustrations, the new version of *East of the Sun, West of the Witch* she found in translation or the newest novel from Miss Hardy, but today she merely gives him a thin smile and hurries out into the graying evening with his worried eyes watching her.

She is halfway across the square, shoving through some sort of rally or protest, when the tears finally spill over, pooling against the wire rims of her spectacles before splashing to the stones below.

Heat hisses through her veins. An unnatural wind whips toward the center of the square. It smells like drying herbs and wild roses. Like magic.

That foolish hope returns to her. Beatrice wets her wind-scoured lips and says the words again. *The wayward sisters, hand in hand—*

This time she doesn't stop—*can't* stop—but returns to the beginning in a circling chant. It's as if the words are a river or an unbridled horse, carrying her helplessly forward. There's a rhythm to them, a heartbeat that skips at the end of the verse, stuttering over missing words.

The spell shambles onward, careening, not quite right, and the heat builds. Her lungs are charred, her mouth seared, her skin fevered.

Dimly Beatrice is aware of things outside herself—the splitting open of the world, the black tower hanging against a star-flecked sky, hung with thorns and ivy, the crows reeling overhead—her own feet carrying her forward, forward, following the witch-wind to the middle of the square. But then the fever blurs her vision, swallows her whole.

None of Mama Mags's spells ever felt like this. Like a song she can't stop singing, like a bonfire beneath her skin. Beatrice thinks it might become a pyre if she keeps feeding it.

She stutters into silence.

The world shudders. The ripped-open edges of reality flutter like tattered cloth before drawing together again, as if some great unseen seamstress is stitching the world back together. The tower and the tangled wood and the foreign night vanish, replaced by the ordinary gray of a spring evening in the city.

Beatrice blinks and thinks, *That was witching.* True witching, old and dark and wild as midnight.

Everything tilts strangely in Beatrice's vision and she tips downward into darkness. She falls, half dreaming there are arms waiting to catch her, sturdy and warm. A woman's voice says her name, except it isn't her name anymore—it's the lost name her sisters used when they were still foolish and fearless—*Bella!*—

And it begins to rain.

Juniper is howling like a moon-drunk dog, reveling in the sweet heat of power coursing through her veins and the feather-soft beating of wings above her, when the tower disappears.

It leaves the square in teeming, shrieking chaos. Every hat is blown askew, every skirt is ruffled, every hair-pin failing in its duties. Even the neat-trimmed linden trees look a little wilder, their leaves greener, their branches spreading like autumn antlers.

Juniper is chilled and dazed, emptied out except for a strange ache in the center of her. A *want* so vast it can't fit behind her ribs.

She looks up to see two other women standing near her, forming a silent circle in the middle of the screaming stampede of St. George's Square. In their faces Juniper sees her own want shining back at her, a hollow-cheeked hunger for whatever the hell it was they saw hanging in the sky, calling them closer.

One of the women sways and says "oh" in a hoarse voice, like she's been standing too long over a cook-fire. She blinks at Juniper through fever-slick eyes before she falls.

Juniper drops her staff and catches her before her head cracks against stone. She's light, feather-fragile in Juniper's arms. It's only as Juniper lays her down and resettles the crooked spectacles on the woman's nose, as she sees the freckles scattered across her cheeks like constellations she thought she'd forgotten, that she realizes who she is.

"*Bella.*" Her oldest sister. And—

Juniper looks slowly up at the other woman, the first cold flecks of rain hissing on her cheeks, her heart thundering like iron-shod hooves against her breastbone.

She's just as pretty as Juniper remembers her: full lips and long lashes and slender neck. Juniper figures she takes after the mama she can't remember, because there's nothing of Daddy in her.

"*Agnes.*" And just like that, Juniper is ten again.

She is opening her eyes in the earthen dark of Mags's hut, already speaking her sisters' names because that's how they were back then, always hand in hand, one-of-three. Mags is turning away from her, shoulders bowed, and Juniper is realizing all over again that her sisters are gone.

Oh, they'd talked about it. Of course they had. How they would run away into the woods together like Hansel and Gretel. How they would eat wild honey and pawpaws, leave honeysuckle crowns on

Mags's doorstep sometimes so she'd know they were still alive. How Daddy would weep and curse but they would never, ever go back home.

But Daddy's mood would lighten, sudden as springtime, and he would buy them sweets and ribbons and they would stay a while longer.

Not this time. This time her sisters cut and ran without looking back, without second-guessing. Without her.

Juniper took off down the mountainside as soon as she understood, stumbling, limping—her left foot was still blistered and raw from the barn-fire.

She caught a single glimpse of Agnes's sleek black braid swaying on the back of a wagon as it jostled down the drive and shouted for her to come back, please come back, *don't leave me*, until her pleas turned to choked sobs and thrown stones, until she was too full-up with hate to hurt anymore.

She limped home. The house smelled wet and sweet, like meat gone bad, and her daddy was waiting for his supper. *Never mind, James.* He'd given her his own first name and liked to hear himself say it. *We'll get along without them.*

Seven years she survived without them. She grew up without them, buried Mama Mags without them, and waited without them for Daddy to die.

But now here they are, wet and hungry-eyed, smack dab in the middle of New Salem: her sisters.

4

> *Little Girl Blue, come blow your horn,*
> *The sheep's in the meadow, the cow's in the corn.*
> *Soundly she sleeps beneath bright skies,*
> *[Sleeper's name] awake, arise!*

> *A spell to wake what sleeps, requiring a blown horn or a good*
> *whistle*

Agnes Amaranth doesn't feel the cold hiss of rain against her skin. She doesn't see the two women crouched beside her, freckled and black-haired, like reflections hanging in a pair of mirrors.

All her attention is inward-facing, fixed on the live thing sprouting inside her, delicate as the first fiddle-head curl of a fern. She imagines she feels a second heart beating beneath her palm.

"*Agnes.*" She knows the voice. She's heard it laugh and tease and beg for one more story, pretty please; she's heard it chasing after her down the rutted drive, begging her to come back. She's heard it in seven years of bad dreams. *Don't leave me.*

Agnes looks down to see her baby sister kneeling below her, except she's not a baby anymore: her jaw is hard and square, her shoulders wide, her eyes blazing with a grown woman's helping of hate.

"J-Juniper?" Agnes becomes aware that her arms are outstretched, as if she expects Juniper to run into them the way she did when she was a child, when Agnes still slept every night with her sister's crow-feather hair tickling her nose, when Juniper still slipped sometimes and called her *Mama*.

Juniper's lips are peeled back from her teeth, her face taut. Agnes looks down to see her sister's hands curled into fists. The shape of them—the familiar white knobs of her knuckles, the twist of tendons in her wrists—chases all the air from Agnes's lungs.

"Where's Daddy? He with you?" She hates the hint of Crow County that surfaces in her voice.

Juniper shakes her head, stiff-necked. "No." A darkness flits across the leaf-light of her eyes, like grief or guilt, before the rage burns it away again.

Agnes remembers how to breathe. "Oh. How—what are you doing here?" Deep scratches score Juniper's wrists and throat, as if she ran through deep woods on a dark night.

"What am *I* doing here?" Juniper's eyes are wide and her nostrils are flared. Agnes remembers what happens when Juniper loses her temper— a serpent the color of blood, flames licking higher, animal screams—and flinches away.

Juniper swallows, draws a shuddering breath. "Had to leave home. Headed north. Didn't expect to run into you two strutting through the city like a pair of pigeons, without a care in the damn world." Her voice is bitter and black as burnt coffee. The Juniper Agnes remembers was all feckless temper and careless laughter; Agnes wonders who taught her to hold a grudge, to feed and tend it like a wild-caught wolf pup until it grew big and mean enough to swallow a man whole.

Her attention snags on the number Juniper just said. "Two?" Surely Agnes is still merely *one*. Surely the baby in her belly is too small to count as a whole person. Agnes's brain feels like a jammed loom, threads snarled, gears grinding.

Juniper narrows her eyes at Agnes, looking for mockery and not finding it, then looks pointedly down.

Agnes follows her gaze and for the first time she sees the woman lying between them, her spectacles spattered with rain. Agnes feels the world collapsing around her, all the years of her life folding together, accordion-like.

Their oldest sister. The one who betrayed her and the one she betrayed in turn, eye for an eye. The reason she had to run.

Bella.

Juniper is shaking Bella's shoulders and Bella's head is lolling, limp. Juniper lays two fingers against her forehead and swears. "She's burning up. Y'all got a place nearby?"

"I haven't seen Bella in seven years. Didn't even know she was in the city." Agnes's lip curls. "Didn't care, either."

Juniper glares up at her. "Then how come—"

But Agnes hears a sound that every person in New Salem knows well, a sound that means *trouble* and *time to go*: the cold ring of iron-shod hooves on cobblestones. Police in the city ride tall, prancing grays specially bred for their vicious tempers and shining white coats.

The sound makes Agnes abruptly aware of how empty the square has become, abandoned by everything except slanting rain and drifting feathers and the three of them.

She ought to run before the law shows up looking for someone to blame. She ought to gather her skirts in two fists and disappear into the alleys and side-streets, just another nothing-girl in a white apron, invisible.

Juniper climbs to her feet with Bella's arm hauled across her shoulders. She staggers on her bad leg, toppling sideways—

Agnes reaches for her. She catches her wrist and Juniper clutches her arm, steadying herself, and for a half-second the two of them are face-to-face, hands wrapped around each other, flesh warm through thin cotton.

Agnes lets go first. She bends and hands her sister the red-cedar staff, rubbing her palm against her skirt as if the wood burned her.

Without quite deciding to, without thinking much at all, she shoves her shoulder against Bella's other side. Their oldest sister sags between them like wet laundry on a line.

Agnes hears herself say, "Come with me."

Beatrice is drifting, burning, floating like a cinder above some unseen fire. Voices hiss and whisper around her. *Hurry, for Saints' sake.* Her feet wobble and slide beneath her, mutinous. Her spectacles swing madly from one ear.

She blinks and sees the coal-scummed walls of west-side alleys passing on either side; laundry strung overhead like the many-colored flags of foreign countries, dripping in the rain; the darkening sky and the hot glow of gas-lamps.

There are two women running beside her, half carrying her. One of them limps badly, her shoulder falling and catching beneath Beatrice. The other swears beneath her breath, fingers white around Beatrice's wrist. Their faces are nothing but bright blurs in Beatrice's vision, but their arms are warm and familiar around her.

Her sisters. The ones she missed most at St. Hale's, the ones who never came to her rescue.

The ones who are here now, running beside her down the rain-slick streets of New Salem.

Juniper never thought much about her sisters' lives after they left Crow County—they'd just walked off the edge of the page and vanished, a pair of unfinished sentences—but she thought a lot about what she'd say if she ever saw them again.

You left me behind. You knew what he was and you left me all alone with him.

Her sisters would weep and tear their hair with guilt. *Please*, they would beg, *forgive us!*

Juniper would stare down at them like God casting the first witch from the Garden, fire and brimstone in her eyes. *No*, she'd say, and her sisters would spend the rest of their sorry-ass lives wishing they'd loved her better.

Juniper doesn't say a word as they lurch through the twisting streets, turning down unmarked alleys and slanting through empty lots. She says nothing as they arrive at a grim-looking boarding house with stained clapboard walls and wooden crosses hanging in the windows. She is silent as they shuffle Bella past the landlady's apartment, up two flights of creaking stairs, through a door bearing a brass number seven and a cross-stitched verse (*Let a woman live in quietude, Timothy 2:11*).

Agnes's room is dim and mildewed, containing nothing but a thin mattress on an iron frame, a cracked mirror, and a rusty stove that looks like it would struggle to heat a tin cup of coffee. Brownish stains bloom on the ceiling; unseen creatures scuttle and nibble in the walls.

It makes Juniper think of a jail cell or a cheap coffin. Or the cellar back home, black and wet, empty except for cave crickets and animal bones and the long-ago tears of little girls. A chill shivers down her spine.

Agnes heaves Bella onto the thin mattress and stands with her arms crossed. The lines on her face are deeper than Juniper remembers. She thinks of witch-tales about young women cursed to age a year for every day they live.

Agnes bends to light a puddled stub of candle. She shoots Juniper a prickly, half-ashamed shrug. "Out of lamp-oil."

Juniper watches her sister stumbling around in the flickering light for a minute before she pulls the crooked wand of pitch pine from her pocket and touches the end of it to the slumping candle. She whispers the words Mama Mags taught her and the wand glows a dull orange that brightens to beaten gold, as if an entire summer sunset has been caught and condensed.

Agnes stares at the wand, her face bathed in honeyed light. "You always paid better attention to Mags than us."

Juniper pinches the guttering candlewick between her fingers and shrugs one shoulder. "Used to. She died in the winter of ninety-one." Juniper could have told her more: how she dug and filled the hole herself to save the cost of a gravedigger and how the dirt rang hollow on the coffin lid; how every shovelful took some of herself along with it, until she was nothing but bones and hate; how she waited for three days and three nights by the graveside hoping Mama Mags might love her enough to let her soul linger. Ghosts were at least seven different kinds of sin and they never lasted more than an hour or two, but sin never bothered Mags before.

The grave stayed still and silent, and Juniper stayed lonely. All Mags left behind was her brass locket, the one that used to have their mother's hair curled like a silky black snake inside it.

Juniper doesn't say any of that. She lets the silence congeal like grease in a cold pan.

"You should have written. I'd have come home for the funeral." There's an apology in Agnes's voice and Juniper wants to bite her for it.

"Oh, would you? And where should I have addressed your invitation? Seven years, Agnes, seven *years*—"

From the bed beside them, Bella makes a soft, hurting sound. Her skin is a damp, fish-belly white.

Juniper snaps her teeth shut and crouches down beside her, peeling one of her eyelids back. "Devil's-fever." Juniper would like very much to know what the hell her sister was doing to get herself burnt up with witching. "You got a tin whistle? Or a horn?"

Agnes shakes her head and Juniper *tsk*s. She says the words anyhow and gives a sharp, two-fingered whistle. A spark of witching flares between them.

Bella's eyes flutter. She blinks up at her sisters, face slack with shock. "Agnes? June?" Juniper gives her a stiff little bow. "*Saints.*" A sudden fear seems to strike Bella. She struggles up from the bed, eyes skittering around the room, lingering on the shadows. "Where's Daddy?"

"Not here."

"Does he know where you are? Is he coming?"

"Doubt it." Juniper runs her tongue over her teeth and lays out the next words like a winning hand of cards, a heartless snap. "Dead men usually stay put." She lets her eyelids hang heavy as she says it, hoping her sisters won't see anything lurking in her eyes.

They stare at her, barely breathing, their faces empty.

Juniper knows how they feel. Even right afterward, when Juniper was scrubbing the guilt and smoke off her arms in the Big Sandy River, she remembers thinking, *Is that it?* Her daddy's death was supposed to feel like vanquishing a foe or winning a war, like the end of the story when the giant crashes to earth and the whole kingdom celebrates.

But the giant had already stomped everything flat. There was no one left to celebrate except Juniper the Giantkiller, all alone.

Agnes lowers herself slowly onto the floor beside Juniper. After a while she says, "So how come you left? Who's watching the farm?"

Juniper answers her second question. "Cousin Dan."

"That dumbshit?"

"He owns it now. Daddy left the whole thing to him. Even Mags's place." A little hut dug into the mountainside with a dirt floor and a cedar-shake roof gone green with moss, worth less than the land it sat on. People in town gossiped and clucked their tongues about Mama Mags, wondering to one another how a person could live all alone like that, but it sounded alright to Juniper. She'd never had any interest in boys or betrothals or the things that came after; she figured she'd spend her days clearing henbit and cudweed from the herb-garden and chatting with the sycamores. In the fall-times maybe she and her red staff would go walking in the hills with a basket over her arm, collecting foxglove and ninebark, snake-skins and bone, sleeping beneath the clean light of stars.

Daddy took that away from her, like he took everything else.

"I—I'm sorry, Juniper. I know you always loved that place." Bella says it soft, as if she's trying to comfort Juniper, as if she cares.

Juniper shucks her shoulders, ducking away from her caring. "How'd you two end up in New Salem, anyhow?"

Neither of them meet her eyes. Bella removes her spectacles and polishes the glass with the bed-sheet. "I w-work for the College, at the library."

Agnes gives a small, humorless laugh and mimics Bella's chopped-short vowels, her schoolteacher voice. "Well, I work for the Baldwin Brothers. At the cotton mill."

Juniper sees their eyes meet, cold and cutting, and wonders what the hell they have to hold against one another. They weren't the ones left in the lion's den. She leans between them. "And how'd you end up in that square today?"

Now they look at her, wide and hungry. Bella touches her own breastbone, as if there's still something lodged there, towing her forward, and Juniper knows they felt it, too: the thing that tugged them together, the spell that burned between them and left a terrible wanting behind it. She can almost see the black tower reflected in their eyes, starlit and rose-eaten, like a promise nearly fulfilled.

Bella whispers, "What was it?"

Juniper whispers back, "You know damn well what it was." Something long gone, something dangerous, something that was supposed to have burned up in the way-back days along with their mother's mothers.

Bella hisses "witching," just as Agnes says "trouble."

Agnes pulls herself to her feet, the sunlit wand drawing deep shadows around her frown. There's no starlight in her eyes, now. "All kinds of trouble. People will be scared, and the law'll get involved. It's not like it was back home, where people mostly looked the other way when it came to witching. You saw the witch-yard in the cemetery? They say in the old days it was ankle-deep with the ashes of the women they burned in this city."

She shakes her head. "And now there are these Christian Union women running around, and the Morality Party has somebody on the City Council—he's running for mayor now, I heard. He doesn't have a chance in hell, but still. Him and his people will eat all this tower business up with a damn spoon."

"But don't you want to—" Juniper begins.

"What I want is to get some sleep. I have an early shift tomorrow." Agnes's voice is clipped and cold as she rummages in a battered trunk. "The police will be out looking, by now. You two should stay here." She tosses a stack of moth-eaten wool at Juniper, not looking at her. "For the night."

For the night. Not forever, not happily ever after.

Of course not.

Agnes spreads her own blanket on the floor and rolls a spare skirt into a pillow. Bella struggles upright, gesturing Agnes to her own bed, but Agnes ignores her.

She lies down on the floor with her body curled tight, a nautilus-shell around her own belly. Juniper glares resentfully at her back before whispering to the pitch pine wand. The witch-light fades and the room darkens from summer-gold to winter-gray.

Juniper lies on the floor beside Agnes and tries to keep her fists from clenching and her teeth from grinding. Her body is strung tight from a night and a day spent running, sleeping only in rattling snatches on the train.

She shuffles and tosses and thinks of their old four-poster bed in the attic. She had trouble sleeping even as a girl, counting whip-poor-will calls and waiting for their daddy's unsteady steps to fall quiet. On bad nights Agnes would stroke her hair and Bella would whisper witch-tales in the dark.

"You up, Bell?" The sound of her own voice surprises Juniper. "You still remember any stories?"

At first she thinks that Bella won't answer her. Will tell her she's too old for tales of maidens and crones and spinning wheels. But her voice rises above the creak and rustle of the boarding house and Juniper can almost believe she is still ten years old, still one-of-three instead of one-alone.

"Once upon a time…"

THE TALE OF
THE SLEEPING MAIDEN

Once upon a time there was a king and queen who longed for a child but couldn't have one. They tried spells and prayers and charms, but after many long years the kingdom still had no heir. In desperation they held a grand feast and invited six witches to bless their kingdom. The six witches granted six fair gifts—peace and prosperity, good health and good harvests, agreeable weather and biddable peasants—but just as the feast was ending, a seventh witch arrived. She was young and graceful and had the sort of face that launches ships and eats hearts. She wore a coal-black adder twined around her left arm and a sharp-toothed smile on her lips.

She told the king and queen that, since they failed to invite her to their feast, she brought a curse instead of a blessing: one day a young maiden would prick her finger on a spindle and the castle would fall into an endless sleep from which no one could wake it.

The king took all reasonable precautions. He ordered all the spinning wheels burned and permitted no unwed women within the castle walls. He kept his throne for one-and-twenty years.

Until the day a strange maiden arrived at the castle gates. The guards should have turned her away, but it had been too long since the seventh witch had been seen, and the Maiden knew the ways and words to make them forget their orders. She wore her familiar like a black-glass necklace around her throat.

The Maiden strode unseen through the castle, smiling as she went, until she climbed to the top of the tallest tower, where a spinning wheel waited for her. She reached her pale finger to the spindle's end.

There are many versions of this story, but there is always a pricked finger. There are always three drops of the Maiden's blood.

Her blood touched the castle floor and a spell drifted through the castle. Every living creature fell into a sudden slumber. Pies burned in the ovens and spears clattered to the floor; cats slept with their claws outstretched toward sleeping mice, and dogs lay down beside foxes.

In the whole castle only the Maiden moved. She stole the king's crown from his brow and settled it on her own head.

The Maiden ruled for one hundred years. She might have ruled forever—who can say what ways a witch might find to live beyond their years?—except that a brave knight heard tales of a cursed kingdom and rode to its rescue. The Maiden retreated to the tallest tower and grew rose-briars around it, vicious and sharp-spined, so thick even the knight and his shining sword couldn't cut through them.

The knight set fire to the tower, instead. As the witch burned, her spell was broken and the rest of the castle woke from its endless sleep. The knight plucked the witch's crown from the ashes and presented it to the king on bended knee. The king pulled him to his feet and announced that he and the queen had finally found a fitting heir.

The knight and the kingdom lived happily ever after, although no rose ever bloomed for miles around, no matter how rich the soil or how talented the gardener. And there were still stories about a young woman who walked in the deep woods sometimes, with a black snake beside her.

5

Sister, sister,
Look around,
Something's lost
And must be found!

A spell to find what can't be found, requiring a pinch of salt &
a sharp eye

Agnes Amaranth lies awake long after her sister's story.

She thinks about witching and wanting and thrones without heirs, babies unborn. She thinks about the second pulse in her belly and the memory of pennyroyal on her tongue.

She must fall asleep eventually, because when she opens her eyes she sees sunrise tip-toeing into the room. Bile bubbles in her throat and she retches into the chamber pot as quietly as she can. Neither of her sisters stir.

Bella's mouth is crimped tight even in sleep, as if her lips are untrustworthy things. The last time Agnes saw her she was weeping silently as she packed her things, watching Agnes with her eyes huge and sad, as if she didn't deserve every bit of what she got. Clearly she's landed on her feet, working in a fancy library with her beloved books.

Juniper sleeps in a heedless, childlike sprawl, all elbows and knees. The toes of her left foot are curled with scars, the puckered flesh reaching up her ankle in a shape almost like fingers. Agnes wonders how long it took to heal and if it still hurts.

Her eyes fall on the battered brass locket lying against Juniper's collarbone. She remembers it swinging from Mags's neck, the way she'd hold it sometimes and look up the mountainside with her eyes misted over. Mags never talked much about the daughter she lost—their mother, who drew her last breath just as Juniper drew her first—but Agnes could see her mother in the shape of her grandmother's silences: the scabbed-over places, the wounded days when Mags stayed in bed with the quilts pulled high.

Agnes lights the stove and cuts butter into a skillet, letting the pop and sizzle wake the others. They stretch and yawn, watching her crack eggs and boil coffee.

They take their tin plates in silence. Juniper eats like it's been days since she saw a square meal. Bella picks at her food, staring out the window. Agnes breathes carefully through her mouth and tries not to look at the slick jelly of the egg whites.

When the food is gone there's nothing to do but leave. Part ways. Settle back into their own stories and forget about lost towers and lost sisters.

None of them moves. Juniper fidgets, trailing her finger through the runny yolk as it dries.

"So." Agnes pretends she's speaking to a stranger, just another boarding-house girl passing through. "Where will you go now?"

She's hoping Juniper will say: *Straight the hell back home.* Or maybe even: *To find good, honest work like my big sister.* Instead her mouth curls with a reckless little smile and she says, "To join up with those suffrage ladies just as fast as I can."

Bella's eyes swivel away from the window for the first time. She covers her mouth with her palm and says faintly, "Oh, my."

Agnes resists the urge to roll her eyes. "Why? So you can wear a fancy dress and wave a sign? Get laughed at? Don't waste your time."

Juniper's smile hardens. "Voting doesn't seem like a waste of time to me." She's still fooling with her egg yolk, swirling it into gummy circles. Agnes's stomach heaves.

"Look, all that 'votes for women' stuff sounds real noble and all, but they don't mean women like you and me. They mean nice uptown ladies with big hats and too much time on their hands. It doesn't matter to you or me who gets to be mayor or president, anyhow."

Juniper shrugs at her, sullen, childish, and Agnes drops her voice lower. "Daddy's dead, June. You can't piss him off anymore."

Juniper's head snaps up, eyes boiling green, hair tangled like a black hedge of roses around her face. "You think I still give a single shit about him?" She hisses it so hot and mean that Agnes thinks she must give two or three shits, at least. "Someone or some-witch worked a spell yesterday. The kind that hasn't been seen since our great-great-great-grandmama's days. It felt..." Juniper's jaw works. She taps her chest and Agnes knows she's trying to find words to describe the swell of power, the sweet sedition of magic in her veins. "It felt impossible. Important. Don't you want to know where it came from? Don't you think it maybe had something to do with the herd of suffragists running around the square?"

"I know that's what the police'll think. Half the papers already call them witches. Don't be a *fool*, June, please—"

Agnes is interrupted by Bella, who lunges from her seat at the foot of the bed to seize Juniper's plate. She clutches it, peering through her spectacles at the trio of yolky circles Juniper has drawn on its surface. "What's this?"

Juniper blinks down at the remains of her breakfast. "Uh. Eggs?"

"The *design*, June. Where did you see this?"

Juniper lifts one shoulder. "On the tower door, I guess."

Bella's head tilts, owl-like. "On the what?"

"You didn't see the door? On my side of the tower there was a door, old and wooden, all overgrown with roses, and there were three circles on it, overlapping. And words, too, but I couldn't make sense of them."

Bella's face goes taut, intent in a way that Agnes recalls from their childhood, when Bella would get to the good part of a book. "What language was it? And did the circles have eyes? Or tails? Could they have been serpents, do you think?"

"Maybe. Why?"

But Bella ignores the question. Her eyes are searching Juniper's face now. They land on her lips, where Agnes can see the dark blush of a bruise and the tattered red of torn skin. Bella lifts her fingertips toward it, her expression filled with wonder or maybe terror. "Maiden's blood," she whispers. Juniper flinches from her touch.

Bella's fingers fall away. Juniper's plate clangs to the floor. "Excuse me. I'm sorry. I have to go. Very sorry." She tosses the words behind her like coins for beggars, a careless jumble, as she reaches for the door.

"What? You're leaving?" Juniper is sputtering, cheeks reddening. "But I just found you! You can't just *leave*." Agnes hears the unspoken *again* hovering in the air, but Bella is already gone, calling back carelessly, "I rent a room in Bethlehem Heights, between Second and Sanctity, if you need me."

Agnes watches her leave with a strange hollowness in her chest. "Well." She scrapes her sister's eggs back into the pan with unnecessary force. "Good riddance."

Juniper whirls. "And why's that?"

"Because Bella can't keep her damn mouth shut! God knows what Daddy would have done if you hadn't—" Agnes shivers hard, as if winter has come early, as if she's sixteen again and her daddy is coming toward her with that red glow in his eyes.

Juniper doesn't seem to have heard her. There's a glassy vacancy in her face that makes Agnes think of a little girl watching her father yell with her hands pressed over her ears, refusing to hear.

Agnes unpeels her fingernails from her palms and carefully doesn't look at the cedar staff propped by the door. "My shift starts soon. I'll talk to Mr. Malton, see if they need another girl on the floor. You can"—she swallows, feeling the bounds of her circle stretch like seams that might split, and makes herself finish—"you can stay here. Till you're on your feet."

But Juniper lifts her chin, looks down her crooked nose at Agnes. "I'm not working at some factory. I already told you: I'm signing up with the suffrage ladies. I'm going to find that tower. Fight for something."

It's such a youngest-sister thing to say that Agnes wants to slap her. In the witch-tales it's always the youngest who is the best-beloved, the most-worthy, the one bound for some grander destiny than her sisters. The other two are too ugly or selfish or boring to get fairy godmothers or even beastly husbands. The stories never mentioned boarding-house rent or laundry or aching knuckles from a double-shift at the mill. They never mentioned babies that needed feeding or choices that needed making.

Agnes swallows all those horseshit stories. "That's all well and good, but *causes* don't pay much, I heard. They don't feed you or give you a place to sleep. You need to—"

Juniper's lips peel back in a sudden animal snarl. "I don't need a thrice-damned thing from you." She takes a step closer, finger aimed like an arrow at Agnes's chest. "You *left*, remember? I made it seven years without you and I sure as shit don't need you now."

Guilt worms in Agnes's belly, but she keeps her face set. "I did what I had to."

Juniper turns away, pulling on her cloak, running fingers through her black-bracken hair. "Bella knows something, seems like. Is Bethlehem Heights a county or a city?"

Agnes blinks. "It's a neighborhood. On the east side, just past the College."

"Don't see why a city should need more than one name. So where's Second and Sanctity?"

"The streets are *numbered*, June. You just follow the grid."

Juniper shoots her a harassed look. "How's that supposed to help if I don't know where—" Her face goes blank. Her eyes trace some invisible line through the air. "Never mind. Don't need a damn grid, after all." She takes the cedar staff and limps into the hall as if she knows precisely where she's going.

Which, Agnes realizes, she does. She feels it, too: a tugging between her ribs. An invisible kite-string stretched tight between her and her sisters, thrumming with unsaid things and unfinished business. It feels like a beckoning finger, a hand shoving between her shoulder blades, a voice whispering a witch-tale about three sisters lost and found.

But witch-tales are for children, and Agnes doesn't like being told what to do. She shuts her door so hard the cross-stitched verse swings on its nail. She listens alone to the uneven thump of her sister's footsteps.

Three circles woven together, or maybe three snakes swallowing their own tails: Beatrice has seen this shape before. Beatrice knows to whom it belongs.

The Last Three Witches of the West.

It's the sign the Maiden left carved into the trunks of beech trees, the sign the Mother burned into her dragon-scale armor, the sign the Crone pressed into the leather covers of books. Beatrice has seen it printed in blurred ink in the appendices of medieval histories and described in the journals of witch-hunters and occasionally mis-identified in Church pamphlets as the Sign of Satan.

It doesn't belong in the modern world. It certainly doesn't belong in the City Without Sin, carved into a door on a tower that shouldn't exist.

Beatrice escapes the labyrinth of the West Babel slums with her skin humming and her fingers shaking. She flags down a trolley and lets the electric whir drown out the rising hustle of the city, the calls of west-side street vendors and the misery of the mills and even the memory of her sisters' faces, fresh and sharp as mint-leaves in her mouth.

(They're alive and whole and their daddy is dead. The thought is deafening, a flood of hope and dread and hurt.)

Mr. Blackwell isn't yet at his desk when Beatrice arrives at the library. Beatrice is relieved; there will be no one to see her pale-faced and rumpled in the same dress she wore yesterday.

She left the window open overnight and her office smells cool and damp, as if she is stepping into a starlit wood instead of a cramped room. The Sisters Grimm lies open on her desk, its pages rippling softly in the breeze.

Beatrice flips to the final page of the final story, traces the verse in faded ink. *The wayward sisters, hand in hand.* She thinks the spell looks somehow even fainter, as if it's aged several decades since Beatrice last saw it; she thinks she might be losing her mind.

She turns back to the title page: *The Tale of Saint George and the Witches.* Mama Mags's version was nothing like the Grimms', all neat and cheery. The way she told it the Last Three had not flown to Avalon in terror, but in a desperate attempt to save the last remnants of their power from the purge. They'd built something—some great construct of stone and time and magic—that preserved the wicked heart of women's magic like seeds saved after the winnowing.

Sometimes Mags said Saint George had simply torched their working along with the Three themselves. Other times she said it had vanished along with the isle of Avalon itself, drifting out of time and mind, lost to the world. *But,* she would whisper with a wink, *what is lost, that can't be found, Belladonna?*

(Mags had always called them by their mother's-names—the old-fashioned second-names given by mothers to daughters—but St. Hale's had found the practice blasphemous. Eventually Beatrice had learned to forget the heathen indulgence of her mother's-name and become merely Beatrice.)

Beatrice has heard similar portents and promises over the years, has even heard it given a name: the Lost Way of Avalon. It's an absurdity, she knows—the Last Three themselves are three-quarters myth and witch-tale, generally only taken seriously by oracles or zealots or the occasional seditious schoolgirl—and Beatrice doesn't see how witchcraft could be bound to a single place or object.

And yet.

Yesterday Beatrice stood beneath the light of strange stars in the shadow of a black tower, where her sister saw the sign of the Last Three.

What is lost, that can't be found? The words Mags taught them along-side a hundred other songs and rhymes. Senseless, silly, utterly insignifi-cant to the grand warp and weft of time.

Unless they aren't. Unless there are words and ways waiting among the children's verses; power passed in secret from mother to daughter, like swords disguised as sewing needles.

Beatrice removes her little black notebook from its drawer and writes out the entirety of *The Tale of the Sleeping Maiden*. She stares out the window, thinking of maidens and drops of blood and tall towers surrounded by roses and truths wrapped in lies.

There's a strange wriggle in the corner of Beatrice's eye. Her gaze flicks back to the desk: there is an odd, many-fingered shadow cast over the Grimms' book.

She draws the page cautiously away. It's unchanged, except perhaps that the ink is a shade paler and the paper slightly thinner. Older.

The shadow-hand retreats as she watches, coiling back into a dim corner of her office and lying still, as if it were an ordinary shadow cast by a bookshelf or desktop.

A cold foreboding spins over Beatrice's skin. She has the sudden urge either to fling the book out the window or clutch it tight to her chest, but before she can do either there's a wooden knock against her office door.

Beatrice flinches, picturing police or witch-hunters or at least Miss Munley, the secretary, but she feels a silent tug and knows, quite suddenly and illogically, who is standing in the hall beating her staff against her door.

Her youngest sister glares at her as she opens it, mouth thin and eyes hot. "If you wanted to run off, you shouldn't've left a breadcrumb trail behind you." She waves her staff in midair, gesturing at the invisible thing between them.

"Oh! It must be a leftover effect of yesterday's—events. A spell was begun but not finished, like thread that wasn't tied off properly." Beatrice can see from Juniper's expression that she doesn't particularly care what it is or how it got there, that she is just a half-step away from an act of violence. Beatrice swallows. "Ah, come in. I'm sorry I ran off this morning."

"It's about that tower, isn't it? You know what it is." Juniper gives her a searching look.

I think it's the Lost Way of Avalon. The thought is heady, dizzying, too dangerous to speak aloud even in the soft-shadowed halls of Salem College. "I don't know. I'm considering some s-some possibilities, is all."

Juniper watches her with a narrow-eyed expression that says she doesn't believe her and is weighing whether or not to make something of it. "Alright. I can help you consider them."

"I'm not sure—"

"And I'm joining the suffrage ladies, like I said. You know where to find them? They got an office somewhere?"

"Three blocks north, on St. Patience. But…" Beatrice wets her lips, unsure how much she should or shouldn't tell her baby sister who has become this prowling, perilous woman. "But I'm not sure the suffragists have anything to do with that tower, or the sp-spell we felt." She stumbles over the word, recalling the hot taste of witching in her mouth.

Juniper shoots her another sideways look. "I might not have a lot of fancy schooling like you, but I'm not stupid. You don't get Devil's-fever from standing around and watching, Bell. Mags said it comes of working witching stronger than yourself." Beatrice is opening her mouth in confession or denial, but Juniper is already looking past her. "Maybe you're right, and they didn't have anything to do with it. Still. Seems to me they're the same thing, more or less."

"What are?"

Juniper's eyes reflect the bronze shine of Saint George's standing in the square. "Witching and women's rights. Suffrage and spells. They're both..." She gestures in midair again. "They're both a kind of power, aren't they? The kind we aren't allowed to have." *The kind I want*, says the hungry shine of her eyes.

"They're both children's stories, June." Beatrice doesn't know if she's telling her sister or herself.

Juniper shrugs without looking away from the square. "They're better than the story we were given." Beatrice thinks about their story and doesn't disagree.

Juniper's eyes slide to hers, flashing green. "Maybe we can change it, if we try. Skip into some better story." And Beatrice sees that she means it, that beneath all Juniper's bitter rage there's still a little girl who believes in happy endings. It makes Beatrice want to slap her or hold her, to send Juniper home before New Salem teaches her different.

But she can tell from the iron shape of Juniper's jaw that she wouldn't go, that she's charted a course toward trouble and means to find it.

"I—I'll take you to the Women's Association. After work."

"And I need a place to stay."

"What about Agnes?"

Frost crackles down the line between them at the mention of her name.

"I see. Well, I rent a room a few blocks east. You're welcome to stay until..." She isn't sure how to end her sentence. Until women win the vote in New Salem? Until they call back the Lost Way and return witching to the world? Until the sullen red is gone from Juniper's eyes?

"Until things settle down," she finishes lamely. Her sister smiles in a way that makes Beatrice suspect that things, whatever they are, will not settle at all.

6

Hush a bye, baby, bite your tongue,
Not a word shall be sung.

A spell for quiet, requiring a clipped feather & a bitten tongue

James Juniper wanted Bella to skip work and head straight to the suffrage ladies, but Bella insisted that she had "obligations and responsibilities" and made Juniper sit on a teetery pile of encyclopedias while she worked, which lasted until Juniper got bored and slipped out the door to wander the hushed halls of the Salem College Library.

It's still early, and there's a stillness to the air that reminds Juniper of walking the mountainside just before dawn, in that silent second after the night-creatures have bedded down but before the morning-birds have started up. It feels secret, stolen out of time, like you might see the ragged point of a witch's hat or the gleam of dragon-scales in the shadows. Juniper closes her eyes and pretends the wood-pulp pages around her are wet and alive, pumping with sap instead of ink. She wonders if her sister ever stands like this—missing home, missing her—and feels a fragile sprout of sympathy take root in her chest.

She hears the rattle-creak of a library cart and opens her eyes to find a prissy, toothy woman hissing at her in a whisper that's several times louder than a regular old speaking voice. She goes on about library hours and permissions and "the stacks," although none of the books looked stacked to Juniper, and Juniper is about to cause what Mama Mags would call "a scene" when an affable-looking gentleman with tufty ear-hair rescues her and herds her back to Bella's office.

Bella blinks up at them through her spectacles and says, "What—oh. I'm so sorry. *Thank* you, Mr. Blackwell. My sister has never been fond of the rules."

There's a little pause, while Bella attempts to glare at Juniper and Juniper attempts to dodge, before the hairy-eared gentleman says softly, "I didn't know you had a sister, Beatrice."

Juniper feels that fragile sprout of sympathy wither and die. The truth is that her sisters ran off and never looked back, never even spoke her name, and they're only together now because of happenstance and a half-spun spell.

Juniper feels Bella watching her and works hard to keep her stupid eyes from filling up with stupid tears.

Mr. Blackwell looks between the two of them with lines of concern crimping his brows. "I never liked the rules much either, to be honest," he offers. Then he bows to Juniper as if Juniper is the kind of lady who gets bowed to. "Lovely to meet you, Miss Eastwood."

He leaves them alone together.

Juniper perches back on the encyclopedia stack to wait and doesn't say anything. Neither does Bella. For a few hours the office is quiet except for the scritch of Bella's pen and the kick of Juniper's heels against book-spines.

At noon Bella screws the cap back onto her ink bottle and stands. "Well. Are you ready to join the women's movement, Juniper?" She gives her a small, not very good smile that Juniper guesses is supposed to be an apology, which Juniper neither accepts nor denies. Instead she shrugs to her feet, toppling the encyclopedias behind her.

Bella looks her up and down—muddy hem to briar-scratched arms—and sighs a little. "There's a washroom down the hall. At least brush your hair. You look like an escaped convict." Juniper barely suppresses a cackle.

It turns out brushing her hair isn't enough. Bella produces a stiff woolen dress from her office closet. It's one of those respectable, pocketless affairs that obliges ladies to carry stupid little handbags, so Juniper can't take so much as a melted candle-stub or a single snake tooth with her. Bella informs her that this is the precise reason why women's dresses no longer have pockets, to show they bear no witch-ways or ill intentions, and Juniper responds that she has both, thank you very damn much.

In the end Juniper goes to see the suffragists entirely disarmed, except for her cedar staff.

She doesn't know what she was expecting the headquarters of the New Salem Women's Association to look like—an embattled army camp, perhaps, or a black-stone castle guarded by lady-knights—but it turns out to be a respectable-looking office with plate-glass windows and oak paneling and a pretty secretary who says "oh!" when the bell rings.

The secretary is Juniper's age, with hair the color of cornsilk and a crookedy nose that looks like it was broken at least once. Her eyes slide between Bella and Juniper and return to Bella, apparently deciding she's the more civilized of the two. "May I...help you?" Her eyes flick back to Juniper during the pause, lingering on the sawed-off edges of her hair.

Bella offers a polite smile. "Hello. I'm Miss Beatrice Eastwood and this is my sister, Miss Jame—"

It is at that moment that Juniper recalls the wanted posters currently spelling out her name in all capital letters across half the city, and intercedes. "June. Miss June...West." She glances at her sister, who looks like a taller, skinnier version of her. "We're just half-sisters, see."

She can feel Bella giving her a what-the-hell-is-wrong-with-you look and ignores it. She sticks her hand out to the secretary. "Pleased to meet you."

Bella clears her throat pointedly. "*Any*way, we—well, my sister—half-sister, I suppose—is interested in joining the Women's Association."

The secretary beams at them in a way that makes Juniper think they don't get fresh blood all that often, says, "Oh, of course! I'll fetch Miss Stone," and skitters into the back rooms. Juniper catches an angled glimpse of desks and stacks of paper, hears the businesslike chatter of working-women, and feels a familiar lonesomeness well up in her throat, a sisterless hunger to be on the other side of that door.

"Please do make yourselves comfortable," the secretary calls as the door shuts.

The two spindly chairs in the office don't look like they can hold anything heavier than a canary, so Juniper stays on her feet, weight hitched away from her bad leg. Bella stands statue-still, hands politely clasped. When did she get all proper, all ladylike? Juniper remembers her as a creature of sighs and slouches and soft-tangled hair.

She watches the clatter of the street through the window, the carriages and trolleys and iron-shod horses. Sober black letters hover over the scene, painted backwards on the inside of the window: HEAD-QUARTERS OF THE NEW SALEM WOMEN'S ASS'N. A thrill sizzles through her.

A day ago she was lost and reeling, spinning through the world like a puppet with its strings cut. And now she's here, with the smell of witching on the wind and the promise of power painted on the window above her. And a whole pack of brand-new sisters waiting just on the other side of the door.

Juniper shoots a sideways look at Bella, all prim and nervous, and hopes politicking proves thicker than blood.

The secretary comes bustling back into the room accompanied by the white-wigged lady who made the speech in the square the day before. She looks older and tireder up close, all cheekbones and worry lines. Her eyes are a pair of brass scales, weighing them.

"Miss Lind tells me you're interested in joining our Association."

Juniper ducks her head, feeling suddenly very young. "Yes, ma'am."

"Why?"

"Oh. Well, I was there yesterday at the rally. I liked what you said about e-equality." The word feels silly in her mouth, four syllables of make-believe and rainbows. She tries again. "And what you said about the way things are. How it's not fair and never has been, how the bastards take and they take from us until there's nothing left, until we don't have any choices except bad ones—"

Miss Stone raises two delicate fingers. "No need to do yourself a harm, child. I quite understand." Her eyes harden from brass to beaten iron. "But *you* ought to understand—whatever your personal troubles—the Women's Association is no place for bloody-mindedness or vengeance. There are no Pankhursts here." Juniper doesn't know what a Pankhurst is. Miss Stone must intuit this from the blankness of her expression, because she clarifies, "This is a respectable, peaceable organization."

"...Yes, ma'am."

Miss Stone pivots to Bella. "And you?"

"Me?"

"Why are you joining us today?"

"Oh, I'm not—that is, you certainly have my sympathies. But I'm awfully busy at work, and I just don't have time—"

Miss Stone has already turned away from her. She addresses Juniper again. "Miss Lind will add your name to our member list and discuss upcoming committee meetings you might join." Juniper tries to look eager, though she finds the word *committee* unpromising.

"And will you be making a contribution to our Association fund?"

"A what now?"

Miss Stone exchanges a look with her secretary as Bella hisses, "*Money*, June."

"Oh. I don't have any of that." Never has, really. What work Juniper did back in Crow County was paid in kind—jarred honey or fried apples or cat-mint picked on the half-moon—and Daddy never let them see a cent of his money. "I'm between jobs, see."

"Between—?" Miss Stone sounds puzzled, as if she is unfamiliar with the concept of jobs, as if money is just a thing a person finds whenever they reach into their handbags. "Oh. Well. No woman is barred from our cause by poverty." She says it all lofty and generous, but her tone hooks under Juniper's skin like a summer briar.

Miss Lind launches into a lecture about all their various letter-writing campaigns and subcommittees and allied organizations. Juniper listens with her temper simmering, bubbling like a pot left too long over the fire.

"And then the Centennial Fair is coming up in May, of course, and we feel it's an excellent opportunity for another demonstration. Get people's minds off th-the equinox." Miss Lind's throat bobs in a dry little swallow. "Anyway. What projects interest you? The campaign for the vote is paramount, naturally, but we also promote temperance, divorce rights, property ownership, and various charitable—"

Juniper tilts her head and says, "Witching." It lands like a barehanded slap, flat and loud. Beside her, Bella makes a soft, pained sound.

"I *beg* your pardon?" Miss Stone's mouth has gone very small and dry, like an apple left too long on the windowsill. The secretary's mouth is hanging wide open.

Juniper is tired of this mincing and dancing, sidestepping around the thing they ought to be running toward. "You know. You saw it: the tower and the trees, and the mixed-up stars." Both of them are blinking at her in horrified unison. "That was real witching, the *good* stuff, the kind that could do a whole lot more than just curl your hair or shine your shoes. The kind that could cure the sick or curse the wicked." The kind that keeps mothers alive and little girls safe. The kind that might still, somehow, find a way to steal Juniper's land back from her dumbshit cousin Dan. Juniper spreads her arms, palm up. "You asked what I wanted to work on, that's it."

Miss Stone's mouth shrivels even smaller. "Miss West. I'm afraid—"

Her secretary interrupts in a nervous little blurt. "The men did it. Those union boys in Chicago last year—they say machines rusted overnight, and coal refused to burn…" Miss Stone casts her the sort of look that turns people into pillars of salt and the secretary subsides.

"The Women's Association is not interested in what some degenerate men may or may not have done in Chicago, Miss Lind." She draws a deep, not very calm breath and turns back to Juniper. "I'm afraid you have entirely misunderstood our position. The Association has battled for decades to afford women the same respect and legal rights enjoyed by men. It is a battle we are *losing*: the American public still sees women as housewives at best and witches at worst. We may be either beloved or burned, but never trusted with any degree of power."

She pauses, her mouth shrinking to the smallest, bitterest apple seed. "I don't know who was responsible for the abnormality at St. George's, but I would turn her in myself before I let such activities destroy everything we've worked for."

Miss Stone extracts a ruffled copy of *The New Salem Post* from the front desk and flings it at Juniper and Bella. The splashy over-sized headline reads MAGIC MOST BLACK, with a smaller line printed beneath it: MYSTERIOUS TOWER TERRORIZES CITIZENS. Some imaginative artist has provided a sketch of a great black spire looming above the New Salem skyline, complete with brooding storm clouds and little bats flapping around the top.

Juniper squints her way through the adjectives and hysteria, skimming past excitable phrases like "terrified wailing of innocent children" and "malevolent apparition" and landing on the last few paragraphs:

While Mayor Worthington's office has claimed there is "no evidence of serious witchcraft" and urges the citizenry to "remain rational," others are less sanguine. There are rumors that the notorious Daughters

of Tituba may be behind the occurrence, although the New Salem Police Department maintains that no such organization exists.

Miss Grace Wiggin, head of the Women's Christian Union, points to the recent and virulent fevers that have run rampant through New Salem and recalls the ancient connections between witchcraft and plague. "Surely we need not wait for a second Black Death before we act!"

Mr. Gideon Hill left us with this sobering reflection: "I fear we have only ourselves to blame: in tolerating the unnatural demands of the suffragists, have we not also harbored their unnatural magics? The people deserve a mayor who will protect them from harm—and there is no harm greater than the return of witching."

Indeed. And Mr. Hill—an up-and-coming member of the City Council and third-party candidate for New Salem mayor—might be just the man for the job.

Juniper tosses the paper back on the desk. "Well," she offers, "shit."

Miss Stone regards her grimly. "Quite."

"Who are the Daughters of Tituba?"

Bella opens her mouth, but Miss Stone answers first. "An unsavory rumor." She stabs a finger at the paper. "Listen, Miss West: you are welcome to assist the Association in our mission. Saints know we need every warm body we can get. But you will have to abandon your pursuit of this, this"—she taps the article—"*devilry*. Am I understood?"

Juniper looks at her—this little old woman with a powdered wig and a big office on the fancy side of town—and understands perfectly well. She understands that the Women's Association wants one kind of power—the kind you can wear in public or argue in the courtroom or write on a slip of paper and drop in a ballot box—and that Juniper wants another. The kind that cuts, the kind with sharp teeth and talons, the kind that starts fires and dances merry around the blaze.

And she understands that if she intends to pursue it, she'll have to do it on her own. "Yes, ma'am," she says, and hears three sighs of relief around her.

Miss Stone invites Juniper to report to the Centennial March planning committee the following Tuesday evening and instructs Miss Lind to add her name to the member list and give her a tour of their offices.

She turns back once before she sweeps into the recesses of the office, her apple-seed mouth unshriveling very slightly. "It's not that I don't understand. Every thinking woman has once wanted what she shouldn't, what she can't have. I wish…" Juniper wonders if Miss Stone was ever a little girl listening to her grandmother's stories about the Maiden riding her white stag through the woods, the Mother striding into battle. If she once dreamed of wielding swords rather than slogans.

Miss Stone gives her shoulders a stern little shake. "I wish we might make use of every tool in our pursuit of justice. But I'm afraid the modern woman cannot afford to be sidetracked by moonbeams and witch-tales."

Juniper smiles back as pleasantly as she knows how and Bella whispers "yes, of course" beside her. But there's a look in Bella's eyes as she says it, a struck-flint spark that makes Juniper think that her sister doesn't intend to give up her moonbeams or witch-tales at all; that maybe she, too, wants another kind of power.

Beatrice Belladonna leaves the New Salem Women's Association headquarters with her cloak pulled tight against the spring chill and an anxious knot in her belly.

She walks down St. Patience thinking about the way her sister looked as she added her name to the list of members, bold and foolish, and the way Beatrice's fingers itched to copy her.

Thinking, too, about the words she found written in the margins of the Sisters Grimm and her growing certainty that, in speaking them aloud, she had touched a match to an invisible fuse. Begun something which could not now be stopped.

Because Beatrice's eyes are on the limestone cobbles, her shoulders hunched around her ears like a worried owl, she doesn't see the woman walking toward her until they collide.

"Oh my goodness, pardon me—" Beatrice is somehow on all fours, feeling blindly for her spectacles and apologizing to a pair of neatly shined boots.

A warm hand pulls her upright and dusts the street-grime from her dress. "Are you all right, miss?" The voice is low and amused, her face a blur of white teeth and brown skin.

"Yes, perfectly fine, I just need my—"

"Spectacles?" A half-laugh, and Beatrice feels her glasses settle gently back onto her nose.

The smudge resolves itself into a woman with amber eyes and skin like sunlight through jarred sorghum. She wears a gentleman's coat buttoned daringly over her skirts and a derby hat perched at an angle Beatrice can only describe as jaunty. The only colored women on the north side of New Salem are maids and serving girls, but this woman is quite clearly neither.

The woman extends her hand and smiles with such professional charm that Beatrice feels slightly blinded. "Miss Cleopatra Quinn, with *The New Salem Defender.*"

She says it breezily, as if *The Defender* were a ladies' journal or a fashion periodical, rather than a radical colored paper infamous for its seditious editorials. Its office has been burned and relocated at least twice, to Beatrice's knowledge.

Beatrice shakes Miss Quinn's hand and releases it quickly, not noticing the way she smells (ink and cloves and the hot oil of a printing press) or whether or not she wears a wedding band (she does).

Beatrice swallows. "B-Beatrice Eastwood. Associate librarian at Salem College."

Miss Quinn is looking over Beatrice's shoulder at the Association headquarters. "Are you a member of the Women's Association? Were you present for the events in the square on the equinox?"

"No. I mean, well, yes, I was, but I'm not—"

Miss Quinn raises a placating hand. Beatrice notices her wrist is spattered with silver scars, round pocks that almost but don't quite make a pattern. "I assure you *The Defender* isn't interested in any of that breathless witch-hunt nonsense printed in *The Post*. You may be confident that your observations will be presented with both accuracy and sympathy."

There's a vibrancy to Miss Quinn that makes Beatrice think of an actress onstage, or maybe a street-witch misdirecting her audience.

Beatrice feels exceptionally drab and stupid standing beside her. She smiles a little desperately, perspiring in the spring sun. "I'm afraid I don't have any opinions to offer."

"A shame. Suffragists have a reputation for opinions."

"I'm not really a suffragist. I mean, I'm not a formal member of the Association."

"Nor am I, and yet I persist in having all manner of opinions and observations."

Beatrice catches a laugh before it escapes and stuffs it back down her throat. "Perhaps you ought to join, then."

She can tell by the flattening of Miss Quinn's smile that it's the wrong thing to say, and Beatrice knows why. She's overheard enough talk at the library and read enough editorials in *The Ladies' Tribune* to understand that the New Salem Women's Association is divided on the question of the color-line. Some worry that the inclusion of colored women might tarnish their respectable reputation; others feel they ought to spend a few more decades being grateful for their freedom before they agitate for anything so radical as rights. Most of them agree it would be far more convenient if colored women remained in the Colored Women's League.

Beatrice herself suspects that two separate-but-equal organizations are far less effective than a single united one, and that their daddy was as wrong about freedmen needing to go back to Africa as he was about women minding their place—but she's never worried overmuch about it. She feels an uncomfortable twist of shame in her belly.

Miss Quinn's smile has smoothed. "I think not. But the equinox, Miss Eastwood. Why don't you tell me what you saw?"

"The same thing everyone saw, I'm sure. A sudden wind. Stars. A tower."

"A door with certain words inscribed on it and a certain sign beneath them." Miss Quinn says it mildly, but her eyes are yellow, feline.

"Was there?" Beatrice asks lamely.

"There was. An old symbol of circles woven together. It's of . . . particular interest to me and certain of my associates. Would you—a librarian, I think you said?—happen to know anything about that sign?"

"I—I'm afraid not. That is, circles are common in all sorts of sigils and spell-work, and the number three is a number of traditional significance, isn't it? It could be anything."

"I see. Although"—Miss Quinn smiles a checkmate sort of smile— "I don't believe I told you how many circles there were."

"Ah."

"Miss Eastwood. I was just heading to the tea shop on Sixth. Won't you join me?"

As she says it, she gives Beatrice a particular kind of look through her lashes, heated and secret. It's a look Beatrice has spent seven years carefully neither giving nor receiving nor even wanting.

(When she was younger she permitted herself to want such things. To admire a woman's peony-petal lips or the delicate hollow of her throat. She learned her lesson.)

She takes an anxious step back from Miss Cleopatra Quinn and her long eyelashes. "I—I'm afraid I must get to work." She attempts a cool nod. "Good day."

Miss Quinn looks neither offended nor discouraged by her abrupt departure, but merely more intent. "Until we meet again, Miss Eastwood." She gives Beatrice a sober tip of her derby hat and spreads her skirt in a gesture that is half-bow and half-curtsy. Beatrice blushes for no reason she can name.

Beatrice walks the three blocks back to the College with her eyes on her boots, not-thinking about moonbeams or witch-tales or the thin wedding band around Miss Quinn's finger.

She barely hears the scintillated whispers of the passersby or the paper-boys darting like swallows through the streets, calling out headlines (*Witches Loose in New Salem! Hill's Morality Party on the Rise! Mayor Worthington Under Pressure!*), and if the shadows on the streets behave oddly—peeling away from dark doorways and coiling out of alleyways, trailing after her like the black hem of a long cloak—Beatrice does not notice.

7

Bye baby bunting,
Mother's gone a-hunting

A spell to end what hasn't yet begun, requiring pennyroyal &
regret

Two weeks after she found her long-lost sisters and lost them again, Agnes Amaranth is standing in a dim back-alley shop just off St. Fortitude. There is no sign or title on the door, but Agnes knows she's in the right place: she can smell the wild scent of herbs and earth, just like Mags's hut, out of place in the cobbled gray of New Salem.

The proprietress is a handsome Greek woman with black curls and dark-painted eyes. She introduces herself, in an accent that rolls and purls, as Madame Zina Card: palmist, spiritualist, card-reader, and midwife.

But Agnes hasn't come to have her fortune told or her palms read. "Pennyroyal, please," she says, and it's enough.

Madame Zina gives her a weighing look, as though checking to see whether Agnes knows what she's asked for and why, then unlocks a cupboard and tucks a few dried sprigs into a brown paper sack.

"Steep the pennyroyal in river-water—boil it good, mind—and stir it seven times with a silver spoon. The words cost extra." Madame Zina's eyes linger on the eggshell swell of Agnes's belly. She's barely showing, but only women in a particular state come to visit Zina's shop asking for pennyroyal.

Agnes shakes her head once. "I already have them." Mags told them to her when she was sixteen. She hasn't forgotten.

Madame Zina nods amiably and hands her the brown paper sack sealed with wax. Concern crimps her black brows. "No need to look so glum, girl. I don't know what your man or your god has told you, but there's no sin to it. It's just the way of the world, older than the Three themselves. Not every woman wants a child."

Agnes almost laughs at her: *Of course* she wants a child. Of course she wants to lay its sleeping cheek against her breastbone and smell its milk-sweet breath, to become on its behalf something grander than herself: a castle or a sword, stone or steel, all the things her mother wasn't.

But Agnes wanted to take care of her sisters, once. She won't bring another life into the world just to fail it, too.

She doesn't know how to put any of her foolish, doomed wanting into words, so she shrugs at Madame Zina, feeling the bones of her shoulders grate.

"Let me read the cards for you. Free of charge." Zina gestures to an armchair that looks like it was once pink or cream but is now the greasy color of unwashed skin. Ragged red curtains droop over the arm.

"No, thank you."

Zina runs her tongue over her teeth, eyes narrowed. "I could read *hers*, if you like." Her eyes are on Agnes's belly.

Agnes sits as if something heavy has hit the backs of her knees.

Zina settles herself across from her and produces a pack of over-sized cards with gold stars painted on their backs and edges gone soft with use.

"Her past." She flips over the Three of Swords, showing a ruby-red heart with three swords run cleanly through it. Agnes thinks of her sundered sisters and the terrible wounds they've dealt one another, seven years old and still unhealed, and shifts uncomfortably in the chair.

"Her present." Zina lays out three cards this time: the Witch of Swords, the Witch of Wands, and the Witch of Cups. Agnes almost smiles to see them. The Witch of Swords even looks a little like Juniper—her hair a wild splatter of ink, her expression fierce.

"Her future." The Eight of Swords, showing a woman bound and blind, surrounded by enemies. The Hanged Woman, dangling upside down like a sacrificial animal on the altar. Agnes avoids her gaze.

Zina sets the deck on the table and taps it once. "You draw the last one."

Agnes reaches out her hand but a sudden wind whips through the open window—night-cool and tricksome, scented faintly with roses—and scatters the deck across the floor. The wind riffles like fingers through the fallen cards before whispering into silence. It leaves a single card face up: the Tower, shadowed and tall.

Agnes's blood burns at the sight of it. "Here—" She claws the cards off the floor and shoves them at Zina. "Let me choose properly."

Zina purses her lips as if she thinks Agnes is being a little stupid, but shuffles the deck. She knocks the edges on the table and presents it again.

Agnes turns the card and the Tower leers up at her a second time. A black spire of ink surrounded by white pinpricks. Up close she sees the border is actually a tangle of thorned vines with smears of dull pink for blooms, like tiny mouths. Or roses.

Agnes stands very abruptly. "I'm sorry. I have to go." She wants nothing to do with that tower or that wicked wind. She knows what trouble looks like when it comes slinking through the open window to tug at the loose threads of your fate.

"Oh, it's not such a bad reading as all that. She'll face trials, but who doesn't in this life?"

Agnes can only shake her head and stumble backward toward the door. She hears Zina call after her—"Come see me when you change your mind. I'm the best midwife in West Babel, ask anyone"—before she is out in the alley, turning right on St. Fortitude.

She walks with one hand fisted in her pocket, palms sweating into the brown paper of the sack, cards hovering behind her eyes like portents or promises: the tower; the heart stabbed thrice over; the three witches.

She can feel the edges of a story plucking at her, making her the middle sister in some dark witch-tale.

Better the middle sister than the mother. Middle sisters are forgotten or failed or ill-fated, but at least they survive, mostly; mothers rarely make it past the first line. They die, as gently and easily as flowers wilting, and leave their three daughters exposed to all the wickedness of the world.

Their deaths aren't gentle or easy in real life. Agnes was five when Juniper was born, but she remembers the mess of stained sheets and the wet-pearl color of her mother's skin. The old-penny stink of birth and blood.

Her father watching with a jagged wrongness in his face, arms crossed, not running for help, not ringing the bell that would bring Mama Mags and her herbs and rhymes.

Agnes should have rung the bell herself, should have slipped out the back door and hauled on the half-rotten rope—but she didn't. Because she was scared of the wrong-thing in her daddy's eyes, because she chose her own hide over her mother.

She remembers her mother's hand—white and bloodless as the blank pages at the end of a book—touching her cheek just before the end. Her voice saying, *Take care of them, Agnes Amaranth*. Bella was older, but she knew Agnes was the strong one.

That first night it was Agnes who washed the blood from her baby sister's skin. Agnes who let her suck on the tip of her pinky finger when she cried. Later it was Agnes who brushed her hair before school and held her hand in the endless night behind the cellar door.

And it was Agnes who left Juniper to fend for herself, because she wasn't strong enough to stay. Because survival is a selfish thing.

Now her sisters are here with her in the sinless city and their daddy is dead. Agnes ought to be relieved, but she's seen enough of the world to know he was just one monster among many, one cruelty in an endless line. It's safer to walk alone. The brown paper bag in her pocket is a promise that she'll stay that way.

She passes a tannery, eyes watering with acid or maybe something else. A butcher shop, a cobbler, a stable half-full of police horses idly stamping iron hooves. St. Charity Hospital, a low limestone building that smells of lye and lesions, built by the Church to tend to the filthy, godless inhabitants of West Babel. Agnes has seen nuns and doctors walking the streets, proselytizing at unmarried women and waving purity pledges. But girls who give birth at Charity's came out grayish and sagging, holding their babies loosely, as if they aren't certain they belong to them. At the mill most women prefer mothers and midwives, when their time comes.

Now St. Charity's echoes with the hacking sounds of the summer fever. Someone has drawn a witch-mark across the door, a crooked cross daubed in ash. Agnes wonders if the rumors are right and a second plague is coming.

She crosses the street and distracts herself by reading the tattered posters pasted along fences and walls. Advertisements and ordinances; wanted posters with rain-splotched photographs; bills for the Centennial Fair next month.

On the corner of Twenty-Second Street the brick has been entirely covered by a single repeated poster, like grim wallpaper. It's crisp and new-looking, the image printed in bold black and red: a raised fist holding a burning torch against the night. Smoke coils from the flames, forming ghoulish faces and animal bodies and distorted words: SIN,

SUFFRAGE, WITCHCRAFT. Smaller, saner lettering across the top urges citizens to *Vote Gideon Hill! Our Light Against the Darkness!*

Three men stand clustered ahead of Agnes, holding paste buckets and stacks of posters, each wearing bronze pins engraved with Hill's lit torch. There's something vaguely unsettling about them—the odd synchrony of their movements, maybe, or the fervid glaze of their eyes, or the way their shadows seem sluggish, moving a half-second behind their owners.

"Tell your husband—vote Hill!" one of them says as she passes.

"Our light against the darkness!" says the second.

"Can't be too careful, with women's witching back on the loose." The third extends one of the posters toward her.

Agnes should take it and bob her head politely—she knows better than to start shit with zealots—but she doesn't. Instead she spits on the ground between them, splattering the man's boots with cotton-colored slime.

She doesn't know why she did it. Maybe she's tired of knowing better, of minding her place. Maybe because she can feel her wild younger sister with her in the city, tugging her toward trouble.

Agnes and the man stare together at the spit sliding off his boot, glistening like the snotty trail of a snail. He stands very still, but Agnes notes distantly that the arms of his shadow are moving, reaching toward her skirts.

And then she's running, refusing to find out what those shadow-hands will do to her, or what the hell kind of witchcraft is on the loose in New Salem.

She runs down Twenty-Second and turns on St. Jude's and then she's back in Room No. 7 of the South Sybil boarding house, panting and holding her barely showing belly. She withdraws Zina's brown paper bag from her apron.

Pennyroyal and a half-cup of river-water: all it takes to keep that circle drawn tight around her heart. To stay alone, and survive.

She did it once before—drank it down in one bitter swallow, felt nothing but rib-shaking relief when the cramps knotted her belly—and never regretted it.

Now she finds herself setting the brown paper sack on the floor, unopened. Lying down in her narrow bed and wishing her oldest sister was here to whisper a story to her.

Or to the spark inside her, that second heart beating stubbornly on.

8

Queen Anne, Queen Anne
You sit in the sun
Fair as a lily and white as a wand.

A spell to shed light, requiring heartwood & heat

Beatrice Belladonna dreams of Agnes that night, but when she wakes only Juniper is there in the stuffy dark of her attic room.

She knows by the damp gleam of Juniper's eyes that she's awake, too, but neither of them mentions their middle sister. There are many things they don't mention.

Yet Juniper keeps sleeping in her room and Beatrice keeps letting her, and she supposes it could just go on this way: Juniper spending her days busy with the Association and coming home with pins and sashes and rolled-up signs that need painting, Beatrice spending her library shifts following whispers and witch-tales toward the Lost Way, never quite telling her little sister what she knows or thinks she knows—maybe because it feels too unlikely, too impossible; maybe because it doesn't feel impossible enough.

Maybe because she worries what a woman like Juniper might do if the power of witching is won back.

Spring in New Salem is a gray, sulking creature, and by the middle of April Beatrice feels like a tall, bespectacled mushroom. Juniper has taken to lighting her pitch pine wand in the evenings just to feel sunlight on her skin, talking wistfully about the bluebells and bloodroot in flower back home.

Beatrice asks her once when she plans to return to Crow County— she's sure their cousin Dan would let Juniper live in Mags's old house for nothing or nearly nothing, even if he is a dumbshit—but Juniper's face closes up like a house with drawn shutters. The witch-light fades from the wand-tip, leaving them in chill darkness. Beatrice adds it to the list of unmentionable things between them.

The next morning Juniper leaves early for the Association and Beatrice reads her paper alone at the breakfast table. She has recently become a subscriber to *The New Salem Defender* in addition to *The Post*. This, she assures herself, is merely part of her increasing interest in political news and has nothing to do with the tingle in her fingertips when she sees the name C. P. QUINN printed in small capitals. She wonders what the P stands for, and if colored women have mother's-names.

Beatrice is assigned to the circulation desk that afternoon. She helps a white-bearded monk with his biography of Geoffrey Hawthorn (*G. Hawthorn: The Scourge of Old Salem*) and lights lamps for a cluster of haggard students who look as if they would rather change their names and flee into the countryside than finish their spring term. By afternoon she's at the desk, supposedly processing recent arrivals—a new edition of Seeley's *Expansion of England*, an account of the East India Company's campaign against the thuggee witches of India; a bound version of Jackson Turner's *The Witch in American History*, which argues that the threat and subsequent destruction of Old Salem defined America's virtuous spirit—but is really watching the whale-belly sky through the mullioned windows, feeling her eyelids hinge shut.

She wakes to an amused voice saying, "Pardon me?"

She unpeels her face from *The Witch in American History* and snaps upright, adjusting her spectacles with mounting horror.

Today Miss Cleopatra (P.) Quinn has her derby hat tucked politely beneath one arm. Her gentleman's coat has been replaced by a double-buttoned vest and her hair is swept into a braided crown. It must be raining, because water pearls over her bare skin, catching the light in a way that Beatrice has no name for (luminous).

Beatrice manages a strangled "What are you doing here?"

Miss Quinn adopts an arch, censorious expression, although a certain irreverence glitters in her eyes. "I was under the impression that libraries were public institutions."

"Oh, yes. That is—I thought—" *You came to see me.* Beatrice closes her eyes very briefly in mortification. She tries again. "Welcome to the Salem College collections. How may I help you?"

"Much better." The irreverence has escaped her eyes and now curls at the corners of her mouth. "I'm looking for information on the tower last seen at St. George's Square, and the Last Three Witches of the West." Her voice is far too loud.

Beatrice makes an abortive movement as if she might launch herself across the desk and press her palm over Miss Quinn's lips. "*Saints,* woman! Anyone could overhear you!"

"So take me someplace more private." She gives Beatrice another of those highly inappropriate *looks* and Beatrice swallows, feeling like a harried pawn on a chessboard.

Mr. Blackwell agrees to cover the circulation desk and watches the pair of them retreat to Beatrice's office with a doubtful expression. He comes from broad-minded Quaker stock, but there are rules about people like Miss Quinn lingering too long in the Salem College Library. The rules aren't written down anywhere, but the important rules rarely are.

Beatrice clicks her door closed and turns around to find Miss Quinn reading the spines of stacked books and peering at the black leather notebook that lies open on the table. Beatrice snaps it shut.

"As I told you on a previous occasion, I'm afraid I don't know anything about the events at the square, or the Last Three. You are of course welcome to search our collections."

"Oh, but I was hoping for a guided tour. From someone with more...intimate information." Her tone is over-warm, over-familiar, over-everything. She's doing what Mama Mags called *laying it on thick.*

Why? What does she know about three circles woven together, three lost witches and their not-so-Lost Way? Beatrice puts frost in her voice. "What do you want?"

"Only what every woman wants."

"And what's that?"

Miss Quinn's smile hardens, and Beatrice thinks this must be her true smile, beneath the dazzle and shine of whatever act she's putting on. "What *belongs* to her," she hisses. "What was stolen." There's a different kind of wanting in her tone now, one that Beatrice believes because hasn't she felt it, too?

She hesitates.

Miss Quinn plants her palms on Beatrice's desk and leans across it. "You and I are both women of words, I surmise. We share an interest in truth-seeking, storytelling. Surely we might share those stories with one another? I am capable of great discretion, I assure you." Her voice is all honey again, oozing sincerity. "Whatever you tell me I will keep just between the two of us. I promise."

Beatrice manages a breathless laugh, dizzy with the clove-and-ink scent of her skin. "Are you a journalist or a detective, Miss Quinn?"

"Oh, every good journalist is a detective." She leans away, straightening her sleeves. "What are you?"

"Nothing," Beatrice says, because it's true. She was born nobody and taught to stay that way—*remember what you are*—and now she's just a skinny librarian with gray already streaking her hair, a premonition of spinsterhood.

Miss Quinn raises her eyebrows and nods at the ratty notebook still clutched to Beatrice's chest. "And what of your work? Is that nothing?"

Beatrice should say yes. She should toss her notes aside and flick her fingers. *Oh, that? Just moonbeams and daydreams.*

Her fingers tighten on her notebook instead. "It's not…much. Just conjecture so far. But I think…" She wets her lips. "But I think I found the words and ways to call back the Lost Way of Avalon. Or some of them."

She flinches as she says it, half waiting for the crack of a nun's knuckles or the cold draft of the cellar.

Miss Quinn doesn't scorn or scold her. "Really," she says, and waits. Listens.

Beatrice isn't listened to very often. She finds it makes her heart flutter in a most distracting fashion. "It's this rhyme our grandmother taught us. I thought she made it up, but then I found it in the back of a first-edition copy of the Grimms' *Witch-Tales*—you're familiar with the Grimms?"

She tells Miss Quinn about wayward sisters and maiden's blood and her theory that secrets might have survived somehow in old wives' tales and children's rhymes. "It must sound ridiculous."

Miss Quinn lifts one shoulder. "Not to me. Sometimes a thing is too dangerous to be written down or said straight out. Sometimes you have to slip it in slantwise, half-hidden."

"Even if I pieced together the spell, I doubt any of us has enough witch-blood to work it. All the true witches were burned centuries ago."

"All of them, Miss Eastwood?" There's a hint of pity in Quinn's voice. "How, then, did Cairo manage to repel the Ottomans and the redcoats both for decades, despite all their rifles and ships? Why did Andrew Jackson leave those Choctaw in Mississippi? Out of the goodness of his black little heart?" The pity sharpens, turns scathing. "Do you really think the slavers found every witch aboard their ships and tossed her overboard?"

Beatrice has encountered wild theories that there was witchcraft at work in Stono and Haiti, that Turner and Brown were aided by super-natural means. She's heard the scintillated whispers about colored covens still prowling the streets. But at St. Hale's she was taught that such stories were base rumors, the product of ignorance and superstition.

Quinn gentles her tone. "Maybe even good Saint George missed a witch or two during the purge. How do you think your grandmother came to know those words in the first place?"

Beatrice has not permitted herself to ask that question out loud. To wonder who Mags's mother was, and her mother's mother. *Witch-blood runs thick in the sewers*, after all.

"Surely it's worth looking for these missing words and ways of yours, at least."

"I—perhaps." Beatrice swallows hard against the hope rising in her throat. "But they don't seem to want to be found." She gestures at her desk, strewn with scraps and open books and dead-ends. "I've read the Sisters Grimm a dozen times, every edition I could find. I've made a good start on the other folklorists—Charlotte Perrault, Andrea Lang—but if there are any secret instructions or notes tucked inside them they're faded, stained…lost."

She doesn't mention the shadow-hand she saw splayed across the page, or the creeping sense that someone doesn't want the words to be found, on the grounds that she wants Miss Quinn to continue thinking of her as a sane adult. "I've *been* looking. But I've been failing."

Miss Quinn does not look particularly distressed. She gives Beatrice a smart nod and sets her derby hat on the desktop. She unbuttons her sleeves and rolls them up, revealing several inches of pox-scarred wrist. "Well, naturally."

"Oh?"

Miss Quinn perches on the same stack of encyclopedias Juniper occupied a few weeks before and extends her hand, palm up, toward Beatrice and her black notebook. Her expression is teasing but her eyes are sober, her hand steady. "You didn't have me."

Beatrice rubs her thumb along the spine of her notebook, stuffed full of her most private thoughts and theories, her wildest suppositions and most dangerous inquiries. Her own heart, sewn and bound.

It should be difficult to hand it over to a near-stranger, even impossible. It isn't.

Juniper didn't have any friends, growing up. The girls at school weren't allowed to visit the Eastwood farm, either because of the whispers of witching that surrounded Mama Mags or the alcohol fumes that surrounded their daddy, or the ugly rumors about just how their mother died (*awful suspicious*, people muttered, *I heard she was fixing to leave him*).

One way or another it was only ever Juniper and her sisters and the green, green mountainside, and after the fire it was just Juniper and the mountain. Juniper figured she wasn't missing much anyhow; her daddy said women were like hens, flocking together and pecking at one another, and Juniper didn't want to be a hen.

But a whole month after signing up with the suffragists to end the tyranny of man, she's started to suspect her daddy was dead wrong.

She doesn't like all of the Association ladies—lots of them are fancy, fur-lined-cloak types who look at Juniper like a yellow dog that wandered into the wrong neighborhood—but even the snotty ones are there for the same reason, have come to lend their white-gloved hands to the same work. It makes Juniper think of the quilting circles Mama Mags used to talk about, where a whole valley's worth of women would huddle in somebody's kitchen and all their tiny stitches would add up to something bigger than themselves.

And not all of them are snotty. There's Miss Stone, who's always busy and never smiles but inspires a fervent, infectious loyalty among her troops; the secretary, Jennie Lind, who keeps to herself but proves to have a surprising weakness for Juniper's witch-tales; a fat, fashionable widow named Inez Gillmore who has more money than the pope and keeps offering Juniper various hats and bonnets to cover her sawn-off hair; an older woman, Electa Gage, who keeps muttering about chaining themselves to public buildings like the English ladies did. Juniper doesn't understand what this is supposed to achieve, but she admires the spirit of it and likes Electa very much.

Sometimes when they're all together, laughing and arguing, it feels like having sisters again. Juniper can almost forget that Agnes is a seething silence on the other side of the city, that Bella is so stiff and buttoned up it's like living with a department store mannequin. Bella's been leaving early and staying late every day, working on some mysterious research that leaves her sleeves stained with ink and her eyes bloodshot. She comes home with a distracted, distant air, her little black notebook clutched in her hand. When Juniper questions her—What's she looking for? Does she know what that sign means? What called the tower to them, and what sent it away?—she evades and delays and never quite says.

Maybe Juniper wouldn't take it so personal-like, except last week she visited Bella's office unannounced and found a colored girl in a men's coat sitting on top of her desk. Bella blushed and said she was "an interested party" but didn't say what she was interested in or why.

After that she figured she'd wait until Bella was sound asleep some night and sneak that little black notebook out from under her pillow and find out for herself what that tower is and who called it. She has certain suspicions.

In the meantime she has Jennie and Inez and Electa and an endless stream of committees and subcommittees to keep her busy. She didn't think throwing down the tyranny of man would take so many meetings, but apparently it does.

After the third or fourth meeting that leaves Juniper facedown on her agenda, praying for the sweet release of her untimely death, Miss Stone takes pity on her and assigns her instead to the practical work of preparing for the march at the Centennial Fair. It's unglamorous to hang flyers and iron sashes and paint slogans, but it beats endless rounds of yeas and nays.

She's crouched in the back rooms of the Association headquarters, painting the final N on a VOTES FOR WOMEN sign and swearing every time the brush bristles break, when the doorbell jangles.

An unctuous voice calls, "Hello? Excuse me?" and Juniper hears Jennie say, "How may I help you, sir?" Timid boot-steps entering the office, then a voice too low for Juniper to catch. She figures she can ignore it—probably just another monk come to complain about their heathen ways or a reporter come to provoke scintillating quotes—until Jennie herself appears in the doorway looking pale. "Miss Stone, come quick!"

Miss Stone marches to the front office with the polite, cold-iron expression Juniper has come to think of as her battle armor. Juniper and the others trail after her like squires or foot soldiers.

In the front office they find a cringing, watery-eyed gentleman accompanied by his cringing, watery-eyed dog. Juniper thinks he looks like an aging, human-sized pill-bug, ready to roll up in a ball if anything startles him.

He and his dog blink up at the ladies now filling the room. "Apologies for calling unannounced, ladies, but I'm afraid I come bearing bad news." He addresses his remarks to no one in particular, eyes skittering from frowning face to frowning face. "I come as a representative of the New Salem City Council. We regret to inform you that the Council has, ah, withdrawn its approval for your march at the Centennial Fair on the first of May. In light of the current climate."

Juniper doesn't see what the weather has to do with anything—wet and gray but warming fast, the promise of summer steaming up from the cobblestones—but she knows horseshit when she hears it.

Miss Stone crosses her arms. "On what grounds, sir? Our petition was approved weeks ago by the mayor's office."

The man smiles at her. It's a repellent expression: wormy and crawling. His dog licks its teeth in a cringing grin. "I'm afraid the Council overrode Mayor Worthington on this issue. We wouldn't want to alarm the citizenry any further with such...antics." He makes a hand gesture that might refer to the march or the Association or the entire concept of women's rights.

Miss Stone starts to say something measured and polite. Juniper cuts across her. "And just who the hell are you to tell us what to do?"

He and his dog swivel toward her, their eyes finding hers in the crowded room. The dog lifts its head cautiously, sniffing the air, and its owner smiles again. She likes his smile even less. "I beg your pardon. This is Lady"—he tugs the leash and the dog flinches—"and I'm a member of the City Council, running as an independent candidate this fall. Mr. Gideon Hill, at your service."

This is Gideon Hill? Juniper has seen his posters plastered all over town, read his nasty quotes in the paper. She thought he'd be somebody substantial—a handsome, square-jawed man like Daddy, capable of charming paint off a fencepost if he put his mind to it. But he's just a stooped, middle-aged man in a creased linen suit, with thinning hair and furtive eyes.

A ripple has gone around the room as the other Association members rustle to one another.

Miss Stone makes another attempt at civility. "We're pleased to meet you, Mr. Hill. We would like to appeal the Council's decision in this matter. We don't want to make any trouble." She ignores Electa's mutter of "speak for yourself" and Juniper's snort.

"I'm afraid it was a unanimous decision." Hill doesn't sound very sorry, though his shoulders are curved inward and his tone is contrite. "It is the Council's duty to protect this city from sin and vice. New Salem must not follow the path of its namesake."

Juniper figures he means Old Salem, the city taken by witches and devils in the seventeen-whatevers. It's a scorched ruin, now, good for nothing but ghost stories.

Hill continues, "Thus the Council is obliged to forbid—"

"And what if we don't give a damn what the Council forbids?" Juniper hears Miss Stone give a soft sigh, but she doesn't care.

Hill looks at her again. She's expecting him to splutter with outrage, to gasp at her daring, but he doesn't. Instead he offers her another smile, even more sickly than the others. "What did you say your name was again, miss?"

And just like that, all the fight goes out of her. Most of the wanted posters are sun-faded and tattered by now, but not all of them, and she knows Hill and his kind would love nothing better than a real live witch to string up.

She swallows. "June W-West."

"And where are you from, Miss West?"

Miss Stone rescues her, sailing between Juniper and Hill like a white-wigged ship. "Thank you for informing us of the Council's decision, Mr. Hill. The Association will take it under advisement."

"Good day, girls." Mr. Hill bows his head and turns away, but his dog doesn't follow. She remains crouched, inky eyes fixed on Juniper, iron collar biting into her throat. Hill gives the leash a vicious tug and she follows her master out the door. The bell tinkles cheerily as they leave.

Juniper limps to the window to watch them go. Mr. Gideon Hill scurries down the street with his hands clasped behind his back and his dog trotting obediently at his heels. In the late afternoon light their shadows are black and long, larger than their owners. As Juniper watches she sees Mr. Hill's shadow ripple strangely, as if it isn't quite under its master's command.

Fear slicks down her spine. She recalls that, by the evidence of the black tower, there is at least one unknown witch in the city working toward ends of her own. But why would she bewitch a sniveling city councilor? Rather than, say, quietly poisoning him in his sleep?

She hears raised voices behind her, catches stray words. *Unfair! Unjust!* And then: *Nothing we can do.*

Someone objects, almost certainly Electa. "Nothing *legal* we can do, you mean!"

Someone else gives a little gasp. Juniper thinks it must be that Susan Bee woman, a mummified Victorian type who wears an honest-to-Eve monocle and treats Juniper like a cleaning girl. "We aren't *criminals*, Miss Gage!"

Electa starts to reply but Miss Stone cuts across her. "Nor can we afford to become so, Electa." There's no heat to it; she merely sounds old, and very tired. "Ladies, do we have a quorum present? Let us discuss our response." She shepherds her flock into the back offices again.

Only Jennie lingers. "June?"

"Mm?" Juniper is watching Hill's shadow disappear around a corner, trying to decide if it seems darker than other shadows, denser.

"They're calling a meeting. Don't you think we ought to join?"

"No." Juniper turns away from the window. "I don't. I think we ought to march at the Centennial Fair."

To her considerable credit, Jennie doesn't gasp or squeal. She looks straight back at Juniper, level and hard, and Juniper sees a fierce spark in her eyes. She wonders for the first time how Jennie's nose got broken, and if she was ever anything other than a part-time secretary with corn-silk hair.

"Miss Stone won't like it," she observes.

"No." Juniper likes Miss Stone, but she's gotten too used to hearing the word *no.* "It'll do her good to see a woman take that *no* and shove it back down somebody's throat."

"The police'll never let us in."

"So we disguise ourselves until the very last second, and disappear before they show up. I know the words and ways." Juniper can tell by Jennie's flinch that she knows what kinds of words and ways Juniper means. And she can tell by the sly shine of her eyes that she doesn't mind it, that she's tired of *no* too.

Juniper smiles, all teeth. "I think you've already got the will."

9

Ashes to ashes, dust to dust
Yours to mine and mine to yours.

A spell to bind, requiring a tight stitch & a steady hand

On the last night of April, Beatrice Belladonna is curled in the round window of her attic room, reading Charlotte Perrault's *Tales and Stories of the Past with Morals* by witch-light. She ought to use a candle or an oil lamp like a respectable woman should, but she's grown used to the honeyed glow of Juniper's pitch pine wand in the evenings. Last week she came home to find a thin strip of holly and a note in Juniper's uncertain hand: YOU OTTA KNOW THE WORDS BY NOW.

Beatrice does. When she works the spell the wand-light is silvery and cool, nothing like Juniper's midsummer blaze. She finds it restful.

It's late. The moon is a pearl over the neat rows of north-side rooftops, and Bethlehem Heights looks like a cuckoo clock running along hidden rails, each piece in its place. Beatrice is thinking of abandoning Perrault, who seems to have no secret rhymes or riddles to offer, when she hears the *thump-thump-clack* of her sister's steps on the stairs.

Beatrice remains curled in the window. "Evening."

Juniper grunts in response, leaving her staff at the door and tossing her half-cloak over the back of a chair, apparently not noticing the bread and broth Beatrice set out hours ago. It's gone cold, the surface skinned with fat.

Juniper shuffles over to the window, scowls out at the pearl moon. She holds a ladies' hat in her hands, fashionable and frothy, purest white. Beatrice can't imagine an article of clothing less likely to be worn by her youngest sister.

"Fair opens tomorrow," Juniper says.

"Yes."

"We're marching at five. After Worthington's speech."

"I thought you said your permit was revoked?"

Juniper gives her a careless shrug, a crow ruffling its feathers.

"I thought that Stone woman was opposed to . . . illegal activities."

Another shrug. "She is."

". . . I see."

Juniper waits, spinning the white hat in her hands. "So. Will you be joining us?"

"Joining what?" It takes Beatrice a second to understand that Juniper is referring to the highly visible and apparently unsanctioned march for women's suffrage. "Oh, n-no, I don't think so. What would the library think?"

She can see Juniper's lip curl, her teeth sharp in the moonlight. "Right. Of course."

Beatrice refrains from pointing out that her position at the library is the reason Juniper has a roof over her head and cold broth to ignore, nor does she invite her sister to trot over to the west side and beg for work in the mills. She merely wants to.

Juniper is still standing beside her, still turning that absurd hat in her hands. "You ought to come watch, at least. It's going to be quite a show." Beatrice hears the satisfaction in her sister's voice and feels a certain uneasiness run down her spine.

The floorboards creak as Juniper turns away. "Invite that colored friend of yours, if you like. Cleopatra."

"Miss Quinn?" (Cleopatra has asked her several times to call her *Cleo*, but Beatrice can't imagine being bold enough to reduce the distance between them to four flimsy letters.)

In the silence that follows, Beatrice pictures herself taking a long morning walk down to New Cairo—the trolleys don't run to the colored end of town—and strolling into the offices of *The Defender*. Casually inviting Miss Quinn to accompany her to a suffrage march, proving herself to be something more than a timid librarian. Perhaps provoking Miss Quinn into one of those sharp, honest smiles, rather than her charming lies.

Beatrice finds herself suddenly more interested in the Centennial Fair. "I suppose—"

But she's been quiet too long. She feels the hot snap of Juniper's temper through the line between them. "Never mind. It doesn't matter."

The door slams shut, limping steps fade quickly, and Beatrice is alone.

She sits in the window for another hour, watching the moon, wondering what it would feel like to fly with moonlight on her bare shoulders, then stands abruptly. She writes a note addressed to Mr. Blackwell, explaining that she will not be able to work her usual shift tomorrow as she has developed a sudden fever.

She lies awake in bed for a long time after, buzzing and nervy. She falls asleep thinking of the place where the trolley lines end.

Agnes is not sleeping. She is tossing and turning, discovering all the new and novel ways in which her body can be uncomfortable. The baby inside her is still small—"the size of a spring cabbage," Madame Zina told her cheerily—but she seems to possess an uncanny ability to find every tender nerve and soft tissue in her body. At night Agnes feels her clawing and kicking, a cat in a too-small cage. She holds her palms flat to her belly and thinks, *Stay mad, baby girl*.

Agnes threw the pennyroyal down the boarding-house privy weeks ago. She did it without drama or debate, as if it were any other brown paper sack of ingredients she no longer needed. When she returned to her room she sat on the floor and trailed her finger in a circle around herself. There were two of them inside it now.

Sometime past midnight she hears uneven steps in the hall and feels an invisible thread winding tight.

Paper rustles. The steps retreat.

When Agnes rises she finds a white square of paper slid beneath her door: COME TO THE FAIR TOMORROW, 4 O'CLOCK. IF YOU GOT THE GUTS.

Agnes knows from the shaky shape of the capitals and the attitude that the note is from Juniper. She doesn't know what's going to happen tomorrow at the Centennial Fair, but, given the electric hum in the line between them, like charged air before a storm, Agnes feels confident it will be deeply stupid and possibly dangerous.

She crumples the note in her fist and pictures tossing it down the privy, too. She wouldn't even need to make an extra trip; she always needs to piss, these days.

Instead she smooths the note flat on the table. She looks at it a long time before she climbs back into bed.

The day before the march, Jennie Lind asked Juniper if she'd ever been to a fair. *Sure*, Juniper told her. Back home they had a cornbread festival every fall. Jennie laughed at her and Juniper thwacked her with a rolled-up poster and Jennie laughed harder.

It's only as Juniper walks under the arched iron entranceway of the New Salem Centennial Fair that she knows why.

The Centennial Fair makes the cornbread festival look like a church picnic. It's like a whole second city sprung up on the north end of New Salem, filled with smart white tents and gaudy stalls and salesmen hawking newfangled contraptions. Electric lights buzz and swing between the tents, singeing the top-hats and hair-dos of the crowd below, and a great metal Ferris wheel spins above them. The air smells rich and fatty, like sweat and fry oil and dollar bills.

Inez buys seven tickets at the booth and passes them around. Juniper, Jennie, Electa; Mary, Minerva, Nell; each of them clutching a white hat in their hands, each of them wearing expressions suitable for the storming of castles.

Juniper had hoped there'd be more of them, but Jennie said they couldn't risk inviting anyone who might turn tail and report their plan back to Miss Stone, so they approached only the most discontented, troublesome members of the Association. Things always come in sevens in witch-tales (swans, dwarves, days to create the world), so Juniper figures they'll do fine.

They spend the day jostling through the Fair, unremarkable in dull olives and sober grays, just seven more citizens come to celebrate the founding of New Salem. They pass knots of mill-girls and flower-sellers, students from the College and men from the tannery, a handful of policemen riding shining white horses. The girls eye them as they pass, linking arms and exchanging looks, perhaps stroking the white brims of their hats. Juniper thinks of wanted posters and murder charges and what could happen if she's caught, and resolves not to be.

They dodge souvenir-sellers offering commemorative plates and historical pamphlets. They buy sausages on little wooden sticks and burn their lips on the grease. They walk so far that Juniper's bad leg aches and she leans hard on her cedar staff.

Her daddy never used a cane, though he should have; he said they were for grannies and cripples, not proud veterans of Lincoln's war. Sometimes when he was deep in his cups he'd give Juniper's staff a mean, slanted look, like it was an old enemy of his, but he never laid a hand on it.

They wander into a tent labeled *Doctor Marvel's Magnificent Anthropological Exhibition!*, which features a number of natives wearing beads and feathers and bored expressions. Juniper pauses for a while to observe THE LAST WITCH-DOCTOR OF THE CONGO, PRESERVED FOR SCIENTIFIC STUDY, who turns out to be a withered African woman with an iron witch-collar locked around her neck. Her skin beneath the collar is whitish and dead-looking, like frostbitten fingertips; Juniper finds she can't meet the woman's eyes. She limps out of Doctor Marvel's tent and tosses her half-sausage away, uneaten.

By four o'clock she and the others make their way to the center stage, where a crowd is gathering beneath red-and-white pennants. Inez slips Juniper a bundle of cloth that might be a parasol but isn't, and the seven of them diverge, pointedly not looking at one another as they edge through the audience. They take places along the fringes, forming a not-accidental circle.

A mustachioed man in a gray suit gives a short speech. There's a polite patter of applause as the mayor replaces him at the podium.

"I must begin of course with a hearty welcome to all of you, the good citizens of New Salem!" The mayor is a saggy gentleman with a red-veined nose and all the charisma of stale bread. Juniper finds Gideon Hill sitting behind him with the rest of the city councilors, sweating in the May sunshine and blinking far too often. Juniper wonders how a man like that—all pinkish and wet, like something recently shelled—could get elected to anything. His dog is curled beneath his chair, her eyes staring straight at Juniper, gleaming red in the first bloom of sunset.

"I must also thank the Council for their unflagging support of this project and valuable oversight."

Juniper isn't listening. She's watching the faces of her co-conspirators—Minerva and Mary looking pale and slightly sick; Inez smoothing the already smooth pleats of her dress; Electa looking bored—wondering if any of them are regretting the decisions that led them here. Wondering if anyone in the crowd has noticed the hats they're clutching to their chests, each of them some shade of white: pearl or lace or clotted cream, beribboned or dripping with baby's breath.

Each of them spelled straight to Hell and back.

But what is there to notice? They're only hats; you can't smell the witching on them unless you get right up close.

Juniper herself carries three hats. She knows neither of her sisters are coming—knows that Bella is too scared and Agnes is too selfish—but still, she brought three stupid hats. Just in case.

Earlier she thought she caught a glimpse of sleek braid, a flash of spectacles, but she can't bring herself to feel along the invisible threads stretched between them. It's better to not quite know, to keep pretending they might have come.

Worthington is leaning over the podium and sweating in a manner that suggests his speech must be drawing to its merciful end. "I say to you now: let us put aside our petty grievances and differences, and celebrate instead what unites us. Let us enjoy the Fair!" The mayor makes a gesture to the brass band perspiring silently behind the stage.

The crowd is applauding dutifully and the first notes of *Salem's Freedom* are rising from the band when James Juniper raises her white hat into the air. Six other hands follow suit.

Juniper and the renegade members of the New Salem Women's Association lower the hats onto their heads and whisper the words.

White cloaks cascade from nowhere and fall over their shoulders, bright and clean. They drape over their day-dresses and in an instant they become a single thing instead of seven separate women.

It's a spell of Juniper's own invention—not exactly *the good stuff*, but not nothing, either. She disappeared the cloaks using Mags's spell for vanishing her potions and herbs when the law came around, which required only a pair of silver scissors to cut the air and a muttered rhyme. Then she had to figure a way to call the cloaks back from nowhere. She lost several of Inez's nicest white wool cloaks, vanishing them into who knows where, before she thought to try a binding.

Bindings are deep, old witching, governed by obscure rules and strange affinities. Even Mama Mags didn't fool with them much; she taught Juniper a rhyme to bind a split seam and promised to teach her more later, except it turned out she didn't have much of a later.

Juniper did her best. She stole loose threads from each of the cloaks and stitched them into the brims of the white hats, whispering the words as she worked—*Ashes to ashes, dust to dust*—jabbing her thumb every fourth stitch and swearing up a storm.

She tested the first one on Jennie, jamming the hat on her head and ordering her to say the words. Jennie paled. "I don't know. I don't think I can." Juniper swatted her with a spare hat. Jennie spoke the words. When the cloak settled over her shoulders—white as snow, white as wings—Jennie looked so stunned, so nakedly joyful that Juniper swatted her again just to keep her from floating away.

Now Juniper sees Jennie's face shining through the crowd, full of that same glee despite the rising panic around her.

The crowd is surging away from the women in white, shouting and screeching. There's a strange note in their voices, fear but also wonder. Witching is a small, shameful thing, worked in kitchens and bedrooms and boarding houses, half-secret. But here they are in broad daylight, calling white cloaks from nowhere. Juniper can feel the terms shifting around them, the boundaries bending. She can see faces—mostly women, mostly young—watching them with fascinated hunger in their eyes. Juniper figures they're the ones who want, who pine, who long; the ones who chafe against the stories they were given and dream of better ones.

She unties the bundled parasol and lifts it high, except it's not a parasol at all. It unfurls into a long banner with the words VOTES FOR WOMEN painted across it in bright red.

The crowd erupts. *Salem's Freedom* devolves into a disjointed series of blats and hoots as the conductor stares, slack-jawed. Mayor Worthington bangs ineffectively on the podium. "What's this now? *Quite* uncalled for—"

His voice is drowned by the thump of blood in Juniper's ears, the burning heat in her chest. She wants to shout or chant or laugh, to shake her banner in their faces and bare her teeth—but Jennie thought they ought to remain quiet, dignified. Silent sentinels rather than wicked witches.

As one, the seven white-cloaked women turn their backs on the mayor and the City Council. Juniper raises her red banner in one hand and grips her staff tight with the other, and marches away from the stage, straight-spined. She feels the others falling in behind her, forming a single many-sailed ship.

The crowd splits like a sea. Mothers tug their children closer and canny salesmen start packing up shop, eyes darting sideways, sensing trouble. Juniper blows them kisses, feeling daring, a little drunk, listening with one ear for the ring of iron-shod hooves. They plan to disappear their cloaks and slink into the crowd before the authorities can arrive, but there are no men's voices, no white horses prancing toward them. Yet.

They pass beneath the high arch of the Fair entrance and into the darkening streets of New Salem proper. Juniper expects the crowd to disperse, but it presses closer against them as the street narrows. The well-dressed families of the Fair are replaced by working folk and young men, the genteel scandal souring into something meaner. A cluster of drunks unslouches from an alley to leer at them, calling lewd suggestions. Someone laughs.

Juniper rests the iron pole of the banner on her shoulder and touches the locket beneath her blouse, the one Mama Mags gave her on her deathbed. At the graveside Juniper dug her dirt-crusted nails along the seam and popped it open like a brass clam, hoping for a message or a note or a voice saying, *It's alright, baby girl, I'm here.* All she found was a thistledown curl of her grandmother's hair.

This morning, Juniper added a pair of snake's teeth.

She doesn't plan to use them, not really. Mags told her they were only for last chances and final straws, when every choice was a losing one—but Juniper's borrowed dress is too fancy and stupid to have pockets and she doesn't like to be without them.

For a dizzy second she hears the scuff of red scales across the floor, the hiss of triumph, of pent-up hate finally set free—but then someone shouts *look!* and she does.

Another group of women is marching down the avenue, headed straight toward them. Juniper blinks twice—are they coming to join them? Is it the rest of the Women's Association?—but then she sees the pale sashes crossing their chests.

"Oh *hell.*" It's those Christian Union women who are always writing nasty letters to the editor and waving signs with slogans like WOMEN FOR A PURE SALEM and MICAH 5:12. How did they turn up so fast? Before the police, even? Juniper didn't exactly advertise her march in the Sunday classifieds.

One of the Union women—a willowy, white-gloved woman Juniper recognizes from the papers as Miss Grace Wiggin—plants herself directly in Juniper's path, chin high and skirt starched. There's a shine to her, a porcelain perfection that makes Juniper want to rub her powdered nose in the mud.

"We, the good and righteous women of New Salem"—Wiggin gestures behind her to the other unionists, as if clarifying which women are good and righteous—"object to the promotion of sin on our streets!" Her voice is high, piercing.

"Oh for Chrissake," Juniper drawls. "Don't y'all have anything better to do?"

"They claim they are harmless! They claim they want justice! But what justice was there in the dark days of our pasts, when thousands of innocents suffered in the Black Plague?"

"Knitting, maybe. Charity work."

Wiggin's jaw flexes. "If we permit these women—these witches!—to march freely down our streets, what comes next? Will our daughters want broomsticks and cauldrons instead of pearls and dolls? Will our sons be seduced by their black arts? Will a second plague strike us down? The Christian Union urges you to vote for Mr. Gideon Hill this November!"

She keeps speechifying, her voice getting higher, more strident. The crowd presses closer, nodding and muttering and sometimes *hear-hear*ing.

Behind her, Juniper hears Jennie curse softly, but she doesn't turn to look because she's looking at something else: Miss Grace Wiggin's shadow.

It's long and dark in the almost-sunset, flung black over cobblestones. At first it mimics Wiggin's own gestures, like a good shadow should, but after a minute its hands fall to its sides. Its shoulders roll, as if stretching out stiffness, and then—like a puppet shedding its strings or a train waltzing off its tracks—it steps away from its owner.

Juniper goes very still. She watches Grace Wiggin's shadow distort, stretching into a creature with too many hands and too many fingers. It finds other shadows—docile, well-behaved shadows lying in their proper place—and pulls them into itself. It swells and blackens; Juniper thinks of things left rotting in the sun.

She remembers asking Mags when she was little if witching was wicked. Mags had cackled. *Wickedness is in the eye of the beholder, baby.* But then she sobered. She said witching was power and any power could be perverted, if you were willing to pay the price. *You can tell the wickedness of a witch by the wickedness of her ways.*

Juniper touches the locket on her chest, full of poison. Mags never told her what went into the making of those teeth, but Juniper found the burned bodies of three snakes in the hearth and saw the bandages wrapped thick around Mags's wrist, and knew the cost was cruel and high.

Now she watches the shadow oozing through the crowd like spilled ink, coiling around ankles and sliding up skirts, and thinks the price for this must have been even higher.

As the shadow spreads, the crowd shifts. Meanness turns to malice; heckling turns to hate. Juniper feels it as a prickle of fear along her arms, the kind that means a thunderstorm is rolling in or your daddy's coming home with a bellyful of liquor.

Juniper sees whitening knuckles, scowling faces, eyes gone empty and dim as closed-up houses. It's as if their souls were stolen along with their shadows.

She looks back to Grace Wiggin. She's smiling so wide and bright that Juniper understands two things in a hurry: number one, that there's a good chance the wicked witch wandering around New Salem is standing right in front of her in a white sash.

And number two, that she's glad, for once, that her sisters forsook her, because at least they won't be here for whatever happens next.

Beatrice is wishing very much that she forsook her youngest sister. She's wishing she didn't invite Miss Cleopatra Quinn to accompany her to the Fair, didn't watch from the fringes as Juniper raised her banner, didn't trail after the white cloaks of the suffragists while the crowd soured like milk around them.

Because then she wouldn't be standing here in the darkening street while a cluster of glassy-eyed men peel away from the crowd and lurch toward her, their shadows twisting and rippling behind them.

Their eyes are on Miss Quinn, a colored woman dressed a little too well, a little too far north. Beatrice sees the shape of slurs on their lips, the promise of punishment in their fists.

She hears Miss Quinn hiss a rude phrase beneath her breath. Then there's a hand in hers—warm and dry, urgent—and Quinn is pulling her sideways, shoving her against the sooty brick wall of a pub.

Miss Quinn removes a stub of white chalk from her coat pocket and sketches something on the wall, a shape made of lines and stars. She whispers a half-song beneath her breath in a language Beatrice doesn't know, then grabs Beatrice by the shoulders and presses her hard against the brick. Miss Quinn places her palms on either side of Beatrice and hisses, "Don't move."

Beatrice tastes witching in the air, feels the sudden heat of it radiating from Quinn's skin. She doesn't move.

The cluster of men is very close now. Their eyes, which had been fixed with eerie, hunting-hound intensity a minute before, now slide harmlessly across Miss Quinn's back.

Beatrice watches them shuffle on, grunting to one another, pointing ahead. And then she looks at Quinn's face (so near to hers that she can see the slide of sweat from her temple, the rust streaks in her yellow eyes) and gasps, "That was—that was *witchcraft*, Miss Quinn!"

"By all means, please say it louder. It's not like there's a riot nearby." Miss Quinn is straightening, dusting chalk from her hands.

"But where—how—?"

"Honestly, did you think yours was the only grandmother who knew words she shouldn't? Aunt Nancy's recipes, my mother calls them." Her voice is light, careless, but Beatrice hears a certain tension running beneath it. "I would be obliged if you would keep this to yourself, Miss Eastwood. We're not supposed to...I don't know what came over me." She gives her head an irritated shake, as if Beatrice had personally forced her to work witchcraft in the middle of New Salem.

"O-of course. I wouldn't want to cause you trouble."

Miss Quinn gives her a taut, crooked smile. "Oh no?"

And if there's more than just exasperation and irony in her voice, a sly heat, Beatrice doesn't hear it.

She's distracted by the echoes of her youngest sister's pain. The pain is followed by fear, and the fear is followed by a terrible, killing rage.

10

May sticks and stones break your bones,
And serpents stop your heart.

A spell to poison, requiring fangs & fury

James Juniper has never in her life hoped to see an officer of the law—in her experience they show up just to hassle your grandmother over a stillborn baby in the next county and stay long enough to clink glasses with your daddy—but she hopes for one now. The crowd is pushing closer, their mutters turning into shouts, their shouts turning into shoves. Miss Grace Wiggin and her followers have melted away, leaving the seven suffragists surrounded by red-faced men and shouting women.

Juniper feels shoulders bracing against hers as the others turn back-to-back, facing the crowd. This isn't right—they were supposed to be a slick spectacle, here and gone again, a scandalous headline for tomorrow's papers. They were supposed to be scared of misdemeanor charges and Miss Stone, not a soul-eating shadow and a vicious crowd.

Someone yanks on Juniper's banner and she stumbles. Her damn leg—the one with the puckered scar wrapped around the ankle, the

silvered, sunken places where muscle and tendon never quite healed—
twists beneath her and she sprawls sideways, palms skinning against the
grit of the street, staff clattering on stone.

She hears Inez call her name, but there are people shoving between
them, and the white cloaks disappear behind bare fists and broad backs.

Juniper looks up to see a man looming over her. A boy, really: scrawny
and underfed-looking, like the leggy weeds that sprout down dark alleys,
his face speckled with youth. His eyes are empty as promises.

He's holding the iron pole of her banner. He lifts it almost idly, as if
he doesn't know what he's about to do.

But Juniper knows. She's had too many hands raised against her,
too many bruises, too many long nights in the lonely black of the cellar.
He's going to hurt her, maybe kill her, because there's no one to stop
him. Because he can.

Juniper keeps a little flame flickering in her chest, a bitter, hungry
thing just waiting for something to burn. Now it blazes high, a tower-
ing, terrible thing. A killing thing.

She claws at the locket on her chest, pops it open. A pair of curved
fangs rattle into her palm and she crushes them, feeling the bone splinter
into flesh. She reaches for her cedar staff, slicks her blood along it.

Her staff is tight-grained and oiled smooth from all those hours
beneath her hand. By all natural laws the blood ought to bead up along
its surface, but Juniper has never cared much for natural laws. The cedar
drinks her blood up, every drop.

The boy is watching her, head a little tilted. He's not afraid—why
would he be? She's just a young crippled girl reaching for her cane, he's
a man with knuckles white around a weapon. Both of them know how
this story goes.

But oh, not this time. This time the girl has the words and ways to
change the story.

He'll be afraid, before the end. Her daddy was.

The words wait in her throat like matches waiting to be struck. Juniper thinks she ought to care about the cost of speaking them—a boy's life, the lives of the fools shouting and shoving nearby, the six other girls who'd followed her into this mess, who didn't deserve to wind up on the scaffold beside her—

But all the caring was beaten and burned out of her, and now she's just hate with a heartbeat.

May sticks and stones break your bones.

Agnes sees her sister fall. She sees her black-feather hair disappear, her white-wing cloak vanish beneath the mass of bodies, and she doesn't move.

She stands on a stoop at the edge of St. Mary-of-Egypt Avenue, watching the crowd become a mob become a riot, thinking: *It's her own damn fault.*

She has one hand on her belly, a half-moon heavy with the promise of a person still-becoming, already precious to her.

Too precious to risk for the sake of a grown-ass woman who should've known better.

Agnes grips the iron railing of the stoop and stares into the heaving crowd, looking for a glimpse of white, some sign of her wild, foolish sister. She knew as soon as she saw the note it would mean nine kinds of trouble.

And yet: this afternoon she rattled north on the trolley. She waited outside the Fair gates, unwilling to waste a hoarded nickel on a ticket. She heard the distant roar of the crowd, saw the VOTES FOR WOMEN banner snapping bright against the sky. Watched her sister limping at the head of a line of women, like a pied piper dressed in white, and felt a swell of something suspiciously like pride in her chest.

Agnes trailed behind them, her feet flat and aching from the weight of the baby. Maybe she was half hoping Juniper would look over her shoulder and see her. Maybe she was just spooked by the souring mutters around her, the resentful curl of lips and the coil of fingers into fists. New Salem is a well-behaved city, as cities go, but Agnes knows trouble when she sees it.

And now here she is, standing on a high stoop beside a cluster of women with low-cut dresses and rouged cheeks. None of them look especially concerned by the heave and froth of the riot below.

Juniper falls. Agnes stays put.

Until she feels her sister's wrath scorching through the line between them.

She knows what Juniper is going to do because she did it once before. She'd been a girl then, full of little girl's venom. She hadn't quite killed him—maybe she didn't quite want to, maybe she lacked the will—and the truth was forgotten in the fire that followed. Lots of things could be forgotten back home, looked away from until they were lost altogether.

Now Juniper is a grown woman with a grown woman's will, and Agnes knows some fool man is going to die.

But it isn't for his sake that Agnes stumbles down the steps and into the riot. Cities forget less easily.

She elbows and claws her way through the crowd, one arm braced around her belly. Someone tears at her hair. A shoulder thuds against her jaw. She doesn't stop.

There's Juniper, looking up from the street with her eyes black and burning. A boy stands above her, iron bar raised high.

Between them, there is a snake. Red as blood, red as lips, red as the rich heart of a cedar tree. It coils around itself, neck arching in a way that makes the boy take a step back, his weapon tumbling from nerveless fingers. Around them a circle of silence grows as the crowd watches, half-hypnotized by the subtle pattern of the snake's scales, the hot smell of witching.

The snake's eyes glow like sun through sap, fixed upon the boy, and Agnes knows it's going to strike. It's going to bury its borrowed fangs into his flesh and he's going to die screaming. And, in a few minutes or days, so will her sister. This city could never suffer such a witch to live for long.

So Agnes does something very, very stupid. She doesn't think as she does it, doesn't ask herself why she would risk her life and more than her life, her everything-that-matters, for the sister who hates her. The sister she abandoned once before.

Agnes steps between the boy and the snake. She meets her sister's eyes.

There's a tilted second when she thinks Juniper won't stop. That she's too full-up with fury to care if her serpent strikes her sister or a stranger, so long as someone pays, someone hurts like she does.

Juniper's eyes flicker, leaf-shadows shifting. She lunges and grabs the red snake by the throat. It twists in her hand, writhing like a live thing instead of a stray scrap of witching, before it goes rigid. And then there's nothing but a red-cedar staff in her sister's hand.

Agnes becomes aware that she hasn't taken a breath in some time. She closes her eyes and sways, tasting the sweet soot of the city's air in her throat, feeling the spark still safe inside her, still alive.

Then a voice behind her—the boy whose life she just saved, the ungrateful little shit—shouts, "*Witches!*"

Juniper is—she doesn't know what she is. Ashes, raked coals. Whatever is left when a fire burns itself out. She's looking up at her sister—and what is Agnes doing here? How is she standing above Juniper with her eyes steady and cool as creek-stones?—when someone shouts *Witches!* and hell, which had already broken loose, breaks looser.

The word swoops through the crowd, batlike. Glass shatters against stone. Screams echo down alleys. Feet rush both toward them and away. Juniper lies there, wrung out with witching and will, until she sees hard hands shove against Agnes's back. Agnes falls, braid arcing, and Juniper hears the hollow smack of her body against the cobblestones.

Then Juniper is scrambling to her feet, swinging her staff in wild circles, shouting, "Get away, get the hell away from her!"

She loops a hand beneath her sister's arm and hauls her upright. "C'mon, Ag, we got to move." She claws the white cloak away from her throat, feels it catch and tangle in the bodies behind her. She limps sideways through the roil of the crowd, tugging Agnes beside her. There's a thin moaning coming from somewhere, like an animal in pain; it's only when Agnes pauses to swear that Juniper realizes it's coming from her sister.

The riot is swirling and thickening around them, rising like floodwater, and Juniper can't find Jennie or Inez or Electa, all the other girls who followed her into this mess. She can't see any way out, any place to run.

Agnes points to a high stoop where three ladies are watching the street through long lashes. One of them is smoking a thin-rolled cigarette. "There!"

Juniper slants toward them, flinging elbows, crushing toes beneath her staff. She climbs the short steps, panting.

A woman in red silk watches her with no particular expression on her face. She removes the cigarette from between her lips. "You ladies in trouble?"

Juniper checks to see that the red-silk woman has a shadow beneath her, and that it seems to possess the correct number of arms and hands. She hitches a sideways, desperate smile at her. "Might be."

The woman gives her a motherly nod. "Then you're in the right place, love." She reaches casually behind her to unlatch the door, knocking it open with one hip. The stale sweetness of perfume and liquor drifts out, and a few jangling notes of ragtime.

Juniper dives into the dimness with her sister's hand in hers.

11

Jane and Jill went up the hill
To fetch a pail of water.
Spill it thrice, say it twice,
Or soon it will get hotter.

A spell against burns, requiring clear water & a strong will

The smell reminds James Juniper of a chestnut in bloom, sharp and sour in the back of her mouth. It hangs heavy in the shadowed hallway and grows stronger as they follow the red-silk lady up two flights of stairs and into a small bedroom. The wallpaper is rich and flowery and the bed is a frosted cupcake of pillows and feather-down.

"This place is awful nice, isn't it, Ag?" Juniper offers. She's thinking of her sister's mildewed room in the boarding house. "Bet it costs a pretty penny, though."

The red-silk lady—who introduced herself with a casual flick of her fingers as Miss Florence Pearl, proprietress of Salem's Sin, No. 116 St. Mary-of-Egypt Avenue—cracks a cackle. Cigarette smoke coils from her nose. "Sure does."

Juniper sees her shoot a knowing wink at Agnes, who snorts, then flinches.

Miss Pearl's eyes narrow. "I'll send Frankie up. Her auntie taught her rootspeak back in Mississippi, she's ten times better than those butchers over at St. Charity's. And dinner—you picky about food? I was almost the whole nine months." She ticks her chin at Agnes's belly, and Juniper notices for the first time the way it's pushed tight against her dress, the way her sister cradles it in her arms.

Oh.

Juniper sees her sister standing above her again, strong and steady, risking herself to save some stupid, vicious boy—and risking a second someone, too.

Agnes shakes her head, lowering herself onto the bed with white lips. Miss Pearl sweeps out.

Then they're alone together with the cupcake bed and the smell of blooming chestnuts and the careful sound of Agnes's breathing. A gluey silence falls between them.

"So," Juniper says, "who's the daddy?" It comes out meaner than she meant it to. She can almost feel Mama Mags's knuckles on the back of her skull. *Mind that tongue, child.*

Agnes shakes her head at the floor, still breathing thin through her nose. "Doesn't matter." She looks up, meets Juniper's eyes. "She's mine."

"Oh." Juniper feels a hot flare in the line between them, fierce and defiant. Is that what mother's love is like? A thing with teeth?

Juniper's mother was never anything to her but a secondhand story from her sisters, a curl of hair in a locket. Juniper never missed her much; she always figured if her mother was worth a damn she would've left their daddy or slipped hemlock into his whiskey, and she didn't do either. Juniper had her sisters, and it was enough. Until it wasn't.

A second silence falls, thicker than the first. Agnes starts to speak just as Juniper asks, "Why did you leave?"

Agnes frowns at the floor. "You're the one who left, as I recall."

"I mean before."

Juniper already knows why she left. Their daddy was a mean drunk with hard knuckles who never loved anything or anyone as much as he loved corn liquor, and there was nothing for miles but coal seams and sycamores and men just like him. Any girl with a single, solitary lick of sense would want to get as far from Crow County as her feet could carry her, unless they loved the wild green mountains more than they loved themselves.

She's just too chickenshit to ask her real question: *Why didn't you take me with you?*

Agnes looks up at her, then away. "Had to, didn't I?"

"I guess." Maybe it's even true; maybe everybody has to survive the best they can. Maybe her sisters couldn't afford to haul a wild ten-year-old girl along with them when they ran. "But later. You could've come back later." Or written a letter, at least. Even a single smudged address would've been a map or a key to Juniper, a way out.

Agnes shrugs one shoulder. "Only if I wanted to spend the rest of my life locked in the cellar. Daddy told me he'd skin me himself if he ever saw me again, and I guess I believed him."

"He—what?"

Agnes looks up again, but now there's a faint crease between her brows. "When he sent me away. He told me he was through with me, that he did his best but God cursed him with wayward daughters, and he washed his hands of us."

Juniper doesn't hear anything but the beginning: *He sent me away.* Her daddy *sent* Agnes away.

What if her sisters hadn't cut and run? What if they loved her after all? It's too huge a thing to think, too dangerous to want. Juniper feels her own pulse rabbiting in her ears, her fingers trembling on the red-cedar staff.

"Why—" She stops, swallows hard. "Why did he send you away?"

The frown between Agnes's brows goes a little deeper. "You don't remember?"

Juniper limps to the bed and settles beside her sister. "I remember I was running the mountain that day." The slant of sun through leaves, the bite of briars, the whip of sassafras and beech leaves against her cheeks. Some days it would take her like that, an animal need to run and keep running, and she would dive through the woods at a pace that would have killed a person who didn't know every stone and gully of that mountain.

"I was running and then I felt..." A tugging in her chest, an invisible need that made her turn around and run even faster. "Well. I remember walking into the old tobacco barn, all dark and hot. You and Bella were there, and so was Daddy..." Juniper feels something vast slide beneath the surface of her memory like a whale beneath a ship. She looks away from it. "I was sick for a while after the barn-fire. Mags did what she could, but my foot must've got infected. I was hot and dizzy for days, and my head ached." It's aching now, a dull warning.

Agnes is watching her face. "Weren't there ever any rumors about me? After?"

Of course there were rumors: people hissed that Agnes was a whore and a hedge-witch, that she cursed the ewes to lamb out of season and lay down with devils before running off to the city to fornicate.

"No."

Agnes grunts, very nearly amused, then sighs long and slow. "Well. It's no secret now: I got myself in a family way. You remember Clay, the Adkins boy?"

There was a whole pack of boys that used to trail after Agnes; Juniper and Bella used to come up with names for them. She thinks the Adkins boy was Cow Pie, or maybe Butter Brains.

"Sure I remember him."

"Well, he and I...I was lonely and he was nice enough, and one thing led to another." Her voice goes young and soft. "Mags figured it out before I did."

Juniper thinks of all the girls she used to see slinking across the back acres to Mags's house, looking for the words and ways to unmake the babies in the bellies. Not all of them young or unwed—some were too old for childbearing or too sick, or had too many hungry mouths already. Mags had helped them all, every one, and buried their secrets deep in the woods. The preacher called it the Devil's darkest work, but Mags said it was just women's work, like everything else.

Agnes is rubbing her thumb over the ball of her belly now. "She... helped me. It hurt, but it was a good kind of hurting. Like shedding a skin, coming out brighter and bigger. Afterward I buried it beneath a hornbeam on the east side of the mountain, and I thought that was the end of it. I told the Adkins boy to get gone and stay that way. I thought nobody would ever know."

Juniper remembers all her daddy's lectures on Eve's curse and original sin, descending into slurred rambles about weak-fleshed women and their whoring ways. She remembers his eyes gleaming red in the gloom in the barn, his bones showing white through stretched-taut skin, and begins to understand. "How did he find out?"

"I didn't tell anybody. Not a soul except Mama Mags." Agnes's mouth twists, venom in her voice. "And Bella, of course. I told her everything back then."

"She never—"

"She did. I was watering the horses because Mags said it was fixing to freeze overnight." Crow County slinks back into her voice, sly and drawling. "Then Daddy turns up and I could see in his face that he *knew*, about me and Clay, about the pennyroyal and the thing beneath the hornbeam. And then I saw Bella creeping along behind him, all pasty white, and I knew what she'd done."

Juniper wants to argue. She remembers the feel of her sisters' hands in hers on summer evenings, the circle they made between them; the promise that was never said aloud but was woven in their hair, written in their blood: that one would never turn against the other. Surely Bella would have died before she broke that trust.

But then Juniper recalls the cold gray of her sister's eyes, the secrets she keeps safe in her notebook, and stays quiet.

"I told him it wasn't true, that Bella was a liar and a—" Agnes swallows hard, skips over something. "But he just kept walking toward me. He wasn't even in his cups—sober as a judge, I'd swear. But he was looking at me like—like…"

Juniper knows exactly how he was looking at her: like she was a colt that needed breaking or a nail that needed hammering, some misbehaving thing that could be knocked back into place. Juniper had seen that look. She came running into the barn, tangle-haired, sap-sticky, arms scored by the reaching fingers of the woods, and saw her sisters huddled against the far wall. Her father prowling toward them like a wolf, like a man, like the end of days—

And then—

That unseen thing swims too close to the surface and Juniper looks away. She goes someplace else instead, cool and green.

Agnes calls her back. "Juniper. June, baby." Juniper returns to the pretty wallpapered room, to the sister who watches her with wide eyes.

Juniper bridles at the pity in that look. "What?"

Agnes takes up her story like a woman knitting past a dropped stitch, leaving a gaping hole behind her. "You remember the fire, don't you?"

For a sick second Juniper thinks Agnes means the second fire, the one she set the night she ran north, before she recalls the shatter of her daddy's lantern as he fell, the spit of oil across dry straw and old timbers, the weeks and weeks of changing bandages and coughing up globs of char and blood.

"Of course I do." She falters a little. "But I don't remember…" How she survived. How could she remember the inside of the barn as it burned—the rafters bright gold above her, the hideous screaming of the horses, the wet snap of flesh—without remembering how it ended?

"When I was younger I was always burning my fingers when I took the pot off the stove." Agnes sounds like she's treading carefully. "Mags gave me some words and ways to keep me safe. I didn't know if they'd do any good, but Daddy was blocking the door and I still had the water for the horses...I threw it in a circle around the three of us and said the words, and it worked. Nearly." Her eyes flick to Juniper's left foot, then away, gray with guilt. "Daddy reached in after you, but we didn't let him take you."

Juniper always thought her scars look like split branches or spreading roots. Now she can see they look more like the fingers of a burning hand.

"Somebody must have heard the horses or seen the smoke. They dragged us all out, piled wet earth over Daddy to put out the flames. Mags took you away—you were all hot and shaking, I thought you might be dying—" Agnes pauses to swallow again, still not looking at Juniper. "We were sent upstairs while people came in and out. The preacher, the sheriff, half the county it felt like. Then Daddy called us down to his bedside and said it was all arranged. In the morning Bella would go to some school up north, and I would go live with our aunt Mildred." Their aunt Mildred was a sour crabapple of a woman who lived two counties north and spent her time collecting tiny paintings of Saints and complaining about the many sins of her next-door neighbors. "I ran as soon as I could. Wound up here."

Juniper wants to ask: *How come you never came back for me?* She wants to ask: *How come you never even wrote?* But she's frightened of the skipped stitches in the story, the things she doesn't want to see.

"Juniper, I—" Agnes is reaching toward Juniper almost as if she means to wrap her arms around her, and Juniper doesn't know if she's going to let her, when someone knocks softly on the door.

The two of them sit straighter, tucking their unruly feelings back inside their chests.

Frankie Black turns out to be a freckled colored girl with velveteen eyes and an accent that makes Juniper homesick. She has Agnes sit up straight and runs her fingertips over the small of her back, pressing and whispering. She lights a honey-colored candle and drips the wax in a pattern of lines and specks. She sings a spell that has a drumbeat rhythm running underneath it, shuffles her feet, *tap-tap-tap*, and straightens up.

It's nothing like Mags's spells, and Juniper watches with narrowed eyes. But Agnes's face loosens as the pain lifts away, so Juniper figures it must be working. It occurs to her for the first time that there might be more than one kind of witching in the world. The thought is an uncomfortable one, far too large; it reminds her of riding the train across the Crow County line and feeling the country unfold like a map beneath her, flat and endless.

"Miss Pearl says you two should stay till morning. There's police out looking for two black-haired women. One of them with child"—her eyes cut to the cedar staff on the bed—"one of them with a demon-snake for a familiar."

Juniper says, "It's not a familiar," at the same time Agnes says, "We can pay. For the room, and the lost business."

Frankie makes a sound somewhere between offense and amusement. "You couldn't afford us, sweetheart. Miss Pearl says we're closed up for the night, anyhow. The men are all riled up, looking to prove something. They can look elsewhere. There's corned beef and rolls if you're hungry." She sets a basket on the dresser top and leaves them alone again.

The honey-candle is sitting in a waxy puddle and the food is nothing but crumbs caught in the valleys of the down comforter before either of them says a word to the other.

Agnes is slouched against the headboard, her body slack in the absence of pain, the baby swimming soft inside her.

Juniper has her arms wrapped around her knees. Her eyes slide over Agnes's belly. "How come you came today?"

Agnes shrugs, because shrugging is easier than talking about guilt and love and the things that still stretch between them after seven years of silence. "How come you invited me?"

Juniper shrugs back, sullen, and counters, "How come you saved that idiot boy?"

Agnes almost laughs at her. For a quick girl, Juniper can be awfully slow sometimes. "I wasn't saving that idiot boy, Juniper."

Juniper narrows her eyes. Her mouth is half-open to retort when she realizes who Agnes was saving. Her face softens.

Juniper glances again at the fragile swell of Agnes's belly. "But—even with—"

"I guess." Agnes attempts a smile. "Mama told me to take care of you." Maybe Agnes owed her, for all the times she'd failed. Or maybe it wasn't about debts or duties at all; maybe it was just that she didn't want to see her youngest sister strung up in the city square.

Apparently she's said something wrong, because Juniper is bristling and sharpening again. "I don't need you to take care of me. I was about to teach that boy a lesson. Teach them *all* a lesson."

Her eyes are seething, shadowed. They make Agnes think of maiden-stories—the kind about young witches who sing ships to their deaths, who hunt the woods at night with their seven silver hounds, who turn sailors into pigs and feast every night.

Agnes wants to be angry at her—for being so careless and cruel and so terribly young—but she can't quite manage it. She's been all of those things herself; she knows the black alchemy that transmutes hurt into hate. She remembers climbing barefoot from the attic window, meeting some poor boy in the woods and tearing at his clothes with more than lust, digging her nails too hard into his skin. It felt so good to be the one hurting, instead of being hurt.

So she doesn't tell her sister to shut her damn mouth and think for a second. Instead she asks, "And then what? After you teach them all a lesson. After you burn them or bite them or curse them. What happens after that?"

Juniper's mouth bows, petulant as a child.

"I know why you'd want to—Saints, so does every woman alive—but think what it costs."

"I don't care," Juniper spits.

She never has. When she found them in the barn that day she hadn't cared what might happen to three nothing-girls found beside their father's corpse; when she led those suffrage ladies into a riot she hadn't cared what kind of hell it started.

Agnes rubs the ball of her belly with a thumb, thinking of the little spark inside it. "I know you don't. But I do." The baby kicks in answer, a butterfly touch, and Agnes tilts her head at her sister. "You want to feel her move? The baby?"

Juniper stares at her like she's never heard the word *baby* in her entire life. She reaches out a cautious hand. Agnes holds it to her belly and they wait together, hushed and still, feeling their hearts beat in their palms. The baby is motionless for so long Agnes is about to give up, until—

Juniper's face splits in half with the size of her smile, eyes gone summer green. "I'll be damned. That was her?"

Agnes nods, thinking how young and bright her sister looks right now, wishing she could stay that way. Wishing there was room for her inside Agnes's circle. "The midwife says she'll come by the Barley Moon, in August. Maybe sooner."

Juniper seems taken aback by this information, as if she thought babies ought to abide by timetables and punch-clocks. She presses her palm to Agnes's belly a second time, and her expression is so hopeful and wide open that Agnes says, "She could use an aunt."

Juniper looks up at her, a quick darting glance, like she doesn't want Agnes to see the hope shining in her face.

"But you've got to be more careful. The march today—it was your idea?"

Juniper takes her hand away. "Yes."

"You saw what happened. The crowd went mad."

Agnes expects Juniper to turn sullen again, but instead her face creases with thought. "I don't think they were in their right minds."

"Oh, don't be so *naive*—"

"No, I mean I saw something...not right. Shadows moving in ways they shouldn't, twisting together. It was witching, but darker and stranger than anything Mags ever did."

Agnes thinks of the shadowless men in the alley and feels the hairs rising on her arms. "But what kind of witch would incite a riot against witches?"

Juniper purses her lips. "That Wiggin woman would. If ever there was a person who would work hard against themselves, it'd be her."

"I heard those Christian Union types all swear oaths against every kind of witching, even the kind to keep dust off the mantel or mealbugs out of the flour."

"Well somebody was messing with shadows."

"All the more reason to be careful."

"All the more reason to be *prepared*. To arm ourselves properly." A fey light comes into Juniper's eyes and Agnes knows she's thinking of that black tower and those strange stars, of long-ago magics and long-gone powers. "Listen, the tower we saw that day. I was thinking—you remember the story Mags used to tell us? Saint George and the Last Three? What if it's *the* tower? *Their* tower? I think that's what Bella thinks, anyway."

But Agnes doesn't want to hear about witch-tales and wishes, and she especially doesn't want to hear about Bella. "Oh, please. It's a children's story. And anyway, you seem well enough armed to me. That snake..." Agnes swallows. "*Was* it a familiar?"

Juniper snorts at her. "Did you forget everything Mags taught you? A familiar isn't a spell or a pet. It's witchcraft itself wearing an animal-skin. If a woman talks long and deep enough to magic, sometimes the magic talks back. But only the most powerful witches ever had familiars, and I don't figure there are any of those bloodlines left." Juniper looks away, and Agnes politely does not mention all the hours Juniper spent in the woods as a little girl, waiting for her familiar to find her.

Juniper gives herself a little shake and shoots Agnes a sickle-moon smile. "But maybe that wouldn't matter, if we had the Lost Way. Just imagine what we could do."

Before she can remind herself that the Lost Way of Avalon is a children's story, Agnes does: she thinks of double-shifts and boarding-house fleas and all the nothing-girls whose highest hope is for a husband like Floyd Matthews, soft-palmed and stupid, and how it would feel to want more. She thinks of her daddy's knuckles and Mr. Malton's leers and how it would feel to be the dangerous one, for a change.

But then she thinks of angry mobs and scaffolds and all the things that would happen next, and the baby girl in her belly.

Agnes meets her sister's gaze as steady as she can. "And what comes after?"

Juniper doesn't look away. "Come with me in the morning," she answers. "Come join the suffragists. And find out for yourself."

Agnes looks into her face, blazing with hope and hunger, young and wild and jagged-edged—and finds she can't answer. Instead she clears her throat and says, "It's late. Time for bed, I think."

Agnes manages not to look at her sister while they ready themselves for bed, unbuttoning and unclasping, taking turns at the chamber pot. It's only in the last second of light, right before Agnes pinches the candlewick between her fingers, that she sees the silent shine of tears in Juniper's eyes.

Juniper curls her spine away from her sister but she can still feel the heat of her, hear the steady rush of her breath.

Long past midnight, when even the ceaseless bustle and clank of the city has finally gone still and Juniper thinks she might be able to hear the distant seesaw song of spring peepers, Agnes rolls over beside her.

"I should have come back for you, no matter what. I was scared."

Of me. Juniper doesn't know where the thought comes from, why it sounds so certain and so sad.

"I'm sorry, Juniper." Agnes whispers it to the ceiling, a prayer or a plea.

If Juniper says anything, Agnes will hear the tightness of her throat, the salt-bite of tears in her voice. So she says nothing.

There's a pause, then: "I'll come with you in the morning, if you'll have me."

Another pause, while Juniper breathes carefully through her mouth. "I'll have you." It comes out too rough, a little strangled, but she hears Agnes sigh in relief.

After that Agnes's breath goes deep and slow and Juniper lies wide awake, thinking about venom and vengeance, praying to every Saint that her sisters never find out how their daddy died.

Bella isn't here—Bella the betrayer? Bella the Judas?—but Juniper wishes she were. She would ask her for a story and fall asleep on a bed of once-upon-a-times and happily-ever-afters and righted wrongs.

She whispers one to herself, instead.

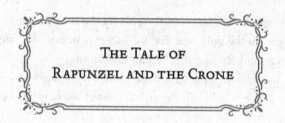

THE TALE OF
RAPUNZEL AND THE CRONE

Once upon a time there was a woodcutter whose wife was with child. But she grew very ill, her golden hair turned brittle gray, and in his desperation the woodcutter went to the local hedge-witch and begged for a cure. The hedge-witch told him of a black tower in the hills covered in green-growing vines even at midwinter. Just three leaves from this vine would cure his wife.

The woodcutter found the black tower and the green-growing vines. He stole his three leaves and brewed them as the witch instructed. Soon his wife was rosy-cheeked and smiling again, her hair the brightest gold. When their daughter was born they named her after the herb that saved her: *Rapunzel*.

But as they named the baby there came a terrible wind from the east, smelling of earth and ash. Knuckle-bones knocked at their door and they found a bent-backed Crone hunched on their stoop. She wore a tattered black cloak around her shoulders and an asp around her wrist, like a bracelet made of obsidian scales.

She came, she said, to take back what was stolen from her. When the woodcutter pleaded that his wife had already eaten the leaves, the Crone shuffled into the house and peered down at the baby girl. The baby girl peered back at her with eyes the color of green-growing vines.

When the Crone left the house that night, trudging through the silent snow, she carried a baby bundled beneath her cloak.

The Crone raised the girl in her high, lonely tower. Rapunzel grew to love the old woman, and, inasmuch as a witch loves anything, the Crone loved the girl. By the time Rapunzel was half-grown the only sign that she had ever belonged to anyone else was her hair: bright gold, long and shining.

One day when the Crone was away, a traveling bard saw the shine of Rapunzel's hair through the tower window. He sang to her:

> My maiden, my maiden,
> Let down your long hair,
> Braided tight and shining bright,
> A way where once was none.

There followed the usual course of events when a handsome stranger sings to a beautiful maiden, and soon Rapunzel was climbing down a golden rope woven of her own hair, reaching her hand out for his.

The Crone returned just as the pair took their first step away from the tower, hands clasped.

"If you would leave me," she told Rapunzel, "you must return what belongs to me."

Rapunzel raised her chin and agreed to pay any price. The Crone bade her close her eyes and touched two cold fingers to their lids. When Rapunzel opened her eyes once more the green-growing color had been taken from them, along with her sight.

The Crone returned to her tower and watched the maiden and the bard stumble together across the hills. Rapunzel did not turn back or call out.

The Crone wept, and as her tears touched the stone floor, the tower trembled and fell. Or perhaps it vanished outside of time and memory and took the Crone with it. Perhaps she waits still for her stolen daughter to call out to her.

The only certainty is the tears themselves.

12

My maiden, my maiden,
Let down your long hair,
Braided tight and shining bright,
A way where once was none.

A spell to escape, requiring three hairs & nimble fingers

When Beatrice Belladonna runs from the riot on St. Mary-of-Egypt's, she knows two things for certain: that her youngest sister is alive, and that her middle sister is with her.

It shouldn't comfort her to know that Agnes is there—she learned long ago that she couldn't trust her when it counted—but it does. If anyone could haul their little sister out of the mess she made and keep her alive through the night, it's surely Agnes.

"If you're finished staring at nothing, I would quite like to keep running for our lives now." Beatrice makes a private note that Miss Quinn grows drier and more cutting under pressure, before bunching her skirts in her fists and following after her.

For a woman born and raised in New Cairo, Quinn possesses an uncanny knowledge of the north side. She leads Beatrice down narrow alleys and nameless back streets, following a winding path that leads them somewhat mystifyingly to the respectable row house where Beatrice rents a room.

"How did you know my address?"

Miss Quinn gives a very unsorry shrug. "Stay inside tonight. The police are awfully scarce this evening, which makes me wonder just who's behind this mess."

Beatrice wants to say, *Thank you for saving me*, or *Be careful*, or *Who exactly are you and what uncanny secrets are you hiding?* but Quinn is already turning away, taking long-legged strides down Second Street.

By the time Beatrice is in her attic room, peering down from her round window, Quinn is gone, vanished entirely from the neat grid of streets below.

Beatrice dreams that night of witches and traveling bards and a golden-haired girl smiling from a tower window. Except her hair isn't golden at all, actually, and her smile is full of secrets.

The following morning, Bella pins her own hair with unusual severity and stares hard at her reflection in the mirror, reminding herself that she is bony and graying and very boring. Then she feels the tug of her sisters through the line—still alive, still together, moving through the city—and wonders if perhaps she is growing less boring the longer James Juniper remains in New Salem.

Beatrice steps into the street just after sunrise, when the shadows lie soft and the air sparks with dew, and hopes very much that Mr. Black-well will forgive her for missing a second day of work.

The headquarters of the New Salem Women's Association are already jammed full of bustling women and urgent whispers. Miss Stone stands behind the front desk like a small general overseeing her troops, wig pinned slightly askew. She is so surrounded by people—a hand-wringing lady wearing a monocle, a roundish woman in a very fine dress, that young secretary girl sporting a bruised jaw and a sullen expression—that Beatrice doesn't think she notices the chime of the bell as she enters.

Until she looks up and fixes Beatrice with an iron glare. "Miss Eastwood, wasn't it? I thought you were too busy for suffrage."

"Oh, I—that is—"

But Miss Stone is already looking back down at the papers spread before her. "If you're looking for that sister of yours, she's not here."

"No, but—"

"And if she has any sense of prudence at all, she will not dare to show her face here again."

Beatrice deduces from this that Miss Stone was previously unaware of Juniper's little spectacle, that she has since become aware of it, and that she suffers from the mistaken belief that Juniper possesses a sense of prudence.

She further deduces that the next several minutes are going to be uncomfortable ones. She manages a faint "Oh, dear" before the bell chimes again and Juniper herself strides into the office with all the swagger and charm of a prize-fighter after a winning match, staff clacking merrily across the floorboards. Agnes comes slinking in after her, looking like a woman with deep misgivings about her choices.

The whispers wither and die. A dozen pairs of eyes land on Juniper. She gives them a beatific smile. "Morning, ladies. Bella! What are you doing here?"

She doesn't wait for an answer. She grabs one of the spindly chairs by the window and perches on the very edge, knees wide and hands crossed atop her staff, still beaming.

The smile dims when she catches sight of the secretary and the swollen bruise along her jaw. "So you made it out alright. The others, too?"

The girl nods, a furtive flash of pride in her eyes. "We think Electa's got a busted rib, but she'll be alright." It occurs to Beatrice to wonder how exactly they all escaped unscathed, and if perhaps the respectable members of the Women's Association have a few words and ways they shouldn't.

Guilt crosses Juniper's face, a foreign expression, but she banishes it with a little shake of her head. "Well. I hope at least we can all agree."

Miss Stone—who has until now been standing perfectly still—clears her throat to ask, "On what, exactly?"

Juniper apparently doesn't hear the tension lurking in Miss Stone's voice like an unsprung trap. She meets her eyes squarely. "That we aren't going to get a damn thing by asking nice and minding our manners. That we need to make use of every weapon we have, or they'll beat us bloody in the streets." Juniper leans forward, that swaggering smile returning. "That it's time for the women's movement to become the witches' movement."

The silence following this statement is so profound that Beatrice imagines she can hear the veins pulsing in Miss Stone's temples.

Juniper speaks into the quiet, heedless. "It was witching that saved me in the street yesterday, and it's witching that will win us the vote. More than just the vote—back in the old days women were queens and scholars and generals! We could have all that back again. My sister— Bella, I mean; this is Agnes, our other sister"—a look of genuine horror crosses Miss Stone's face as she contemplates the prospect of another Eastwood—"anyway, Bella has been doing some research about that tower we saw on the equinox. I think it's . . ." Juniper's eyes cross Bella's, and Bella knows that Juniper has guessed what the tower is, what the sign of three circles must mean. "I think it's important. That it might bring witching back to the world."

Juniper looks around at the stone-still women. "What do you say?"

None of them answer. Miss Stone exhales a very long sigh into the silence and lowers herself into her chair. She leans back, regarding Juniper with an almost bewildered expression, as if she can't understand how someone so young could be so powerfully irritating. "Miss West. The Women's Association has no interest in your wild theories or dangerous ideas."

The smile slides off Juniper's face like frosting off a too-hot cake. "Well, as a member of the Women's Association, I think—"

Miss Stone produces a bitter *ha* of laughter. "Oh, you are certainly no longer that."

"Excuse me?"

"I, as president of the Association, do officially expel you from our company, and deeply regret ever having granted you membership."

Juniper is standing now, fingers white around her staff. "How *dare* you—"

Miss Stone counts on her fingers, voice very cool. "You organized an illegal assembly against the will of the Association. You made a public demonstration of witchcraft. You endangered the lives of the six fools who followed you into your treason. Saints only know what else you did—the rumors are nearly too wild to believe. Perhaps you have a pair of black horns on your head. Perhaps you can fly. Perhaps you set a demon-snake on an innocent child." Beatrice flinches. No one notices.

"Look, you wanted to get people's attention, and we got it. If you're going to get upset that I *defended* myself, I don't—"

Miss Stone raises her voice very slightly. "Miss Wiggin, the head of the Women's Christian Union—and, I might add, the adopted daughter of a member of the City Council—was injured in the riot. She claims it was an act of witchcraft, and I am disgusted to say I am unsure whether she is lying."

Juniper's mouth is open again, but Miss Stone ignores her. She leans forward over the desktop, hands knitted. "I have dedicated the better part of my life to the uplift of women. I was there at Seneca, at the very beginning." Her fury seems to have blown itself out like a summer storm, leaving her winded and tired. "They laughed at us. Derided us, mocked us, printed vicious cartoons in every paper. We kept working. We built organizations all over the country, saw suffrage laws passed in three states, brought attention to the plight of our sex—but now they are no longer laughing, Miss West. Now—thanks to you and your accomplices—they are afraid. And we could lose everything."

Juniper strides forward and places her palms on the desk, wearing a look of such blazing intensity that Beatrice feels it scorch her cheeks as it passes. "Or we could win it all. If we stop worrying so much about what a woman should and shouldn't do, what's respectable and what's not. If we stand and fight, all of us together. Imagine if there'd been seventy of us marching, instead of seven!" Miss Stone looks faintly ill at the thought. "There's this book Bella used to read us when we were little, about these three French soldiers—what's the thing they said?" She throws the question sideways to Beatrice.

Beatrice clears her throat, cheeks pinking. "All for one and one for all."

"That's it." Juniper's face is lit now by some internal glow, a passion like the sun itself. "It has to be all for one and one for all, Miss Stone."

Every eye is on the young woman with the crow's-wing hair and the long jaw and the summer-green gaze—like and not like the feral girl-child Beatrice remembers—and for a wild moment Beatrice thinks they're going to listen to her.

Miss Stone laughs. It's not a cruel laugh, but Beatrice sees it hit Juniper like a slap. "Goodbye, Miss West. I can't wish you luck, for the sake of the city."

Juniper straightens from the desk, all the glow gone from her eyes, face pinched tight, and gives the room a mocking bow. She limps out the office door without looking back. She never let their daddy see her cry, either.

Agnes follows. She pauses to hold the door behind her and looks up at Beatrice, almost as if she's waiting for her. As if they are still little girls tumbling into the farmhouse, one-two-three, holding the door carelessly open behind them for the next one. "Well?" Agnes sounds annoyed, whether with herself or her sister Beatrice can't tell.

Beatrice feels Miss Stone's eyes on her face. "I don't know you, Miss

Eastwood, but you seem a respectable woman. That sister—*those* sisters of yours will lead you astray."

Beatrice hesitates. She thinks about the fates of girls who go astray in all the stories, the hot iron shoes and glass coffins and witches' ovens. (She thinks about St. Hale's, a prison built especially for straying girls.)

But then Beatrice looks at Agnes still waiting for her, half scowling, and thinks about what else awaits those gone-astray girls: the daring escapes and wild dances, the midnight trysts and starlit spells, a whole world's worth of disreputable delights.

Beatrice bows her head as she leaves. "So I hope, Miss Stone."

Agnes is just about to give up and close the damn door behind her, to hell with Bella and the suffragists both, when Bella finally makes up her mind. She goes sailing past Agnes, spine uncrooked, cheeks pink with some private pleasure. Their eyes meet, then slide away.

Juniper is already stamping down the street, clacking her staff with such aggression that passersby scuttle aside. "Those *thrice*-damned *boot*-licking *shit*-witches! Too cussed cowardly to take a damn stand—to hell with them!" She spins to face the plate-glass window of the Association headquarters and crosses her fingers in a gesture of such exceptional rudeness that Bella chokes, *"June."*

Juniper spins back to face her sisters. Her eyes are bright and green as fox-fire. "So. What do you say?"

"To what?"

Juniper looks at Bella like she wants to grab her by the shoulders and shake her. "To *witching*! To the Lost Way of Avalon!"

Bella shushes her, casting worried looks at the genteel bustle of the street: mothers with their hats just so and children with their clothes starched stiff, maids with baskets of fresh white laundry and gentlemen checking their pocket-watches. It strikes Agnes suddenly how ludicrous it is that they should be plotting the second age of witching in the middle of a sunny, orderly street on the north end, surrounded by clerks and investors and clean limestone. Surely it calls for a haunted moor or a misted cemetery.

Bella says, low and urgent, "Juniper, I don't know what you know or think you know about that tower, but I assure you I don't have the secret recipe for Avalon stuffed in my socks."

Juniper crosses her arms, runs her tongue over her teeth. "I know you know more than you've told me."

"I—I—" Bella stutters, and Agnes marvels that she grew up in their daddy's house without learning how to lie properly. "Yes. Alright. I found some...words, the day the tower appeared. I don't know what came over me, but I spoke them aloud. And then..." She gestures upward, recalling the splitting seam of the sky and the dark tower.

Juniper stares hard for another second, then grins. "You *snake*. I *knew* it was you. Why didn't you tell me?"

Bella fumbles for an answer, but Agnes perfectly understands why a person might hesitate to give a vicious, vengeful girl the key to a mysterious and boundless power. There were stories in the old days about whole cities put to sleep, kingdoms frozen over in endless winter, armies reduced to rust and ash.

Juniper waves away Bella's stutters. "Doesn't matter now. The real question is: why haven't you done it again?"

"Because it wasn't a complete spell. It's missing some of the words, and all of the ways."

"Then find them! What exactly have you and your lady friend been up to, all those late nights in the library?"

A flush creeps up Bella's neck. "She's not my—Miss Quinn and I have been searching. We've collected some scraps, some possibilities, but we have nothing but theories, so far."

"So let's test them." Bella looks doubtful and Juniper presses on, heedless. "Listen. Ever since the equinox the three of us have been bound together, haven't we?"

Bella *tsks*, sliding her spectacles up her long nose. "An effect of an unfinished spell, I told you."

"And how come the three of us were pulled into that spell in the first place? After seven years apart, what drew us together just when our oldest sister got stupid and read some words out loud?" Juniper's voice lowers. "And before that—didn't you feel something tugging you toward the square?"

Agnes remembers it: a line reeling her in, a finger prodding between her shoulder blades. She feels it still, an invisible hand chivying her toward her sisters despite her better judgment.

"Mags always said anything lost could be found. Remember that song she taught us? *What is lost, that can't be found?*"

Bella blinks several times and murmurs, "I do, yes."

"Well, I think maybe magic *wants* to be found. And I think maybe we're the ones who are supposed to find it."

"What, like *fate*?" It's the first thing Agnes has said since they stepped outside, and both her sisters flinch from the venom of it. "Like *destiny*?" Fate is a story people tell themselves so they can believe everything happens for a reason, that the whole awful world is fitted together like some perfect machine, with blood for oil and bones for brass. That every child locked in her cellar or girl chained to her loom is in her right and proper place.

She doesn't much care for fate.

Even Juniper looks a little cowed by whatever she sees in Agnes's face. "Maybe not. Maybe it's just luck that Bella found that spell. That the three of us wound up in St. George's Square. On the equinox. A maiden"—she taps her own chest. "A mother"—she nods to Agnes. Bella casts her such a baffled, owlish look that Agnes suspects she didn't notice the swell of her belly until this very second. Her mouth makes a small, perfect O.

"And a crone." Juniper points at Bella, who makes a disgruntled sound. "Like the Last Three themselves."

None of them speak for a moment. Juniper limps a little closer, until they stand in a tight circle of three, heads nearly touching. "Maybe Agnes is right, and that's all horseshit. But what if it isn't? What if we could make every woman in this city into a witch, just like that?" Juniper snaps her fingers. "No more reading witch-tales in books, Bell— you could write them yourself! And no more shit-work for shit-money, Ag. No more being *nothing*." Her voice thickens on the last word.

Juniper breathes hard through her nose and asks them a second time: "What do you say?"

"Alright." Bella looks stunned by the sound of her own voice. "Yes."

Juniper swivels to Agnes. "And you? Will you help us?" Her jaw is set, her eyes shining, and Agnes marvels at the contradiction of her: bright-eyed and black-hearted, vicious and vulnerable, a girl who knows so little of the world and far too much. A part of Agnes wants to say yes just so she can keep an eye on her.

Except she doesn't get to choose for herself anymore. She smooths her blouse over her belly. "I can't start any trouble. For her sake."

Juniper looks down at her hand. "Oh, I think you've got to. For her sake." She meets Agnes's eyes, challenging. "Don't you want to give her a better story than this one?"

Agnes does. Oh, how she does—to see her daughter grow free and fearless, walking tall through the dark woods of the world, armed and armored. To whisper in her ear each night: *Don't forget what you are.*

Everything.

Agnes's throat is too full-up with wanting to speak. Bella offers, tentatively, "You know the Mother herself started all sorts of trouble, in the stories. I wish..." Her voice lowers. "I think it might have been better for us if we'd had a more troublesome mother."

Agnes looks between them, her wild sister and her wise sister.

She nods her head, once.

Juniper is whooping and thumping Agnes too hard on the back, already badgering Bella about the Lost Way, and Bella is shushing her to no discernible effect, when footsteps sound behind them.

Agnes turns to see the secretary girl from the Women's Association, with her cornsilk hair and blue-bruised jaw. As she approaches, Agnes sees she's not as mousy as she'd thought: her eyes are hard, shining with newborn conviction.

"Jennie?" Juniper asks. "What—"

"I want to join." Jennie says it very fast, like a person diving into cold water before they can change their mind.

"That's nice," Juniper says. "Join who?"

Jennie frowns as if she thinks Juniper is making fun of her. "You." Her eyes skitter to Agnes and Bella. "Your new society."

Bella starts to say something calm and reasonable, like, *There's been some sort of misunderstanding! We're not forming a society at all. Sorry for your trouble*, but Juniper is already reaching out a welcoming hand, smiling with all the glee of a missionary contemplating a convert.

"Why, Jennie. You can be our first member."

Bella makes a wheezy, punctured-tire noise. "I'm not sure—I don't know—" But Juniper has an arm slung over Jennie's shoulder and Jennie is smiling a shy smile.

"Well." Bella sighs. "There were really four musketeers, anyway."

PART TWO

———— ❦ ————

HAND

IN

HAND

13

Tell your tale and tell it true,
Cross my heart and hope to die.
Strike me down if I lie.

A spell for secrets kept and told, requiring bindweed & blood

T he Calamitous Coven."

"No."

"Eve's Army."

"No! It ought to be about, I don't know, *sisterhood* or *union*—"

"The Ladies Union of Giving the Bastards What's Coming to Them."

"James Juniper, if you can't be serious, at least be quiet."

Juniper subsides, slouching lower against the wall. As a clandestine society of would-be witches, Juniper had anticipated that their first order of business would be exciting and magical, like burning the Sign of the Three across City Hall or turning the Hawthorn River to blood.

Her sisters and Miss Jennie Lind apparently thought otherwise. The four of them have been stuck in Agnes's cabbagey room at South Sybil for hours now, discussing safe houses and membership oaths and other disappointingly unwitchy subjects.

Jennie is even taking honest-to-Eve *notes*, sitting on Agnes's bed with Bella's little black book propped on her knees. She's the one who suggested their society have a name, although she has so far ignored each of Juniper's excellent suggestions.

"The Sisters of Sin."

Jennie's pen doesn't move.

"What about—" Bella begins, then bites her lip. "What about the Sisters of Avalon?" It takes less than a second's silence for Bella to begin backtracking and hand-wringing. "Perhaps not. It sounds a bit like the Daughters of Tituba, doesn't it, and we hardly want to be mistaken for make-believe. And it's so provocative to associate ourselves so openly with the Last Three—"

But Agnes is smiling and Jennie's pen is moving across the top of the page, and Juniper can feel the name settling over them, shining in their faces. Juniper has a goosefleshed premonition that it will be printed in papers and on wanted posters, whispered through the alleys and mill-floors, passed like a lantern from hand to hand. *The Sisters of Avalon, they call themselves. Did you hear?* The looks exchanged, the flash of longing in their eyes.

"Excellent." Jennie finishes the last flourish of the name. "And what about titles and duties? Should they be elected positions, do you think?"

Juniper finds that this somewhat dampens the shine of their new name. "Positions?"

"Well, I mean—secretary, treasurer, president, vice president, press liaison, head of recruitment…" Jennie ticks them off on her fingers.

"Saints, there's only four of us."

"Sounds like a problem for the head of recruitment."

Juniper flicks a ball of lint at Jennie and Jennie dodges without taking her eyes from her paper. Bella offers, tentatively, "I—I could be the press liaison. I have a—contact in the newspaper business." Bella doesn't look at any of them as she says it, and Juniper wonders if she means that colored woman in the gentleman's coat, and why that should cause her to blush such a vivid pink. She recalls a little uneasily that there were rumors back home about her oldest sister, too.

Jennie writes something in the notebook. "Full name?"

"Beatrice Eastwood."

Jennie hesitates. "Why do your sisters call you Bella?"

Juniper says, "Because that's the name our mama gave her. Beatrice *Belladonna* Eastwood." Bella shifts uncomfortably and Juniper sighs at her. "Honestly, if we can't use our mother's-names in a secret society of witches, when can we?"

Jennie finishes writing and turns an expectant eye to Agnes, who looks very close to rolling her eyes. "I can...ask around, I suppose." She makes a circle with her index finger, indicating either the South Sybil boarding house, the neighborhood of West Babel, or the entirety of New Salem. "Does that make me in charge of recruitment?"

"Name?"

"Agnes Eastwood." Juniper tosses a second ball of lint at her. "Oh, fine. Agnes *Amaranth* Eastwood."

Jennie records this, too, then says brightly, "And who's president?"

There's a brief exchange of glances between the sisters. Juniper asks, "What does it mean to be president, exactly?"

Jennie makes a seesaw motion with her head, cornsilk hair swinging. "Not much, really, if we agree to a collective decision-making process." The phrase recalls the endless meetings of the Women's Association. Juniper gives an involuntary shudder.

"But in the Association...Miss Stone was the heart of us." There's a gray note in Jennie's voice, like regret, and Juniper shrugs away a prickle of guilt. It was Jennie's own damn choice to follow her out the Association door. "She was our direction. We all steered the ship, but she was our compass." Jennie looks at Juniper as she finishes, frowning a little.

Juniper looks away. "Well, we can vote on it later. Let's talk about getting some girls signed up, O head of recruitment."

But Bella says anxiously, "I'm not sure how many people we ought to recruit. What would we be recruiting them *to*, exactly?"

Juniper says, "Hell-raising," just as Jennie says, "Yes, we'll need a constitution, and a declaration of intent."

Juniper considers for several consecutive seconds and offers, "To raise hell?"

The other Sisters of Avalon ignore her. She tries again. "To bring about a second age of witching. To get back what was stolen from us."

"That might be a little...much, don't you think?" Bella clears her throat over Juniper's muttered *you're a little much*. "How about: to restore the rights and powers of womankind?"

Jennie writes it down while Bella frets, because Bella always frets. "Without the Lost Way we don't have any powers to restore. I'm not sure anyone would sign up for the sake of m-moonbeams and witch-tales." Her hands are twisting in her lap, chapped and ink-stained.

Agnes is standing by the window, looking out at the gray alley. "You're forgetting a whole street full of people just saw a woman set a viper on a boy because he gave her a little trouble."

"A *little* trouble—"

Agnes continues. "By now the city will be rotten with rumors. People will be scared, scandalized...but some of them will want to know more. They *need* to know more, if what June says is true."

Juniper had told them about the shadows at the riot and the sick shine of Miss Wiggin's smile. She doesn't know how convinced they are, but she had seen them sidestepping shadows and looking twice at dark doorways in alleys.

"And who knows?" Agnes continues. "They might have some witching of their own. Every woman has a handful of spells from her aunt or cousin or mama."

Jennie objects. "Not every woman."

"Well, *most* women, then."

There's a stiffness in Jennie's face, a wordless denial.

Bella is watching her. "And how did you and the other girls escape the riot, exactly, if it wasn't witching?"

The stiffness cracks. Jennie chews her lip, cheeks pinking. "It was nothing. Just a little spell." Her cheeks slide past pink and head straight for scarlet. "To...tie shoelaces together."

Juniper cackles, because the image of dozens of rioters tripping over their own feet is delightful, but Bella asks, boringly, "That sounds like men's magic. Or boys' magic, at least."

Jennie isn't looking at any of them, face draining to blotched white. "I...had...a brother." Even Juniper hears the past tense and shuts the hell up.

Agnes wades into the hush. "Well, wherever you learned it, I think your friends are grateful." Jennie gives her a twist of a smile. "And even a boys' prank had some use. Maybe our words and ways don't seem like much all scattered around the way they are, but if we put them together..."

Agnes trails off, but Bella continues in a hushed voice. "I could collect them. Record them. The first grimoire of the modern age..." For reasons that are obscure to Juniper, the prospect of so much writing and reading makes Bella's eyes shine and her frets vanish.

The rest of the evening is a series of debates and schemes. Jennie recalls that the Women's Association ran regular ads in *The New Salem Post* encouraging interested parties to visit their headquarters, and suggests the Sisters do the same. Agnes notes dryly that they don't have headquarters, that they wouldn't want anyone to know where it was if they did, and that *The New Salem Post* would never run an advertisement for witchcraft anyway.

Bella makes a *hmm*ing noise and mutters that there may be "other reputable papers" in the city, if they had some means of ensuring their invitation reached only sympathetic eyes. A thought seems to strike her.

"Do you think 'cross my heart and hope to die' could be altered for mass-production?" She snatches her notebook back from Jennie and sinks for some time into her own notes, murmuring to herself.

By nightfall the members of the Sisters of Avalon have gone their separate ways: Bella to present their proposal to Miss Quinn and the staff of *The Defender*; Agnes to rustle up witch-ways from someone called Madame Zina; Jennie to check on Inez and Electa and the other members of Juniper's small rebellion, and invite them to join a much bigger one.

Juniper lingers in Agnes's room. She steals a handful of salt from a pot on the table and tosses a line of it across the threshold and window ledge, thinking of Mags. *Honey to keep things close, salt to keep things out.* She thinks, too, of those wrong-shaped shadows rolling and oozing through the streets, prying at shutters and sliding under loose-hung doors.

Juniper limps to the bed, where Bella's little black notebook lies open. She flips through the pages and squints at Jennie's tidy writing.

Beatrice Belladonna Eastwood, Press Liaison.

Agnes Amaranth Eastwood, Recruitment.

Jennie Gemini Lind, Secretary/Treasurer, with the mother's-name written in a shaky, uncertain hand, as if she wasn't sure of the spelling.

And, at the very bottom of the page, neat and firm:

James Juniper Eastwood, President.

As a rule, Agnes walks out of the Baldwin Brothers Bonded Mill and keeps walking. She doesn't linger to chat or laugh, she doesn't head to the dance halls or evening sermons or markets with the other girls; she keeps her eyes on the pavement and walks the hell home.

But on the eleventh of May, just as the afternoon is softening like butter into a warm evening, she waits.

She leaves the dim tomb of the mill and leans against the heat of the brick, shifting her weight from one foot to the other, trying to lift the baby off her bladder. Mr. Malton isn't the sort of boss to grant extra privy-breaks to a girl just because, as he says, "she can't keep her knees shut." He's been eyeballing Agnes's belly as it grows, pressing hard against the bar of the loom. Just this afternoon he tapped it with his red-sausage finger. "You get three days for bearing. When she's four she can work in the rag-pickers' room."

Agnes closed her eyes so he wouldn't see the white lick of rage in them.

Her daughter will not grow up in the sunless dark of the mill, breathing dust and fumes, huddling next to the steam pipes in winter to keep warm. Her daughter will not be nothing.

Agnes unclenches her jaw in the alley. There are knots and strings of women gathering nearby, but she doesn't look at them. Instead she looks at the thin stripe of sky above, the hungry green of the weeds reaching thin fingers between the cobbles, crabgrass and chickweed and dusky deadnettle. Agnes can't recall if there were this many weeds last spring.

There's a cluster of women forming down the alley, a copy of *The Defender* spread between them. None of them, Agnes imagines, are regular subscribers to New Cairo's radical colored paper, but the Sisters of Avalon purchased several dozen extra copies of this particular issue and distributed them through the boarding houses and mail-rooms of the west side.

Agnes catches a raised voice. "It's nonsense, is what it is. Pure fancy. Somebody's idea of a joke."

"Or," suggests another, conspiratorially, "it's a trap. The police never did find that snake or the witch who made it, did they? Maybe they think they're being clever."

There are low, doubtful mutters at this, and Agnes figures this is more or less the opening she's been waiting for. She wishes she had wit or zeal to convince them, but she's not her sisters, so she merely stalks toward the gathered women and waits for them to notice her squared shoulders. "It's not a trap," she says quietly. "Or a trick."

All of them stare at her the way you'd stare at an alley cat that suddenly sang opera. Agnes understands why; she hasn't spoken a single spare word to them other than "bobbin's busted" or "watch your shuttle" in five years of working shoulder-to-shoulder.

One of them huffs loudly, but another one shushes her. Agnes chances a glance of the shusher's face and recognizes her vaguely as the new girl who got her hair caught in the loom last spring. The machine sucked her into itself, slick and fast, as if her body was just another thread. She screamed, and under the screaming was the wet rip of hair from scalp—until Agnes sliced through it with a pair of shears. The girl fell to the ground, weeping and moaning, stuttering her thanks. Agnes told her to pin her hair up if she wanted to keep what was left of it. She'd never learned her name.

The girl is a year older now, a year harder. Her hair is pulled tight beneath a gray kerchief and her eyes are the color of coins. "That so?" She says it level and flat, like a woman paying off a debt.

Agnes meets her eyes. "Did any of you try it yet?"

Embarrassed shuffling. A clucked tongue. The rustle of a hastily folded newspaper shoved down someone's apron-front.

On the sixth page of that newspaper, in the section generally reserved for advertisements selling pomades and tobacco and Madame CJ Walker's Wonderful Scalp Ointment, there was a half-page of solid black ink. In large white capitals are the words:

WITCHES OF THE WORLD

UNITE!

The text below invites women of all ages and backgrounds to join the Sisters of Avalon, a newly formed suffrage society dedicated to the restoration of women's rights and powers. Interested parties are instructed to prick their fingers and smear the blood across the advertisement while chanting the provided words, which would—if the blood belongs to a woman, and if that woman bears the Sisters no ill intent—reveal a time and location.

A Miss Inez Gillmore purchased the ad on behalf of the sisters, signing the check with a merry flourish that Agnes both envied and resented. Bella and Juniper provided the spell, fussing for days with bindweed and blood and ink, their fingertips gone purplish red from repeated needle-pricks. And Agnes provided the location, against all her better judgment. Who would ever suspect the shabby, respectable South Sybil boarding house as the site of seditious organizing?

Agnes gestures to the poorly hidden newspaper. "Try it. Speak the words. Feel the worth of them." They were the words the three of them had used as girls to leave messages for one another, the ones they didn't want their daddy to see: *Meet me at the hollow oak* or *Staying at Mags's tonight.* "It's true witching, stronger than anything your mother taught you."

One of the women—Agnes thinks it's the same broad, ruddy-cheeked woman who laughed with her over Floyd Matthews—gives a quiet, doubtful *huh*, as if her mother taught her a thing or two.

Agnes holds both palms up in surrender, but continues, "And there's more where that came from. Lots more." Well, *some* more, at least. "Think what you might do, with a little real witching."

Agnes can see her words working on them, tugging at the loose threads in their hearts. These were women who were never tempted by the suffragists or their rallies or their high-minded editorials in the paper. Oh, they wanted the vote—what woman didn't want it, aside from Miss Wiggin and her fellow fools?—but these were women who knew the difference between wanting and needing. The vote couldn't feed their children or shorten their shifts. It couldn't cure a fever or keep a husband faithful or stop Mr. Malton's reaching fingers.

Maybe witching could.

The girl with the tight-pinned hair and the coin-colored eyes chucks her chin at Agnes. "You one of them, then?"

Agnes flinches a little at that *them*, at being one of something rather than simply *one*, but she ducks her head in a nod.

The broad woman makes another derisive sound. "Well, good for you, eh?" Her accent is cold and jaggedy, like snow-cut mountains. "I would never risk my children in such a way." Her eyes linger pointedly on Agnes's rounding belly, flick once to her ringless finger. There are murmurs of agreement from some of the others.

Shame bubbles acidly in Agnes's throat, followed very quickly by anger. She regards the big woman: mouth thin and hard, red veins cracked under milky cheeks, eyes like iced-over lakes. "How many children do you have, ma'am?"

She puffs out her chest. "Six daughters, all healthy, all hard workers."

"And your daughters. They're safe, you think?"

The frozen eyes narrow. Agnes presses. "They'll grow without knowing hunger or want or a man's hand raised against them? They won't go blind in the mill or lose their fingers packing meat?"

Now the woman's shoulders are straining against the seams of her blouse, her face reddening. "Well, they will not get themselves"—she says a long, chilly word that sounds like it must be Russian for *knocked up*—"without a husband, that's for damn—"

Agnes cuts her off. "And their husbands will treat them kindly? They won't lose their paychecks in barrooms or gambling halls, they won't die young, they won't beat their wives for back-talk or a burned dinner?" Agnes knows she's going too far, saying too much, but she can't seem to stop. "And if they do, will your daughters keep their own daughters safe?" Her voice cracks and bleeds like a split lip. If their mother had been a true witch instead of merely a woman, would she have saved her daughters from the man she married? Would she at least have *lived*?

Agnes swallows hard into the silence. She can feel glances winging past her. "It's a risk just to be a woman, in my experience. No matter how healthy or hardworking she is." A great weariness washes over her as she says it, a grim bone-tiredness that makes her want to walk away and keep walking, until she finds someplace soft and green and safe to have her child. But no such place exists. A voice very like Juniper's whispers, *Yet*, in her ear.

None of the women answer her. Agnes is turning to leave, feeling like she should go find Jennie and tell her she needs a new title because she's a piss-poor recruiter, when the woman in the gray kerchief says, "What's your name?"

"Agnes." She hesitates a half-second before adding, "Amaranth." There's a quick hiss of breath around her. Mother's-names are things shared between friends and sisters, not offered in grimy alleyways to strangers.

The kerchiefed woman raises her chin. "Annie Asphodel." She nods to the women around her. "And this is Ruthie and Martha. The big one is Yulia." Yulia merely crosses her arms a little harder, eyes still narrow and frozen.

Annie snaps her fingers and holds out her hand to Martha, who withdraws a crumpled copy of *The Defender* from her apron and hands it over. Annie removes a pin from her hair, its point gleaming sharp in the buttery light.

She gives Agnes a hard little nod, like one soldier to another. "We'll be seeing you, Agnes Amaranth."

Beatrice and her sisters chose nine o'clock in the evening because nine o'clock is a woman's hour. The dinners have been served and the dishes dried and stacked, the children tucked into bed, the whiskies poured and served to the husbands. It's the hour where a woman might sit in stillness, scheming and dreaming.

But on the seventeenth of May, some of them are doing more than dreaming.

Beatrice sees them from the scummed glass of the window in No. 7 South Sybil. They come in ones and twos and sometimes threes, their shadows like soft velvet beneath the gas-lamps, their cloaks pulled tight around their shoulders. It isn't chilly, but there's a fretful wind chasing them down the streets, plucking hairs loose from their pins and tugging at skirts.

It's hard to tell in the gloom, but Beatrice thinks some of the women are very young, their hair plaited and their steps eager, and some of them very old. Some of them stride quickly and others skitter like mice across a kitchen floor. Some of them have apron-strings and patched elbows showing beneath their cloaks; some of them gleam with pearls and rings.

She hears the creak of the boarding-house door, the patter of feet on stairs, the rush of eager whispers in the hall. A helpless panic tremors through Beatrice and she glances to her younger sister, mute and beseeching. Juniper advises her to get her panties untwisted and sit tight, but she rests an awkward hand on Beatrice's shoulder as she says it. The damp heat of her palm tells Beatrice that she feels it too: the sense that they're teetering on an unseen edge, perched at the beginning of an untold story.

There's an uncertain knock at the door. "C'mon in," Juniper calls, and they do: Misses Electa Gage and Inez Gillmore followed by a gaggle of other girls stolen from the Women's Association; a knot of grim-looking mill-girls with colorless kerchiefs and skeptical expressions; an unsmiling girl with long black hair and cedar-colored skin; a pair of rather disreputable-looking sisters who introduce themselves as "Victoria and Tennessee, spiritualists, magnetic healers, and mediums."

Miss Quinn appears at the head of a stately delegation of black women who regard the room with expressions of deepest skepticism. Quinn shoots Beatrice her cat's grin, causing Beatrice to stand up, forget whatever it was she intended to do, then sit back down and study the backs of her own hands for a while.

She hadn't been at all certain that Quinn would come. She'd helped them with their advertisement, working with Juniper and Beatrice long after the offices of *The Defender* should have closed to set the spell into ink and lead. It was only after the last page had rolled through the press that Quinn glanced sideways at Juniper. "And am I invited to this meeting, Miss Eastwood?"

"Sure."

Quinn's face remained very neutral. "How very...broad-minded of you."

"Well, all for one and one for all," Juniper declared nobly. She ruined this immediately thereafter by adding, with some relish, "Daddy'd roll over in his grave if he could see us. He fought for the Yanks but only because they gave him fifty dollars and a bottle of rye."

Miss Quinn tilted her head. "Tell me, Miss Eastwood: how much of all this"—she gestured to the stacks of still-warm newspapers, the witch-ways scattered across desktops—"is designed purely to spite your dead father?"

Juniper ran her tongue over her teeth with a simmering expression that made Beatrice wince in anticipation, but in the end said only, "Come to the meeting, Miss Quinn. Bring your friends."

Quinn had.

Beatrice watches them covertly as they settle into their seats. There's a camaraderie among them, an unusual deference to Quinn's posture, which confirms certain of Beatrice's theories.

Following the riot on St. Mary-of-Egypt's, Beatrice watched Quinn more closely. She considered the keenness of her interest in their researches and the words and ways she already possessed; the times she left abruptly or disappeared for days in a row, never quite saying where she'd gone; the mildly scandalized whispers about "that colored journalist" who was often seen entering and leaving all manner of unlikely places across the city; the several occasions she accidentally referred to herself as *we* instead of *I*.

Beatrice is no detective, but even a librarian might consult a bound volume of minutes from the annual convention of the Colored Women's League. She might run her finger down the member list at the back and

144 ALIX E. HARROW

pause at *C. P. Quinn*, wondering if perhaps the League was interested in less respectable activities than their literature suggested.

Beatrice is distracted by a flurry of new arrivals: a mother and daughter whispering in Yiddish; Madame Zina the midwife; a trio of women in alarming dresses who greet Juniper and Agnes as if they are old friends.

Juniper beams. "Glad you and the girls could make it, Miss Pearl."

"Who are they?" Beatrice asks Agnes in an undertone.

"Whores," Agnes whispers back. Beatrice had not previously been aware that one's entire body could blush.

Miss Pearl and her girls take seats at the very front. One of them—a freckled, honey-colored girl—glances back at Miss Quinn. They exchange a charged look so fleeting that Beatrice is half-convinced she imagined it.

By ten after nine there are so many women crammed into Agnes's room at No. 7 that it shouldn't logically contain them all. Beatrice knows that, in fact, it doesn't.

Over the previous week Agnes approached the other occupants of the South Sybil boarding house. No. 12, it transpired, was the home of a truly astonishing number of sisters and cousins and second cousins from Kansas who had charmed their room to be rather larger on the inside than it was on the outside. They gave Agnes the necessary ways and words, and now No. 7 is large enough for six rows of borrowed chairs and two dozen women. It no longer seems quite so gray and miserable, and the wet-earth smell of witching has chased away the smell of overcooked cabbage. Yesterday Beatrice even saw a robin nesting in the eaves outside the window.

Nearly all the chairs are full. There are no more taps at the door. The whispers and shuffles of the women fall away in eerie concert, replaced by an expectant stillness. Eyes swivel to the front of the room, where Beatrice and her sisters sit.

Beatrice sees Juniper's throat bob as she stands, fist tight around her staff. She glances back at her older sisters, suddenly looking young and raggedy and not at all like the president of a suffrage society. Heat passes down the line from Agnes to Juniper, a rush of secondhand strength.

Juniper squares her shoulders and turns back to the room full of waiting women. "Welcome," she begins, her voice clear and bright, "to the first meeting of the Sisters of Avalon."

Juniper introduces Beatrice and Agnes and Jennie. She thanks the gathered women for answering the advertisement and reads their mission statement from a creased page held in her hand, stumbling a little, sounding like a schoolgirl reading from the Bible.

She folds the paper and fixes them with a green-lit gaze. "That's why we're here." Her voice is steady now. "How about you all tell me why you're here?"

A nervous silence follows. It lingers, escalating toward the unbearable, until a flat voice calls from the back, "My brother gets fifty cents a day at the mill. I get a quarter for the same damn work."

"The courts took my son," hisses someone else. "Said he belonged to his father, by law."

Miss Pearl offers, "They arrested two of my girls on immorality, and not a one of their customers." The end of her sentence is lost in the sudden flood of complaints: bank loans they can't receive and schools they can't attend; husbands they can't divorce and votes they can't take and positions they can't hold.

Juniper holds up a hand. "You're here because you want more for yourselves, better for your daughters. Because it's easy to ignore a woman." Juniper's lips twist in a feral smile. "But a hell of a lot harder to ignore a witch."

The word *witch* cracks like lightning over the room. Another silence follows, tense and electric.

A voice cuts through the hush, hard and foreign-sounding. "There's no such thing as witches. Not anymore." It's the big Russian woman from Agnes's mill, arms crossed like a pair of pistols across her breast.

"No," Juniper parries. "But there will be."

"How?"

Juniper looks again at her sisters, and Beatrice knows from the jut of her jaw that she's about to say the thing which they agreed she shouldn't say, at least not on the first meeting, and that there's nothing at all she can do about it.

She smiles benevolently down at the Russian woman. "By calling back the Lost Way of Avalon."

The faces of the gathered women contort into two dozen separate species of shock: shocked outrage, shocked disbelief, shocked confusion, shocked hunger. Then the room erupts as the ones who know the story relate it to the ones who don't, as a handful of women gather their skirts and scuttle for the exit with horrified expressions, as Miss Quinn laughs softly into the chaos.

Juniper arcs her voice high over the noise. "We don't have all the ways and words yet, but we will soon." Beatrice wonders how she manages to sound so sure, so confident, as if they are likely to find the map to an ancient power tucked in their skirt pockets. "In the meantime, we propose an exchange. Each of you knows a spell or two or three, maybe more. Share them with the Sisters, and together—"

The Russian interrupts again. "Spells to clean laundry and scour pots! *Feh.*"

"I know a spell that can kill a man stone dead," says Juniper, softly. "Would you like to hear it?" The Russian doesn't answer. "I bet some of these other ladies know more than they've said. And even small spells are worth something. You heard about those union boys in Chicago? Look what hell they raised with nothing but a little bit of rust." Beatrice refrains from noting that they were men, and thus far less likely to be hunted, tried, and burned by a jury of their peers.

One of the other mill-girls, a kerchiefed woman about Agnes's age, says, unexpectedly, "My cousin was there, with Debs and the Railway Union. He's back home now, at least for a while. I could...talk to him, if you like."

Someone else sneers, "*Men's* magic. Wouldn't do a damn thing for us." Jennie fidgets in the front row, cornsilk hair sliding to cover her face.

Juniper addresses the sneerer. "And who told you that? What if your daddy or your preacher or your mama was dead wrong?" She nods to the kerchiefed girl. "You—Annie?—talk to your cousin. Why not?" She throws her gaze around the rest of the room. "Why not at least try? Join us. Learn from us, teach us, fight with us, for all that *more* you want." She gestures behind her, to where Beatrice's notebook lies open on the table. "Add your name to the list and swear the oath if you're interested. If not"—her eyes slant to the door—"head on home. Forget you ever dreamed of anything better."

In the silence that follows, the Russian woman climbs to her feet. A pair of girls stand with her, so broad-shouldered and blue-eyed they can only be her daughters. There's a long moment when Beatrice is certain the three of them are headed for the door, that half the room will follow, unswayed by the shine of Juniper's smile. That the Sisters of Avalon will fail before it even begins.

The big woman stalks to the table. She grips the pen in awkward fingers and signs her name on the page, right beneath the heading written in Jennie's neat hand: THE SISTERS OF AVALON.

Then Juniper is grinning and many chairs are scraping, many women are climbing to their feet. They form a rough line leading to the table and the book, their eyes bright, their chins high, their voices stuttering over the words of the oath: *Tell your tale and tell it true, cross my heart and hope to die, strike me down if I lie.*

Only Miss Quinn and her companions remain sitting.

Beatrice threads her way across the room and perches beside them.

"An excellent showing, Misses Eastwood." Quinn nods.

"Thank you. Won't—will you join us?"

Quinn's eyes meet hers very briefly, a yellow flick, and Beatrice can't name the thing she sees in them. Regret? Guilt? "Oh, I think not."

There's a rustle beside her as the oldest of her companions climbs to her feet: a small, very brown woman wearing a wide-brimmed hat and a black-lace veil. There's something familiar about her that Beatrice can't place. "I'm afraid we are not interested in"—she makes a gesture at the chattering women, the packed room—"publicity."

"What are you interested in, then?"

A flash of teeth behind the veil. "Power, Miss Eastwood." She nods regally and her companions stand beside her. "Please do let us know if you find any."

The woman adjusts a handbag on her elbow and Beatrice imagines for a spine-prickling second that she sees an animal peering out of it—a sleek, furred creature with ember eyes—but then the woman and her handbag are gone, leaving behind the faint, peppery scent of cloves. Quinn follows shortly after.

Beatrice watches them go, wondering precisely what goes on at meetings of the Colored League.

She stations herself beside Juniper and watches the list of names growing longer. Some of their mother's-names are the usual sort, alliterative and botanical—*Annie Asphodel Flynn, Florence Foxglove Pearl*—but some of them are strange and foreign. *Gertrude Red Bird Bonnin. Rose Chava Winslow. Frankie Ursa Black.* She wants to ask what they mean and where they come from, wants to follow them back to the ways and words used by their mother's mothers.

The Russian woman stumps over to Juniper and crosses her arms again. Beneath the permanent scowl of her face there's a little of the same glow Beatrice sees in the rest of the room: hunger, or hope.

"Not many of us," she observes gruffly.

Juniper claps her on the back, slightly too hard. "Oh, there will be, Yulia my friend. I got an idea."

Beatrice looks up to meet Agnes's eyes. She and Agnes are still wary with one another, careful as cats, but at this moment Beatrice is certain they are both wondering the same thing: whether there is anything in the world more sinister than their youngest sister in possession of an idea.

"About this idea of yours," Bella begins.

It's past midnight and No. 7 South Sybil is finally empty again. Agnes rolled out spare quilts for her sisters and told them gruffly that it was too late to walk halfway across the city. Juniper is curled on her side, tired enough not to care how hard and flat the floor is, hovering right at the bleary edge of sleep.

She produces an eloquent *hnnngh* in response.

"Is it a dangerous idea?"

"Nah."

"If you were to estimate the size and scale of the riot the idea would provoke—the number of innocent bystanders it would put in St. Charity's—"

Juniper hurls a pillow at Bella and is satisfied by her subsequent squawk. "I was thinking of a few demonstrations, is all. Nothing dangerous." She thinks unwillingly of Electa lowering herself carefully into her seat, clutching her cracked rib. Of Jennie's bruised jaw going from midnight blue to dawn yellow. Of her sister asking *what comes after?*

"Demonstrations of... witching?" Bella asks.

"No, of knitting. *Yes*, witching." Juniper folds her arms behind her head, watching the play of shadows through the gap beneath the door. A pair of legs walking past, doubling back, pausing in the hall. "Something to show them what we can do."

"Who is 'them'?"

Juniper shrugs, invisible in the dark. "The women who think we're lying or stupid or selling them snake oil. The men who think they can beat us in the street. Everybody, I guess."

There's a long pause before Bella says, with unflattering shock, "That's... not a terrible idea."

"Why, thank you."

"It would certainly help with recruitment, and the larger our organization becomes the more collective knowledge we possess. Of course we'll need to be quite clever in our selection of spells—" Bella's voice is warming with the kind of scholarly enthusiasm that means she could keep going for hours or possibly weeks, when a second pillow whumps into her and Agnes grates, "Go to *sleep*, you ingrates."

The ingrates go to sleep.

Whoever was standing in the hall must have left, because the light shines unbroken now. It's only in the final blurred seconds before she closes her eyes that it occurs to Juniper that she never heard their footsteps.

14

Moly and spite a woman make,
May every man his true form take.

A spell for swine, requiring wine & wicked intent

I t's Beatrice Belladonna who finds the words and ways for their first demonstration. Well, who else would it be? Who else spends their days wrapped in ink and paper-dust? Who else dreams in threes and sevens, in once-upon-a-times and witch-tales?

She finds it in an obscure translation of Homer, tucked between a verse about cruel arts and noxious herbs. Beatrice is no Classicist, but she's certain she's never seen these lines in any other version of the *Odyssey*. She assumes they are the addition of the translator, a Miss Alexandra Pope.

Juniper claps her hands and cackles when Beatrice shows her. "Hot damn, Bell. Who will it be? The mayor? That Gideon Hill bastard?"

Agnes says, "Jesus, June, you're a menace," and Beatrice says, a little shyly, "I was thinking perhaps Saint George?" Her sisters agree.

And so, on the last night of May, when the moon is a blacker blackness in the sky above them and the air smells hot and rich with summer, Beatrice leads the Sisters of Avalon to St. George's Square.

They flit through the alleys and side-streets of New Salem in ones and twos, there and gone again. Instead of their usual skirts and aprons they wear gowns sewn from scraps and bits, pieced together by the girls who are cleverest with needle and thread.

Juniper had waved an illustrated copy of the Sisters Grimm at them as they worked. "We want them long and loose, witchy as all hell. And for Saints' sake, make sure they have pockets."

Beatrice thinks they did well; in their dark cloaks and long gowns the Sisters look like shadows or secrets, like fables come to life.

They gather in the white-paved square. Saint George stands over them, tall and bronze and cold, the hero who saved them from the plague and the wicked rule of witches.

Beatrice meets his metal eyes and has no difficulty at all summoning the will.

The words come next. Then the red splash of spilled wine. The bright scorch of magic as it burns its way into the world, shared between them and stronger for it. Beatrice staggers a little with the force of it.

When they smell the hot reek of molten bronze, they run.

It's the lamp-lighters who find it first. They arrive with their ladders and dousers just before dawn, leaning for a moment against the linden trees that have never quite been the same since the equinox, ragged and twisting.

"Thought I'd gone mad," one of them tells *The New Salem Post*, several hours later. "Thought my eyes was playing tricks."

But his eyes are not playing tricks. On the plinth where Saint George once stood, proud and princely, there is now something lumpen and squat, vaguely shameful: a bronze pig, bearing a brand of three circles woven together.

--◇◈◇--

The following afternoon Miss Cleopatra Quinn marches into Beatrice's office at Salem College and lays three newspapers across the desk. BELOVED STATUE SUFFERS UNCANNY ATTACK, reads one headline. THE WITCHES ARE COMING! declares another. *The Defender* offers the more measured SAINT OR SWINE? AVALONIANS STRIKE A BLOW FOR WITCH-KIND.

"My, my, Miss Eastwood. I wasn't aware I was fraternizing with such a troublemaker." Beatrice assures herself that Miss Quinn means nothing in particular by the word *fraternizing*.

"It was nothing," Beatrice murmurs, barely blushing.

"Hardly nothing. You have the whole city's attention, now."

They do: the Women's Christian Union, the Ladies' Temperance Society, and the New Salem Women's Association issued a joint letter of condemnation the previous week, and Mr. Gideon Hill is holding rallies each Sunday afternoon. A "modern-day coven," he calls them, seeking to bewitch young maidens and seduce God-fearing husbands. (*Just the reverse*, Beatrice thinks, and then spends several minutes shocked at her own wickedness.)

And their numbers are growing. Agnes says they knock at all hours of the day and night: too-young girls run away from home, lost-looking mothers with babies in tow, grandmothers with sly smiles and witch-ways tucked in their pockets.

"Juniper wants another demonstration before the half-moon," Beatrice says. "I haven't found anything suitable—just the usual trifling spells to darn socks or shine silver—but Agnes thinks she might have what we need. It comes from that old witch-tale story about a boy who buys an enchanted bean from the Crone. Do you know it? One of the mill-girls told Agnes a rhyme that went with the story…"

But Beatrice trails away because Quinn isn't listening. She's looking out the window with her brow knit. "I hope you and your sisters know what you're doing. I hope you understand that this kind of trouble"—she nods out to the square, where city workers are even now gathered around

Saint George's plinth, scratching their heads over the problem of relocating several possibly accursed tons of bronze pig—"demands a response."

"From who?"

"The law. The Church. Every man whose wife looks at him sideways, not quite laughing, picturing him as a pig instead of a man. Every man who has ever wronged a woman, which is just about every man." Her voice is tense, her arms folded. Beatrice doesn't think she's ever seen Quinn look worried.

"Well," Beatrice says with forced cheer. "That's why we're looking for the Lost Way, isn't it? Here are the materials we requested last week." She gestures to the teetering stack of crates behind her desk.

Quinn turns away from the window, the worry banished by a childish eagerness. "The Old Salem papers?"

It was Quinn who connected Old Salem with the Lost Way. She was skimming through an antique book of nursery rhymes when a scrap of paper slid from the pages. It seemed to be the end of a much longer letter, just a few precious lines:

> is true. What was lost has been found. Even the stars are not the stars I knew as a girl. Come soonest, my love. If we burn, let us burn together,
> S. Good

> October 10, 1783
> Salem

Beneath the signature were three circles looped together, dotted with ink-drops that might have been eyes.

Quinn showed it to Beatrice and she felt a great wave move through her as she looked at it, an electric thrill that ran from her spine to her scalp. This was not a myth or a children's story; this was ink-and-cotton proof that the Eastwoods were not the first wayward sisters to call the tower and its strange constellations.

She met Quinn's eyes and found them molten gold. "October tenth. Mere weeks before Old Salem fell."

Beatrice wished she shared Juniper's talent for profanity. She settled for a hoarse, insufficient "Oh *my*."

Old Salem, where witching rose again in the New World, despite centuries of shackles and stakes. Where Tituba and Osborne and Good and the rest of them had worked their wonders and terrors, walking the streets with black beasts at their heels. Where men feared to tread and women feared nothing at all.

Until the honorable Judge Geoffrey Hawthorn arrived with his troop of Inquisitors. Legally speaking, they ought to have announced themselves and made their arrests, separated the sinners from the sheep, held lengthy trials, and permitted each witch to confess her sins as she was bound to the stake. Hawthorn felt it would be more efficient to skip to the end. He and his men came in the night, silent except for the snap of lit torches.

The city burned for days, along with every woman and child and unlucky cat inside it. The papers reported ash falling as far away as Philadelphia, where children played in the drifts, like snow.

Now Old Salem is nothing but a black blight a hundred miles north, occupied by crows and foxes and black trees. Sightseers still trickle through, Beatrice has heard, paying a nickel each for haunted carriage rides through the ruins.

Beatrice looks again at the stacked crates, which comprise the College's entire collection of documents relating to Old Salem, and which Mr. Blackwell provided with only the slightest raising of his eyebrows and a mild "For the Hawthorn manuscript, I presume?" Beatrice made a gesture that might have been a nod.

None of it is properly transcribed or annotated, most of it is charred or scorched or merely unutterably dull, but somewhere between all the ledgers and receipts and housewives' cookbooks there might—*might*—be the words and ways that lead them to that rose-eaten tower.

She slides her spectacles up her nose and braces herself for a very long day. "We should begin with an initial catalog, I think. Are you staying? I'll take the top two boxes, if you'll take the third."

But Miss Quinn isn't looking at the boxes. She's watching Beatrice with several conflicting emotions in her face. "Or," she says, coming to some invisible conclusion, "you could accompany me to the Centennial Fair and buy me as many of those little fried cakes as I can eat. We deserve a day off, don't you think?"

There is very little Beatrice would like to do more than escort Miss Cleopatra Quinn to the Fair and buy her little fried cakes.

A minute later the two of them are strolling into the honeyed heat of the afternoon, strolling north across the square. Quinn shakes her head as they pass the bronze pig.

"Oh, please. You seem to be perfectly capable of witching when it suits you, I notice—" But Beatrice is unable to continue this line of inquiry because Miss Quinn tucks her hand casually, almost thoughtlessly, around her elbow, and Beatrice becomes incapable of further speech.

They stride up St. Mary-of-Egypt's, attracting sideways stares and sneers, not quite managing to care. They purchase a pair of yellow paper tickets and stride beneath the high iron arch of the Centennial Fair, where Beatrice buys Quinn a truly upsetting number of fried cakes. Afterward they share a watery beer, fend off two fortune-tellers, and win a gaudy brass ring with a glass diamond at a spin-the-wheel game.

Beatrice presents it to Quinn with a giddy flourish and Quinn laughs. "Oh, I think one is enough for me." She taps her own wedding ring. "I don't make the same mistake twice."

Beatrice slides the ring onto her own finger, instead, and doesn't feel anything in particular (a leaden weight, say, or a numbing chill) sinking in her stomach.

When she looks back up, Quinn has stationed herself in the line for the Ferris wheel, and is gesturing for Beatrice to catch up. Beatrice isn't sure she's interested in being stuffed into a small glass cage and dangled above the city, but the line shuffles forward and Quinn says, "Oh, hush," and soon they are smashed hip-to-hip, spinning up into the hot blue of summer.

The cabin smells of stale beer and there's something unfortunate smeared across the windows, but it doesn't matter. The city lies distant and foreign beneath them, like the surface of the moon, and the wind rushes clean and bright over their skin. Beatrice closes her eyes and wonders if this is how witches felt astride their broomsticks, like hawks who slipped their jesses, who may never return to the leather fist waiting below.

The wheel creaks to a stop. Beatrice and Quinn sway together in the wide-open sky, wind-kissed. Quinn's hand is still resting lightly on Beatrice's arm, and Beatrice is paying no attention to it (the pearl shine of her nails, the smudge of ink on her sleeve, the warm smell of cloves rising from her skin).

Beatrice twists at the brass ring around her own finger. "Your husband," she blurts, and feels Quinn go still beside her. "Is he—does he know how you spend your afternoons?"

Quinn's smile is far too knowing, smug as a sphinx. "Oh, I doubt it. He's often away."

"I see. And do you—" Beatrice suddenly cannot imagine how she intended to conduct the rest of the sentence.

Quinn is still smiling. "We have an arrangement. Mr. Thomas is a very *understanding* man." She places a peculiar emphasis on the word, as if passing Beatrice a note written in a code she doesn't know.

"Good. That's good. That is, I didn't think there were any understanding men."

Her tone is too bitter; Quinn's sly smile fades a little. "Your father really did a number on the three of you, didn't he."

The two of them have talked extensively about Miss Quinn's past: her childhood in a crowded row house in New Cairo, all smog and sun and hopscotch; her aunts who petted and spoiled her and braided her hair; her mother who still runs a spice shop and comes home smelling of paprika and peppers; her father who used to cut out each of Quinn's articles from *The Defender* and paste them into a scrapbook, with which he assailed guests and neighbors at any opportunity.

But Beatrice hasn't much mentioned her own family, for the same reason a person doesn't much mention carrion at the dinner table.

Beatrice attempts a casual shrug. "I s-suppose." She plucks at the brass ring on her finger. "He was—he could be very charming. I once saw him talk a pair of men out of a blood-feud with nothing but a smile and a round. But he could also be..." *A devil, a monster, a wolf on two legs.* "Different."

Quinn makes a carefully neutral noise and Beatrice knows she could stop there, if she liked. She could skip over the rotten places in her past as she usually does and remain unblemished a little longer.

But the two of them are alone far above the city and Quinn's hand is still on her arm, and surely a woman who turned a Saint into a pig might manage to tell the truth, however small and sordid.

Beatrice wets her lips. "It wasn't only my father. It was—St. Hale's." Just saying the name sends a sick swooping through her stomach, as if the cabin has broken loose from its moorings and gone plummeting earthward.

Quinn sucks a sharp breath between her teeth. "That place has... an unfortunate reputation. Beatrice, I'm sorry."

Beatrice can barely hear her over the memory of hot wax hissing on the back of her bent neck, the ache of her knees on the chapel floor. Her hands bound together in forced prayer, cords cutting deep. A dozen clever cruelties that drove every desire from her body save one: to make them stop.

Beatrice finds that she's twisting violently at the brass ring. It slips from her finger. "Oh dear, pardon me—"

Quinn scrabbles after it but the ring falls between the steel seams of the cabin and twinkles downward. It vanishes in a final flash of cut-glass diamond.

A small silence follows while Beatrice reassembles herself, parentheses braced once more like a pair of cupped hands around her heart. "I apologize. I do not mean to be so hysterical."

"I don't know what they told you at St. Hale's, but a few tears hardly make a woman a hysteric."

Beatrice had not been aware that she was crying. She scrubs too hard at her cheeks, feels the wind whip them dry. "In any case, you are mistaken. My father did not send me to St. Hale's." Beatrice says it calmly, but there's acid in her throat. "My sister did."

Quinn startles beside her. "Juniper?" she whispers.

"Certainly not. June is the loudest of us, but hardly the most dangerous. And she was only a girl when it happened."

Quinn doesn't move or speak or ask questions. She simply listens, as if her whole being is bent toward the listening, as if Beatrice is someone worth listening to.

Beatrice swallows very hard. "Our father was angry with Agnes for…" There would be a kind of justice to it if Beatrice spilled her sister's secrets, one bloody eye traded for another, but she finds she can't do it. "Our father was always angry. Or maybe not always—Mother said he used to laugh, and take her dancing, until the war…Well. I never saw him dance. One day he came for Agnes, and Agnes threw me before him like a bone to a wolf."

Agnes had looked at her with her eyes ringed white and her teeth bared. In her face Beatrice had seen the sudden certainty of her own death: the red of her blood, the black of the cellar, the gray of her gravestone. She was an animal with its leg caught in a wire trap, deciding whether to turn its teeth against its own flesh or just lie down and die.

And Beatrice watched her sister choose. *I saw Beatrice with the preacher's girl last Sunday.*

Until that day, until the very second Agnes opened her mouth to exchange her life for Beatrice's, they had been one another's keepers. But no longer.

Beatrice looks out over the city without seeing it. "I was in St. Hale's by the following Sunday. I believe our local preacher assisted with the tuition costs."

Quinn stays quiet a little longer, maybe waiting for more of the story, maybe just waiting for the wind to dry the wetness on Beatrice's cheeks. Then she asks, "And yet—you trust Agnes now?"

"...Yes." Or at least she trusts that her sister wants the same thing they want: more.

"Although she broke that trust before."

"Surely trust is never truly broken, but merely lost." Beatrice's lips twist. "And what is lost, that can't be found?"

She feels the amber heat of Quinn's gaze on her face, scrutinizing her. "Perhaps you should trust less easily, Miss Eastwood." There's a harshness in her voice, but she loops her arm not-very-casually through Beatrice's as she says it, and Beatrice does not pull away.

The wheel spins them back to earth, the bright-smelling wind replaced with the greasy fug of the Fair. As they stroll back beneath the high arch of the entranceway, still arm in arm, Quinn asks, lightly, "So. Tell me about this second spectacle."

And Beatrice—who perhaps should trust less easily—does.

15

Fee and fie, fum and foe,
Green and gold, see them grow!

A spell for growth, requiring buried seeds & fool's gold

It's Agnes Amaranth who finds their second spell. She's talking with Annie before the shift bell rings, whispering about ways and words and spells half-hidden in witch-tales, and Annie scoffs. "You think there's witchcraft hidden in pat-a-cake songs? Secret spells in the tale of Jack and the Giant?" Agnes watches her with narrow gray eyes and says, "Maybe so. Tell it to me."

Later that evening Agnes walks past the black remains of the Square Shirtwaist Factory on St. Lamentation. She read in the papers that forty-six women died in the fire, and another thirteen leapt from the high windows. "It's company policy to lock the doors," the owner argued in court. "So the girls don't get shiftless." He and his partner had paid a fine of seventy-five dollars.

Standing there, looking up at the burned carcass of the factory with heat gathering in her fingertips, Agnes notices that there are survey stakes spaced neatly around the lot. Scraped earth. The beginnings of a scaffold. She understands that the factory will be rebuilt, locked doors and all—that the sisters and cousins and mothers of the dead girls will work atop their ashes—and she knows, then, what their second spectacle will be.

On the tenth of June, Agnes and the Sisters of Avalon walk two-by-two down St. Lamentation. They wear their billowing black gowns, their skin gleaming white and olive and clay-dark beneath the gas-lamps, and carry seeds in their pockets: rye and rose, wisteria and ivy.

They plant their seeds in the ashen dirt of the Square Shirtwaist Factory, and toss glittering handfuls of fool's gold into the lot. They speak the words. They're silly words, stolen from a tale about a boy who trades his milk cow to a witch for a handful of magic seeds, known only by women and children and daydreamers: *fee and fie, fum and foe.*

The Sisters feel the sweet rush of witching in their veins. They leave before the first green finger pokes through the black earth.

By dawn the burnt carcass of the factory is nearly hidden by leaves and roots and reaching tendrils, as if several wet springtimes have passed in a single night. By noon there is nothing left of the building except the occasional right angle poking through the vines, a scattering of burnt nails among the tall grasses. Birds roost among thick twists of green, and the leaves hum with wingbeats and small, scuttling things. A sign is scratched into a bare patch of earth: three circles, twined together like snakes.

The workers gather nervously at the perimeter, muttering and scowling and crossing themselves. Several of them tilt their caps back to squint up at the thing that was once a construction site—the three-leafed ivies where the scaffold once stood, the tendons of wisteria where the brand-new punch-clock once sat with its stingy second-hand and cold heart—and stroll home, whistling off-key. One of them—a big, brash man with a bronze pin on his chest—begins to hack and slash at the green-grown mountain, shoving his way inside it; he does not emerge, and no one goes looking for him.

The next morning there's a black-suited officer waiting beside Mr.

Malton at the mill. The girls are asked to turn out their pockets and shake out their aprons before entering, "in light of recent events." Agnes complies, unhesitating, and a scattering of seeds spills into the alley, some tufted white and some dark and shining as beetle's eyes.

"Flower seeds," she says innocently. "For my window box, sir." She sweeps her lashes low over her eyes in a way that has always made men very stupid. The officer waves her inside.

Three days later Agnes is sweating on the corner of Thirteenth and St. Joseph, squinting at the folded square of paper in her hand: *August S. Lee. The Workingman's Friend.*

She thought at first "the workingman's friend" was some sort of title or tiresome motto, but Annie informed her it was a place: a barroom on the upper west side frequented by socialists, unionists, populists, Marxists, libertine college students with wispy mustaches, unemployed men with beards, and every other species of malcontent.

"August'll be there, stirring up trouble." Annie shakes her head. "He was throwing bricks through bank windows before he could talk, his mother used to say."

"And yet he refuses to meet with us."

"He wishes us all the best, but says he has 'serious matters' to attend to—like drinking the town dry, I suppose. Well, you know how they are." Agnes did.

But she also knew that Mr. August S. Lee was in possession of words and ways that she wanted very much, and that young men in dim barrooms were not known for their reticence, especially if there was an admiring young lady looking up at them through her lashes and saying, "Oh! How *shocking*!" at regular intervals. Agnes coiled her hair like a sleek black adder atop her head, allowing a few strands to wisp artfully around her face, and chose a half-cloak the precise color of her eyes, before going to find The Workingman's Friend.

It proves to be less of a barroom and more of an unswept basement. She descends a narrow set of steps and finds the air blue with cigar smoke and fumes, the summer evening sun replaced by the yellow hum of electric lights.

There's an easy rumble of talk in the room—the comfortable conversation of men with cheap beer and nowhere in particular to be—but it falls quiet as Agnes steps forward: a woman, alone and young, her cloak parted around a pregnant belly.

She approaches the bar and asks for a Mr. August Lee. The barman points to a high-backed booth with a slightly helpless expression, like a cornered spy betraying his comrade's location.

Four men are seated at the table, blinking up at her with expressions ranging from mild terror to smeary delight. Agnes smiles sweetly at them. "Hello, boys. I'm here to speak with Mr. Lee." They blink at her with varying degrees of inebriation and she adds, gently, "If your name is not Mr. Lee, *shoo*."

Three of the men shoo. They leave behind a long, rangy man with summer-straw hair and a suspicious squint. His face is young but hard-edged, with a skipped-meal sharpness: arrowhead cheeks, knife-blade nose, scarred jaw. Agnes might have noticed that he was handsome, if she had any time for handsome men.

Mr. Lee looks up at her. She sees his eyes perform the usual up-and-down over her form, pausing only briefly on her swollen belly, before resting on her face.

He offers a grin that's clearly supposed to be dashing, but the scar along his jaw pulls it crooked and wry. "Do I know you, miss?"

She offers another honeyed smile. "May I sit?" She wedges herself into the booth without waiting for a response. "My name is Miss Agnes Amaranth. I'm here to ask—"

A sudden suspicion crosses his face. "If you're a teetotaler, you're wasting your time. That Wiggin woman has already come around twice this month, and I'm not interested in salvation."

"Oh! I'm not here to talk about your vices or faults, Mr. Lee." Agnes imagines it would be quite a long conversation.

The dashing grin reappears. "Glad to hear it."

"I'm here," she says pleasantly, "to talk about witchcraft." The smile freezes, hanging half-formed on his face. "I represent the Sisters of Avalon. You may have heard of us?"

It takes a beery two seconds before his eyes widen. "Oh *hell*. You're that women's club Annie's been on about."

"Oh, you have heard of us! How lovely. Well, I'm here because we've heard the most *fascinating* rumors about the Pullman Strike in Chicago." His face stiffens when she says the word *Chicago*, and he rubs at the scar along his jaw. Agnes pretends not to notice, fluttering on with girlish innocence. "Some people said work was delayed by means that were…uncanny. Rusted machines, furnaces that never burned hot, timber that rotted overnight." She leans forward conspiratorially, looking up at him through the long black of her lashes. "We were hoping you might be willing to tell us more about it. Share some of your ways and words."

Mr. Lee watches her for a long, considering second before settling back in his seat, one arm flung along the back of the bench. He sips the foamed gold of his beer and asks neutrally, "Was that your girls, at the Square Shirtwaist Factory? And St. George's Square?"

Agnes, who feels vaguely that it would be unwise to confess criminal activity to a near-stranger, merely smiles.

He lifts his beer in a mocking toast. "Quite impressive. Showy. I've seen your sign all over town." Agnes has seen it, too: three circles drawn in soot on alley walls or scratched into the sides of trolleys; three flower wreaths hung together in a shop window, their edges overlapping; three loops embroidered into the tags of sweatshop shirts. The Sign of the Three had spread through New Salem like the underground roots of some great, unseen tree, tunneling beneath the cobblestones and surfacing in every mill-house and kitchen and laundry room.

Agnes tries to hide her too-sharp smile with an airy "Yes, it has gotten some attention, hasn't it?"

"And there's your problem, Miss Agnes Amaranth." Mr. Lee's tone is so perfectly condescending Agnes thinks he must have taken lessons. She pictures whole classrooms full of young, handsome men practicing their pitying smiles. He continues, "See, in Chicago we weren't interested in *attention*. It wasn't a damn stage-play. It was a *war*. Not a show."

Agnes permits herself to imagine his expression if she were to grab his beer and toss it in his smug face. She bends her lips in another simpering smile. "Still, Mr. Lee. Surely it wouldn't be *too* terribly taxing to spend an evening or two in consultation with us? We would be very grateful students, I promise." Agnes thinks of Juniper, who might show her gratitude by permitting Mr. Lee to leave the premises on two feet rather than four, and fights back a laugh.

Mr. Lee is still sprawled against his bench, unmoved. He cocks his head at her. "Does all this"—he waves his beer at her, indicating everything from her eyelashes to her pinned-up hair—"generally work for you? Sweet looks and wiles?"

Agnes straightens very slowly, her simper flattening into cold appraisal. "Generally, yes."

He shakes his head ruefully. "I'm sorry to disappoint you. Annie said you were a hell of a looker"—Agnes feels a sudden rush of warmth toward Annie—"and hard as a coffin nail"—the warmth subsides substantially—"which is frankly more interesting. I sympathize with your cause, truly I do. There were women standing on the train tracks in Chicago, too, and we were grateful. But it comes down to the laws of nature."

"What laws, precisely?" There's no honey in her voice at all, now.

Lee takes another drink, thumbs foam from his upper lip. "Women can't work men's magic."

Agnes feels invisible thunderclouds rolling nearer. "No?"

"It's no insult. It's just the way we're made. A man would make a mess of women's witching, wouldn't he? All those fiddly charms for housework and keeping your hair just so..."

The thunderclouds crackle closer, raising the hair on her arms. "Have you ever tried it?"

He looks mildly affronted, as if she'd asked whether he sometimes wore corsets and lace. "Of course not."

"Give me a man's spell to try, then, right here and now."

Her tone cuts through the indulgent laze of Mr. Lee's expression. He sits a little straighter in his seat, his eyes on the iron line of her mouth. "Does your father know where you are?"

She gives him a cold shrug. "Dead."

"Your husband?"

Agnes raises her left hand and wiggles her ringless fingers.

"Huh. What about the baby, then? Are you sure a woman in your condition should be—"

Agnes lowers all her fingers except one, causing Mr. Lee to snort into his beer.

He mops the splatters with his sleeve, grinning in a helpless, boyish way that makes him seem suddenly much younger. He looks at her and mutters something that might be *sweet damn*.

Agnes feels an answering smile tugging at her lips, but she hammers it flat. "I have a proposal for you, Mr. Lee." There is a voice in her head telling her this is a very stupid proposal; she ignores it. "If I can perform a spell of your choosing to your satisfaction, you will agree to assist us however you may."

Mr. Lee crosses his arms and adopts an unconvincing expression of reluctance. Agnes would bet a week's pay that he was the sort of boy who never turned down a dare or backed down from a bluff. "And if you fail?"

"Then I leave you in peace."

"Seems a shame. I don't care much for peace."

"What, then?"

His eyes flash wickedly. "A kiss."

She isn't surprised: he's a flirt and she's a woman with demonstrably questionable morals, and in her experience there's rarely anything else a man wants from her. But she's surprised to feel a flicker of disappointment—that he's so predictable, perhaps. Or that she's tempted.

She folds her hands primly. "I'm afraid my kisses are not for sale, Mr. Lee."

"Then what do you propose?"

She pretends to consider. "I could refrain from telling your cousin that you propositioned a young lady in such an uncouth fashion, if I lost."

The humor fades slightly from his face. Annie has come to work on several occasions with bruised knuckles; Agnes suspects there's a short temper beneath her kerchief and apron. "A compelling counter-offer," Mr. Lee murmurs. "I accept."

He drains his beer and stands, setting the glass back on the table with a showman's flourish. He winks. "Watch closely, now."

He fishes in his breast-pocket, produces a single green-tipped match, and holds it over the empty glass. He chants a string of foreign-sounding words—Agnes thinks they might be Latin or Greek—and snaps the matchstick.

There's a delicate *ping* as the glass cracks and splinters, fissures running through it like frost. It remains standing, held together more by habit than anything else.

A few men are watching from the bar now. They grunt approval. August presents his matchbox to Agnes as if it's a bouquet.

She unwedges herself from the booth and stands. Her fingers brush his as she selects a match.

She clears her throat and says coolly, "The Sisters of Avalon meet at the South Sybil boarding house, Mr. Lee." His eyes kindle with admiration. "Knock at Number 7 and say the word *hyssop*." It's the secret code she and her sisters used as girls: *hyssop* meant all's well; *hemlock* meant run and hide.

Agnes holds the match above the fractured glass and stumbles her way through the words. A flicker of heat licks up her spine. She says the words a second time, pouring her will into them: her aching feet and her heavy belly, her hope and her hunger, her bone-deep weariness with handsome young men who barter for kisses like coins. Heat scorches beneath her skin, fever-hot. Her daughter kicks hard in her belly—*Sorry, love*—

She closes her eyes and snaps the matchstick.

A cracking, shattering sound fills the bar, followed by several unmanly yelps and a great deal of swearing.

Agnes keeps her eyes shut tight, swaying slightly, smelling a sudden green scent like fresh-cut tobacco.

When she opens her eyes she finds a gray wool vest several inches from her nose and two arms held high on either side of her face, shielding her. The heat fades and leaves her cold and dazed, terribly tempted to press her forehead into the heat of that gray wool vest.

Mr. Lee steps back with a slight crunch of glass beneath his boots. His eyes are very wide. A red line gleams across his cheekbone, and another two or three score his forearms. Shouts and grumbles rise around them as men wave the shattered handles of beer mugs at them in an unfriendly fashion.

Mr. Lee dusts splintered glass from his hair and meets her eyes. "Well now, Miss Agnes Amaranth. What was that address?" He smiles as he says it, wry and crooked and a little abashed. The smugness has been replaced by an intent gleam in his eyes.

"South Sybil Street. Come after dark and keep quiet in the hall—the landlady disapproves of gentleman callers."

She turns to leave, picking her way through glittering shards and spilt liquor, and he calls after her, "May I bring flowers?"

Agnes does not look back as she leaves, so that he cannot see her smile. "I'm sure you may bring whatever you please, Mr. Lee, so long as you bring magic also."

Juniper is sitting cross-legged on the bed, tossing a slightly wizened apple from palm to palm while Bella reads from one of her dustiest and most dull-looking books, when Agnes returns to South Sybil.

She's sweaty and cross, with glittering specks caught in the dark swirl of her hair. "Any luck?" Juniper asks her.

Agnes gives a dark *ha*. "I found Mr. Lee, if that's what you mean. But there's nothing lucky about him—he's arrogant, feckless, probably criminal—not *nearly* as handsome as he thinks he is—" Agnes is frowning at her own reflection in the cracked shard that serves as her mirror. She tugs and fusses at her hair, dissatisfied in some unfathomable fashion.

"To hell with him, then," Juniper says mildly. "We'll find some other boy to teach us men's magic. Somebody's bound to have an uncle or a brother—"

"No!" Agnes's voice is several degrees sharper than is strictly warranted. "That is, Mr. Lee has already agreed to help. He'll be here soon, maybe tomorrow evening." She casts a disgruntled look around the room, eyes lingering on the tumbled piles of papers and books, the frayed lengths of black cloth, the herbs strung in drying bundles before the window, and the Mason jars rattling with seeds and bones. South Sybil bears an increasing resemblance to Mama Mags's house.

"I'm going out," Agnes announces.

"What for?"

Agnes gestures vaguely behind her as she sweeps out. "A vase."

Juniper watches her go with her jaw slightly slack. She looks at Bella and finds her eyes crimped behind her spectacles. "What's so funny?"

"Nothing. It's just—our sister has always had low taste in men." Juniper finds this so baffling and absurd that she can think of no response.

She changes the subject instead. "I saw Cleo here earlier. What did she bring us?"

Bella blushes. Juniper has noticed lately that she blushes often at the mention of Cleo Quinn. "Oh, I asked if she could find us anything about Miss Grace Wiggin. Since you continue to insist that she's a wicked witch of nefarious powers."

"She *is* a wicked—"

"Miss Quinn made some inquiries. Grace grew up in the Home for Lost Angels—the orphanage," she clarifies, in response to Juniper's blank stare, "before she was adopted at sixteen by an older gentleman who had no heirs and a generous inheritance from an uncle. A gentleman who is now a member of the City Council."

"Who?"

"A Mr. Gideon Hill."

Juniper puzzles over this for a while, wondering if it clarifies anything or merely obscures it further. "So. She's just campaigning for her daddy? Writing to the papers and waving banners and making a nuisance of herself?"

Bella shrugs.

Juniper returns to her apple-tossing, whispering words to herself, only some of which are profanities. Sometimes she pauses to inspect the apple closely, as if looking for worms, then resumes her whispering. She touches the apple with various objects—coins and bones, red strings and crow feathers, to no discernible effect.

Nearly an hour later she taps her thumbnail against the skin of the apple and grins at the delicate *tink-tink* sounds it produces. "Well, I hope our sister has her head on straight by the full moon."

Bella makes a distracted *mmm?* noise without looking up from her book. Juniper sets a small, heavy object in its pages. Bella peers at it through her spectacles and gives a soft gasp. "What—how—"

"Electa taught me one of her mama's old songs. I thought there might be something to it." She plucks the heavy thing from her sister's book and holds it up to the light. It's round and lustrous, glowing yellow as butter: a small, golden apple.

Juniper grins at it, this thing that fell out of storybook and song to shine in her palm, real as anything. "Think I found our third spectacle."

16

Ferrum rubigine, pernay o chronoss.

A spell to rust, requiring salt, spit, & considerable patience

The night after Agnes Amaranth shattered every stein and bottle in The Workingman's Friend, Mr. August Lee knocks at the door of Room No. 7 in the South Sybil boarding house.

Agnes is bent over a map of New Salem with a handful of other Sisters, debating the best routes to approach their third spectacle, when a man's voice husks, "Uh, *hyssop*," from the hall. The room falls still. Worried glances dart like swallows between them.

Juniper rises from the bed, reaching for her red-cedar staff the way a man might reach for a loaded pistol. "It's fine, June. It's just Annie's cousin."

Juniper has already whipped open the door to reveal the lanky, shockingly dapper Mr. Lee. His shirt appears to have been ironed and his summer-straw hair looks as though it suffered a recent encounter with a comb; in his left hand he holds a red burst of carnations.

He touches a polite hand to his cap. "Evening, ladies. I'm here at the request of a Miss Agnes Ama—"

"We know who you are. What're these?" Juniper snatches the carnations and inspects them. She plucks a few petals and crushes them between her fingers, sniffing suspiciously. "Don't think my Mama Mags ever used these in her witching. What properties do they have?"

Mr. Lee is struck briefly silent by the uncivil young woman and her green-lit glare. "It's not—they're not a *spell*. They're *flowers*, for Miss—" Mr. Lee looks a little frantically around the larger-than-it-ought-to-be room and finally spots Agnes leaning her hip against the kitchen table, fighting a smile.

She loses. "Let him in, June. Give me those." Agnes rescues the flowers and arranges them in a chipped porcelain vase. They sag forlornly over the edge, looking distinctly misused. "So glad you could join us, Mr. Lee. You've already met my younger sister, Miss James Juniper. This is Miss Beatrice Belladonna, Misses Victoria and Tennessee Hull—"

Agnes circles the room, introducing both her sisters and Sisters. Mr. Lee, in an attempt to recover his footing, assays a charming smile at a pair of girls from Salem's Sin; they return looks of such surpassing coldness that Agnes almost feels sorry for him. He redirects the smile to Bella, whose polite but profound disinterest is somehow even more crushing. Mr. Lee's gaze swings back to Agnes in desperation.

She gestures to one of their mismatched chairs. "Shall we begin?"

In the end Mr. Lee's first lesson in men's magic is not so much a lesson as a hostile interrogation. Bella perches in a seat next to him with her little black notebook propped on her knees, interrupting every six or seven seconds with probing questions and obscure remarks ("How do celestial movements alter the efficacy?" "Are all your spells in the imperative rather than subjunctive mood?"). As Mr. Lee fumbles through answers that are mostly long pauses and pained expressions, Juniper sits on his other side, mangling the words at the top of her voice and complaining when they produce no obvious results ("Some good men's magic is. What's Latin for *horseshit*, Mr. Lee?"). It's clear that whatever work Mr. Lee did in Chicago—Annie said he was a lineman who became one of Debs's left-hand boys, charged with arson and inciting to riot by the state of Illinois—it hadn't prepared him for two hours with the Eastwood sisters.

Looking harassed, Lee withdraws a pinch of salt and a bent nail from his vest pocket and chants at the nail in rough-cut Latin until it looks marginally flakier and redder, as if it contracted a sudden rash.

"Neat," Juniper sneers, "if you've got a year or two to spare."

Lee slaps a hand on the table, his charm hanging in ragged tatters around him. "Listen. This exact spell took out a mile of track in Chicago and got me beaten damn near to death. When you're out on the front lines—"

Agnes thinks he might be warming up to a real speech, full of aggrieved passion and chest-thumping, when one of the other girls at the table gives a soft, devastating snort. "You wouldn't know a front line if it bit you, boy." It's Gertrude Bonnin, the clay-colored woman from one of the Dakotas.

Mr. Lee looks at her, not so much offended as despairing, and Juniper slings an arm around Gertrude's stiff shoulders. "Our girl here fought in the Indian Wars out west, *Mister* Lee. She and a bunch of other girls busted out of their boarding school—using Saints only know what kind of witching, because she won't tell us—and joined their mamas and aunties on the front lines."

Gertrude pats Juniper's arm and says, without a trace of apology, "Not every word and way belongs to you."

"What about the uplift of women around the globe? What about the universal union of our sex, and the comradeship of womankind?" Agnes is fairly sure Juniper's store of three-syllable words has just been exhausted; she suspects her sister is quoting from a pamphlet they received from the Witches' Franchise League in Wales. It was accompanied by a substantial donation to their cause from a Miss Pankhurst and an invitation to the summer solstice ritual at Stonehenge.

Gertrude gives another of her devastating snorts. "When I see you out west, standing beside us against the U.S. cavalry, I'll consider us comrades."

Juniper flicks the bent nail at Gertrude in response and mutters about stubborn Sioux girls and useless men. At this point the Hull sisters intervene, insisting that they wouldn't need Mr. Lee at all if instead they summoned the dead souls of their ancestors for instruction. Juniper makes a lewd suggestion about where Victoria can stick her crystal ball, and the tone of the evening descends thereafter.

Mr. Lee watches the rising debate with his jaw slightly slack and his blond hair tousled. Agnes sidles closer and pitches her voice beneath the noise of the room. "What's the matter, Mr. Lee? Is this not how you pictured our little women's club?"

"I...not entirely." He scrubs a hand over his jaw. "What's all this?" He nods at a pile of black felt and silken scraps, a scattering of dark feathers.

"Oh, nothing that would interest you, I'm sure. Just another *show*."

For some reason this provokes another of his bright, boyish grins. "*My* what sharp teeth you have, Miss Eastwood," he murmurs. "Will you be sprouting wings? Riding broomsticks across the Thorn?"

Bella, who was apparently eavesdropping, begins to say something about the absence of historical evidence that witches specifically preferred *broomsticks*, and that such stories likely refer to any number of spells for flight or levitation—but Agnes interrupts her on the grounds that it's boring and no one cares. "That information is for Sisters only, Mr. Lee."

"August, please." He looks up at her with a dare in his eyes. "And how would one petition to join the Sisters of Avalon?"

Agnes never liked to back down from dares, either. "Bella. The roster, if you please?"

Bella hesitates for a long second before sliding her little black notebook across the table. Lee writes his name beneath the others—AUGUST SYLVESTER LEE—and tosses the pen down like a dueling glove.

"And now your oath, sir. Prick your finger and draw a cross, then repeat after me."

"Witchcraft? Are you sure a man can work it?"

"Are you sure you're a man? You strike me more as a mouse."

August barks a laugh before he pricks his finger and speaks the words. The two of them grin a little giddily at one other until Juniper squints over at them and mutters darkly, "Oh, for the love of God."

Later—after most of the Sisters of Avalon have slunk back through the halls of South Sybil and out into the damp green darkness of the June night, after August left with a tip of his hat so low it was nearly a bow and Agnes watched him go with a hand on her belly, reminding herself the price a woman paid for wanting—Bella clears her throat.

She's standing at the door with her black notebook tucked beneath her arm, looking back at Agnes with deep lines around her mouth. "Be careful, Ag." It's almost a whisper. "I heard Annie saying he's just here for a month to lie low. I don't think he's the type to stick around."

"It's not—it's none of your damn business," Agnes hisses back.

"I just didn't want you to form any attachments that might be... unwise."

"And what about the lovely Miss Quinn? Is *she* a wise attachment?"

Bella's face goes gray, her shoulders hunching around some unseen wound. "I—I don't know what you mean." She sweeps from the room.

Then Agnes is alone, feeling like a snake or a shard of glass, something that hurts if you hold it close.

At the next meeting of the Sisters, Beatrice chooses a seat beside Miss Frankie Black. They work side by side, stripping lace and buttons from a pile of old skirts and donated blouses. There are more Sisters now, in need of more witch-robes.

Beatrice engages Frankie in an airy discussion of family and background, basking in the southern sprawl of her accent, before asking casually if Frankie happens to know Miss Cleopatra Quinn.

Frankie looks at her slantwise. "Yes."

"Oh, I thought you might. And are you...close?"

"Quite close, at one time." Frankie's voice is very even, but Beatrice's heart gives a double thump at that *quite*. She thinks of all the things Quinn doesn't tell her, the work she doesn't share.

"Well," she says lightly, "I've just lately become acquainted with her. She's quite..." She trails away, unsure what word she meant to say (*enigmatic, compelling, consuming*).

Frankie turns to face her directly. There's an unmistakable shine of pity in her eyes. "Look, you should know before you get your heart broke: Miss Cleopatra has...*other* interests, and they will always come first."

"Other—?" Beatrice would give any sum of money to prevent herself from blushing. "The Colored League, you mean?" She abhors the note of desperate optimism in her voice.

The pity deepens. "No, not the Colored League."

"She's a member, is she not?"

"I don't believe she's been to a meeting in months. Maybe ever."

"Then I—I don't know what you mean." But Beatrice does.

She feels her elaborate theory—that Quinn was a clandestine operative for a women's rights organization—collapsing like underbaked bread. There was a much more obvious reason that a beautiful woman with an *understanding* husband might make private calls at unlikely places, might disappear for periods of time without saying where. Beatrice remembers her first meeting with Quinn, the blinding smile, the daring derby hat, the effortless charm.

A woman like that could do much better than a bony librarian. Beatrice wonders wanly if she was the only woman to escort Miss Quinn to the Fair.

Frankie sniffs and reaches out to pat her hand. "Don't fret. You're hardly the first."

Following her conversation with Frankie, Beatrice is more careful. She no longer permits Miss Quinn to loop her arm through hers or accompanies her in public. When their eyes meet—gray to gold, cloud to sunlight—Beatrice looks away after a single second (she counts in her head, *one-one-thousand*, drawing the syllables long and slow).

The last time Quinn visited the library, Beatrice suggested stiffly that there was no need for Miss Quinn to make the trip up from New Cairo quite so often, as they had finished reviewing the Old Salem materials and found nothing more exciting than a few desiccated rose petals and a pale tatter they thought was lace, but which turned out to be the shed skin of some long-dead snake. Everything else—the court transcripts and diary entries, the ledgers and letters—was either painfully mundane or mysteriously fragmented. A promising journal with the final pages ripped out; a little girl's letter to her aunt with entire passages faded away to nothing; an account from one of the Inquisitors who burned the city, which ended: *After the fire died and the screams faded—and I tell you I shall hear them till Judgment Day—Judge Hawthorn had us comb the ashes for days. Whatever he sought he did not find.*

"If the secret to calling back the Lost Way exists, we may be reasonably certain it's not in the Salem College Library." Beatrice met Miss Quinn's eyes (*one-one-thousand*). "Surely your time would be better spent pursuing—other possibilities."

Quinn opened her mouth as if she might object, but the expression on Beatrice's face made her close it. "As you wish, Miss Eastwood." It's only after she's gone that Beatrice notices she left her derby hat behind.

Beatrice spends the rest of the week working alone. She transcribes the chapters she is assigned; she adds more witch-tales and rhymes to her little black notebook and fills page after page with notes and theories and failed experiments (*Solstice and equinox offer amplification? Maiden's blood & Crone's tears—Mother's ???*); she squints at innocent shadows as they glide across the floor and keeps her threshold lined with salt. Mr. Blackwell blinks as he steps across it and asks Beatrice mildly if she's been feeling well.

If a certain scent lingers in the air, Beatrice doesn't notice (cloves; newsprint; machine oil).

She sees Miss Quinn a handful of times—at meetings of the Sisters of Avalon, flitting in and out of South Sybil as they plan their third spectacle—but somehow never quite remembers to return her derby hat; Quinn does not retrieve it.

By the eighteenth of June the summer heat has finally sunk through the limestone and wood-paneling of the library, so that sitting in her office feels like sitting in the damp interior of an animal's mouth. Even the books look rumpled and disheveled, pages swollen.

Beatrice works until midafternoon, sweaty and glazed and lonely. Her eyes slide to the derby hat on her desk.

She stands and tucks it under her arm. It may be unwise to form any particular attachment to Miss Quinn, but surely Beatrice might enjoy her company. Occasionally. She informs Mr. Blackwell that she's going home early and strides out into the bright haze of the square.

The trolley deposits her at the southernmost tip of Second Street, where the neat cobbles give way to hard-packed dirt and the stately homes are replaced by hasty tenements, and scuttles north again. Beatrice proceeds on foot, stepping across the invisible line that divides one neighborhood from the next—although New Cairo isn't so much a neighborhood within New Salem as it is an assault upon it.

Instead of a neat grid of streets there's a haphazard tangle; instead of pulled curtains and closed windows there are balconies crowded with flowerpots and laundry and bright awnings; even the churches are suspiciously cheery, ringing with raised voices rather than tolling bells and dour chants. The city has retaliated—passing fussy little ordinances and fines for broken windows, stuffing the entire neighborhood into a single odd-shaped voting district—but New Cairo persists in growing. *The Jungle*, Beatrice has heard it called, with a sour smile, or *Little Africa*; Beatrice thinks they're frightened to say the word *Cairo* aloud, as if it might summon golden tombs and witch-queens from the air.

The offices of *The Defender* are six blocks south, in a sooty red building that hums with the constant churn of the press. The secretary looks up as Beatrice enters. "Cleo isn't in, Miss Eastwood. Check Araminta's, on Nut Street." He says *Nut* strangely, almost like *night*.

After several wrong turns and two consultations with bemused passersby, Beatrice still walks past it twice: Nut Street is a long, crooked alley, deep-shadowed and cool even in the afternoon heat. Red-painted doors and dark windows line the walls, bearing discreet signs: LESLIE BELL, TAILOR; M. LAWSON'S CURATIVES; ARAMINTA'S SPICES & SUNDRIES. Beatrice taps at the door. After a long silence, she turns the handle.

She smells the spices first: a hundred shades of cinnamon and sage, clove and cardamom. The air itself glows reddish-gold, flecked with motes of pepper and paprika. The shop is filled with rows of tiny wooden drawers and brown paper packages, sacks of garlic and jars of ruby peppers. The floorboards sigh little puffs of saffron and salt as she crosses them. There's another smell lying beneath the spices, colder and stranger and wilder, that Beatrice can't name.

Beatrice edges toward the counter in the back, empty except for a small copper bell. Beatrice is reaching for it when she hears her own name, followed by: "—certain she isn't holding anything from me. She doesn't suspect anything. She's just...cautious."

Beatrice goes very still, her hand outstretched, her lungs half-full. She knows that voice.

Someone else says something, low, indistinct. It must be a question, because the first voice responds: "Tomorrow night. The Rose Moon. I told them a full moon was a foolish time for going unseen, but they're getting cheeky, less careful. Foolish."

Tomorrow the Sisters of Avalon work their third act of witching. Right now there are black gowns hanging ready in a dozen dressing rooms and boarding houses; words and ways waiting on a dozen tongues.

Another question, too soft to make out. The voice that Beatrice knows so well—the voice that has teased and tempted her, that has argued with her over worm-eaten books and stained letters—answers: "The witch-yard, in the city cemetery. Three hours after midnight."

It sounds like a report, as a soldier might give to a general. Or a spy to her master.

Beatrice has been betrayed once before. She is familiar with the cold that spreads from one's chest to one's fingertips, numbing the flesh, muffling the pulse. It's like that old tale about the witch so monstrous she turned men to stone with her gaze, except Beatrice is the monster and the stone both.

It's only when she hears a clatter that Beatrice realizes her body is moving. She's stepped backward into a shelf, toppling jars. Peppercorns scatter across the floor like buckshot.

The voices in the back room go abruptly silent. A soft curse, hurried footsteps—

Beatrice is already running, shoving past long strings of drying herbs and necklaces of shriveled flowers, sending more jars tumbling in her wake. She has one hand on the door when she hears her name again. She looks back over one shoulder.

Behind the counter, obscured by jangling ropes of herbs and yellow clouds of spilled spice, her face wrenched and taut, stands Miss Cleopatra Quinn.

(She's beautiful. Even here, even now—her sleeves rolled to the elbow, the tendons of her throat standing rigid beneath her skin, betrayal dying on her lips—there's a glow to her, as if she carries a lit candle in her chest.)

Their eyes meet. Beatrice can't tell how many seconds pass; more than one, certainly.

"Beatrice, please—"

It's the third time she's heard her name in Quinn's mouth, and everyone knows the third time is the last. Beatrice drops the derby hat still clamped foolishly beneath her arm.

She runs. No one follows.

Juniper listens as Bella tells her the whole sorry thing. Juniper stays quiet for a while after, running her tongue along her teeth, watching her sister pace and fret. "S'too late to call it off."

Bella's shoulders are bowed in a U around her chest, her face white and raw. "I should have asked her to take the oath, should never have trusted her. She practically told me not to." She wrings her hands. "If we left now we could get to Agnes and the Hull sisters, probably a few others before midnight...Oh, what should we do?" If she wrings her hands any more violently Juniper thinks the skin will rub clean off.

She crosses her ankles. "Depends."

"On what?"

"On who she talked to." Juniper catches Bella's eyes and pins her, asks her flat-out, "Do you think your girl ratted us out to the law?"

Bella stops pacing. She stands framed by the round glow of the window, eyes on the smogged stars. "No," she whispers. Juniper can't tell if she really means it or merely wants to.

But Juniper doesn't care. She wants the cool whip of the night on her cheeks, the black tangle of robes behind her, the heat of witching in her blood. Damn the danger.

She stands, her smile wide and wicked. "Then it's time we get ready."

17

Intery, mintery, cutery-corn,
Apple seed and apple thorn;
Feather fine, five-fold
Turn it all to gold.

A spell for a golden apple, requiring five feathers & pricked
thumb

James Juniper is just a girl, most of the time. The rest of the Sisters of Avalon are just maids or mill workers, dancers or fortune-tellers, mothers or daughters. Everyday sorts of women with everyday sorts of lives, not worth mentioning in any story worth telling.

But tonight, beneath the Rose Moon of June, they are witches. They are crones and maidens, villains and temptresses, and all the stories belong to them.

Juniper likes the city at night better than its daytime self. At night the noise and clatter soften enough to hear the rush of wind through alleys, the padding of stray cats, the chitter and dart of bats. The earth feels closer beneath the cobblestones and the stars shine stubborn through the smog and gas-light. Juniper can almost pretend she's running through the woods back home, tangle-haired and barefoot. Maybe it's just the solstice getting closer; Mags always said the holy days are when witching burns brightest, when even mice and men can feel the hot pulse of it beneath the skin of the world.

The cemetery is locked after dark, the gates high and sharp, but tonight they are witches. Juniper tosses her cedar staff over the top, then braids three hairs together and whispers the words. The Sisters climb the black silk rope, long and supple, and thud into the soft earth of the cemetery one after the other. They slip like shadows among the graves.

The witch-yard is tucked on the eastern edge of the cemetery: a half-acre of weeds and scraggled grass, without so much as a cracked headstone or a wooden cross. A witch was never buried beneath her name; instead, her ashes were sown with salt to prevent her soul from lingering longer than it should, then scattered over unhallowed ground. Juniper looks at that barren, sour earth and feels a leaden weight in her limbs: grief, maybe, for all the women they burned before her.

The fence around the witch-yard is less a fence than a suggestion; their skirts snag on rusted iron and sagging posts as they step across it. They flock to the center, where a single stunted hawthorn claws the sky.

Stillness falls. The cemetery is silent except for the rustle of wind through black-dyed cloth.

Juniper looks from face to moon-silvered face: Agnes with her belly hard and full; worried-looking Bella; Frankie Black and Florence Pearl, their arms long and bare; Jennie Lind and Gertrude Bonnin; a dozen other girls with eyes like bared blades and bloody promises, standing on the ashes of their ancestors.

Juniper wishes, with a poisonous twist in her stomach, that her daddy could see them. A girl is such an easy thing to break: weak and fragile, all alone, all yours. But they aren't girls anymore, and they don't belong to anyone. And they aren't alone.

Come and get us now, you bastard.

Her fist is tight around the feather in her pocket, and for a red second she wants to snap it. What good are golden apples? They should be raining brimstone or poisoning wells, making every man in New Salem shake in his damned boots. Last week they'd found a spell to call storms, a sailor's rhyme about red skies at morning and red skies at night, but Agnes shook her head. "I thought you wanted to recruit more women to the cause."

"It'd recruit the hell out of me," Juniper said, truthfully.

"Yes, well, you're a plague and a calamity and you should be locked up for the safety of the city." Agnes held the apple up to the window, where it glowed a rich, impossible yellow. "All of us grew up on stories of wicked witches. The villages they cursed, the plagues they brewed. We need to show people what *else* we have to offer, give them better stories."

Now Agnes clears her throat at Juniper's side. She steps forward to bury five apple seeds at the base of the hawthorn. She kneels in the dirt, hair loose and shining around her shoulders, lips forming the words for growth and greening. Some of the others whisper them with her. *Fee and fie, fum and foe.*

The hawthorn creaks. It groans and whines in a manner not unlike Mama Mags on a cold morning, when frost creeps white up the mountainside. Then it grows. The knobbled branches swell; the roots twist through the earth; the dry curls of leaves turn glossy emerald. Buds sprout, unfurl, bloom, fade, fall—an entire springtime in a second. Fruit swells, hard and green and then waxy red, ready for the plucking.

When Agnes stops speaking, there is an apple tree in the witch-yard where the hawthorn once stood, its crown spread high and proud, its boughs heavy with unnatural fruit.

Juniper puts her thumb to her mouth and bites until she tastes warm copper. She reaches for an apple and smears her blood across its flesh, red on red. Beside her she sees the others mimic her, hands lifting up, blood running down their wrists, feathers clutched tight.

They speak the words together, and it's just like Bella said it would be: stronger for the sharing. Grander, wilder, hotter—the witching burns into the world and the apples blush gold. Except it's not just the apples: yellow creeps up stems and twines around branches, runs along the branched veins of the leaves. Juniper and her Sisters keep speaking the words and the magic keeps burning and the gold keeps spreading until the entire tree stands bright and metal, as if Queen Midas herself strolled out of legend to trail her fingers along its bark.

The chanting stops. Silence falls, broken only by the calls of night-birds and the *clink-clink* of wind through golden leaves. The tree seems to emit its own buttery light, like a torch burning in the night, and Juniper sees the shine of it reflected in the upturned faces of the Sisters of Avalon. Each of them has the awed, slack expression of a woman who has witnessed an impossibility: a miracle, a revelation. A better story, glowing gold in the darkness.

Juniper glances sideways at Agnes, who looks younger and softer in the golden light. Juniper reaches for her hand without thinking, the way she did when they were girls, except now her palm is tacky with her own blood. "So maybe you were right," she whispers.

"Of course I was." Agnes folds her fingers around hers and squeezes once.

Juniper limps forward. With the scuffed end of her staff she scrapes a sign into the dirt: three circles, bound one to the other.

She's about to tell them all to head home when something rustles in the grave-strewn dark at Juniper's back. *A fox*, she thinks, *or a cat*.

But the rustle spreads. It echoes from every direction, a sudden swell of sound. Juniper spins to see shadows standing, black-cloaked figures rising from behind gravestones with silver badges glinting on their chests. She sees hands reaching, dark cloths whipped aside, and then the witch-yard is flooded with the blinding light of a dozen lanterns.

The light hits them like the stroke of midnight breaking some invisible spell. The glow of the golden tree turns sickly yellow and the wheeling stars become pale pinpricks above them. The wind dies, the night-birds fall silent. The witches are made into mere women once more.

Juniper swears, eyes stinging. Around her she hears the gasps and screams of the others—her sisters and Sisters, the girls and women who followed her into this—

Trap. She thinks the word and feels the iron bite as it closes around her.

She's still tear-blind and staggering when she hears a man's voice echoing weirdly off the gravestones. It's a familiar voice—oily, too high—but it's only when Juniper hears the soft whimper of a dog that she realizes who it belongs to: Mr. Gideon Hill.

"For the safety of our fair city and the good of her people"—she can hear the smile in his voice, cloying and gray—"I hereby place James Juniper Eastwood and her accomplices under arrest, to be tried for the crime of murder by witchcraft."

The first thing Beatrice feels is a rush of very foolish relief: there's been some sort of mistake! Surely none of them, whatever their sins and faults, are murderers.

Then Beatrice sees her youngest sister's face—bloodless and hard, her eyes flicking through every expression except surprise—and thinks perhaps she is mistaken in that assumption.

The second thing she feels is the familiar chill of flesh turning to stone, the numbness that follows betrayal. These men were huddled in the cemetery past midnight, waiting. Forewarned.

One of the figures scuttles forward, his lantern held high: a middle-aged, unremarkable man with a dog skulking at his heels like a reluctant shadow. It takes Beatrice far too long to recognize him, given that his face is plastered on campaign posters across three-quarters of the city. The Gideon Hill of the ads and newspapers is noble, even dashing, with ruddy cheeks and flaxen hair. In the lantern-glare he seems to have no color at all.

His eyes flick to the golden tree behind the Sisters and his lips twist in the patronizing cousin of a smile. "Most impressive, ladies." The eyes move to the ground, where Juniper scratched the sign of the Last Three, and the smile vanishes. His voice rises. "You have besmirched our fair city with your sinful ways. But no longer!" Beatrice is busy turning to stone and drowning in panic, but she spares a second to think, *Besmirched?* and wonder exactly which pulpy novels Mr. Hill has been reading. "James Juniper, come with us if you please. The rest of you will be taken in for questioning."

Beatrice knows enough about witch-trials to hear the violence waiting beneath the word *questioning*: the hiss of hot iron on flesh, the crack of a whip.

The line of men at Hill's back seems to hesitate. They shuffle and murmur, perhaps reluctant to lay hands on black-gowned women meeting beneath the full moon, perhaps remembering all the stories they heard as boys.

Mr. Hill stamps his foot at them. "Sergeant, tell your men—"

But Juniper cuts him off. "Easy now, Hill." Her voice is a slow, careless drawl, nearly friendly; it reminds Beatrice of the sheriff talking their daddy down from some drunken rant: *Easy now, James.* "No need to get hysterical."

Juniper strolls away from the golden tree and limps over the fence, leaning heavy on her staff, just a young crippled girl with cropped hair. She lifts one hand in sarcastic surrender. "Do you think you brought enough boys, Sergeant? Or do you want to run back for a couple more?"

Her expression is scornful, a little bored, as if this is all a lot of fuss and mess, but Beatrice feels her terror shrieking through the line between them and knows it's nothing but stubbornness and guts keeping her standing.

Juniper ought to remember that there are places where guts don't matter. Dark cellars, little white rooms where they lock you up until you lose the dangerous habit of courage.

Beatrice takes a half-step toward her, but Juniper turns back to face the women still circled around the tree. "Ladies," she says, and smiles. It's such a Juniper-ish smile—fey and foolish and dangerous, like an animal spinning to face its hunter, bare-toothed—that Beatrice knows abruptly what she's about to do. She hears Agnes shout *no!*

"*Hemlock.*"

Juniper flings herself backward into Gideon Hill. They topple—him swearing, her howling and thrashing, swinging her staff—and the Sisters of Avalon scatter like a broken string of pearls.

Beatrice watches them running in a dozen directions, screaming, stumbling, leaving scraps of black hung on the broken spokes of the fence. They dodge through the headstones, some of them caught by reaching hands, borne to the earth, some of them vanishing like smoke into the night. Beatrice knows she ought to be running with them, but she's still made of stone, unmoving.

There's a tangle of bodies where Juniper once stood. Beatrice catches the shine of boots, the sick thud of fists on flesh. Hill struggles free. He stands panting, wiping blood from his split lip with an absent expression, as if he doesn't feel any particular way about being violently tackled by a witch.

A pair of officers lumber toward the tree where Beatrice stands still as limestone. She thinks distantly that it might be nice to burn, because at least she'll never have to see Miss Quinn's cat's grin and wonder why she betrayed them.

Someone shoves her between the shoulder blades, hard.

"*Run*, damn you!" Agnes hisses.

Beatrice runs.

Agnes should have started running as soon as she heard the first scuff of cloak on stone, as soon as she understood they'd walked into a trap.

She stayed. While Juniper flung herself at Gideon Hill, while Bella stood there like a damn statue, while her little sister's blood turned thick and gelid in her palm.

The last time Juniper got herself in trouble, Agnes had rushed to save her without a second thought. But this time the men are wearing badges on their chests. This time Agnes will wind up in a jail cell, and she knows what happens to women who go to jail with babies in their bellies: they lose them. Either before birth, from rough treatment and poor food, or after it, when some flint-faced doctor rips the baby from their bodies and takes her away, still squalling. Agnes's daughter would end up in the New Salem Home for Lost Angels. If she isn't over-lain or shipped out west, Agnes might see her sometimes playing in the alleys, pox-scarred and undersized, with bitter black stones for eyes.

No. Not for anything. Not for the vote or the Sisters or even her own true-blood sisters.

She gives Bella a good shove and runs without looking back, one arm wrapped tight around her belly. Hands reach for her and she twists away from them. They tangle in her long cloak and she scrabbles for the clasp, sending it winging free behind her.

Each footfall is a slap against her stomach, jarring her hips. Her hair clings sweaty and tangled against her neck. She dodges behind a white pillar of stone and doubles over, heaving, choking back coughs.

There are boot-steps and raised voices behind her, growing nearer.

She fumbles a candle-stub from her pocket and draws a shaky, desperate X of wax on the stone. It's men's magic—"good for a quick getaway," Mr. Lee had said, smiling his crooked smile. She gave him an arch look. "And are you often in need of getaways, Mr. Lee?"

"Oh, weekly, Miss Eastwood."

Across the room, Juniper made a *blech* sound.

Now Agnes pants the string of Latin he taught them. Lightness fills her, as if her bones are hollowing out. A black twist of hair unpeels from her neck and floats lazily upward, as if gravity has briefly forgotten its business.

She runs again. This time she's a thrown stone skipped across a pond, a gull skimming above the waves, there and gone again. The sounds of pursuit fade behind her.

Agnes braids a rope of hair for herself and climbs back over the cemetery gate. She runs alone through the quiet streets, her feet weightless and silent. She thinks of the Hanged Woman lying flat on Madame Zina's tabletop, of Juniper disappearing beneath a wave of knuckles and boots.

She slows, staring down at the palm where her sister's blood is cracking and flaking. *Don't leave me,* Juniper begged her. *Take care of them,* her mother told her.

But hadn't that been her mother's job, first? She failed her daughters; Agnes will not fail her own.

She closes her fist and keeps running.

Beatrice is aware that she isn't going to make it. It's too dark and the graveyard is too full of humps and hollows and tilted stones, and she can't see through the blur of tears in her eyes.

She hears the pound of footsteps behind her, the rush of heavy breathing.

She dodges behind a marble mausoleum and presses herself against the door, the iron rings digging into the soft meat of her back. It isn't much of a hiding place—any second now an officer is going to stumble around the corner and see the shine of her spectacles in the moonlight, and she's going to burn beside her sister for a crime she didn't commit.

Behind her, the door gives way. It caves inward and hands reach out to pull her inside. She has time to think, calmly, that this must be a fear-induced hallucination, because it's only in story-papers that the dead come alive on the full moon and pull sinners down into their graves—

Before a warm, dry hand presses over her mouth. It smells of cloves and ink.

"Stay quiet. And stop biting me, woman."

Juniper knows better than to bait a mad dog or a drunk, and she knows from the glassy-eyed faces of the police officers that they're a little of both. But she also knows there are times when every choice is a losing one, when you just have to go in swinging and hope you make it out alive.

She keeps her staff swiping and her legs kicking, tangling the officers in the long sweep of her robes as she flails. She chants *A tangled web she weaves* in a breathless whisper, crushing the cobweb in her skirt pocket and reveling in the yelping and swearing of men who have just felt spider-silk gumming across their eyes and mouths.

One of them shouts, "It's her! The witch! She got me once before—" and something cracks across her spine hard enough to knock the air from her lungs. A fist smashes against her ear with a hollow-melon sound and she finds herself facedown in the dirt.

She smiles into the ashes. *Run, girls.*

Boots and batons land in a panicky hail across her body, blending together into a single pulsing pain. She hears a terrible splintering sound and worries for a moment that it's bone before the shattered pieces of her red-cedar staff fall before her.

"Oh, that's enough of that, isn't it?" She hears the smile in Hill's voice.

Juniper opens streaming eyes to see his face queerly doubled above her, pale and grayish against the night. She grins up at him, knowing from the copper taste in her mouth that her teeth are slimed with blood. She makes a sideways hat-sweeping gesture from the ground. "Fancy seeing you again, Mr. Hill."

It might have passed as nonchalant and unbothered, except she has to swallow hard against the bile rising in her throat. She closes her eyes against the red flare of pain.

She feels silken fingertips beneath her chin, pressing upward, and opens her eyes to see Hill smiling down at her. His expression seems—wrong. Pleasant, relaxed, nothing like a cringing bureaucrat out hunting witches past midnight. "Oh, Miss Eastwood, what a delight you are."

It's the sincerity in his voice that does it, slicing through her defiance and making her feel, for the first time, truly afraid.

Hill lifts his eyes to the men gathered around him, panting and bruised, one of them holding the halves of her staff with a blackening eye and an aggrieved expression. "Take this one to the Deeps, boys."

18

May she snatch me through the doors of Hell
And take me down with her to dwell.

A spell for opening certain doors, requiring stars & scars

Standing in the stale dark of a tomb, surrounded by the muffled stamp of boots and held tight against the woman she is reasonably sure is her enemy, Beatrice Belladonna thinks of several questions she would like to ask. *What are you doing here?* seems like a logical starting place, or maybe *Why did you betray us?*

Instead she says something like *grrrg*, because Miss Cleopatra Quinn's hand is still clamped around her jaw. She wriggles and Quinn relents very slightly, lifting her palm a cautious inch away from Beatrice's lips.

"Cle—Miss Quinn!" she hisses. "What—how—are there *coffins* in here?"

Beatrice can't see Quinn's expression because her back is pressed against her chest and also because the tomb is the lightless black of the space between stars. The air feels thick and sour on her skin. A stale breeze exhales from somewhere.

"No."

"What are you—"

Quinn cuts her off with a low rasp in her ear. "Not here."

Beatrice doesn't understand where else they might find opportunity to talk, as the cemetery is full of baton-wielding witch-hunters and the sun will be rising soon. She imagines spending an entire day in the tomb, a grown woman reduced to a little girl locked in the dark again. Panic claws up her throat.

"Listen, I c-can't stay in here. I have to get out." That wind blows again, damp as breath on her neck.

Quinn's arms unwrap from her chest. One palm rests lightly on her shoulder. "Hold on." Beatrice hears the shush of fabric and the snick of a struck match before her eyes sting with sudden light. Quinn touches the match to the narrow tip of a wooden wand. She whispers the words and the wand glows a rich, tiger's-eye gold. Her face emerges from the blackness like a fire-lit dream, all dark hollows and honeyed planes, the witch-light burning in her eyes.

The light spreads, filling every cobwebbed corner of the mausoleum, and Beatrice discovers why she felt a breeze blowing inside a stone tomb.

"*Stairs?*" Her voice is an octave higher than she'd like it to be.

Quinn holds a finger to her lips and turns back to the door. She sings a short hymn and presses her wrist—the scarred wrist, pocked with white slashes and circles—against the aged wood. Heat flares, driving back the damp chill of the tomb. A lock creaks into place.

Then Quinn takes Beatrice's hand in hers and pulls her down the narrow steps and into the long, serpentine tunnel that runs beneath the New Salem cemetery.

For a long time after they descend, Beatrice hears nothing except the nervous pant of her own breath and the shush of her skirts along the dirt, and sometimes the scuttle of some many-legged creature dodging Quinn's wand-light. Several times she knocks her head on the sloping ceiling or scrapes an elbow along the wall, but no dirt shakes loose. The tunnel walls feel smooth and unyielding, as if they were carved from granite rather than clay and root-riddled soil. There are no struts or beams, no wooden trusses beneath her trailing fingers. Beatrice grew up in Crow County; she knows enough about mineshafts and cave-ins to understand that this is impossible.

"What is this place?" Her own voice sounds over-loud, shouting back at her from the too-close walls.

"Why," Quinn answers, with a showman's sweep of her wand, "the Underground Railroad, of course."

"Really? You mean these tunnels go as far as—"

Quinn's laughter echoes through the tunnel. "No, not really. Saints. No one dug a hole all the way to Canada." Her shadow flickers as she shakes her head. "These tunnels are only under New Salem."

"Oh," Beatrice says, intelligently.

"This city was built in a huge hurry, did you know that?" Beatrice did. After the burning of Old Salem there had been a great rush to rebuild, as if the fresh-paved streets were ropes to bind the unruly past. "City Hall and the College were built within a year, along with half a dozen churches, all those boring square houses on the north end... Who do you suppose built all that?"

Beatrice has read any number of pamphlets and historical texts about the founding of the city but can't recall anything about the workers. "I don't know. I suppose it would have been—"

"Slaves." Quinn's tone is perfectly even, but her spine is rigid. "Slaves, in the nation that so recently fought for freedom. Slaves, building the City Without Sin."

Beatrice feels a queasy flick of shame. "I didn't—"

"But their work was plagued with delays and setbacks, missing tools, mistakes. Because they were busy building something else beneath all that marble and money. Something that would let them move through the city without fear, whenever they pleased." Quinn gestures with the wand at the endless tunnel around them, smooth and hollow as the burrow of some vast snake. "They taught their sons and daughters, and the secret was passed down to us."

Beatrice is quiet for several steps before asking softly, "Who is *us*?"

Quinn stops walking. Her shoulders lift and fall in a steadying sigh. "The Daughters of Tituba."

If her voice wasn't so flat, so entirely empty of humor or mockery, Beatrice would think she was being laughed at. It's like claiming to be a vampire or a valkyrie, a monster out of myth. The Daughters of Tituba were a rumor, a whisper, a penny-paper story. They were the reason husbands went astray and graves were robbed. In the least reputable papers they were drawn with bones tied in their hair and teeth strung around their throats, red-lipped and wild. *The Last Living Descendants of the Black Witch of Old Salem*, the captions read, *Still Hungry for Vengeance?*

Miss Quinn does not possess a necklace of teeth or a bone hairpiece, as far as Beatrice knows, and if she hungers for anything it's only the same small, impossible thing that Beatrice wants: the truth, laid bare. The story told straight.

"I didn't think they were real."

"Real enough." Quinn is still standing with her back to Beatrice. "I wanted to tell you. Truly, I did. But we're sworn to silence on the graves of our mothers and their mothers across the sea. I couldn't."

"But Frankie said—oh." Beatrice recalls the phrase *other interests* and everything she thought it implied. She finds her embarrassment overcome by a sudden buoyancy. Not the Colored League; not a string of lovers, after all.

Quinn turns. "Frankie Black?"

"We spoke. I understood—that is, I thought you and she were..."

Quinn's eyebrows are higher than usual. "We were. But I made it clear that the Daughters came first, and she objected."

"Oh."

"Beatrice—I'm sorry." Beatrice doesn't think she's ever heard Quinn apologize.

She half reaches for her before she remembers what else Quinn ought to be sorry for. She makes her voice cold and hard, pretending her flesh is stone once more. "We were betrayed. They were waiting for us, and J-Juniper is..." Her breath catches. "Agnes and the others ran, but I don't know how far they made it." She feels the distant spark of her middle sister and knows that she, at least, is safe.

Quinn's mouth is grim, her shoulders heavy. "I'm sorry," she says again.

"*Was it you?*" The words come out ragged and bloody, as if they ran through dense briars on their way to her lips. "Did you tell the police? Make some trade or deal with them?"

Miss Quinn's eyes go wide. She takes a careful breath before saying, very slowly and soberly, "The Daughters have been interested in the Lost Way of Avalon for a very long time. So much of our power was stolen from us—although we kept more than you thought—and the idea that it might be restored to us in a single instant...well. When the tower was called to the square I was sent to investigate the suffragists. And I found you: a librarian with a clever face and hungry eyes who knew more than she ought to. I assisted you. Pursued and encouraged you." Her eyes flick over Beatrice's face, furtive, guilty.

"Because you were ordered to."

"Yes." It should feel like a victory—the hero forcing the spy to confess her sins!—but Beatrice feels nothing but an oily shame. To think that she believed Miss Quinn was interested in her...friendship (she never thought Miss Quinn was interested in friendship).

Beatrice wishes without much hope that the tunnel will collapse and bury her before she cries, but instead she hears a soft curse and feels Quinn's fingers clasping hard around her wrist. "I spied on you. I lied to you. I told the Daughters everything you discovered or planned or even suspected." Quinn's voice thickens, low and urgent. "But Beatrice, I swear it wasn't me who betrayed you."

The tunnel fails to collapse; Beatrice cries. In a small, blurred voice, she begins, "Then who—" but breaks off. She thinks of Agnes, hard-eyed and harder-hearted, who would do anything at all to save her own skin. But if she'd betrayed them, why had she come tonight? And what about the oath they all swore with pricked fingers and crossed hearts, whose breaking would have certain obvious and rather grue-some effects?

Beatrice swallows a knot of salt and snot. "Why did you come?"

"For the same reason I came to your first two spectacles. Because you—the Sisters were walking into harm's way, and I wanted to be there in case…they needed me." Miss Quinn—the brash liar, the spy who wields her charm like an edged weapon—cannot quite meet Beatrice's eyes as she says it.

"And where are you taking me now? To your superiors? Am I a captive?"

Quinn lets go of her wrist very quickly. "No. Never. I'm not…" She looks tired and sorry, stripped bare. "Saints, I've butchered this. I'm trying to say that I'm sorry, and I will not lie to you again. I remain a faithful Daughter." Beatrice hears the capital D, the weight of a century of secrets and witching. "But I hope to become a Sister, too. If you'll have me."

Beatrice just stands there, looking into Quinn's yellow eyes (*one-one-thousand*). She wonders if trust, once lost, can ever truly be found again, and if she's being a fool (*two-one-thousand*). She decides she doesn't care, that maybe trust is neither lost nor found, broken nor mended, but merely given. Decided, despite the risk (*three-one-thousand*).

"I'm afraid I left my notebook in my office," Beatrice murmurs in a slightly underwater voice. "But I believe there's room on the roster."

Quinn smiles, wide and relieved, witch-light dancing in her eyes. Beatrice clears her throat and adds, "Does this tunnel come out any-where near the College?"

The mischief returns to Quinn's smile, curling the corners and add-ing a devilish pair of dimples. She turns and strides deeper into the dark.

"Not directly. Have you heard of the night market of New Cairo, Miss Eastwood?"

The tunnel branches and spreads like the root of a hollow tree. They turn right, then right again; twice Quinn stops to sing them past locked doors or other, less visible barriers, and once she pricks Beatrice's finger and daubs her blood on a pale stone before they walk on. The walls turn slick and wet for a while, cold as a river-bottom, and then they climb upward again. They pass steps leading up to every possible entryway: sewer grates, narrow closets, trapdoors, granite slabs that would take witchcraft to move aside. The doors are marked with strange signs, arrangements of stars and lines rather than words.

Beatrice is aware that she ought to be investigating and questioning, possibly taking notes, but she feels dull and heavy, as if the line leading to Juniper is an anchor pulling her under.

Quinn rises in front of her and Beatrice follows her up a narrow staircase. The steps are stone, softened and scooped with years of use, leading to an ordinary-looking door.

Quinn hesitates before it, glancing back at Beatrice with a calculating expression. She unfastens her cloak and tosses it over Beatrice's shoulders instead. Bella tries very hard not to notice the heat of her fingertips as she pulls the hood high and tucks stray hairs beneath it.

"Tuck your hands in your sleeves, please. No need to start talk."

The door opens into an alley, velvet-blue and fresh-smelling after an hour spent deep beneath the city. It's not yet dawn, the moon still a silver dollar above them, but the alley is crammed full of people. Women with white wraps over their hair and gold-flashing bangles on their wrists, men wearing linen cloaks and swinging canes, the white flash of teeth and the blue shine of skin. Stalls line both walls, overflowing with wares, clinking with coins: a marketplace, held by moonlight.

Beatrice is too busy staring and blinking to hear what Quinn is saying. She gives her hood a sharp tug. "The Daughters ought to know what happened at the cemetery tonight. May I make another report?"

Beatrice nods and Quinn catches the eye of a woman standing just outside the door, arms crossed. "Is she in?"

The woman gives a half-bow that must mean yes. Quinn turns left and Beatrice trails behind her, head bent to hide the freckled milk of her face. During her daylight visits to New Cairo she's felt noticed, perhaps a little out of place, but she's never felt so thoroughly foreign. She wonders if this is how Quinn feels on the north end, as if her skin has transformed into an unreliable map, bound to lead people to all sorts of wrong conclusions.

The stalls they pass seem to contain both ordinary contraband—home-brewed liquor and home-cooked remedies in brown glass jars, crates of cigars that look like they've never met a customs agent—and much less ordinary goods: curled leaves and pale roots; furs and feathers; the black glisten of beetles' wings and the ivory gleam of bone. Witch-ways, sold by wizened grandmothers and laughing girls, women with neat aprons or sweeping skirts or babies wrapped and bound to their chests, sleeping through the moonlit market.

Quinn moves easily down the alley, receiving nods and waves and tips of more than one hat. She seems subtly different, taller and grander. Nothing about her has ever struck Beatrice as fearful, but there's always been something armored about the way she moves on the north end. Here she is a queen, and royalty requires no armor.

Quinn steps sideways through another door. It's only as Beatrice follows her and sees the sign—ARAMINTA'S SPICES & SUNDRIES—that she realizes it's the same shop she visited only hours before.

Araminta's Spices & Sundries is a very different sort of establishment by moonlight. There are black wax candles dripping onto bronze saucers and green bottles lining the shelves with labels like *Hellebore, collected after rain* and *Hen's teeth*. The other-smell has grown stronger, wilder and darker, unmistakable for anything except what it is: witching.

"Does this happen every night?" Beatrice doesn't know why she whispers it.

"Lord, no. Only on full moons." Quinn leans an elbow on the counter and dings the brass bell three times. "It's famous, in certain circles. People come up from miles away, hoard their goods and recipes all month..."

A small, regal woman shuffles up to the counter wearing a wide-brimmed hat hung with lace. Her face behind the veil is all cheekbone and chin, bones and angles, but the cheeks lift in a smile when she sees Quinn.

"Evening," Quinn greets her. She nudges Beatrice, who lowers the dark drape of her hood.

The woman stares at Beatrice for a long, still second before sighing, "Oh, *Cleo*," very much like a mother whose daughter has brought home a particularly unlovely pet and begged to keep it.

Quinn answers with crisp formality. "The third spectacle was an ambush. I saw at least four of the Sisters taken into custody, including their leader. Her blood-sister." She tilts her head at Beatrice. "When I understood what was happening I...intervened."

The woman behind the counter—Araminta?—murmurs something like *obviously*.

"With your permission, we'll stay here till dawn." The woman's eyes slide between them again, a little too knowing; Beatrice squirms. "And then in the morning I'll take her...wherever she likes."

"The Hall of Justice, I suppose," Beatrice sighs, and finds herself the object of two identical yellow stares. "T-to sort all this out."

Araminta begins to laugh then, a rolling cackle, and does not stop for a long time. "Oh, sweet Saints preserve us. You're going to march straight into the lion's den and do what? Ask them real nice to give your sister back? *This*"—she waves a knobbed knuckle at Beatrice but addresses Quinn—"is exactly the kind of foolishness I was talking about. *This* is why we're better off keeping to ourselves."

"Excuse me," Beatrice says stiffly. "My sister has been arrested on false charges"—well, probably false—"and they can't hold a woman indefinitely without hard evidence."

This only provokes an even longer, more extravagant laugh from Araminta. She's thumbing actual tears from her eyes by the time it subsides.

Araminta turns away to face a gilded cage that sits behind the counter. She extends two fingers through the bars to stroke the creature inside it: a rabbit, whose fur is such a deep and starless black that it seems to swallow the candlelight like an open mouth.

Araminta addresses Beatrice over one shoulder. "They can do exactly whatever they want, child. I'd bet my eye-teeth your sister is already in the Deeps." She catches sight of Beatrice's face and the carved lines around her mouth soften very slightly. "I'm sorry for it. Truly, I am. But it's too late for her now."

It's not the harshness of the words that undoes Beatrice; it's the pity lurking beneath them. Terror closes like cold water above her.

If Quinn or Araminta says anything further, Beatrice doesn't hear it. She is distantly aware of an arm around her shoulders, shepherding her behind the counter and up a narrow flight of stairs; a warm room that smells of spice and skin; a bed spread with saffron quilts.

She lies awake listening to the murmur of voices in the street and the tocking of a clock somewhere in the house—*too-late, too-late*—until Quinn's voice tells her to sleep, and she does.

Beatrice dreams of cellars and locked doors and wakes with her own fingers clawing at her throat.

Dust motes dance above her, suspended in sunlight. Pigeons burble at the window. She is alone, though there's a hollowed-out warmth in the bed beside her, as if someone has lain next to her in the night. Her spectacles are folded neatly on the bedside table.

Beatrice looks at them, picturing the hands that placed them there and feeling a dangerous tenderness creep over her, before she realizes the thing she doesn't feel: her youngest sister. The line between them has gone slack and dead as a cut tendon.

She finds Miss Quinn in a galley kitchen on the first floor, patting a round of biscuit dough with flour-dusted fingers. She listens to Beatrice's tearful babbling patiently, cutting neat rounds of dough with a tin can, sliding them into the oven with an iron *skree*. Then she folds Beatrice's fingers around a hot mug and gently refuses to escort her to the Hall of Justice. "After all the trouble I took to save you? No. You're going to eat your biscuits and change out of those witch-robes, then go home. Tomorrow you'll go to work as if nothing has happened."

"But—"

Quinn touches the back of her hand, very gently. "You're no good to her locked in the cell beside her. Please."

Beatrice eats her biscuits and changes out of her witch-robes. She follows Miss Quinn two blocks east into a white-tiled salon full of chattering women who dip their heads to Quinn and raise their eyebrows at Beatrice, and through the back to a door that reads SUPPLIES. A cool, deep smell seeps around its edges. Beatrice is not surprised when Quinn presses her scarred wrist to its surface and whispers the words.

The tunnel twists north, rumbling sometimes as trolleys or hooves clatter overhead. Beatrice keeps feeling along the line that led to her youngest sister, like a woman tonguing the gap where a tooth once was.

"W-why is it called the Deeps?" she asks, as Quinn pauses to scrawl some complicated sign on the tunnel wall.

"Because it's waist-deep down there. At least after a bad rain."

Beatrice makes a sound somewhere between a whimper and a question mark, and Quinn clarifies. "They built the prison on the riverbank, where the land was soft and boggy—there's a reason none of our tunnels lead to the east bank—and it sinks an inch or two every year. The lowest cells always have standing water in them. There's no way to get dry or clean. I knew a man arrested for loitering who came out with his feet dead white, just rotting away in his boots..." Quinn's voice trails into the tunnel-dark.

"Were you...close?"

"Cousins," Quinn answers, with that same iron shape to her spine. Beatrice is quiet after that.

The tunnel ends in a spiral staircase and a narrow, arched door. Beatrice stumbles after Quinn, sun-blinded, and finds herself standing in the genteel bustle of Bethlehem Heights, half a block from her rented room. No one appears to notice them, and Beatrice wonders if Quinn has cast one of her strange glamors over them before she understands that the door they stepped through is tucked discreetly at the corner of a handsome manor house: a servants' entrance. In their neat ironed dresses she and Quinn are just a pair of maids, all but invisible—*nothing*. It occurs to Beatrice for the first time that there's a certain power in being nothing; she thinks of that old tale where the clever Crone tells a man her name is Nobody, and when asked who cursed him the man cries, "Nobody!" while the witch escapes.

"Go home. I'll meet you at the library tomorrow." Quinn gives her a last amber look and disappears.

Beatrice counts very slowly to twenty, then turns on her heel and heads due west toward the New Salem Hall of Justice.

Because she isn't as much a fool as Quinn and that Araminta woman seem to think, she stops first at a certain disreputable establishment on St. Mary-of-Egypt's. She asks for Miss Pearl and finds herself shuffled into a spare, practical powder room on the first floor. Pearl's eyes are puffed and bluish, her nails still grimed with grave-dirt. She lights a thin cigarette as she listens to Beatrice's request and nods once. "The bastards took Frankie, too. Ask after her, won't you?"

When Beatrice leaves Salem's Sin she is a crone in truth: her eyes are filmy blue and her hair is the yellowed ivory of a pulled tooth. Her flesh stretches thin and frail over her cheekbones. Some of it is clever powders and dyes and some of it is more, the words and ways a whore might use either to attract attention or divert it. She was rather hoping to be disguised as a busty blond or a sultry Jezebel, but Miss Pearl recommended wrinkles. "Men stop seeing you altogether, after a certain age."

The clerk at the front desk of the New Salem Hall of Justice doesn't even look up as she approaches, so perhaps Pearl was right. He remains bent over a stack of paperwork, scratching idly at his pimpled chin, apparently unbothered by the sickly smell that rises from the floorboards: a stagnant reek, like still water and old meat.

She raps her knuckles on his desk and he looks up at Beatrice with bored, pinkish eyes.

"I am looking for information regarding a woman taken into custody early this morning. A Miss James Juniper Eastwood."

A dim spark of interest. "She one of the witches they brung in?"

Beatrice gives the clerk her most severe librarian's glare and is gratified to see him straighten reflexively in his seat. "What she is or isn't remains to be proven in a court of law, sir. What I would like to know is where she's being held, on what charges, and in what specific condition. I am also interested in the whereabouts of a Miss Frankie Ursa Black and Miss Jennie Lin—"

"S'not public information, ma'am." He shrugs. "Didn't look too good when they drug her in, though."

Cold sloshes in Beatrice's stomach. She gathers herself. "I would like to speak to your supervisor immediately, young man. A girl has been arrested and apparently injured, without due process or a fair trial—"

Her outrage attracts the attention of the officers lounging in the back office. One of them slouches to the front. "What's it to you, woman?"

Beatrice transfers her milky glare to him. "I am Miss Eastwood's landlady, if you must know. And I take considerable offense when one of my tenants is arrested on false charges."

The officer grunts at her. "There's nothing false about her charges, ma'am." He scrounges lazily through the detritus of the front desk and produces a poster with WANTED FOR MURDER & SUSPECTED

WITCHCRAFT printed in large capitals beneath a drawing of a woman's face. Her hair is an untidy sprawl of ink rather than the chopped-short nest Beatrice knows, but it's unmistakably Juniper. The artist captured the defiant line of her long jaw, the wild gleam of her eyes.

Beatrice swallows. "I'm not sure what this proves, precisely, but—"

The officer slides another paper across the desk: a yellowed page from *The Lexington Herald*. MURDER BY MAGIC, it reads, CROW COUNTY VETERAN FOUND DEAD.

Beatrice doesn't need to read the article, because she already knows what it says. She found out seven years ago what Juniper was, what lay coiled beneath her skin, waiting to strike. Her daddy should have remembered it, too, but maybe he got soft or stupid over the years. Maybe one day he took too much from her, some last precious thing, and left her with nothing to lose.

Beatrice skims *The Herald*: *untimely death*; *signs of the uncanny*; *daughter seen fleeing the property*.

She slides it back across the desk and the officer shakes his head. "What kind of woman would kill her own father, eh?" He taps the paper twice. "This'll be in *The Post* first thing in the morning. I wouldn't go around telling folks you rented a room to a murderess, if I was you."

Beatrice notices a brass badge shining dully on his chest, showing a torch raised high, and understands that Miss Quinn was right. That there will be no bail or due process, that the rule of law has given way to the rule of men and mobs. That it's too late.

She retreats, and watches the men forget her as soon as she leaves their sight. Outside the air is thick and gray with the promise of rain. Beatrice tries hard not to think of Juniper down in the Deeps, all alone with the rising water. At least the cellar was dry, most days.

Beatrice doesn't know where she's walking until she is standing in the wood-paneled hall of the Salem College Library, blinking dimly at her office door. Her sanctuary, her one safe place.

But there's something subtly wrong. It takes her a frazzled moment to realize that her nameplate—the cream-colored card with her name in neat script—is missing from its brass holder.

Her door is locked.

She stares at it for several seconds before retreating to the washroom and scrubbing the disguise from her face. Her own eyes are clouds looming back at her in the mirror.

Miss Munley is working at the circulation desk today, shuffling stacks of paper in a way that is meant to communicate that she's very busy and harried and doesn't have time for nuisances like Beatrice.

"E-excuse me, ma'am?" (After St. Hale's, Beatrice's words developed a tendency to clot and stick in her throat, like sour milk. It took years to make them flow cleanly again.) "My office seems to be locked."

Miss Munley doesn't look up at her. "It is no longer your office, I'm afraid." Her voice is as crisp and neat as the turn of a staple.

"Why?"

She taps her papers on the desk to neaten the edges and meets Beatrice's eyes. "Because—in light of recent information provided to us by a concerned citizen—you are no longer employed by the library."

The numbness creeps over her again, the chill of betrayal. Someone betrayed more than the time and place of their doomed spectacle; someone whispered names and positions. But then why isn't Beatrice down in the Deeps beside her sister?

"I see." Beatrice's voice sounds like it's coming through an especially battered phonograph, warbly and tinny. "May I retrieve my personal effects?" What would the police make of her stacks of children's tales and folklore, her scribbled words and ways—her black leather notebook, ringed with salt?

"No. In fact we have been instructed to inform the authorities if we see you on the premises." Miss Munley slants an unreadable look at Beatrice and adds, "So I would advise you to leave the premises at once. Before I see you."

Beatrice leaves the premises. She stands in St. George's Square, unmoving, unmoored.

She wants very badly to go home, but the little attic room has never been her home. Her home was always witch-tales and words, stories into which she could escape when her own became too terrible to bear. It was the soft quiet of the stacks and her too-small office and the scratch of her pen across the page. All of it, lost.

It begins, gently, to rain.

Beatrice is very familiar with despair. It's followed her since St. Hale's, trailing like a loyal black dog behind her, nipping sometimes at her heels. Now she greets it calmly, almost gladly, like a childhood friend.

Agnes knows despair. She first met it on the night her mother died—a black hound that curled on her chest, bending her ribs inward—and has often heard the pad of its steps following her up the boarding-house stairs.

Now she feels its eyes watching her from the shadows of the mill-house floor.

She stands clustered with the other girls, murmuring and whispering. Annie is there, pale and puffy-eyed, and Yulia, with her lips white and thin. Her eldest daughter is there beside her, but the next-eldest is missing. Caught, as she fled the witch-yard? Struck by the summer's fever, like so many other girls?

Mr. Malton glares out at them from eyes like peppercorns, small and dry. Agnes can tell he's skipped his morning drink, can almost feel the blood thudding resentfully in his ears.

"You've all read the papers, by now." They haven't, because a quarter of them can't read and another quarter can't read English and none of them can afford the over-sized special issues the paper-boys are running up and down the streets, but the mill already hums and hisses with rumors. Only Agnes and the other Sisters kept their mouths shut and their eyes down this morning.

"There are witches walking among us once more. They caught the ringleader early this morning—some madwoman from down south, I heard—but some of them still roam free." Malton waves a creased page of newsprint in the air. Agnes does not permit her eyes to follow it. She can feel the soft heat of Bella somewhere to the north, but nothing but a cold absence where Juniper should be.

Malton wheels, fixing them with his red-veined stare. "And I have it on good authority that some of them might even be standing right in front of me, posing as good honest working-women in order to seduce others to their cause."

Agnes does not flinch, does not breathe. *What authority?*

"So I'm here to offer you girls a warning: if I get so much as a whiff of witching—or unionizing, suffrage, any of that trash—I'll take it straight to the police, make no mistake." His eyes rake them, and Agnes catches the wet gleam of fear beneath all his bluster. She wants very badly to make him more afraid.

"As it is," he finishes, "you've all earned yourselves a week without work."

Gasps and curses ripple through them. A week without pay means hungry children and cold stoves and maybe angry husbands.

Someone shouts, "You can't do that!" and Malton spits back, "The hell I can't." His nose throbs an unhealthy purple. "The Baldwins have agreed: we can run on scabs and day-workers for a week while you girls take some time to consider your situations. Decide where your loyalties lie."

The mill seethes around Agnes. Women exchange bitter glares of blame and suspicion, eyeing one another as if they would gladly tie the witch to the stake themselves if they found her. Annie and Yulia are standing very still, not looking at one another or at Agnes.

Eventually the women form a resentful line out the door, apron-strings hanging loose. Agnes trails at the back, trying to look as if she's merely worried about late rent.

Just before she steps into the alley Mr. Malton's hand reaches out to stop her, pressing against the bowl of her belly. "Hold on a minute, girl."

He's far too close to her. She smells the sour sweat of him, feels his breath against her cheek. "Don't think I've forgotten your little trick." It was one of the first spells Mags taught them: a nettle-leaf and a sharp needle and a man would be too busy yelping and swearing to want you any longer.

His palm is sweating through her dress. "Should I go to the authorities, do you think? Should I tell the police what you are, Miss *Eastwood*?"

His fingers dig like nails into the swollen meat of her stomach, biting deep, just because he can. Because she can't stop him. Because she is nothing and he is something.

Rage licks hot and red up her spine, followed by a sick wave of shame. What a fool she was to think witching could change anything. Their mother had known plenty of words and ways, and what good had it done her?

Agnes swallows rage and shame both—and oh, she's grown tired of the taste of them—and answers, "No, Mr. Malton."

"Good girl." He gives her stomach a hard, careless pat, like a man might give a horse.

Agnes walks blind down the alley, rain slicking her hair against her throat, and despair follows her. It's almost a relief when she feels its teeth against her throat.

Juniper has never met despair. She's caught glimpses of some black creature edging nearer—when her sisters abandoned her, when she lay down on the fresh-turned earth of her grandmother's grave—but she's driven it back with fire and fury, every time.

But now she hears its claws clicking down the cobbled streets behind her. Coming closer.

She knows better than to let the fear show on her face. The officers around her are hungry for it, waiting to lap at her terror like tomcats at a bowl of milk.

Juniper declines to feed them.

She keeps her eyes blazing and her teeth bared as they prop her in front of an accordion-box camera. As a fist snarls itself in her hair and forces her to face the camera's glassy eye.

She keeps her chin raised as they rip the locket from her throat and the dress from her back and leave her shivering in her shift. As eyes rove across the pimpled white of her flesh, skinning her.

She keeps her spine straight as they drag her down stone steps, past the leering, greenish faces of drunks and derelicts, pickpockets and prostitutes. As they fling her into ankle-deep water that smells of oil and shit.

Juniper stands with her wet shift half-slicked to her body and cold mud splattered over one cheekbone, staring into the low glare of a gas-lamp with her fingers curled into fists.

"That all you got? Weak-ass chicken-shitted sons of—"

Hands fall on her again, wrenching her arms behind her back. She braces her belly for the blow and prays briefly that they won't bust anything important. *Three bless and keep me.*

But the blow never comes: instead she feels chill metal press against her throat. She swears and arcs against the man behind her, but she hears the rasp and click of rusted tumblers turning in a lock, and a piercing, deadening cold sluices through her veins.

They release her. Her bad leg crumples beneath her and her knees splash back into the reeking water. She reaches for her own throat with trembling fingers and finds an iron collar, locked tight.

Back in the olden-times witches were punished with bridles to stop their tongues from speaking the words, shackles to stop their hands from working the ways—and collars. To break their will.

The hot heartbeat of magic is gone. So are the lines that lead to her sisters, but Juniper thinks dully that it doesn't matter; they won't come for her, now that they know.

Dimly, she hears the slosh of booted feet and the low, mean sound of laughter.

Then she is alone in the dark. When her daddy died—when she killed him and set fire to what was left of him, so that no ghost or spirit might linger a single second longer in the world—she thought at least she would never be locked down in the dark again.

She was wrong.

Despair creeps toward her out of the deeps, the color of night, but Juniper does not let it take her. Instead—her voice tangling with the trickle of water, echoing against wet stone—she tells it a story.

THE TALE OF
THE WITCH WHO SPUN STRAW
INTO SILVER

Once upon a time there was a foolish miller who bragged that his daughter was a witch who could spin straw into silver. The king, who was even more foolish than the miller, sent his guards to fetch the girl and tossed her into a cell full of straw. He ordered her to spin it all into silver before dawn or face the stake, and left her alone to weep.

Just before midnight a creaking voice asked the miller's daughter, "Why do you weep so?"

"Oh," she answered, "because my father is a fool and I will surely burn tomorrow, for I am no witch."

An old, old woman lurched out of the shadows, dressed in tattered rags and carrying a black-wood staff. A pair of rubies were set into the staff's head, like the red eyes of a snake.

"Ah," she said to the miller's daughter, "but I am. What will you give me if I turn this straw to silver?"

With the girl's golden necklace clasped around her neck, the Crone sat down at the spinning wheel.

At dawn the king was very pleased to find a room full of spun silver, enough to build a statue or a ship. He was so pleased, and so foolish, that he locked the girl in an even larger cell the following night and demanded that she perform the trick again.

The miller's daughter wept, and soon she heard the shush of a tattered cloak along the floor. She and the Crone haggled briefly, and this time when the Crone sat down at the wheel she wore the girl's diamond ring on her finger.

By morning the cell was full of silver and the king, who was by now beginning to dream of entire armadas, locked her in a third cell, larger still.

The miller's daughter wept, a little perfunctorily, and the Crone appeared. But there were no necklaces or rings left to barter. The Crone asked for the girl's firstborn child, instead, and the miller's daughter—who did not want to burn at the stake, who counted her own life more heavily than that of a child not yet thought of or wanted—agreed.

The straw was spun. The king was pleased. So pleased, in fact, that he made her a king's wife instead of a miller's daughter.

In time the king's wife became a prince's mother. On the child's name-day the Crone appeared to claim her debt. The king, seeing the Crone with her black-wood staff, realized the secret behind his wife's miraculous spinning and spurned her, so that the king's wife lost her crown and her child in the same hour.

The woman wept, and the Crone took pity on her. "If you can find my tower within three days' time, I will forgive your debt," she said, and vanished.

For two days the woman walked the high hills of her kingdom, barefoot, ragged, her gown stained with milk. On the evening of the third day the last of her milk ran from her breasts and fell like pearls to the earth. The pearls ran together, forming a line, which became a pale, milky snake with red rubies for eyes. The mother—or, in some tellings, the Mother—followed the snake deeper into the woods.

Perhaps, among the darkest and oldest trees, she found a tower. Perhaps a fire was burning in the hearth and bread was waiting on the table, and her son lay wrapped in black rags, sleeping gently. Perhaps she and her child lived in the tower happily ever after.

Neither the Mother nor the Crone was ever seen in the kingdom again.

19

Mirror, mirror, on the wall,
Tell the truth, reveal all.

A spell to see, requiring a mirror & a
borrowed belonging

Beatrice Belladonna expects despair to hurt, but it doesn't feel like much of anything. She thinks of Jonah in the belly of the whale and the little red witch inside the wolf and wonders if either of them felt a little relieved to be eaten, to be taken away from the world and permitted to curl in the suffocating black, alone.

Beatrice sleeps. She dreams—of locked cells and spun silver, of white snakes and black towers—and wakes sweating in the stale heat of midday. She wills herself back to sleep, staring at the pulsing dark of her own eyelids until she slips into a dazed, dreamless place.

The next time she wakes the attic is all slanting shadows and twilit windows, and Miss Cleopatra Quinn is sitting at the end of her bed.

(Beatrice is abruptly aware that her left cheek is sticky with spittle and that she is wearing her oldest and most mortifying nightdress, the one with little bonneted ducks embroidered at the collar.)

"I believe in the story it's a kiss that wakes Snow White from her sleep, but I've always found that a little presumptuous." Quinn's voice is light, but her eyes on Beatrice are heavy with worry. "I tried to visit your office at the library today."

Beatrice licks sleep-gummed lips. "It's not my office anymore."

"So I was made to understand." She adds, after a pause, "I'm sorry."

The next pause is much longer and emptier. The interior of Beatrice's skull feels dim and cobwebbed, like a closet she prefers not to open.

Quinn strokes the brim of the derby hat in her lap. "*The Post* reports five arrests—Frankie, Gertrude, Jennie, the oldest Domontovich girl— all of whom are charged with general mayhem, the promotion of sin, and public witchcraft. Juniper has . . . additional charges, of course. As far as I can tell, most of the girls were shipped four miles south to the women's workhouse. Except Jennie, who I can't seem to find, and Juniper, who is in the Deeps."

Beatrice wonders vaguely what Quinn expects her to do with this report. Cry, perhaps. But even crying seems messy and troublesome compared to the clean relief of sleep.

Quinn continues in a clipped, professional voice. "Your sister's trial is set for the middle of next week, but the Deeps are not a healthful place to linger, and the solstice is the day after tomorrow. I don't think we can afford to wait."

Beatrice lets this rattle through the cobwebby closet of her brain for a while before asking, cautiously, "Wait?"

"To retrieve your sister from the custody of the New Salem Police Department," Quinn clarifies. "To rescue her."

It takes far too long for Beatrice to recognize the rusty, bitter sound coming from her mouth as a laugh. "You and Miss Araminta assured me it was too late and sent me home like a schoolgirl. Now you're proposing some sort of daring rescue?"

Small, pitying lines appear between Quinn's brows. "As I recall, we merely discouraged you from visiting the Hall of Justice and asking if they would give your sister back, pretty please. None of us would leave a sister, or a Daughter, to rot in the Deeps if we could help it."

Beatrice scoots herself upright in bed, muscles cramped from an entire day spent in stubborn sleep, no longer caring about her mortifying nightdress (she still cares). "But we *can't* help it! We have no legal recourse. No financial recourse—I am no longer even employed! No witching sufficient to sway a jury or dig a tunnel or disappear a woman from a locked cell." Bella makes a hopeless gesture at the room. "I would like to s-save my sister. Even knowing what she did, what she is. But it is not possible."

The pity in Quinn's face turns tart. "Very true, Beatrice. So don't you think it's time we considered the impossible?"

"I don't—"

"Oh, for Saints' sake, woman." Quinn swats her blanketed legs with her derby hat. "Get out of bed. Use whatever remains of your common sense. All summer we've been inching closer to the thing that could turn the world upside down. That could give us back what we lost, make the impossible possible again."

Hope flutters in Beatrice's chest, broken-winged. It hurts far worse than despair. "But our theories are so tenuous. Mere…moonbeams."

Quinn swats her again. "They are perfectly scholarly! Considered, documented, based on reliable sources—"

"*Children's* stories! Nursery rhymes! Nothing respectable, nothing verifiable!"

"Must a thing be bound and shelved in order to matter? Some stories were never written down. Some stories were passed by whisper and song, mother to daughter to sister. Bits and pieces were lost over the centuries, I'm sure, details shifted, but *not all of them*." Quinn stands, pacing. "Towers and roses. Maiden's blood. Crone's tears. Mother's milk. Would you really deny your own discoveries? Surely you are not such a coward."

"Oh, I assure you I am."

"You *aren't*—"

"But even if I agree with you about the ways, we don't have all the words." Bella turns her hands palm up, a gesture of surrender. "We don't even have my *notes* anymore."

She's interrupted by a polite tap at the door. A polite, familiar voice calls, "Miss Eastwood? I'm so sorry for the lateness of the hour. But you left your notebook at the library, and I thought I ought to return it."

There's a brief silence while Quinn's eyebrows climb and Beatrice peels out of her sheets and tugs a robe over her horrible nightdress. "H-*Henry*?" Beatrice kicks aside the line of salt and unbolts her door to find Mr. Blackwell blinking affably on the stairs. In his hand he holds a small, shabby book bound in black leather.

Beatrice snatches it and strokes the familiar pleats and cracks of the spine. "Oh, thank you! I thought it would be confiscated by the authorities, in light of the accusations leveled against me." Beatrice recalls herself and adds, "Not that the accusations are true. They're quite false."

"Are they?" Mr. Blackwell asks mildly.

Beatrice is blinking her way toward some confused combination of denial and confession when Miss Quinn steps into view at her shoulder. "No. Although I don't think our Beatrice has been holding congress with demons, do you?"

"Ah, Miss Quinn, a pleasure." Mr. Blackwell looks distinctly unsurprised to see Quinn in Beatrice's room. "Well, I'm sorry to interrupt, ladies. I only wanted to return the book"—Beatrice clutches it tighter to her chest—"and wish you both the best of luck."

"With—what?" Beatrice asks.

"Well." Mr. Blackwell gives a slightly embarrassed cough. "With calling back the Lost Way of Avalon. I presume."

It occurs to Beatrice that she has gone slightly mad. Surely she did not actually hear Mr. Henry Blackwell—head of Special Collections, possessor of tufty ear-hair and a rather grand collection of bow ties—wish her luck with the restoration of witchcraft.

Quinn reaches over her shoulder to pull the door wider. "Why don't you come in and have a seat, Mr. Blackwell."

Mr. Blackwell sits at Beatrice's wobbly kitchen table, not looking at Beatrice's robe and nightdress, smiling politely at his own thumbs.

"Did you overhear us?"

"Oh, come now, Miss Eastwood," he scoffs gently. "I approved all your requests for materials. I loaded the carts myself and wheeled them to your office and scratched them out of the log afterward. Witch-tales and folklore. Old Salem and Avalon. Every instance of significant magic after the Georgian Inquisition. I put the pieces together." He transfers his polite smile to Beatrice. "I may not be a witch, Miss Eastwood, but I'm quite a tolerable librarian."

Something in Beatrice's face—the numb creep of betrayal—compels him to add, even more gently, "I have not told a soul and do not intend to. My ancestors broke with the Church after they witnessed the atrocities of the first purge. My own grandmother harbored witches who fled from Old Salem and slaves who fled from the Old South. My mother would return from the grave to haunt me forevermore if I did not at least offer you my assistance now, such as it is."

Trust less easily, Quinn advised her. But Beatrice has never learned how. "We're trying to save my sister and we don't know how. She's locked in the Deeps facing trial for murder by witchcraft."

Mr. Blackwell makes a considering sort of face. "And did she? Murder someone, I mean."

"I don't know," Beatrice lies. Then, "Probably." And, even quieter, "Yes, I think she did."

"Was it a necessary act? A just act?"

"I don't know." She thinks of her daddy's charming smile and red eyes, of the iron squeal of the cellar hinges. "Yes."

Mr. Blackwell nods genially at his own knuckles. "As a man of God

I disapprove, but as a mere *man*, well... I wonder sometimes where the first witch came from. If perhaps Adam deserved Eve's curse." His smile twists. "If behind every witch is a woman wronged."

Beatrice is too busy staring at him to object when Quinn slides the black leather book out of her grasp and opens it to a page of signatures beneath the heading THE SISTERS OF AVALON. Quinn produces a pen and adds three words to the bottom of the page before sliding it across the table to Mr. Blackwell.

"There's still room, if you'd like to become a formal member."

"Oh, how generous of you. That is, I wouldn't like to intrude—" Beatrice notes with some astonishment that Mr. Blackwell's ears have gone pink with delight.

"Not at all," she murmurs. "The more the merrier." And, with the sensation that she's experiencing a very vivid and unlikely dream, Beatrice guides Mr. Blackwell and Miss Quinn through their oaths and inducts them to whatever remains of the Sisters of Avalon. Quinn does not flinch or hesitate as she crosses her heart. Her eyes on Beatrice are a pair of promises, brightest gold.

In the quiet that follows, Mr. Blackwell says, "So. There is, I assume, some reason you haven't snapped your fingers and called the Lost Way in order to save your sister."

Beatrice tugs her robe tighter around her shoulders, feeling tired and shabby and not at all like someone who could restore the ancient power of witching or stage a daring rescue. "We have the will, and at least some guesses about the ways. But we're missing the words." She flips through her black notebook, trailing her fingers over the rhyme as if it might sprout extra lines and verses. "We've looked in every book of witch-tales, every children's songbook, every scrap relating to Old Salem. If the words ever existed, they're well and truly lost now."

Mr. Blackwell does not look especially displeased to be faced with an unsolvable puzzle; he looks instead like a man receiving an early birthday gift. "Well, you know what they say: if you want to find something lost, you ought to look where you last found it." He beams across the table. "Ladies, I have a suggestion."

It's been a long while since Agnes felt lonely. When she first came to New Salem the loneliness was like a cold shackle around her ankle, weighing her steps, tugging her back, but in time she stopped feeling the weight of it.

Now she can almost hear the clank and drag of chains at her heels as she paces. Her room at South Sybil is still unnaturally large, full of the ghostly echo of women laughing and teasing and whispering to one another.

Her pacing is interrupted sometimes by tentative taps on the door and whispers of *hyssop*. Girls who want to know when the next meeting will be and if Juniper is all right and if Agnes knows any good curses for Hill's men, who prowl the city with brass badges on their chests.

Agnes ought to tell them to burn their gowns and forget about witching forever, but the words catch in her throat like stale bread. It's the way the girls look at her—scared but not quite scared away, still hungry and hopeful—or maybe it's the glow in their eyes when they say Juniper's name.

She tells them to go home. To lie low. She lets them keep their hope a little while longer, and they leave her alone.

Except she's not really alone. She never is, now. She whispers to her daughter as she walks, snatches of songs and half-forgotten rhymes, promises she knows she can't keep. *It'll be alright. I'll keep you safe.*

In the deepening gray of the second evening her pacing is interrupted by three bold thuds at the door and a man's voice. "Hello? Hyssop."

Only one man knew that word. Agnes doesn't move.

Mr. August Lee knocks again. "Miss Eastwood? Agnes?" A slight pause. "I see your shoes in the hall."

She moves stiffly to the door and opens it a slim, miserly crack.

August's haystack hair is standing on end, his eyes wide with relief.

"Oh, thank the Saints. Your name wasn't in the papers, but I wasn't sure whether…" He trails away in the face of her hollow stare. "May I come in?" He holds up a grease-blotched newspaper, and Agnes catches the hot smell of gravy and meat.

She steps away from the door and settles herself on the edge of her bed, swallowing the sniveling gratitude in her throat. A strong woman wouldn't cry just because someone was worried about her.

August fetches a tin plate and unwraps the newspaper to reveal a pair of folded hand-pies, still hot. He hands them to her and she doesn't cry about that either, or mention that she's eaten nothing but boiled eggs and cold coffee for two days. She doesn't think any man has ever brought her hot pies, ever thought of her body as a thing to be taken care of rather than merely taken.

He hovers uncertainly until she takes a bite and makes an involuntary, animal noise somewhere between a growl and a groan. Then a crooked smile flicks over his face and he sits beside her, slightly too close.

"I should have come earlier. I'm so sorry, Agnes."

The tone of his voice and the angle of his body tells her he would quite like to put his arms around her. Agnes stiffens. "I'm alright."

She's not alright: she's hungry and heartsick, haunted by the slack line that once led to Juniper, and she can't seem to make herself wash her sister's blood from her hand. But the concern in August's voice makes her teeth hurt, like too-sweet tea.

"I should have gone with you. Or stopped you from going altogether."

"What makes you think you could have stopped us?" Agnes hears the chill of her own voice and tries half-heartedly to warm it. "It wouldn't have mattered if you were there. They were waiting for us."

He shakes his head. "One of your Sisters must have blabbed."

The chill returns to her voice, doubled in its absence. "They didn't."

"Well, maybe they didn't mean to. But you know how girls gossip."

The chill quadruples. "They didn't," she says again. "Because if they did, their own tongue would've split in two as the words left their lips, and the whole city would know them for the snake they are."

August blinks at her, eyes round and boyish. "But how—oh. The oath." His hand makes a concerned gesture toward his own lips, as if he'd like to check the condition of his tongue.

He recovers with visible effort. "Still. I wish I'd been there to protect you." He looks at her through the pale haze of his lashes, warm and handsome, perhaps a little expectant. She says nothing.

The longer she says nothing the more troubled his look becomes, like an actor whose leading lady is departing from her script, refusing to play her part. Now is the moment she's supposed to fall weeping into his arms. She's supposed to be distraught, delicate, undone; he's supposed to comfort her in her hour of need, and in her gratitude—well, who knows?

Agnes imagines leaning close and sinking her teeth into his lip, biting until the taste of blood overcame the taste of tears on her tongue. She'd been so taken by him, so seduced by the admiration in his eyes. But she should have known no man ever loved a woman's strength—they only love the place where it runs out. They love a strong will finally broken, a straight spine bent.

August's hand moves to cover hers on the bed and she pulls away. "I think you should leave." Her voice is so far past cold it might qualify as glacial.

"What did I—why—" He recoils, his face so baffled and hurt that a familiar fear brews in her belly. Will he leave when she asks, or will he linger, wheedling and wanting?

She wets dry lips and wishes for a pocketful of nettles. "*Get out.*"

He does, pausing only for a sorry-looking dip of his head. Agnes sighs shaky relief.

She carries her plate back to the table. It's only as she reaches for the newspaper to wrap the remains of her pies that she sees the face staring up at her from the front page: sharp teeth and wild eyes; a doubled trail of dark ink running from her nose; a stranger's fist snarled in her hair, baring her throat before the camera like an animal before the knife.

Juniper.

Juniper sleeps. At first her dreams are all witch-tales and towers, but then they're simply home: the honeysuckle taste of the air and the undersea shadows of the woods in midsummer; the hollow boom of thunder on the far side of the mountain and the clean taste of creek-water on her tongue. She didn't know cleanness had a taste before she came to New Salem and saw the Thorn sludging past, its waters clotted with gray froth and refuse.

Now that water seeps from the stone walls of her cell and trickles into her dreams. She is standing in Mama Mags's house, the light prisming through rows of Mason jars, the smell of witching on her tongue. Mags is there, her hair its usual nest of bone-colored bracken, her eyes like river-stones. She's asking Juniper a question—*The locket, girl, where's my locket?*—and then there's water around Juniper's ankles, cold and grease-slick, rising fast—

Juniper wakes. For a bleary second she thinks her own dream woke her, or the furtive splishing and rippling from live things in the shadows of the cell, but then she sees the glow: lantern-light, growing brighter. Someone is coming down the steps.

Her heart clangs against her ribs. They can't be back yet. The hours run strangely in the Deeps, but Juniper can tell by the weight of silence above her that it's very late, long before dawn. Surely she has more time.

But the light swells like a scream. Someone is coming.

She isn't ready. The first time, two officers held her arms while a third delivered timid, random blows to her body, seeming half-afraid that she would transform into a serpent or a harpy. They asked her questions— Who were her co-conspirators? Where did they meet? When had she last lain with the Devil?—and seemed spooked by her silence.

The second time, they'd brought a professional with them, an expressionless man in a leather apron who did not seem afraid at all. He placed a finger against the iron collar around her throat and whispered a word. Then he merely waited while the iron grew hotter and hotter, steaming in the damp, drawing red lines of blisters around her neck. He stopped only when she begged.

He left without asking her any questions at all. The cooked-meat smell of her own flesh lingered for a long time after.

The lamp-light rounds the final turn of the stairs. Boots slosh in ankle-deep water. A face moves toward her, glowing pale in the darkness of the Deeps.

Gideon Hill. Alone, except for the dog walking like a collared shadow beside him.

He stops outside her cell, lantern raised in one hand, watery eyes watching her. She looks back at him and slouches purposefully back against the damp stone of the wall, arranging her bad leg across the rusted iron of the bed-frame. "You gave me a scare," she drawls. "For a second I thought it was somebody important."

She expects him to snarl or spit or curse her as a sinner; she can't figure why else a city councilman would be ruining his suit in the fetid dark of the Deeps.

He laughs. It's a genuine laugh, low and appreciative. It sends a chill prickling down Juniper's spine, like a warning.

"Excuse my delay. It's so difficult to make time to visit the condemned, during the middle of a campaign." His voice is fuller than she remembered it, round and rich. Maybe it's just the echo of the walls around them.

She crosses her arms behind her head, speaking to the sagging ceiling. "It's rude to come calling after supper, my daddy taught me."

"I was concerned the presence of your jailers might inhibit your honesty. I wanted to speak more...frankly."

"Well *frankly*, Mr. Hill"—Juniper does not look away from the ceiling, does not change her tone in the slightest—"you can go fuck yourself."

Another low laugh. Then a sibilant mutter too soft to hear, the clink of a tugged leash.

Juniper startles at the sudden sloshing of boots beside her: Gideon Hill and his dog are standing inside her cell. The door remains closed and locked behind them.

Juniper feels the fine hairs of her arms stand on end. All the scathing swagger drains away from her.

He draws so close she can smell the fresh moonlight on his suit and feel the heat of his hound's breath against her bare skin.

He smiles down at her. It isn't the craven, cringing smile she remembers from the Women's Association, or even the hearty, false one that beams from thousands of campaign posters. This smile is all canines and red gums. It seems to be stolen from someone else entirely; Juniper would very much like to know who.

"You girls have done very well." Juniper wants to write the word *girls* on a ribbon and strangle him with it. "You chose nice, visible subjects, ideal for stirring up a fuss. It will cost the city a considerable sum to replace the statue of Saint George, by the way."

Juniper doesn't think she's ever cared less about anything. She watches him through narrowed eyes, wary as a cat.

He shrugs at her silence. "I can't say I'm sorry, honestly. It was always a terrible likeness. But what I want to know is—"

"I'm not telling you a single name. So why don't you save yourself some time and slither on home."

Hill flicks a disinterested finger. The gesture has more authority than Juniper thought Hill had in his entire body. "I'm not interested in names. Your friends are far more useful to me playing witch, putting the fear of God in the common folk. If I wanted them locked up with you, they would be."

Juniper's fingernails cut crescents into her palms. "How did you know about the graveyard? Who blabbed?"

Hill makes a soft, pitying sound. "No one, James."

He holds a hand in front of his lantern. It casts a five-fingered shadow against the scummed water between them, perfectly ordinary, until the edges ripple outward. The fingertips lengthen like claws or roots. His dog whines at his heels and he gives her a sharp, vicious kick.

Juniper stares at the shadow with the rising, queasy sense that she got it all terribly wrong. There is indeed a witch running loose in New Salem—the kind who deals in shadow and sin, in ways and words so wicked even Mama Mags wouldn't have touched them with a ten-foot pole—but it sure as hell isn't Miss Grace Wiggin.

It's the man standing with her in the prison cell, smiling his not-right smile, looking nothing at all like the stoop-shouldered bureaucrat Juniper met at the beginning of the summer. His hair is still thinning and his eyes are still pink-rimmed and too wet, but it's like his body is a house with a new owner. Everything is subtly rearranged: his limbs move differently in their sockets and his muscles are pinned differently to his bones. The only thing that remains unchanged is the furtive flick of his eyes.

Hill smiles at her again, flexing the fingers of his shadow-hand. "Everything casts a shadow, Miss Eastwood, and every shadow is mine. There are no secrets in this city."

His hand remains still, fingers splayed, but its shadow twines itself into a shape Juniper recognizes: three circles, interwoven. The lines are uneven, interrupted by bulges that might be the heads of snakes as they swallow their tails.

"The signature you left at your greatest works, I believe." His voice is softer now. "Not many people know it, these days. Tell me: where did you find it?"

Juniper gives him the sullen shrug that used to drive her daddy to drink. "Thought you knew everything."

"There were certain warded places, certain materials I couldn't... I'm a busy man. I can't watch everything."

Salt to keep things out. She grins at him. "Guess there's one secret in this city, then."

"Did someone teach it to you? Was it written somewhere?" The furtive thing in his eyes is writhing right beneath the surface, a grub beneath the soil. "What else have you found?"

"Maybe we found an ancient scroll. Maybe a fairy told it to us. Maybe we're the secret great-great-granddaughters of the Last Three themselves."

The flesh of his face goes taut, the sick smile stretching into a grimace. "The Three died screaming, along with their daughters. Tell me the truth, child."

Juniper leans forward and spits in the water between them. It lands with a satisfying spatter of scum and snot.

He dabs at his pant leg, sighing a little. Juniper doesn't see the shadow until it seizes her.

His shadow-hand oozes up her leg like a liquid spider. She swears and scrubs at it but her fingers pass through it as if it isn't there. It scuttles up her belly and across her chest, wraps cold fingers around her throat. Dull heat gathers in her collar, mounting as the shadow-hands tighten.

Hill watches her gasp and claw at her throat. "Clever things, these collars. They dampen magic, but they don't actually prevent its presence—they merely react to it. An invention of Saint Glennwald Hale, in the sixteen-hundreds."

Her blisters hiss and pop against the hot metal. A scream gathers in her throat, but she meets Hill's eyes and clamps her jaw against it.

He gives another short sigh, as if this is all rather tiresome and distasteful, and Juniper feels the oily creep of his shadow climbing higher. It moves up her neck and slides chill fingers between her lips, prying apart her teeth and oozing like oil down her throat. She gags.

"For the last time, girl: Where did you see their sign? What else have you found?"

The shadow slides deeper, questing and clawing, and she feels words pulled from her, rising like vomit in her throat. "We saw it on the tower door."

"On Alban Eilir?" Juniper stares up at him, bewildered, gagging on shadows, and he amends, "The equinox. The tower on the equinox?"

"Yes." The word is stolen from her, pulled out between reluctant teeth.

"You and your sisters are the ones who called it, were you not?"

"Yes."

"And you have been trying to find the necessary means to make a second attempt?"

"Yes."

"And have you succeeded?" Juniper hears the shift in his voice, catches the pale grub of fear in his eyes, and understands that this question is the one he wants answered more than any other, the real reason she's locked in the Deeps with a shadow-hand between her teeth.

She fights as the confession is dragged out of her, feels the edges of the word slicing the soft meat of her throat. It leaves her lips with a splutter of blood. "*No.*"

She can almost see the tension unwind from Hill's frame. The shadow retreats, coiling like a snake from her mouth, leaving Juniper to retch helplessly into the water below. It's not just the black taste of the shadow in her mouth—it's the invasion of it, the queasy betrayal of her own body. Even on his worst days her daddy could only touch the flesh-and-blood of her; her will remained her own.

Somewhere above her Hill is straightening his cuffs, wrapping the dog-leash neatly around his palm. "So I suspected. But some of your spells have been . . . substantial, and I wondered if somehow—but no."

She feels his hand on her cheek, chill and damp, and lacks even the energy to spin and bite it.

"Thank you, Miss Eastwood. You've quite put my mind at ease." He wades back to the cell door with his dog picking her way delicately behind him. They pass like ghosts through the iron.

"What *are* you?" Juniper wishes her voice didn't shake as she spoke, that there wasn't acid sick drying on her shift.

The warm glow of his lantern is already spiraling back up the steps. He calls back, "Merely a man, Miss Eastwood. And perhaps—if you and your sisters keep stirring up trouble—a mayor. We'll see in November."

Juniper curls around herself in the center of the iron bed-frame trying to tuck her bare flesh away from the shadows. She dreams herself home again, but this time she is running endlessly down the rutted clay of the drive, calling after her sisters. They do not answer.

Agnes is not dreaming. She is awake, pacing again, when she hears the second knock on her door.

She already knows who it is. She felt her sister coming nearer through the line between them, like a fish reeled in to shore, and only Bella is capable of tapping quite that timidly at a door.

But when she opens the door she finds two women standing in the hall: Bella, accompanied by the woman she still insists on referring to as Miss Quinn, although the rest of the Sisters have called her Cleo for weeks now.

Cleo hurries across the threshold as if she doesn't like to be out in the open. Bella follows after her, sliding the lock behind them.

"It's the middle of the night," Agnes observes. She adds, half against her will, "I heard the police were hassling women walking the streets at night."

Bella waves this concern away. "Oh, we weren't on the streets. And we're in something of a hurry. We're taking the earliest train north in the morning, and I needed to give this to you before we depart." She withdraws a glass vial from her sleeve and extends it to Agnes.

Agnes does not take it. She can see three droplets clinging to the glass, clear as water. "What is this?"

"Crone's tears. You'll need to provide mother's milk, of course, and find some way to get a drop or two of Juniper's blood. We really ought to be together to conduct the ritual properly, but we'll have to hope the Lost Way of Avalon isn't too particular about the details."

"The Lost—" It's only then that Agnes understands what her sister intends to do, what madness has come knocking at her door in the middle of the night. "I thought we didn't have the words."

Cleo shrugs rather casually. "Your sister and I are going on a research expedition."

Bella nods briskly. "May we count on you to be ready on the evening of the solstice?"

Agnes considers for a long moment. Her daughter is very still inside her, as if she, too, is waiting for her answer. "No."

Bella *tsks* at her. "Well whatever you have planned, surely you can skip it. This is worth missing a shift."

"No," Agnes says, and finds her eyes sliding away from Bella's as she says it. "I meant: you may not count on me."

She hears Cleo gasp, but not Bella. Perhaps she isn't all that surprised that Agnes would disappoint her. "This is our baby sister we're talking about," she says softly.

"And do you know what our *baby sister* did? What she is?" Agnes read the article beneath Juniper's bloodied face, understood why Juniper ran away from the only place she ever loved.

"Yes." Bella is watching her with those steady, storm-cloud eyes. "We are all what we have to be, to stay alive. Cowards. Traitors." The eyes flash, lightning behind the clouds. "Even villains, sometimes. Surely you can't hate her for it."

Agnes looks away again. "No."

"Agnes, she *needs* us—"

"Oh, don't pretend this is about anything but you and your books and your cleverness. You just want to be *right*, to snap your fingers and see one of your precious stories come to life." She fires the words like arrows; by the stricken chill of Bella's face, she knows they were well aimed.

Bella spins on her heel and strides to the cracked mirror hanging in its frame. She whispers to it—*Mirror, mirror, on the wall, tell the truth, reveal all*—a rhyme Agnes knows well, stolen from her favorite witch-tale as a girl, and rubs something across its surface. Agnes thinks it might be a lock of hair the color of crow feathers.

Heat in the air. The wild smell of witching. Then Beatrice removes the mirror from its nail and brings it to Agnes. "Just a little spell I learned from a story," she sneers, and tilts the surface so that Agnes can see the image inside it.

It should be the ceiling of South Sybil—sagging plaster, brownish stains spreading like the map to a foreign country—but it isn't. It's a woman's body, doubled along every fracture of the mirror, lying pale and still as bone. Her eyes are closed, the lids bluish, translucent, like the eyes of cave-creatures. She is nearly naked, bruises blooming darkly through her tattered shift, left foot twisted and pale with scars. A collar is clamped tight around her neck, and the skin beneath it is the color of uncooked meat.

Agnes prefers the Juniper that grins up from *The Post*, all teeth and defiance. This Juniper is just a girl, young and fragile and half-broken.

Bella's breath mists the surface. "I know you've always chosen your own hide over ours. I know you've never much cared what happens to us, but—"

"I always cared, Bell. Always." Agnes swallows the salt-promise of tears in her throat, hardens her voice. "But it never fucking mattered that I cared. I couldn't stop him, couldn't protect you—couldn't even protect myself—" The tears threaten again, and Agnes breaks off.

There's a pause, and after it Bella's voice has softened very slightly. "Maybe this time we can make it matter. Miss Quinn and I will find the words. Juniper has always had will to spare. We need you to gather the ways. Will you do it?"

Agnes doesn't want Bella to speak softly to her. She wants to keep that bitter coal burning hot between them, because once it cools she'll have nothing left but terrible guilt. She hadn't wanted to betray her, to spill Bella's secrets to their daddy, but surviving always comes at a cost.

Agnes looks again at the girl in the mirror, eyes tracing the dark blush of bruises, the shine of old scars. Juniper's lips move in her sleep. *Don't leave me.*

Agnes feels the taut scab of her sister's blood dried on her palm. She closes her eyes. "Yes."

Bella gives her a cool nod and sets the mirror on the table. "Wait for my sign."

"But then I'm through. If we—after we save her, I'm done with witching and women's rights and all the rest." She rests her palm on the full moon of her belly. "The cost is too high."

"Fine." Bella's lip curls very slightly before she turns away. "It's funny. Mama always said you were the strong one."

She unbolts the door and steps back into the deeper dark of the hall. Cleo moves to follow her and Agnes reaches for her sleeve. "Where are you going? To look for the words?"

"Why, the last place we know for certain the words were spoken." Cleo removes her sleeve from Agnes's hand, lips curling. "Old Salem."

20

Hark, hark,
The dogs do bark,
When witches come to town.

A spell to raise the alarm, requiring a gnawed bone & a strong
whistle

Beatrice Belladonna always wanted to see Old Salem. It makes regular appearances in her favorite penny-papers—a burned city full of charred bones and the wailing ghosts of witches—and even in more academic texts it retains a certain Gothic drama. It's always drawn with dense thickets of cross-hatched ruins and brooding trees, the stubborn black shapes of crows lurking in the corners, as if the artist had tried unsuccessfully to shoo them off the page.

As soon as Mr. Blackwell spoke its name, Beatrice felt a bone-deep certainty that he was right. Surely they could not fail to find their missing words in such a place—steeped in the oldest and wildest of witchcraft, oozing with mystery and memory.

But by the time she and Miss Cleopatra Quinn arrive in Old Salem, her certainty is sagging.

Perhaps it's the journey itself. It's difficult to feel particularly magical after fifty miles spent with one's forehead pressed to the window of a crowded train car, watching the landscape blur past like a spun globe, followed by another twenty miles suffocating in the back of a stagecoach. Miss Quinn is obliged by the cruel absurdity of Jim Crow to ride out front with the driver, and without her Beatrice feels herself growing drab and doubtful.

The final four miles are spent swaying in the back of a coal-colored wagon with LADY LILITH'S AUTHENTIC OLD SALEM EXCURSIONS painted on the side in faux-medieval script. Lady Lilith is a bored, fifty-ish woman with artificially dark hair and a disconcerting habit of hawking and spitting at regular intervals. The other passengers are similarly unmagical: a vacationing family from Boston who cast disapproving looks at Miss Quinn, a honeymooning couple uninterested in everything except one another, a trio of boarding school girls of the kind who wear black chokers and worship the Brontë sisters.

The sky is such an unblemished blue it looks strangely unfinished, as if a careless painter has forgotten to add clouds and birds and slight variations in hue. Beatrice feels obscurely that the day should be gray and wintry, the wind howling as they approach the gravesite of the last witches of the modern world.

Lilith's mules turn from the pocked highway down an even more forgotten-looking road made of moss-eaten cobbles and mud. The woods rise like water around them, cool and silent; even the newlyweds cease their giggling. The air smells green and secret, surprising Beatrice with a rare pang of homesickness for Crow County; she supposes a person doesn't have to love their home in order to miss it.

They trundle on in near-silence, Beatrice wondering fretfully how much farther it is and whether their quest has any hope of success, until Miss Quinn points into the shadowed wood at a low, lichen-covered wall made of blackened stone. Another wall runs beside it, sketching a square in the undergrowth. Beyond that Beatrice sees the rotten remnants of a doorway, the ghost of a lane, and understands abruptly that they have already reached Old Salem. They are driving now through its remains.

"Excuse me, ma'am." Miss Quinn interrupts Lady Lilith mid-hawk. "Do you think we might explore a bit on our own?"

Lady Lilith hauls her mules to a halt and eyes Quinn, scratching speculatively at the three white hairs coiled on her chin. "S'haunted," she observes. "Dangerous, to let tourists go wandering off. I might get in trouble."

Beatrice begins to explain that she is a former librarian and Miss Quinn is a journalist, and that they intend to take the utmost care in their explorations—which are in fact a matter of life and death for someone they love dearly—but Quinn produces a neatly folded dollar bill and presses it into Lady Lilith's damp palm. "If you could come back before dusk, we'd very much appreciate it," Quinn says, then climbs out of the wagon and extends a hand to help Beatrice down after her.

Lilith flicks the reins and Quinn and Beatrice are alone in the soft green ruins of the city.

They wander wordlessly through the woods, pausing to scrub moss from walls or scuff leaves away from stone roads. The trees around them strike Beatrice as implausibly ancient, surely older than a century. Crows and starlings watch them with mocking eyes, as if they know what the women are looking for and where it's hidden, but are disinclined to help.

Beatrice is no longer sure precisely what they are looking for—a signpost with an arrow pointing to the Lost Way of Avalon, perhaps, or a book titled *On Restoring the Power of Witches and Rescuing One's Sister from Certain Death*; some instruction or spell that has survived a century of rain and sun and morbid tourists. The sudden absurdity of the idea curdles Beatrice's stomach. She glances sideways at Quinn, wondering if she regrets signing her name in that notebook.

They walk on in silence. Sometimes Beatrice finds a patch of moss that grows in unlikely spirals, or a stone that bears an uncomfortable resemblance to a man with his arms raised to ward off some unseen blow. Somewhere in the middle of the city they find a bare circle of black-scorched stone, untouched by moss or grass or even fallen leaves, and the wind whips cold and tricksome against Beatrice's cheek—but there are no helpful letters carved into the earth, no books hidden beneath loose cobbles.

By the time Lady Lilith's wagon rattles back down the narrow road, the forest is gold and blue with early twilight, and tears are gathering behind Beatrice's eyes. When she blinks she sees her sister's body swimming in the darkness of her eyelids.

"Will you be staying at Salem Inn, misses?" Lilith asks them perfunctorily. "We offer two meals in the historic dining hall without additional payment and a free ticket apiece to the Museum of Sin, recently reopened to the public following some difficulties with mold this spring."

Beatrice feels the faintest, dimmest spark of hope. Quinn is making some polite excuse about urgent business back home when Beatrice steps forward and asks, "How much just for the museum?"

In the Deeps, Juniper waits.

She doesn't know what she's waiting for anymore, but she keeps doing it anyway.

She has visitors, sometimes, but never the ones she wants. An officer arrives twice a day to hang a pail of something whitish and congealed inside her cell. Grits, Juniper thinks, or the aggrieved ghost a grit might leave behind if it was murdered in cold blood. When she asks for water the man points downward, to the putrid gray of the water at their feet. He laughs.

In the mornings a woman in rubber boots comes to carry out the piss pot. The first morning Juniper badgers her with questions—Where are the others? How many did the bastards get? Has she no pity, no shame, aiding the enemy of all womankind?—until the woman calmly tips the contents of the pot into Juniper's grits. The second morning Juniper keeps her damn mouth shut; the third morning the woman brings her a hard biscuit and a tin cup of water.

Her tormentors don't return. Juniper is relieved at first, before she remembers that time is a tormentor, too. Down in the cellar the hours used to come alive around her, stalking and prowling in the dark.

By the evening of the third day, Juniper is cold and hungry and so thirsty her throat feels barbed, as if she swallowed briars. She sits on the bed and watches the stairwell, still waiting. A habit, maybe, from the seven years she spent hoping her sisters would come home.

She's given up on hope, but she can't seem to leave the habit of waiting behind.

Beatrice suspects that Lady Lilith's Museum of Sin—boasting *More Than One Hundred Genuine Relics of Witchcraft*—has not eradicated its mold problem as thoroughly as Lilith claimed. There's a damp, living smell to the place; Beatrice imagines saplings pressing up beneath the floorboards, vines digging green fingers into the plaster.

The museum is a series of low-ceilinged rooms draped in patchy velvet and black-dyed gauze, crowded with shelves and glass cases of Genuine Relics. At least three-quarters of the items are transparent frauds—Beatrice is confident that the witches of Old Salem never wielded wands with fake rubies glued to their handles, and the dust-furred skeleton labeled *American Dragon (Juvenile)* is most likely a small crocodile with vulture wings wired to its back—and everything conceivably authentic is too trivial to matter. There is a set of silver thimbles, charred and iridescent from some great heat; an iron skillet containing the "burnt remains of its owner's last meal"; a little girl's smoke-stained sewing sampler.

"Well." Beatrice sighs. "It was worth a try. I don't suppose Lady Lilith will refund us our dimes."

Quinn is peering into cases and reading brass labels with every appearance of fascination. "Whyever should we want a refund?"

"You're being very sporting about this, but it's clear—"

"My family has been free for three generations," Quinn interrupts. She tilts the derby hat back on her head in order to more closely examine a box containing, allegedly, the femur of an unidentified witch. "But my grandmother was born on a farm called Sweet Bay." Quinn squints as if she's reading a label, but her eyes don't move. "A rice plantation."

"I'm—so sorry."

"I'm sure you are. But what is *sorry* worth, in the face of Sweet Bay?" Quinn is still staring at that brass label, but the perfect calm of her voice is splintered, bleeding through the cracks. "My grandmother didn't need your *sorry.*"

"I—"

Quinn straightens abruptly and moves to the next case, mending the split seams in her voice. "She didn't need anyone, in the end. She and her sisters made it north, with the help of Aunt Nancy's recipes. She taught my mother how they used to speak in codes and symbols, to keep their secrets safe. The Daughters still use some of them, because we aren't strong enough to risk working in the open. Yet." Beatrice wonders precisely what Quinn and the Daughters might do with the Lost Way of Avalon, and then whether she really wants to know.

"Anyway. What my mother taught me is this: you hide the most important things in the places that matter least. Women's clothes, children's toys, songs…Places a man would never look." As she speaks she is levering open one of the glass cases, running long fingers over the hinges of a woman's sewing box. "If the witches of Old Salem had the spell to restore the Way, do you really believe they would have advertised it? Left it listed in the index of a grimoire?" She shakes her head, abandoning the sewing box for the child's sampler hanging on the wall, yellowed and stained. "You're thinking like a librarian, rather than a witch. Ah! Come see."

It appears to Beatrice to be a perfectly ordinary piece of embroidery: a crooked house framed by a pair of dark trees, with three lumpy women standing in the foreground beside a scattering of animals. Clumsy letters run across the top: "Workd by Polly Pekkala in The Twelfth Year of her Age, 1782." A border of dark vines curls around the edges.

"I don't see—oh." There is a twist in the vines along the top, a hiccup in the pattern. The vines loop back on themselves to make three circles, interwoven.

Beatrice squints through her spectacles at the little scene. Upon closer inspection each of the animals in the yard is purest black, with red knots for eyes, and the figures are all women. One of them has a stitch of red dripping from her finger; the second holds a swaddled bundle to her breast, either a baby or a large potato; the last has a line of pale French knots running down her cheeks. *Blood, milk, and tears.*

Beatrice feels warm, weightless, as if she is hovering several inches off the warped floorboards. It's the way she feels in the archives when she catches a glimmer of gold and brings it into the light, shining softly. She knows by the look on Quinn's face that she feels it, too: the specific, almost spiteful joy of finding the truth buried beneath centuries of dust and deceit and neglect.

Their eyes meet and Beatrice forgets to count the seconds. Something warm and nameless wings between them.

(It is not nameless.)

Quinn is running her fingers over the empty linen of the sky above the little house. She breathes a small *ha!* of satisfaction and reaches for Beatrice's hand. She guides it to the sampler's surface. Beatrice is so worried she might sense that unnamed thing in the sweaty heat of her palm, the staccato flutter of her pulse, that she almost misses the subtle, irregular bumps of stitches beneath her fingertips.

She peers closer. There are tiny, nearly invisible words written in white thread.

> *The wayward sisters, hand in hand,*
> *Burned and bound, our stolen crown,*
> *But what is lost, that can't be found?*

The rhyme their Mama Mags once sung to them, the verse hidden in the Sisters Grimm. Except this time the words keep going:

> *Cauldron bubble, toil and trouble,*
> *Weave a circle round the throne,*
> *Maiden, mother, and crone.*

Beatrice shivers as she reads the last line, wondering if she and her sisters are meant to walk this winding path, destined by blood or fate. She waits to be overcome with some grand sense of destiny before recalling that she is merely an ex-librarian standing in a fraudulent museum that smells of mold, trying to save her wicked, wild sister.

Quinn pulls the black leather notebook from Beatrice's pocket and flips to the page with a spell concerning barking dogs and gnawed bones. "The solstice begins at midnight. I believe it's time to call your sister."

21

The wayward sisters, hand in hand,
Burned and bound, our stolen crown,
But what is lost, that can't be found?

Cauldron bubble, toil and trouble,
Weave a circle round the throne,
Maiden, mother, and crone.

A spell to find what has been lost, requiring maiden's blood,
mother's milk, crone's tears & a fierce will

*W*ait for my sign, Bella told her, but Agnes doesn't know what sign she's waiting for. In the stories, witches were always sending messages by raven or whispering secrets into the hollow curves of conch shells, so Agnes rattles around South Sybil, squinting out windows, looking for letters in the smoke-bitten stars or words written in the rising steam.

When the sign comes, Agnes cannot miss it.

It begins as a lone keening from the street below, the plaintive howl of a street-dog. Then the street-dog is joined by its brothers, by yips and barks and rumbling growls that rise from every quarter of the city in an uncanny wave. It's as if every dog in New Salem has joined a single, mottled wolf-pack. The noise of the dogs is followed by the human shrieks and curses of alarmed pedestrians and angry owners.

"Saints, Bell. I hear you." The line that leads to her oldest sister is stretched thin by the miles between them, but Agnes can still feel the echo of Bella's will behind the working.

Agnes gathers the ways—three glass jars, the waxen stubs of seven candles, a book of matches, and a cast iron skillet that is the closest thing she has to a cauldron—and wraps them tight in a canvas sack.

Then she and the sack and the baby swimming silent inside her step out into the howling noise of the night. The streets are so full of people—baffled policemen and shouting men, irritable mothers holding screaming infants, escaped toddlers clapping their hands with delighted cries of "DOGGY!"—that no one pays much attention to Agnes.

"Nothing to be concerned about," one officer is repeating, loudly and falsely. "Just a flock of geese passing by, or a cat." But Agnes can tell from the white sheen of his face that he doesn't believe it. That he can feel the rules of the real shifting beneath his feet, the orderly world of New Salem warping and cracking like a snow globe tossed in a bonfire.

She pulls her cloak hood high and winds through the alleys with the bag clanking gently at her side and Mama Mags's stories echoing in her ears, the ones about sisters and spells worked on solstice-eve. In stories the sisters are always set one against the others—the beautiful one and her two ugly sisters, the clever one and the fools, the brave one and the cowards. Only one of them escapes the wicked witch or breaks the terrible curse.

Their daddy was a curse. He left them scarred and sundered, broken so badly they can never be put back together again.

But maybe tonight—just for a little while—they can pretend. Maybe they can stand hand in hand, once lost but now found. Maybe it will be enough to save their wild, wayward sister from a world that despises wayward women.

Agnes walks until the howling of the dogs quiets to whimpers and whines, until the moon hangs high and clear above her, until her steps echo in the empty dark of St. George's Square. Mama Mags taught her that magic likes to burn the same way twice, like deer following a trail or water running to a river. Perhaps the tower will come easier to the place they last called it; perhaps this time it will stay.

She kneels beneath the empty plinth where Saint George once stood and places the candles around her like the pale flowers of a fairy ring. She sets the jars before her, three in a row, and waits.

It is midnight when Beatrice returns to the ruins of Old Salem.

Old Salem at midnight is not the same city they visited at noon. The skeletons of walls and streets are clearer by moonlight, their bones drawn in silver and shadow beneath the moss. The wind has risen, banishing the idle warmth of summer, whistling strangely through the alleys and corners of the lost city. It tugs at Beatrice's hair, playful as a schoolgirl.

She and Miss Quinn stand in the bare circle of earth in the middle of the lost city. Seven candles flicker around them, drawing upward-slanting shadows over their faces, guttering in the untrustworthy wind.

Miss Quinn nods approval. "Thoroughly witchy, Miss Eastwood. You could hardly ask for better."

"I thought perhaps the Way would have an affinity for the city, if it stood here once before. I suspect we'll need all the help we can get." There are supposed to be seven candles made of pure white wax, instead of five mismatched stubs stolen from Lilith's inn (one of them is decorated with small, malformed bats; two of them are melted to their willow-patterned saucers). She and her sisters are supposed to be standing shoulder-to-shoulder, hand in hand; they're supposed to be real witches, with familiars and broomsticks and pointed hats, instead of three desperate young women.

"Truly, this is madness. It cannot succeed. Even supposing we have the words and ways, I am not at all suited for this sort of thing. I lack the blood, the conviction, the courage—"

Quinn gives a tart cluck of her tongue. "Please do stop pretending you are a coward. It grows tiresome."

"*Pretending*—"

"You fret and worry, but your hands are steady as stones." Quinn's arms are crossed, her chin high. "You have not stammered once since we arrived in Old Salem."

Beatrice closes her mouth. "I suppose not."

Quinn takes a step nearer, her face gilded gold. "Would a coward form a secret society of witches? Would she transfigure statues and hex cemeteries? Would she stand in the ruins of a lost city on the solstice?"

Beatrice feels as if the earth is tilting beneath her feet or the sky is tumbling around her ears, some fundamental truth is coming undone. "Perhaps she wouldn't." It comes out a near-whisper. "But she might still fail."

"And yet you will try anyway."

"Yes."

"For your sister."

Or perhaps for all of them: for the little girls thrown in cellars and the grown women sent to workhouses, the mothers who shouldn't have died and the witches who shouldn't have burned. For all the women punished merely for wanting what they shouldn't have.

Beatrice settles for another "Yes."

"I deceived you, it's true, but Beatrice…" The challenge in Quinn's face softens, replaced by a wistful tenderness that Beatrice finds far more dangerous. "I beg you not to deceive yourself."

"I see." A brief silence follows, while Beatrice recovers her straying voice. "Call me Bella." Beatrice was the name of her father's mother, a dried-out onion of a woman who visited once a year for Christmas and only ever gave them turgid novels about the lives of the Saints. A Beatrice couldn't stand in this wild wood by the light of the not-quite-full moon, working the greatest witching of her century; a Beatrice couldn't meet Quinn's eyes in the candlelight, with the wind whipping her hair loose across her face. Perhaps a Belladonna could.

"Oh, are we on first-name terms now?" Quinn's lips are a teasing curve, but that tender thing lingers in her voice.

"Of course we are." Bella swallows once, too hard. "Cleo."

She finds she can't look into Quinn's eyes as she says her name. She looks down at her notebook instead, rubbing her thumb across the words. "If anything untoward happens, you should run."

"No, thank you," Quinn says politely.

Bella tries again. "If it goes awry…" They both know it would be unwise for Quinn to be found in a scene of obvious witchcraft beside the burned husk of a white woman.

"Then I advise you not to let it go awry." Quinn catches her eyes. "I am not here as a spy, Bella. Or even as a member of the Sisters of Avalon. I'm here as your…friend." Her grin tilts. "And because I am the most curious creature ever cursed to walk the earth, to quote my mother, and I would very much like to be there when the Lost Way of Avalon comes back to the world."

"Your mother seems a wise woman," Bella says, and adds, a little daringly, "I'd like to meet her, someday."

"But you already have!" Quinn sighs at Bella's slack expression. "I did tell you my mother ran a spice shop."

Bella considers objecting on the grounds that Quinn never said her mother ran a secret apothecary disguised as a spice shop while actually leading a clandestine society of colored witches, but instead says, "Oh."

Quinn gives her a consoling pat. "She thought you were very sweet."

Bella closes her eyes in brief and mortal mortification. "Well. It's time, don't you think?"

Quinn's hand slips into hers, warm and dry. Bella wets her lips, feels the cool whip of wind on her tongue, and says the words a coward never would:

> *The wayward sisters, hand in hand,*
> *Burned and bound, our stolen crown,*
> *But what is lost, that can't be found?*

It's seven minutes past midnight when Juniper's collar begins to burn.

She splashes to her knees in the dark waters of the Deeps, fingers scrabbling at the hot iron, teeth gritted on howls and curses.

She heard the dogs, earlier—even buried beneath ten thousand pounds of stone and iron she could hear that mad chorus, sense the wicked heat of witchcraft in the air—but her collar had remained dull and cold against her blistered throat. Now it blazes, and beneath its heat she feels the lines that lead to her sisters, taut and singing with power.

Her lip splits beneath her teeth. Blood runs hot down her chin, too hot, and drips to the cold water below. Juniper hears the delicate *splish* as it lands and remembers her blood falling to the limestone cobbles of St. George's Square—then the whipping wind, the dark tower, the wild smell of roses—Bella's fingers on her mouth: *maiden's blood.*

She knows, then, what her sisters are doing.

"Oh, you *fools.* You beautiful Saints-damned sinners—" She curses them and cries as she curses, because she knows they are doing it for her. Even though they abandoned her once before, even though they know now what she is—a murderess and a villain, worse than nothing—

It hurts even to think it. *They came back for me.* She feels something snap in her chest, as if her heart is a broken bone poorly set, which has to break again before it can heal right.

For a moment she pictures herself standing arm in arm with her sisters, triumphant before the Lost Way of Avalon. She knows it will never be. Because—though she can sense the rightness of the words and ways, though she feels her sisters' will scorching down the line between them—Juniper knows they will fail.

Bella calls. The magic answers.

> *Cauldron bubble, toil and trouble,*
> *Weave a circle round the throne,*
> *Maiden, mother, and crone.*

The heat gathers first in her palms, spreading like fresh-caught flames up her arms, burrowing into the hollow of her throat. The invisible lines between Bella and her sisters—the bindings left behind by that half-worked spell months before—hum like fiddle strings beneath the bow.

The wind rises, and with it comes the calling of night-birds and the feral smell of magic.

> *The wayward sisters, hand in hand—*

She feels Agnes a hundred miles away, lit like a torch in the center of New Salem, the cobbles growing hot beneath her heels. She feels her hands steady on the glass vials, and the bright hiss of tears and milk and blood as they fall.

> *Burned and bound, our stolen crown—*

But where is Juniper? The line between them is thin and weak, far too cold.

Bella kneels on the bare earth of Old Salem, still speaking the spell, magic burning through her. Steam rises from the soil as it boils beneath her.

> *But what is lost, that can't be found?*

The words feel true in her mouth, like keys sliding into invisible locks. But the heat is consuming her. She pictures her veins glowing hotter and hotter until she ignites, until she is a bonfire with a woman's voice.

She feels Agnes burning with her, arms wrapped tight around her belly, hair rising around her in the same wind that whips dirt and dead leaves around Bella.

But she doesn't feel Juniper. There are only two of them, and two is not enough.

The last time she worked this spell—when she was just a librarian named Beatrice who found a few words that shouldn't exist—she had grown frightened and fallen silent. Without the words the spell suffocated like an airless fire, and the only price was a little Devil's-fever, quickly cured.

But now she is Belladonna Eastwood, the oldest sister and the wisest, and Juniper needs her.

She circles back to the beginning of the spell in an unbroken chant. The woods dim around her, vanishing in the rising haze of heat. Her lips keep moving, desperate prayers mixing with the words.

—oh hell—Three bless and keep us—weave a circle round the throne—

Distantly, she feels cool fingers across her brow, palms cupping her face. A thumb traces her cheeks and she turns blindly toward it. If she is going to die, let it be with the sweet frost of those fingers against her lips, the taste of ink and cloves on her tongue.

There comes a point when Bella knows she should turn back. It's like wading into the creek after a storm, the water rushing around your ankles, knowing if you take another step it will pull you under.

Bella takes another step. She goes under.

She is fire. She is pain. She is a crack in the world through which something else—magic or God or the heat of every unanswered wish and impossible dream, burning eternal on the other side of everything—pours through.

She thinks she's probably dying.

The something-else pauses. It considers her, this dying woman kneeling in a circle of spent candles, her lips still shaping the words that are killing her.

Somewhere very far away, an owl calls.

Bella opens her eyes. Through the haze of heat and tears she sees a shape gliding through the trees, silent as smoke, blacker than the blackest night. Its eyes are a pair of embers burning nearer.

Quinn gasps, but Bella's lips crack into a smile, because——though she is burning, though she is failing—at least she has come this far. At least she has knelt in the bones of Old Salem and watched her familiar winging toward her.

Bella draws a breath. She begins again.

The wayward sisters, hand in hand—

Juniper hears the words echoing down the line, tastes them gathering in her mouth. She keeps her teeth clamped tight.

The spell needs her. She feels it boiling too hot, gathering like lightning with nowhere to strike. But if she speaks, the collar around her throat will kill her.

If she doesn't speak, the spell will kill her sisters.

Let it go, for the love of Eve, save yourselves.

They don't let it go. Because they are fools, because they are desperate, because they will not abandon her a second time.

Juniper closes her eyes and whispers several very filthy words.

She thinks a little bitterly of all the lofty reasons she wanted to restore the Lost Way—to reclaim the power of witches for all womankind, to break the shackles of their servitude, to set this whole damn city on fire. And in the end she's going to do it because she wants to save her dumb-shit sisters, who are only doing it to save her in turn.

She wonders if all great acts are secretly done for such small reasons;

she wonders if the cleaning lady will be the first to find her in the morning, facedown in the Deeps with a red ring around her neck.

She gathers her will around her—a wild, clawing thing, hungry and desperate and half-starved—and speaks the words.

The collar glows dull orange in the darkness, but the borrowed words still tumble from her mouth in a steady stream. The orange deepens to ruby, painting the cell in blood and shadow, and Juniper feels herself falling backward. The collar hisses as it hits the water. Her mouth fills with the sour taste of sewer. Her will doesn't waver.

Something vast slides invisibly into place, a great key turning in a lock, and the world splits open.

Magic comes roaring through the crack, through the three women who stand in Salem's past and present. Juniper feels the heat of it crack the cobbles beneath Agnes's feet and blacken the earth beneath Bella; around her, the Deeps boil.

And the collar around her throat—built to punish street-witches and fortune-tellers, women with nothing but the half-remembered rhymes of their mothers—burns from red to white to black, and then crumbles into gray ash.

The heat fades.

Juniper feels the tower standing tall, rooted like a tree in the middle of New Salem. And she feels her sisters: Agnes, her forehead pressed to heat-cracked stone and her arms doubled around her belly, laughing and sobbing; Bella, held tight in someone else's arms, too stunned even to feel relief. Alive, both of them.

Juniper lies back in the cooling waters of the Deeps and closes her eyes, listening to the distant beating of their hearts. It's a peaceful, easy sound, as familiar as rain on the roof.

She thinks she might stay like this, suspended, drifting away from the burned-meat smell of her own flesh and the pain too huge to feel, but a voice is calling her. It's a familiar voice, querulous and cracked with age. It tells her to wake up, to get on her feet.

Juniper doesn't much want to, but she knows better than to disobey that voice. She wakes up; she gets on her feet. She tries not to feel the brush of air against the raw mess of her throat.

A ghostly hand touches hers. Juniper knows the hand is a fever-dream or a mirage, a product of the pain pulsing like wine through her skull—but it feels familiar. Warm and knob-knuckled, paper-fleshed.

The hand pulls her forward, folds her fingers around a broken shard of stone. Then it places the edge of the stone against the wall and drags it in a slow, grinding circle. *Weave a circle round*, Juniper thinks, drunkenly, and mumbles the words again. Her voice sounds wrong in her ears, clotted and strangled.

The stone falls from her fingers as she closes the circle. The scratched shape begins, very faintly, to glow.

She squints at it, stupidly, until the voice clucks its invisible tongue at her and says, *Go on, girl.*

Juniper places her palm inside the soft shine of the circle. The cell vanishes around her, whipping into the starlit night.

22

One for sorrow,
Two for mirth,
Three for a funeral,
And four for birth,
Five for life,
Six for death,
Seven to find a merry wife.

A spell for healing, requiring willow bark & silkweed

Beatrice Belladonna is mildly surprised to discover that she is not dead.

She is slumped sideways in a ring of white wax with someone's arms held fast around her and someone's voice in her ear. "Oh, thank the Saints," it breathes, and Bella realizes who the arms and the voice belong to. She considers fainting again, simply to luxuriate in the feeling of Quinn's body against hers.

"Bella, I think—I think it wants your attention." With a small, private sigh, Bella opens her eyes.

There is an owl standing on the bare earth before her, except that no natural owl has ever had feathers so black they seem to swallow light, refusing even to reflect the dappled silver of the moonlight. No owl has ever possessed eyes the color of coals: a deep, solemn red. Behind those eyes Bella senses an echo of that vast thing that paused to consider her, as if the owl is a cinder spit from a much greater fire.

Witchcraft itself wearing an animal-skin, Mags used to say.

"Hello," Bella says shyly. How should one greet a familiar? What does one say to magic fashioned into a shape that suits you?

Her familiar does not answer, regarding her with that red gaze. It lifts one foot, and Bella notices for the first time the thing clutched in its obsidian claws: a jagged, charred stone.

It uncurls its talons and the stone rolls toward Bella. Behind her Quinn makes a small, weary sound, like a woman who has seen quite enough strange and uncanny things for one evening and hopes they will soon desist.

Bella takes the stone. The owl watches her. "Th-thank you?" Bella offers. She doesn't know if normal owls possess the ability to blink at one in a manner both disappointed and long-suffering, but this one apparently does.

It loses patience with her and launches itself abruptly skyward. Bella struggles upright. "Wait! Come back, I'm sorry!"

But it doesn't leave. It merely sweeps in a low circle above them, wings angled. Three times it circles—Bella thinks of the Sign of the Three and the resonance of form, the repetition of drawn circles in folklore—before it cuts back toward Bella with talons outstretched. She braces for the blow, but the claws rest lightly on her shoulder. The owl weighs no more than the idea of an owl, a suggestion of bone and feather.

It calls, low and plaintive. Bella digs the point of her stone into the dark earth and drags it in a wide circle, whispering the words once more. *Weave a circle round the throne*. The circle begins to emit a soft, pearled light, like foxfire. Quinn makes her weary sound again.

Bella takes her hand and draws it earthward. She presses their palms against the night-cool earth, one beside the other, and Old Salem vanishes.

They leave nothing behind them but pooled wax and burned earth, and the faint, sweet smell of roses.

Agnes is not dead, and neither is her daughter.

She kneels in the place that was St. George's Square. But now the street-lamps glimmer weakly through a forest of twisted trees, impossibly far away. Stars wheel in wild patterns above her, nearer and brighter than Agnes has ever seen them in New Salem. The sky is broken by an immense blackness, a stone tower overgrown with ivy and climbing roses, its door marked with three winding circles.

Agnes is looking up at the tower, touching her belly and thinking dreamily, *Happy birthday, baby girl*, when two women appear in the place that was once St. George's Square. If Agnes had not recently seen an entire tower appear from thin air, sliding into reality like a fish reeled from sea to air, she might have found this quite shocking.

"Bella!" She is standing beside Cleopatra Quinn at the tower door, their palms pressed to the woven circles. "How did you—is that an *owl*?" A tall shadow perches on her oldest sister's shoulder, regarding Agnes with hot-ember eyes.

"Yes, I think so," Bella burbles. Her own eyes are feverish and over-bright, spinning in a manner that causes Agnes some concern. "*Strix varia*, I suspect, though with the coloring it's difficult to be sure. Ovid thought them vampires and ill omens, the silly man—just look how handsome he is!" Bella pauses in this delirium to draw a finger down her owl's breast. A thought seems to strike her. She wheels, looking up at the vastness of the tower, then back to Quinn and Agnes. "Do you feel anything? Any particular power awakening?"

A small, uncertain silence falls as the three of them wait for some mysterious and ancient magic to flood their veins, filling them with the lost majesty of their fore-mothers.

"I don't think so," says Agnes.

"No," says Cleo.

"Neither do I. Well, perhaps there's some ritual or key inside—a series of clues which reveal a secret chamber, like one of Miss Doyle's mysteries! Or perhaps if we read the inscription aloud—" Bella bends closer to the door, where words are written in foreign-looking script. "*Maleficae quondam, maleficaeque futurae.*"

Nothing happens.

Before Bella can try anything else, a fourth woman appears at the tower door. Her shift hangs in ash-streaked tatters, clinging to damp flesh, revealing the dark blooms of bruises. Her head is bowed, face hidden by a black tangle of hair. Her breath is a wet rattle.

The woman straightens. As she turns, Agnes sees the red ruin of her throat, a mess of bloody pink and dead white that she can't look at very long.

Juniper is beaming at them, lips cracked, teeth bloody. Her eyes are a deep gray-green, like the shadows of summer leaves, softer and sweeter than Agnes has ever seen them—until they land on the creature perched on Bella's shoulder.

"Oh, *horseshit.*" Juniper's voice is somehow both wet and scorched, terrible to hear. "How come you get one before me?"

Then, with a strange, boneless grace, she collapses.

Bella is not dead. But, but she thinks her sister might be.

Agnes reaches her first. "June? June, baby? *Help* me, damn you! Get her inside!" It takes Bella a long moment to realize Agnes is addressing her, and another to crouch down beside her sister's broken-doll body. She hesitates to touch her—she's an open wound, a collection of bruises and burns and abuses—but between them Bella and Agnes haul her awkwardly upright.

Quinn pulls hard on the iron ring of the tower door. It opens easily, as if some tidy caretaker has kept its hinges oiled all these centuries.

Bella and Agnes lay their sister on the cool flagstone floor with her hair haloed around her and her throat gaping like a second mouth.

Bella looks a little wildly into the shadows, hoping for a glowing chalice or an ivory wand or perhaps a magical potion labeled *Drink me!*

There is nothing. Only soft darkness cut with silver shafts of moonlight, and a faint, dry smell that makes Bella's heart lift inexplicably in her chest.

Agnes's voice is hesitant, swallowed by the vast dark above them. "Someone will see, soon, and then they'll come for us. What do we do?"

But Bella isn't listening. She is breathing in that smell—dust and parchment, leather and cotton, ink made from oil and oak-gall and soot—with a wild suspicion swelling in her chest.

She fumbles a matchbook from her skirt and drags the tip across the flagstones. The light flares, reflected in the deep amber of Quinn's eyes, illuminating a too-small circle of flagstones. At the very edge of the circle Bella can make out the faint outlines of shelves lining the tower walls. The glass shine of jars. Long benches and scarred tables scattered with leaves and bones and nameless things, as if some untidy woman had been brewing witch-ways just hours before.

Bella stands, lifting the match higher in trembling fingers, wishing for a lamp or torch or even a candle.

From her shoulder, the owl ruffles its feathers. It stretches forward—Bella doesn't know if a true owl could extend its neck to such an uncanny length, or if the rules are different for familiars—and plucks the guttering match from her fingers. It makes a neat toss-and-catch motion with its head and swallows the match whole, flame and all.

"Oh! Don't—" Bella makes a helpless gesture, far too late. Golden light is blooming in the shadowed center of the owl, like a candle seen through smoked glass. It glows brighter, spreading until the owl shines the deep gold of a well-tended fire, only the very tips of its claws and wings still edged in black. It spreads its wings and takes luminous flight.

Three faces turn upward to watch as it spirals upward through the tower. In its shining wake they see an endless staircase that circles and twines along the walls, so aimless and haphazard it looks grown rather than built. Landings and ladders sprout from the stairs like branches, lustrous and worn smooth with use, and doors nestle in the shadows, although Bella can't imagine they open onto anything but empty air. And nestled between them—in leaning stacks and on tidy shelves, in calfskin and cracked leather, their pages gold-limned by the owl's light—there are books. More books than Bella has ever seen, in a lifetime devoted to books.

Her owl fades back to pooled ink as the match burns out. It roosts somewhere high above them, invisible but for the red gleam of its gaze.

Bella closes her eyes. There's an odd bubbling in her chest. It takes her a moment to identify it as giddy laughter. The Lost Way of Avalon isn't a miracle or a magical relic or a fanciful artifact. It's merely the truth, written and bound, preserved against time and malice. It's—

"A library," Quinn breathes.

"A *library*?" Agnes is the only one of them still crouched beside Juniper, her fingers bunched in the damp white of her shift. "What the hell are we supposed to do with a *library*?"

Bella is drifting toward the nearest shelf, squinting at the moonlit label written in antique calligraphy. *Jinxes—Mortal, perilous, purely amusing.* The next label reads: *Weatherworking—Storms, floods, locust-plagues,* directly above *Changelings—Made from clay, stone, dealings with fae folk.* The one beneath that is *Medicinal—Burns, bites, bruising.*

Quinn reads them over her shoulder. Even in the dimness Bella can see the keen shine of her eyes, the hunger of her half-smile as she looks at the books. She is a woman who understands the value of words, especially the ones they don't want you to say.

Bella reaches for a volume bound in cherry-wood with brass hinges along the spine. The title is burned into the cover in square capitals: *THE BOOK OF MARGERY MEM, Being a Translation of her Curative Receipts.*

Bella steps into a sliver of moonlight as she opens it, sees the lost words and forgotten ways preserved in a thousand tidy lines of ink. Witchcraft, pure as dragon's blood and bright as stardust, unspoken for centuries.

"With this, Agnes, we could do more or less anything we pleased. Speak with wolves or bring stones to life or turn Mayor Worthington into a weevil." She turns back to Agnes, still crouched over Juniper's still body, white with worry. "But we'll begin with saving our sister."

Juniper doesn't much miss her body; it's a broken, burnt thing, so full of pain there's hardly any room left for her. She drifts above it instead, watching with detached affection while her sisters fret over the red mess of her neck, peel the cotton shift from her bruised flesh. That Quinn woman stands above them with dried herbs in one hand and a book in the other, reading aloud.

Her words tug at Juniper. She tries to ignore them, but they reel her downward, closer and closer to the shipwreck of her body. Then her sisters take up the words in tear-streaked voices. *One for sorrow, two for mirth, three for a funeral, four for birth—*

Bella lays a sprig of green across Juniper's throat, still speaking the spell, knocking her knuckles on the stones.

The words are a trap. They pin her inside her own body alongside every bruise and burn. Her screams are hoarse, thin things.

The pain eases with each knock of her sisters' knuckles, each round of *one for sorrow, two for mirth*. A blissful coolness follows behind it, like creek-water on a hot day.

Juniper lies still, listening to the even beat of her blood and the tiny, invisible motions of skin reknitting and blisters shrinking. Her sisters are talking above her, their voices falling from some great height down to her ears.

"They'll be here soon." That's Agnes, tense with fear.

"Who?" Bella sounds profoundly un-Bella-like, giddy and pleased and thoroughly unworried. Juniper wonders if she's drunk.

"*Everyone!* Police, mobs with pitchforks, Hill and his friends! We have to go!" There's something very important Juniper needs to tell them about Hill, about witchcraft and stolen shadows with watching eyes, but the thought sinks into the blessed coolness and vanishes.

Bella sobers. "I am not leaving this library for those depraved people to discover." *Library?*

Agnes makes a wordless growl, but Quinn says calmly, "Hide it, then. If you can bind hats to cloaks and hide them away, why not a tower?"

There is a small silence, while the words *ashes to ashes, dust to dust* rattle loosely through Juniper's skull. Then Bella says, "That is—quite brilliant, Cleo," with such admiration in her voice that it's almost indelicate. "But one of us will need to leave, to work the binding and find a safe place to hide it. And draw the Sign to give us a way back out."

"I'll do it," Agnes offers quietly.

Bella's voice cools for some reason. "Of course. I had forgotten you were already leaving."

Juniper finds the voices above her blurring together after this, devolving into a jumble of plans and mutters and *hurry now*s. She would be content to lie there, basking in the absence of pain, except—

"Wait!" Her voice is still all kinds of wrong, thin and hoarse. "Thank you. For saving me."

There's a shush of skirts and Agnes's face appears above her. "Hush, baby." Her voice is warm and low and bossy as hell, just like when they were girls.

"I didn't think you'd come. Now that you know about Daddy."

"It's true, then." Agnes sounds neither surprised nor especially upset. Just tired.

Juniper swallows and gasps a little with the pain of it. "It's true."

"Oh, June." Bella kneels on her other side, her face long and sharp beside Agnes's. "Why? After all those years."

"He got sick. He was always getting sick after the fire—weak lungs, the doctor said. This time was worse. He spent weeks laid up in bed, coughing up blood and slime." Juniper remembers sleeping on the floor by his bed so she could tend to him in the night, listening to the wet rattle of his breath. "The doctor said there was nothing he could do. He had a lawyer come draw up a will and gave Daddy a brown bottle for the pain. Whatever it was made him…" Strange. Feeble. Not himself. He looked at her sometimes with his eyes all wet and shining and called her by her mother's-name. Once when she was setting his dinner tray on his lap he'd touched her wrist in a way that made her stomach twist sickly. That night she slept outside, letting the cold wind scour her clean.

Her sisters' faces are grave and silent above her. Juniper closes her eyes. "One day near the end he started carrying on about sin and regret and how he was sorry I wasn't born a son. He said at least Dan would do right by the farm. And that's when I knew he'd taken it from me, all of it." Even now, the ghost of that rage is enough to choke her. That land belonged to her, by birthright and blood.

Bella begins, softly, "So that's why."

"No." Juniper swallows again, feels the pucker and rip of the wound in her throat. "I wanted to, but I didn't. Till he started apologizing for… other things. The cellar. The two of you leaving. Our mother." Her voice wobbles on the last word. Juniper doesn't know why; she's never even met the woman, never known her as anything but a curl of hair in Mama Mags's locket, the reason her sisters wore black on her birthday. "He said he—that he—"

Juniper had understood then that her daddy—her flesh and blood, her enemy, her only-thing-left—was a murderer. And then, as the snake's teeth bit into her palm, she understood that she and her daddy had one thing in common.

A warm hand slides into hers. Bella starts to speak but Juniper cuts her off. "Did you know? The two of you?"

Above her Juniper feels her sisters look at one another and then away. "Not really," Bella says just as Agnes says, "Yes."

There's a brief pause before Agnes amends, "When her pains started,

Mama told me to go ring the bell, but Daddy caught my wrist…" Juniper hears the bitter guilt in her voice. "I don't know if he meant for it to happen. But he knew how hard her births had been before."

"You should have told me," Juniper says, but she doesn't know if she means it. What would it have been like to grow up knowing that? Is this the reason her sisters were always a little less wild than she was, a little more frightened?

"You should have told *us*," Bella answers, a little waspishly. "Before you were dragged off to prison."

"I thought if you knew what I did, what I am, you might…" *Hate me, leave me, turn around and never come back.*

"But surely you didn't think it would surprise us. After what we saw." At Bella's words, Juniper feels that unseen something swimming up from the deeps of wherever it lives inside her. She wants to look away from it, to send it back down where it belongs, but she's tired and hurting and cracked wide with confession. It looms closer.

Agnes is shaking her head. "She doesn't remember, Bell."

Juniper doesn't want to ask. She asks. "What don't I remember?"

Agnes meets her eyes, gray to gray. "The day in the barn. When Daddy found out—what he found out." Her eyes flick to Bella, bitter cold, then back to Juniper. "We were trapped against the wall. He was coming closer. And then there you were, standing between us, scrawny and fierce. You told him to leave us alone, or else, and he laughed at you. So…" Agnes trails away, but Juniper remembers.

Juniper remembers: the arc of her spine as she looked up at her father.

Juniper remembers: the snake teeth waiting always in her pocket, ever since Mama Mags folded her fingers around them and told her to keep them secret and safe, just in case.

Juniper remembers: something snapping inside her. Her patience, her tolerance, her last straw.

May sticks and stones break your bones and serpents stop your heart. She didn't have her cedar staff back then. But she had a tobacco-stake from the barn floor, crusted with dirt and chickenshit, and she had the words.

And she had the will. Almost.

At the very last second, as she watched her daddy writhing on the barn floor, a snake the color of dust wrapped around his ankle, her will had wavered. Maybe she didn't hate him quite enough; maybe she just didn't want to hate herself.

Afterward, when she was alone except for the wet crackle of her daddy's breathing, she sent the memory of that snake down into the deepest oceans of herself, where she couldn't see it, because her sisters were gone and she couldn't stand to know it was her own fault.

Juniper feels tears trickling down her temples, burrowing in her hair. Her daddy had been different after the fire: slower, more cautious, less likely to raise a hand in anger. She thought it was gratitude, maybe, for all the putrid hours she spent changing his bandages and spoon-feeding him. But he was kind to her for the same reason a man is kind to a mad dog: for fear of her teeth.

Turns out he wasn't quite scared enough.

"That's why you never came back, then." Because they saw what she was. A monster, a murderess. A dragon red in tooth and claw, and only princesses were rescued from towers. "That's why you never wrote."

But Bella's voice cuts across hers. "I did write, June. Once a week at first. When you never wrote back, I thought you must want nothing to do with me. I thought maybe you'd heard...rumors." Juniper tries hard to focus on her face, a hovering smear with sad eyes.

Agnes echoes her. "The first thing I bought when I got to the city was a postcard. You never answered, and after a while I stopped trying."

"But—oh." Juniper wonders if her daddy paid the postman to lose those letters, or if he burned them himself. She wonders if she ever shoveled their ashes from the woodstove, unknowing, and if her daddy watched her when she did.

Their closeness had always bothered him. When they were little he was forever playing them one against the other, favoring the youngest, blaming one for the sins of her sisters, finding the cracks between them and wedging them wider. But it never seemed to stick. The three of them remained a single thing, inviolate. So he split them apart and spent seven years tearing at the last threads that bound them together.

But—Juniper looks up at her gray-eyed sisters, here with her now—he failed.

"Agnes. Bell. I—"

"I do hate to interrupt, but it's nearly dawn. Our time is short." Quinn is standing in the doorway, pointing out to the thin line of gray visible on the horizon.

Juniper's sisters get to their feet. Juniper wishes they would come back. She wants to ask what happened to the other Sisters and how they called back the Lost Way and if they think it's possible that Mama Mags's ghost visited her in the Deeps—but the stones are so cool on her skin and the air is so heavy on her eyes.

She wakes once, briefly, when a hand touches her cheek, and Agnes says, "Goodbye, Juniper." Then, more stiffly, "Goodbye, Bella."

"You know where to find us if you change your mind."

Juniper doesn't know if Agnes replies, because she drifts away.

There are still voices around her, murmuring and whispering, but they don't belong to her sisters. They belong to three someone-elses, and they sound like the soft sighs of turning pages, the rustles of rose petals one against another, the silent touch of strange stars.

Agnes looks behind her once before she leaves the tower.

Bella stands with a pair of silver shears in one hand and an open book in the other, that eerie owl perched like a gargoyle on her shoulder, looking like the Crone herself come back from the dead. Juniper lies pale and still on the flagstones, a maiden laid out for sacrifice.

The sight of them tugs at Agnes. She wants to turn back and take her place between them, play the part of the middle sister and the Mother—but she doesn't.

She pushes through the door and kneels briefly beneath the shadowed trees. She scoops a palmful of earth and leaf-litter into a glass and whispers the words over it: *Ashes to ashes, dust to dust.* She prays it is enough.

The night is quiet except for the whisper-touch of leaves and the distant toll of church bells ringing the solstice-morning service. The branches of trees drag against her skirts like friendly fingers, half-familiar; she remembers all the times she chased Juniper through thickets of mountain laurel and holly back home.

Agnes slips from the woods and takes three steps before she realizes she is not alone: there are birds roosting on every lamp-post and iron bench, crowding the sills and rooftops of the College and City Hall, silent as falling feathers—

And there is a woman standing several feet in front of her, right where the cobbles turn to dark, leaf-strewn earth.

Her face is tilted up to look at the tower, her skin ivory in the unsettling shine of constellations that have doubled in number and abandoned their usual patterns, unnaturally bright despite the electric orange glow of the city.

She isn't wearing her usual white sash or her starched skirt, and her Gibson Girl hair has deflated somewhat, but Agnes knows that face: Miss Grace Wiggin, head of the Women's Christian Union and famed crusader against suffrage, witchcraft, alcohol, gambling, prostitution, immigration, miscegenation, and unionizing.

Agnes goes very still, feeling like some wild creature caught in the lamp-light. Wiggin's face turns toward her slowly, as if she has difficulty tearing her eyes from the tower. Tears glitter in them, and a quarter-teaspoon of longing.

"Did you do this?" Her voice is thin, lost-sounding, nothing like the shrill clarion call Agnes remembers.

Agnes inclines her head, feeling an unsteady surge of pride. *I did this, with my sisters.* They called it from bottomless time, sang it straight into the middle of sober, sinless New Salem. Grace Wiggin and her ladies-in-waiting seem suddenly less worrisome, almost humorous.

Wiggin's eyes focus on her for the first time, her lip curling. "And did you not fear for the soul of your child? Have you no mother's natural instincts?"

Agnes considers slapping her. "What about you, Miss Wiggin? Do you not fear for your reputation, out alone at night? Have you no shame?"

An odd, childish flash of guilt crosses the woman's face. "I was out for a walk. I happened to be looking up and saw the stars shifting, changing, and the birds gathering... Then I smelled the roses."

Mags always said the solstices and equinoxes were the times magic burned closest to the surface of things, when any self-respecting hedge-witch or wild-hearted woman ought to be outdoors, with moonlight on her skin and night around her shoulders.

What is a proper young woman doing out on the summer solstice, watching the sky? Why do her eyes keep reeling back to the tower, like moths to flames?

Agnes is struck by the sudden suspicion that Grace Wiggin doesn't hate witching at all. "It's beautiful, isn't it?"

"It's vile. Wicked." But the words have a hollow, learned-by-rote ring. Agnes waits, watching the tense roll of muscles in Wiggin's face, wondering how long the woman will keep talking rather than screaming for help, and if it will be long enough for Bella to make the tower disappear.

That longing look is back in Wiggin's eyes, stronger now. "My mother used to make my dolls dance, when I was a girl. I begged her to teach the words to me and she did, and more besides. I liked to learn them. It made me feel—" She doesn't say how it made her feel, but Agnes knows: like her voice had power, like her will had weight.

"What happened to her?"

Bitterness seeps into Wiggin's face, aging it. "She was caught killing the unborn." Agnes thinks of Mags and the narrow path back to her house, Madame Zina with her gauzy veils and fake card-readings. "They made me go to the hanging. I was a Lost Angel, after that."

An ungainly tenderness takes root in Agnes's chest. She rebels against it—surely her circle needn't be large enough to include women like Grace Wiggin, for the love of God—but it's as if Wiggin's face has become a window, or maybe a mirror. Agnes can see the frightened, hurting girl she once was, with a heart full of hate and nowhere to send it.

"Listen. You don't have to keep doing...what you do. You don't have to keep helping a man like Gideon Hill just because he—"

The sound of his name shatters the fragile thing between them. Wiggin's eyes are shards of flint; her fingers clutch the shawl tighter around her shoulders. "How *dare* you—Mr. Hill is the noblest—the bravest—" A fervent, unnatural rage chokes her words.

Agnes is wondering if Wiggin is going to attack her, clawing and hissing like a cat, when the tower vanishes.

The stars and the tangled woods and the dark earth—all of it falls out of the world like coins dropping into an invisible pocket. Nothing remains of the Lost Way of Avalon except a mischievous wind, and the feral scent of magic and roses in the air. Wiggin staggers sideways, mouth open in horror. She spins back to Agnes with her skin waxen and yellow in the first streaks of true dawn. "You'll burn for this," she hisses. "He'll make sure of it."

And then she screams. "Help! Someone help! There are witches in New Salem!"

Agnes runs, pausing only to draw an X on the cobbles and whisper August's spell into the dawn. Her hair rises from her shoulders and the baby's weight lifts from her hips, and she runs with the vial knocking against her thigh and Wiggin's voice ringing in her ears like a curse, or a prophecy.

She runs west, keeping to the side-streets and narrow alleys, dodging the lamp-lighters and night-soil men, hiding in doorways when she hears the ring of hooves on stone. At the cemetery she pauses, chewing her lip, before climbing the fence and winding her way back to the witch-yard, where their golden tree still stands, grand and gleaming, far too heavy to move.

Agnes buries the glass vial of earth among its roots. She scores a symbol into the soft metal of the tree's trunk—three circles, intertwined—and whispers the words. The sign begins to glow, very faintly, and her fingers hover above it, wanting to touch it and be drawn back to the tower and the woods and the wild story her sisters are writing together.

But Agnes is through with all that. She saved her sister, and now she must survive for her daughter.

She walks home, weary and sore-footed. At first she hides when she sees officers riding past on their tall grays, but soon she realizes they hardly notice her. She is nothing, once again.

23

London Bridge is falling down, falling down,
iron bars will bend and break, bend and break,
My fair maiden.

A spell for rust, requiring saltwater & joined hands

Juniper wakes to a series of mysteries. The first mystery is her own
skin, which she remembers as a battered, mistreated thing, like a
worn-out suit of clothes. But it feels whole and smooth beneath her
hands. Even—her fingers tremble as they reach her throat—the place
where the iron collar burned itself to ash. It ought to be a scabbed, gluey
ruin, weeping yellow and red, but there's nothing but knots of taut flesh.

The second mystery is the room, which is round and sunny, and
which she has never seen before in her life. There are three beds set
beneath three arched windows, and three woven rugs overlapping on a
wooden floor. Juniper thinks a little giddily of witch-tales about three
bears and lost maidens. There's a just-rightness to the room that Juniper
can't quite name, until she realizes it reminds her of the attic where they
slept as girls. It was the only part of the house she was sorry to burn.

The third mystery is the most subtle and the most troubling: the light is all wrong. It feels like the middle of the day, but the sun falls slantwise through the windows, heavy and gold as a ripe apple. It's autumn sunlight, Juniper is sure of it, and she wonders dizzily if she slept through summer.

She finds no answers in the quiet dancing of the dust motes, or in the green tendrils of ivy and rose that curl over the window ledges. She rustles in a chest at the foot of her bed and finds a wide-sleeved robe in undyed wool, with a single silver clasp in the shape of an S, or maybe a snake. She pulls it over her head, ignoring the pop and groan of muscles that would prefer to lie back down in the featherbed, and climbs down the ladder.

It ends at the top of a staircase that corkscrews downward. Along its dizzy route there are doors and alcoves, chairs piled with cushions and windows with wide benches beneath them. And books. An amount and variety of books that Juniper finds frankly excessive.

Juniper limps in slow spirals through the tower, badly missing her red-cedar staff, trailing one hand along the spines: soft calfskin, brittle leather, ragged cotton, burlap, eelskin, iron, titles stamped in gold and char, something that whispers sweetly as she touches it and something else that stings. She's a little surprised she doesn't find her oldest sister lying on the steps, expired from sheer glee.

Then, as she passes a delicately carved door, Juniper hears Bella's voice. "—was thinking we ought to start with the medicinal texts. The fever is horrendous this year, and think what a coup it would be if we cured it!"

Juniper is standing halfway up a tower, right against the stone of the outer wall. By every natural law, there should be nothing but empty air behind the little carved door. But when she opens it she finds a smallish room paneled in dark oak, with a wide table presently buried beneath scrolls and books and scattered ink-pens. Bella leans over one side, spectacles perched on her nose, and Quinn sits at the other, lips quirked at some private joke.

"June!" Bella straightens. "When did you get up? What possessed you to walk down all those stairs on your own?" She shuffles Juniper over to a chair with much muttering and flapping of hands.

"I'm fine," Juniper says, but her voice sounds like the drag of a match-tip against stone, harsh and grating. She fends off an offered shawl and cushion. "Jesus. Morning, Cleo."

"Morning."

"Where's that big black bird of yours, Bell? And how do I get one?"

Bella circles the table and resettles herself on the arm of Quinn's chair. "Strix, you mean? He comes and goes as he pleases. Sometimes he vanishes altogether, back to the other side."

"Huh. And where's Agnes?" Juniper reaches for her without thinking, forgetting that the spell that bound them is done and over now. But the invisible line between them is still there. She can feel Agnes somewhere in the city, toiling away.

It takes Juniper far too long to realize that Bella has not answered her, that she's even now shuffling a stack of pages on her desk rather than meeting Juniper's eyes. "Agnes is...no longer an active member of the Sisters of Avalon. By her own volition."

"What?"

"She got scared and quit," Quinn clarifies.

Juniper feels a petulant heat in her throat. It was supposed to be the three of them together again, one for all and all for one. "But she was here. She called back the Lost Way with us. And you're telling me she just split?"

Bella says, softly, "She's got more than just her own neck to look out for, remember." It's the closest Juniper has heard Bella come to defending their sister. "And it's more dangerous now. Look." Bella unfolds a waxy-looking poster from a stack on her desk and hands it over.

Juniper meets her own eyes on the page: her face is sketched in charcoal, standing between her sisters. Juniper is drawn tangle-haired and snarling, like the kind of witch who lives in the woods and runs with wolves; Bella is sharp-boned and thin, like the witch who lives in a spun-sugar house and eats little children; Agnes is all curves and lips, more like the witch who lures men to her bed and leaves them cold and white in the morning. The caption reads: THE SISTERS EASTWOOD: WANTED FOR MURDER & MOST WICKED WITCHCRAFT, and offers a generous reward for information regarding their whereabouts.

Juniper looks down at their monstrous faces and feels a bitter twist in her gut. If it's a villain they want, who is she to deny them?

Bella folds the poster away. "There are rumors, too, Quinn tells me. Hysterical theories about your escape and a black tower seen on the solstice. The square is still full of birds, apparently. A few churches have begun holding nightly vigils against the return of witching—they're telling their congregations that the fever is a punishment sent by either God or the Devil, they can't seem to agree which—oh, quit grinning like that, June, this is serious!"

"Jesus, Bell, lighten—"

"There have been nineteen arrests since the solstice." Quinn speaks very slowly and clearly, as if she thinks Juniper might need things spelled out in one-syllable words. "Mostly harmless street-witches—an abortionist, a fortune-teller, a woman who claimed to speak with the dead. There have been raids, too, women beaten bloody for nothing but a few feathers in their pockets or a questionable spice-rack."

Juniper is not grinning anymore. She hears Agnes asking her what comes after, what it costs. "Are the Sisters alright?"

Quinn makes a little yes-and-no bob of her head. "Four of them are still in the workhouse, as far as I know; I still haven't found Jennie. A few others have had unpleasant encounters with the police. The Hull sisters were among the nineteen arrests."

Juniper can't think of anything to say, can hardly think around the queasy guilt crawling up her throat. Quinn isn't finished. "There are calls for the mayor's resignation. The City Council has formed a committee to investigate the rise of witchcraft, headed by Mr. Gideon Hill. Who has climbed rather dramatically in the polls."

At the sound of Hill's name Juniper stops feeling guilty or queasy or guilty; the only thing she feels is afraid. "He came to visit me in the Deeps," she rasps.

"Who did?"

"Gideon Hill. And he's not—he isn't—" She swallows against the memory of those shadowy fingers pressing between her lips. "He's a witch."

Bella and Quinn are quiet as Juniper stutters through the story, but she can tell she isn't getting it right. She tells them what happened—how he melted through the bars, how he pulled confessions from her, how he laughed—but she can't seem to tell them how it was. How his eyes flicked, furtive and fearful, how a stranger stood behind his face. How the shadows slid like oil between her teeth.

"Well," Bella said, adjusting her spectacles. "I suppose if men's magic has proved somewhat efficacious for us, it stands to reason a man might master a little witchcraft."

"It wasn't a little witchcraft. He said every shadow was his, he said—"

"A bluff, surely. It would require an unthinkable degree of power to control a city full of shadows. And the ways would be ghastly, I imagine. We'd have heard about it if there were dozens of white lambs going missing, or piles of bones found in the City Council chambers, don't you think?"

Juniper sets her jaw. "I know what I saw. We ought to figure out what the hell he is, at least. And send a message to Agnes and the other Sisters, warn them that he knows their names, probably where they live, where they work."

Bella taps the folded-up poster again. "I suspect Agnes knows. She was already planning to leave South Sybil, I believe, and work under a different name. I recommended the ladies at Salem's Sin, should she need to disguise herself." There's a gentleness to her tone, as if Juniper is a fretful horse that needs settling. "She could not be more cautious than she already is."

Juniper looks away, around the wood-paneled room that shouldn't exist. There's a narrow, mullioned window on the east wall, and the light that shines through this one is wintry and pale, as if it looks out at the month of January rather than June.

"So. This is it." Juniper makes a *ta-da* gesture with her hands. "The Lost Way of Avalon. Is it—did we—" The question she wants to ask is a childish one, but she can't help herself. "Are we witches now?"

Neither of them laugh at her, although Quinn's mouth quirks again. Bella sweeps her hand grandly at the piled books and notes on the table. "We certainly have sufficient ways and words to become so, don't we? An entire library of spells and hexes, curses and charms, poisons, potions, conjurings, recipes...Quinn and I are developing a system to catalog and translate them all." Bella gives a small, contented sigh.

"Translate them?"

"Well, relatively few of them are in English, and none in what you might recognize as modern English. There are a few texts in Latin and Greek, but significantly more in Arabic, classical forms of Persian, a Turkic language or two, even something I think must be a written form of Malinke, from Old Mali. And then once we translate them there are the witch-ways to contend with. Herbs that are native to the Old World, for example, but which do not thrive in the new one, or ingredients which no longer exist—dragon's tooth, siren's scale, that sort of thing. It will take considerable time and effort, but already we've found a stronger spell for warding and another for rust—" Bella pauses in this rhapsody to squint worriedly at Juniper. "What's wrong?"

Juniper gives a shrug that tugs at the fresh scar around her neck. "Guess I just didn't figure the Lost Way of Avalon would be a bunch of schoolwork."

Bella clucks her tongue at her. "The Last Three Witches of the West spent their final days assembling the world's greatest library of witchcraft, which Agnes and Quinn and I went through considerable difficulty to retrieve. I'm so sorry it disappoints you."

"But even after you translate all these spells from Greek or hiero-glyphs or what have you, are you sure we can work them? A woman would need a good helping of witch-blood, wouldn't she?"

"Well, as to that...Cleo and I are no longer convinced that magical prowess is a matter of inheritance." Bella actually gives a little clap as she says this, as if she simply cannot contain herself.

Juniper looks to Quinn, who translates, "We don't know that blood counts for a damn thing, when it comes to witching."

Juniper makes a skeptical *hunh* that provokes her sister to rustle through a stack of scrolls. She unrolls one of them and points rather theatrically at an illustration painted in rusty red and brown. It shows a woman surrounded by spikes of flames, her mouth open in a silent scream, her skirts already alight. Beneath her feet, where Juniper might expect to find dry brush or logs, is a heaped, charred pile of books.

Bella gives the illustration an aggressive tap. "Why were witches sentenced to burning, anyway? Why not hanging or beheading or ston-ing?" Back in Miss Hurston's one-room schoolhouse Juniper was taught that witches were burned to remind folks of the hellfire that awaited them in the next life, but Juniper supposes Miss Hurston also believed that bad behavior could be cured by prayer and regular thwacks with her yardstick, so perhaps her information was flawed.

Her sister leans closer, eyes bird-bright behind her spectacles. "What if they didn't start as witch-burnings? What if they were book-burnings, in the beginning?"

Juniper shrugs. "I guess."

Bella makes a noise like an irritable cat. "Think, June! What did Mags tell us every spell requires?"

"The words, the will, the way."

"Where in that list does it mention a woman's heritage? Her blood?" Bella gestures a little wildly to the carved door, to the tower behind it full of endless shelves of books. "I don't think they were burning blood-lines out, at all—I think they were burning *knowledge*. Books, and the women who wrote them. I think...I think they stole the words and ways from us, and left us nothing but our wills."

Bella's face is full of fierce intent, but Juniper feels as if something inside her has been punctured and is slowly deflating. Some part of her had been childishly hoping they were the long-lost great-granddaughters of the Mother, descendants of Morgan le Fay or Lilith or Eve herself. But perhaps they weren't born for greatness, after all; perhaps no one was.

Bella is still theorizing, speaking mostly to herself now. "I think the Maiden and Mother and Crone weren't especially powerful for any reason other than the knowledge they kept. I wish..." Her voice goes a little sheepish, young-sounding. "I wish I could ask them. It would be infinitely more convenient than translating and transcribing all this."

Juniper thinks privately it would be infinitely more convenient if the lost power of witches had turned out to be an enchanted broomstick or a potion you drank at the half-moon, rather than a bunch of books in dead languages.

She plucks moodily at Bella's notes, admiring a diagram of a woman spitting flames from her mouth. "Is this a fire-starting spell?"

"It seems so, yes."

"Can I try it?"

"Can you start a magical fire in a tower full of paper and leather?"

Juniper considers. "What if it were a very *small* fire?"

Bella shoos her from the room with instructions to eat and return to bed.

Juniper limps the rest of the way down the endless stairs, glaring a little resentfully at the spines of books she can't read, watching the strange slant of the light through the windows. She finds the bread and cheese but takes it outdoors to eat, resting her spine against the sun-warmed stone of the tower.

She thinks of Agnes, back at some loom, head bowed. Of Frankie and Victoria and Tennessee and all the others stuck in the workhouse, caged like crows. It doesn't sit right, that Juniper should be here beneath the twisted boughs of Avalon, hurt but now healed, while the women of New Salem are left to cower and creep, undefended, with nothing but their wills to protect them...

So give them the words and ways. It's like someone whispers it in Juniper's ear, in a voice like rose-leaves rustling. Juniper wonders if the Deeps shook something loose in her skull, or if the tower is haunted, and then decides she doesn't care because the ghost has a damn good point.

She wanted the Lost Way to be a miracle-cure, a waved wand that turned every woman into a witch. But if there isn't any such thing as witch-blood—if none of them are born for greatness and all they have are moldering stacks of books and an overgrown tower just south of somewhere—perhaps they have to make the miracle themselves.

When Juniper comes clattering back up the stairs and announces her intention to slip back into New Salem and spread the good word of witchcraft among its women, like Johnny Appleseed if he had a bag of spells instead of seeds, Bella is not especially surprised. Juniper has always been the wild one.

Bella feels the spark of her spirit burning in the line between them, white-hot—the line which shouldn't exist, which is the subject of several pages of Bella's notes and queries and theoretical musings—and knows she will have to lock her sister in the top of the tower if she wants to stop her, and even that would merely delay her; Juniper isn't the sort of maiden to wait around for rescue.

"This is a very bad idea." Bella says it mostly out of the dim sense that she would like to have the opportunity to say *I told you so* after the dust settles. "The witches of Old Salem called back the Lost Way and started slinging spells and cursing enemies left and right, and look how that turned out."

Juniper shrugs. "So I'll be more careful than they were."

"You don't have a reputation for careful, June."

"Why did we do all this, exactly? Why did we call back the Lost Way?" Juniper's hands are on her hips, her head tilted, defiant. The skin around her neck has a raw shine to it and her voice is lower and smokier than it used to be, as if she keeps a hot coal in her mouth.

(At St. Hale's they taught Bella that pain was the greatest teacher; how is it that Juniper never seems to learn?)

"To save you," Bella answers. Beside her, Quinn adds something beneath her breath that sounds suspiciously like *you ungrateful wretch*.

A guilty blush rises in her cheeks, but Juniper's hands remain on her hips. "Sure, yes. But I meant—why was I in the Deeps in the first place?"

"Murder?" Quinn suggests, and Bella lets out half a laugh before she catches it.

Juniper waves a harassed hand at the pair of them. "They threw me in the Deeps because we were stirring things up. We were reminding this city that we were witches, once, and might be again." Her voice husks lower. "And it was *working*. People were listening. More than listening—how many names are written in your notebook? Nineteen arrests, you said. Should we hide away while our Sisters suffer for our sins? Are we such cowards?"

The word *coward* wraps tight around Bella's throat, a blouse that no longer fits. She meets Quinn's eyes. *I beg you not to deceive yourself.*

"No," she says steadily, "I am not."

Quinn exhales. "Well, that's good. Seeing as I have already supplied the Daughters with at least half a dozen spells."

Juniper cackles while Bella gapes. "You already—but—" She feels old and stuffy and librarianish—and a little betrayed.

Quinn sobers. "I didn't tell anyone where I got them, or how to find us. I think my mother at least suspects the Lost Way is no longer lost, but you have no need to worry. We know all about secrets on the south side."

"I . . . see. Well." Bella draws a deep breath. "It's hardly fair to favor our Daughters over our Sisters. Shall we even the score?"

Juniper smiles so widely her lip cracks and bleeds.

That evening, just as dusk purples toward night and the first stars open like white eyes above them, Juniper opens the tower door. Her pockets bristle with witch-ways and her cloak drapes dark and long behind her. She hardly seems to feel the wounds and bruises still mottling her flesh.

The problem with saving someone, Bella thinks, is that they so often refuse to remain saved. They career back out into the perilous world, inviting every danger and calamity, quite careless of the labor it took to rescue them in the first place.

"Where will you go first?" Bella asks.

Juniper looks over her shoulder with a fey wink. "Oh, I don't want to spoil the surprise. You can read about it in the papers tomorrow."

SUSPECTED WITCHES ESCAPE FROM SAINT JUDE'S WORKHOUSE FOR WOMEN; FIVE WOMEN NOW AT LARGE

June 24th, 1893, *The New Salem Post*

...the five women—four of whom were taken into custody on the last full moon, in the midst of a Satanic ritual conducted in the heart of the New Salem cemetery—were still in their cells at the workhouse on the evening of the twenty-third. In the morning the guards found their doors locked but the cells empty. One witness on the street reports seeing six bats flit from the workhouse that night; another claims it was an owl carrying a long golden rope. All of them agree that they saw a dark-haired woman with a pronounced limp in the vicinity.

Our readers are asked to report any sightings of this young woman or the escaped suspects—Victoria V. Hull and Tennessee T. Hull; Frankie U. Black; Gertrude R. Bonnin; and Alexandra V. Domontovich—to the New Salem Police Department.

BREAK-IN AT THE HALL OF JUSTICE

June 26th, 1893, *The Times of Salem*

The New Salem Hall of Justice ought to be the safest place in the city to store one's belongings, but officers confirmed this morning that the personal effects of Miss James Juniper Eastwood—including a number of ungodly herbs and potions as well as an antique locket containing human hair—have been stolen...

Several other alterations were made to the Hall during the night, including the disappearance of several warrants and bonds, and the vulgar alteration of several officers' badges.

DOCTOR MARVEL'S ANTHROPOLOGICAL EXHIBITION SHUTS ITS DOORS

June 29th, 1893, *The New Salem Post*

Following the disappearance of most of its occupants, Doctor Marvel's Magnificent Anthropological Exhibition will be closed to the public.

This beloved attraction, designed to educate the public about the many fascinating peoples of the world, is no stranger to difficulties and irregularities. Doctor Marvel himself recounted to *The Post* the many occasions on which his subjects have resisted his efforts to educate the public. "Had a pair of Indian witches last summer that ran off three or four times before I found their little satchel of shells and bones. And a little Hungarian girl last Christmas cursed her handler so that the smallest ray of sunlight burned his flesh. But I've never had anything like this."

At approximately ten-thirty last Sunday evening, the Last Witch Doctor of the Congo began to laugh. She continued laughing until several staff members left their beds to investigate, and found all the members of the exhibition missing. Where the Witch Doctor ought to have lain, they found only rusted chains and a white, grinning skull; each staff member who saw the skull that night has since been plagued by bad dreams and poor sleep.

A DECLARATION FOR NEW CAIRO

July 4th, 1893, a letter from the editors of *The New Salem Defender*

The recent raids conducted by the Police Department have left seven buildings burnt in New Cairo and ruined the livelihoods of several hardworking families. The editors of this paper soundly reject the Council's argument that such raids are necessary for public safety and note that none of them produced any evidence of witchcraft at all.

...If the authorities of New Salem insist on maintaining this adversarial position toward our neighborhood, perhaps it is time for New Cairo to follow that hallowed American tradition: secession.

24

Maiden, Mother, and Crone,
Guard the bed that I lie on,
One to watch,
One to pray,
One to keep the shadows at bay.

A warding spell, requiring salt & thistleseed

Agnes Amaranth is nothing, these days.

She used to be something—the city is wallpapered with her face, beautiful and terrible, her name written large above her crimes—but neither the face nor the name now belongs to her. Thanks to the ladies of Salem's Sin, Agnes's hair is the dull, forgettable color of sewer-water, and her face is pocked and rough as the surface of the moon. Mr. Malton barely glanced at her when she turned up back at the Baldwin Brothers mill, asking for work. He shoved the record book across the desk and she wrote the first name she thought of: Calliope Cole.

Each time someone says the name she startles, because she hasn't heard her mother's name since she was a girl. She gains a reputation in the mill as being flighty, perhaps a little simple.

She doesn't mind. She keeps to herself, the way she used to before this summer of sisters and witching. The mill-girls are content to ignore her.

Or at least most of them are. Yulia offered her a friendly, knuckle-grinding handshake on her first day, then squinted hard at the familiar gray of her eyes. "Ha," she grunted. "It's clever, using a different name. We should find a new meeting house, too, yes?"

Agnes shrugged. "I suppose you should. I wish you luck."

Agnes watched Yulia's face curl from confusion to disdain. "I see. They locked my girl up for a week, fed her stale bread and rancid butter, and *she* is not afraid."

Agnes refrained from saying anything untoward—like *Good for her* or *She should be* or *What about you? Aren't you afraid for your daughter?*—and eventually Yulia left her alone.

She must have told the other Sisters not to bother with Agnes, because after that they turn their backs to her as she passes, noses high. Only Annie Flynn still offers her the occasional cordial nod. Once she even stopped Agnes in the alleyway to invite her to the first meeting of the Sisters since the disaster of the third spectacle. "Your sisters will be there, I heard."

"Tell them... Give them my love."

"I will." Her gentleness was somehow worse than Yulia's derision. "My cousin has been looking for you. May I tell him where to find you?"

Agnes made a jerky, uncertain gesture that might have been a nod.

She's staying now at Three Blessings Boarding House, which smells exactly as cabbagey as South Sybil but costs two cents less a night. She might have paid extra for a private room, except that she'd taken her carefully hoarded coin jars to the cemetery and left them beside the golden tree. They were gone the next day.

The following night Agnes found her jars returned to her window ledge. Instead of coins they were full of thistleseed and salt and feathers, with tight-rolled scraps of paper tucked in the lids. She unrolled them to find words and ways written in her oldest sister's neat script: spells for sending messages by mockingbird and binding wounds, for soothing fussing babies and getting milk-stains out of shirt-fronts, for "keeping the shadows at bay." Agnes read that last one several times before she cast salt and thistle across her threshold and whispered the words. Afterward she stuffed the little scraps of paper beneath her mattress. She keeps meaning to burn them—what if the boarding house is raided? What if one of the other girls finds them?—but she never does.

At night she dreams of sisters; during the day she tries hard to forget them.

It's difficult to forget when every story in the city—every rumor, every whispered conversation, every article—seems to be about them: the girls who busted out of prison, the woman who turned her husband into a pig, the witch doctor still running loose. But those were merely the stories witnessed by a sufficient number of people to be printed in the papers. Agnes hears dozens of less credible stories: colics cured and bones mended; lightning called and locks picked; machines busted and debts forgotten. None of the women appear to have any difficulty working the spells they are given. Agnes wonders if their witch-blood was awakened somehow by the return of the Lost Way, or if witch-blood never mattered much in the first place. She wonders what theories Bella and Quinn are working on and if Juniper has earned her familiar yet, if the Sisters are planning any more spectacles and if Gideon Hill has spies among them—

The baby thumps inside her. *Never mind, baby girl. It's just you and me.*

By the beginning of July the mill is so hot four girls faint before noon. At five Agnes lines up with the other girls, their cheeks boiled red, their hair slicked to their necks. Even Mr. Malton hardly has the energy to pinch or leer, but merely sits, fanning himself and sweating whiskey.

Agnes passes him with her head down, sewer-colored hair draped in front of her face.

She steps into the alley and takes a single breath of clean summer air.

"Agnes! Is that you?" Mr. August Lee is waiting for her, sleeves rolled to his elbows, hair tousled gold. He's blinking uncertainly at Agnes's hair and pox-marks.

She dips her head to him. "It's Calliope, if you please, sir," she says, but she meets his eyes with her own, thunder-gray, and relief spreads over his face.

He takes two steps forward, swaying as if he wants to step closer but doesn't quite dare. "Of course. My mistake. Listen, I was hoping we could talk."

"About what?"

"I only wanted to apologize. And help, maybe."

Agnes knows she should tell him and his tousled hair to leave her alone, to go home and forget her name, but it's been so long since she's spoken to anyone but the fleas in her mattress. She nods once and takes the arm he offers.

The evening is thick and blue. It's too hot to remain indoors for long, so the occupants of the West Babel tenements are crowded on stoops and balconies, summer-drunk. Several of them greet Mr. Lee by name; a few of them watch the sway of Agnes's belly and raise their eyebrows at him. He doesn't seem to care.

Mr. Lee steers her three blocks west to a pair of double doors, through which a great deal of noise and music and light are pouring out. Agnes arches her brow at him. "I'm in no condition for dancing, Mr. Lee."

"Of course, Miss Calliope. But no one will overhear us here."

They settle at a table in the dimmest corner of the dance hall, nearly invisible beneath the haze of tobacco and ether. Mr. Lee seems content simply to watch her in silence, his hands pressed to the frost of his beer glass, until she asks, "Why are you here, Mr. Lee? I thought you'd be back in Chicago, by now."

He looks out at the press and swirl of bodies and doesn't answer directly. "I grew up in West Babel, did you know that? My folks split a room with Annie and her family—twelve of us packed like fish into two rooms. My father worked for Boyle's, over in the Sallows." Boyle's is a meat-packing factory crouched on the west side of the Thorn, all grease and offal and missing fingers. "People said he was a fighter, but he wasn't really. He was a dreamer, always on about the eight-hour day and workers' rights and utopia. It's just that dreamers generally wind up fighting. He started having men over to our place, drawing up charters... He was a half-step away from a real union when they got him."

"Who got him?" Agnes doesn't know why he's telling her all this, but she likes the warmth of his voice when he mentions his father. She wonders what it would feel like to mourn your daddy rather than merely outlive him.

Lee takes a drink, sets his glass precisely back in the damp ring it left behind. "Boyle's men, we think. They said it was an accident, that he was fooling around on the line. But we saw him, after. I don't know how a man could contrive to hang himself on a meat hook without a little help." Another drink, much longer. Agnes wants to cover his hand with hers. She presses her fingers flat to the table. "Lawyers from the plant came to see us a few days after. They asked my mother to sign some papers swearing that her husband's death had been his own doing. They sat at our kitchen table and handed her a pen. She looked at me— I was fourteen, old enough to know the truth—and then she looked away. She signed their paper and that was that.

"I wasn't at home if I could help it, after. I fell in with Dad's old friends, went looking for trouble. Found some, in Chicago." He rubs the scar along his jaw. "And it was—well, it was awful, to tell the truth. Uglier and meaner than I thought it would be. But it was grand, too, to be part of something. To find a fight worth having."

There's an earnestness in his voice that makes him sound young and desperately naive; Agnes wonders if he's a dreamer, too. She asks again, lower, "So why are you still here?"

That sweet smile, hitched sideways by his scar. "Because I found an even bigger fight, I guess." His eyes flash up to hers. "And a woman who won't look away."

Her stomach sours with shame. *Wouldn't I, August?* Agnes doesn't say anything for a long time, digging her thumbnail into the soft wood of the table and thinking about when to fold and when to fight. She realizes her thumb is sketching three woven circles and stops.

"When is she due?" Lee is looking at the dent where her belly presses against the table.

"Barley Moon. The midwife says she's big, though, so it could be sooner." Agnes doesn't mention the flutter of fear in her belly, the memory of her mother's skin whiter than wax. Maybe Mama Mags could have saved her, but maybe not. Mags told her once their family lost more women to the birthing bed than they did men to the battlefield.

Lee's voice goes a little lower, almost fearful. "Who was he?"

It takes Agnes a long minute to understand who he's referring to; she hasn't thought twice about Floyd Matthews all summer. "Nobody. A nice boy from uptown."

"Did you love him?" She can tell by the braced shape of his shoulders that the question matters a great deal to him; she wishes it didn't.

"No, August. I didn't love him." His whole body seems to exhale. "But the more interesting question is: did he love me?"

"Did he love you?" he asks obediently. There's a puzzled crease between his brows.

"Only some of me. And I'm tired of making do with some, with half-measures."

Agnes watches his mouth open and close and then open again, and she's suddenly sure he's on the verge of making some declaration or vow because he thinks, poor fool, that he loves all of her. Because he doesn't know how cold and cruel she is beneath the softness of her skin, doesn't know the anything-at-all she would do to survive.

She stands up from the table, pushing her chair back. "I'd have done the same thing your mother did." She aims it like a slap, and he rocks back with the force of it. "Did you never think what would have happened if she'd fought? How easy it is for lawyers to take a child away from a woman alone? Did you never think what it must have cost to choose her living son over her dead husband?"

She sees from the sudden white of his face that he never has.

"Sometimes you can't fight. Sometimes you can only survive."

He swallows once. "And yet you're still fighting."

Agnes draws her half-cloak back over her shoulders. "If you and your boys want to help the Sisters, talk to Annie or Yulia. Not me."

"Wait—why? What are you doing?"

She looks back once before she leaves, a last greedy glance at the tangle of his hair and the angle of his scar. "Surviving."

Juniper is a ghost, these days.

She is a silhouette on the windowsill, an apparition in the alley, a woman there and gone again. She is a pocketful of witch-ways and a voice whispering the right words to the right woman, the clack of a cane against cobbles.

She is rarely out in daylight, and she finds she likes the city better by night. It's stranger and wilder, full of soft voices and scurrying feet. It reminds her of running the mountainside after dark, surefooted and free, certain that if she ran fast enough she would become a doe or a vixen, anything but a girl.

Now she runs along alleys rather than deer trails and ducks beneath laundry-lines rather than pine boughs. Now she runs *toward* rather than away, and she no longer runs alone.

There are fewer Sisters of Avalon than there once were—some of them were caught, some of them left town a half-skip ahead of the law, some of them were just scared—and they no longer have anything like headquarters. Instead they meet wherever they may: an attic above a hat shop that smells of glue and felt; Inez's gilded parlor, where they drink wine from golden goblets and laugh themselves sick; a church basement that makes Juniper's heart race in her throat.

Juniper and Bella bring the Sisters spells written out in plain English and the words disappear up sleeves and down boots. Later they are whispered by those who can read to those who can't; stitched into handkerchiefs and hems; tucked into the pages of romance novels so frivolous that no man is likely to touch them. In return the Sisters give them bread and soft-baked potatoes, hot pies wrapped in dish towels, baskets of apples. They don't ask where the Eastwoods live or how they disappear so thoroughly that neither the police nor the angry mobs—nor those eerie, unnatural shadows—can find them. They look at Juniper and Bella with shining eyes, waiting for the next trick, the next miracle, the next proof that witching has returned.

For tonight's miracle, Juniper requires help.

She strides down a dark street, leaning on the slender cane that is the piss-poor replacement for her cedar staff, and two women walk beside her: a young nurse named Lacey Rawlins who works at St. Charity Hospital, and Miss Jennie Lind.

Jennie had turned up at the Sisters' last meeting, looking—different. Her skirts were fancier and frothier than Juniper remembered, and she wore a chestnut wig instead of her own cornsilk-colored hair, but mostly it was her eyes that struck Juniper. They were colder and harder, like twice-beaten iron.

"Where the hell have you been?" Juniper asked, thumping her so hard on the back that Jennie coughed a little.

"They sent me to a...different workhouse, then released me into the custody of my family. Took me a while to get away." She looked over Juniper's shoulder and smiled at Inez. "Inez gave me a place to stay, and all this." Jennie gestured at her fine skirts.

Juniper hadn't said anything then, but she'd had herself a little think about it later. Why would Jennie be sent someplace different than all the other girls? And why would she be released without trial?

Before the Sisters left that evening she pulled Jennie aside. "Are you, by chance, the daughter of some fabulously wealthy member of New Salem society? Who pulled strings to spring you the second you got caught? And who you have now broken ties with?"

Jennie blinked at her once, then murmured, "Oh, we broke ties a long time ago." She fingered her crooked nose.

"Huh. Well, next time you're home steal a couple of candlesticks for us. We could use the cash."

A genuine smile. "Yes, ma'am."

Now Jennie follows behind Lacey as they creep through the doubled iron doors of St. Charity Hospital.

It looks nice enough inside—halls of green tile and white plaster, rows of doors with neat-painted numbers—except there don't seem to be any windows. The smell turns Juniper's stomach: lye and lesions, stained sheets and stale air.

Lacey pauses before a door at the end of the hall. Juniper tries not to look very closely at the smears of rust and yellow on its surface. She can almost feel the heat of fevered bodies behind it. "Ready?" Lacey asks, and they are.

They work three spells that night.

The first is for sleep, requiring crushed lavender and an old prayer. *Now I lay thee down to sleep.* Only when the rustling of bodies falls still do they creep through the door and into the sick ward.

The second spell is for driving down a fever, requiring a red thread tied around fingers slack with sleep. Juniper and the others move from bed to bed to bed, endless doubled lines of them, occupied by women and children and ruddy-cheeked men. This strikes Juniper as strange—surely any natural illness ought to fall hardest on the youngest and oldest.

The third spell is for healing, requiring willowbark and silkweed and knocked knuckles. This one proves more difficult than the others. Juniper hisses the words, veins hot with witching, and feels them vanish into the air, as if swallowed down some cold, invisible throat.

A chill creeps up Juniper's spine. She looks at the dark twist of shadows and wonders if somehow Gideon is watching her even now, if he's working against this small act of mercy.

Juniper had asked around about Gideon Hill and found his life bafflingly ordinary. As a boy he went by his first name—Whitt or Wart or something equally unfortunate—and spent his time reading novels and daydreaming. Then his favorite uncle passed away, leaving him a considerable sum of money and a pitiful black dog, and Hill had sobered considerably. There was no missing interlude of years when he might have disappeared to study ancient magics in the libraries of Old Cairo, no wicked grandmother who might have passed on her witching; no indication at all that Hill was anything but a balding, middle-aged gentleman who wanted to be mayor.

Now Juniper grits her teeth and speaks the spell again. She bends her will against whatever-it-is that opposes them, joining hands with Jennie and Lacey, and the magic burns reluctantly into the room. Lungs clear around her, bruises fade from beneath tired eyes, pulses steady.

Juniper grins at the bodies now sleeping soft and well in their cots, leaning heavily on her spindly cane. She can already hear the headlines shouted by news-boys tomorrow (WITCHCRAFT WORKS MIRACLES! FEVERS CURED!).

She limps into the night with her Sisters at her side.

SIGNS OF WITCHCRAFT AT CHARITY; FEVER WORSENS

July 12th, 1893, *The New Salem Post*

Miss Verity Kendrick-Johnson, a spokesperson for St. Charity Hospital, has confirmed to *The Post* that the patients of the first floor ward were found with definitive signs of witchcraft about their persons, and denied that any member of their staff would have participated in such devilry.

Miss Kendrick-Johnson further advises people seeking miracles to look elsewhere; none of the bewitched patients have shown the slightest signs of improvement. Their condition may in fact have worsened, and several of the weakest patients have since passed away. "Put your faith in science and the study of man," recommends Kendrick-Johnson. "Not stardust and sin."

ARREST MADE IN CONNECTION WITH THE PORTER CASE

July 6th, 1893, *The Times of Salem*

...the police have taken Miss Claudia Porter into custody in connection to the disappearance of her husband, Mr. Grayson Porter. Mr. Porter, a respected member of the Rotary Club and benefactor to this very publication, has been missing since the 25th of June. "Check the stockyards," Miss Porter reportedly advised her arresting officers, cackling, "It takes a pig to find one."

NEW LEADERSHIP NEEDED

July 15th, 1893, a letter to the editor of *The Post*

In light of the daily headlines about malfeasance and witchcraft running loose—in light of Mayor Worthington's failure to produce even a single one of the Eastwoods—it seems clear to this letter writer that the city of New Salem is in need of new leadership. I call upon the Mayor to step down from his post, that we might elect a brighter light against our present darkness.

    Sincerely,

    Bartholomew Webb

25

Hush little baby, don't say a word,
Mother will call you by mockingbird.

A spell to send a message, requiring a mockingbird pinion & a
great need

Over the following weeks Agnes doesn't think of Mr. Lee at all. She doesn't look hopefully down the alley at the end of every shift; she doesn't feel anything in particular when Mr. Malton flips the page of his calendar to the correct month, or let her eyes linger overlong on the capital lettering at the top (AUGUST). The trick to being nothing is to want nothing.

The shift bell rings. Agnes lines up with the other girls, treasuring the way Mr. Malton's eyes skip right past her sewer-colored hair and scarred-up face. They fall instead on the girl behind her in line.

The girl started just a few days ago. She's nothing, too, but not the right kind. She's young and hungry-looking, bones raw beneath cream-colored skin. Agnes can practically smell the desperation rolling off her.

So can Mr. Malton. "You. Ona." He picks her from the line like a housewife choosing a chicken at the market. "Come back to my office for a moment."

Mr. Malton saunters to the back of the mill, keys jangling on his hip, and Agnes stops in the doorway, jaw gritted, willing Ona not to follow him.

Ona's eyes cross hers once, flint-black, and then she trails after him like a lamb behind the butcher.

Agnes looks away. It isn't hard; she's had years of practice. She simply turns her head aside and walks on, with Mama Mags's voice in her ears: *Every woman draws a circle around her heart.*

She can't seem to make herself step out into the alley. She's caught on the threshold, too stupid to leave, not quite stupid enough to turn back. Instead of Mags's voice she hears her sister's: *Don't leave me.* She thinks of Mr. Lee, in love with a woman who won't look away.

Agnes turns around. Maybe because there are witch-ways burning in her pockets, or because her own daughter might grow up to look a little like Ona. Or because she is a damn fool.

Mr. Malton's office door is locked. Agnes whispers to it and the latch rusts to nothing in her hand.

The room smells of shoe polish and alcohol. Ona is perched on the meanest edge of her seat, shoulders set, her eyes obsidian. Malton looms over her, one hand on his desk, the other on the back of her chair.

He looks up at the squeal of hinges, the faint patter of rust on the floor. His lip curls at the sight of Agnes with her pox scars and her swollen belly.

"What the hell do you think you're doing?"

"Leave," Agnes tells the girl in the chair. She can see from the resentful flick of Ona's eyes that she's resigned to doing what she has to, and that she doesn't care to have it witnessed. "*Now,* girl," Agnes growls, and Ona slips around her and vanishes into the mill, a raw-boned shadow.

Malton is staring, slack-jawed. He turns to Agnes with an ugly gleam growing in his eyes, a lust that has nothing to do with want. "Care to explain yourself?"

Agnes takes a twist of her hair between her fingers and hisses the words. The false color melts away, her pox scars fade, and she stands before him wearing her true face once more. "Good afternoon, Mr. Malton."

He jerks so violently he falls backward into the chair. Agnes thinks how quickly she might grow used to men flinching rather than flirting.

Malton gapes at her, fishlike, before gasping, "Begone, witch!" and fumbling for the silver cross beneath his shirt.

Agnes tuts at him. "Pretty sure that only works on vampires." She leans closer, enjoying the way he presses himself against the office wall, as if she has a deadly nimbus around her body. "If you scream, I swear they'll find a pig wearing your suit when they come running."

She doesn't technically have the ways to work the spell, but it hardly matters. She can tell from the panicked bulge of his eyes and the dry bob of his throat that he believes her. She is a witch, and a witch's words have weight.

"Very good. Stay put." She steps around him, rustling through drawers until she produces a sheet of paper and a pen. She writes a short list, tapping her chin briefly with the pen, then rummaging in her pockets for a dry curl of bindweed.

She circles back to face Mr. Malton. "If you want to leave this office on two feet rather than four, you will do three things for me." She raises one finger. "First, you will speak of this to no one."

Malton whimpers.

"Second, you will issue every person in your employ a raise of a dime a day, effective immediately."

The whimper goes higher.

"And third—and listen to this part very closely—you will never touch an unwilling woman again, in this mill or outside of it, for as long as your miserable life shall last."

His whimper is now so thin and high it could be mistaken for a boiling kettle.

"Now, swear to it." She coaches him, stuttering and stumbling, through her three conditions. Then she stabs the pen into the sweating meat of his thumb and presses bindweed to the blood. "Mark it on the page and repeat after me."

His voice is a thin warble as he says the words. *Cross my heart and hope to die, strike me down if I lie.*

The sweet heat of witching slicks through Agnes's veins like whiskey. Oh, how she missed it, the drunken drumbeat of power in her chest, the thrill of working her will onto the world.

The muscles of her belly tighten, a ripple of not-quite pain. Agnes hardly feels it.

"If you break any of these vows, your heart will stop in your chest and you will fall down dead, and neither Heaven nor Hell will let your cursed spirit enter." This is a bald-faced lie, but Mr. Malton goes white as cotton. "So behave yourself."

The air outside the mill is gentle and golden with five o'clock sun. The light doesn't seem to come from anywhere in particular, as if the city itself emits a faint sepia glow. The wind that trickles down the alley is cool for summer, smelling of fallen leaves and char, and Agnes wants suddenly to follow it all the way back to the dark tower where her sisters are waiting.

Her belly ripples again, a little stronger, and she rests a palm against it. She's wondering if she ought to worry, if perhaps witching isn't healthy for a womb this far along—when warm wetness trickles down her thigh.

Oh hell.

She stumbles backward, bracing a hand against the brick as a bright peal of pain tolls through her. The wetness trickles faster.

Madame Zina's is nine blocks north and west. Agnes closes her eyes very briefly.

She pulls the hood of her half-cloak over her face, tucking the dark shine of her hair beneath it. She hobbles north, not thinking of the wet-pearl sheen of her mother's skin or the wrong-thing in her daddy's face as he watched her, or of all the dead mothers in Mama Mags's stories.

She thinks instead of her sisters, of June's face as she felt the kick of her niece against her hand.

She's coming, June.

Bella is alone in the tower when she feels it: a tremor of pain echoing down the line from somewhere into nowhere. *Agnes.*

She is sitting cross-legged on one of the tower landings, reading in the last light of the autumn dusk, her black notebook held open by a tin cup of coffee. The pain echoes in her empty womb, spreads up her spine.

It might be nothing. Bella knows women often have false pains toward the end, and that Agnes isn't due until the Barley Moon. But the pain has a certain weight to it, a portentous taste like thunderclouds gathering. Bella finds her fingers straying to a shelf several feet away, where a brass label reads *Birthing—early, breeched, stillborn.*

The pain comes again, a little louder.

Bella gathers an armful of books from the birthing shelf and spirals back down the stairs to the first floor. Without precisely thinking about what she's doing or why, she begins to flick through the texts, gathering ways and making notes. Clean linens and jasmine flowers. A silver bell and powder-white shells. A gnarled tooth smaller than a pearl.

She waits. The pain finds a rhythm, cresting and falling. Bella circles the tower, straightening shelves that don't need straightening, trying to feel through the line whether Agnes is alone or with friends, scared or safe.

Somewhere above her she feels the heat of red eyes watching her.

"It's fine, Strix. I'm sure she's fine." Her voice has a thinness to it, like the first fragile stretch of ice across the Big Sandy. She wishes Quinn were here.

The air twists in a way that means someone has arrived at the tower door. It opens, and a wild-haired silhouette limps inside, cane tapping the flagstones.

Bella knows from the pale green of Juniper's eyes that she feels it, too, that she's worried. "Should we go to her?" Bella whispers it.

Juniper rolls her head back and forth. "She knows where to find us, if she wants us."

"Yes."

Bella perches at a workbench. Juniper circles the tower in her rolling gait. Strix watches from above.

Eventually Juniper trails to a halt and sits beside Bella on the bench. Her hand brushes not quite accidentally against Bella's and Bella holds it. They wait together for the next peal of pain.

Agnes knows before she knocks that Madame Zina will not answer. The door hangs crooked in its frame and the curtain-rod is slanted across the window. Someone has drawn an ashen X across the glass.

Agnes knocks anyway, because she doesn't know what else to do. Because she walked nine blocks with her thighs chafing and her stomach clenching and unclenching like a fist, and a shiver is starting in her spine.

The door swings inward at her touch. Beyond it the room is dark and tumbled, a nest of toppled jars and strewn herbs. Maybe Zina ran before they came for her, or maybe she's shackled in the Deeps, but she sure as hell isn't here. There are other midwives on the west side, but so many of them have moved or closed up shop—

The pain swells, crests, fades. It's hard to think anything in its wake except animal thoughts: run, hide, go home. But Agnes doesn't have a home, just a narrow bunk at Three Blessings Boarding House with a few spells stuffed beneath the mattress.

She thinks for no reason of Avalon: that black tower, star-crowned, and the endless spiral of books. *You know where to find us*, Bella told her before she left.

Agnes finds her feet moving before she knows where they're carrying her.

She doesn't count the blocks as she walks back east. She merely sets her jaw and keeps going, feeling the bubble and burst of blisters on her feet, the bloody chafe of her thighs. The pain comes more often now and lingers longer, and she is obliged to stop and press her back against the warm brick while passersby cast her looks of concern and alarm. She keeps her hood pulled high.

The New Salem cemetery is locked after sundown, but the gate is open, swinging loose on its hinges. Agnes looks at it, swaying where she stands, feeling the same way she felt when she saw Zina's crooked door. *No.*

There are men thronging the graveyard, their expressions both urgent and vacant, shovels and lit torches in their hands. They seem to be gathered at the witch-yard, shuffling and laboring around a vast, gleaming tangle. It takes a long second for Agnes to recognize it as the roots of a golden tree, ripped up.

No, no, no. The earth around the tree is churned and torn and wrong in some way that Agnes doesn't understand. She stares, swaying a little, until she realizes that none of the gathered men seem to cast a shadow across it.

Agnes wheels away, hands flying to her hood. She walks blindly, taking turns at random, trying to think of someplace to run or someone to run to, but the pain returns and she finds herself on her knees in the middle of a nameless street, thinking, *There's no time*.

She knows it as if there's a wound clock somewhere in the center of her, ticking away seconds. The baby is coming too fast and she is crouched here like an animal with nowhere to go, no one to help her. She drew her circle too tight.

She fumbles in her pocket and finds a pair of silver-brown feathers, their edges ruffled and split. She stares at them for far too long, trying to remember what they might mean, what she might do with them—before the pain sends her thoughts running for cover again.

When it subsides she's still holding the feathers. She remembers the words to an old lullaby written in her sister's tidy hand: *Hush little baby, don't say a word, Mother will call you by mockingbird.*

Agnes whispers the words to the feathers in her hand, along with a name, and feels the fever-flick of witchcraft under her skin. The feathers flutter upward, caught by an uncanny wind, and vanish into the falling night.

Agnes doesn't know if the message will find him, or if he will answer, or if she is a fool to trust the fickle heart of a man—but the pain comes to chase the worries away.

Time behaves strangely after that. It skitters forward then leaps out of sight, leaving her stranded in her own private eternity. She knows she ought to stand up, run, find shelter, but all she can do is curl over her belly and hiss curses between her teeth.

Footsteps. A concerned voice. "Are you all right, miss?"

Agnes tries to say she's fine, thank you, just resting, but the words are lost in a moan.

A hand guides her elbow. Her hood slips aside as she stands, and she hears a sharp gasp. "Oh, Saints preserve us—you're—"

Someone shouts her true name down the street.

The pain swallows her again. When she emerges the street is full of people and horses and men in black uniforms. "Agnes Amaranth Eastwood! You are hereby under arrest for the crime of witchcraft!"

Rough hands roll her onto a canvas stretcher, and shackles snap around her wrists. Agnes fights, writhing and kicking, pulling so hard against her cuffs that something pops wetly in her wrist, but it does her no good.

She falls back, panting, and hears voices conferring. They use words like *hysterical* and *agitated*, and then one of the men is pressing a foul-smelling rag across her mouth.

The street goes gray and distant, as if she is peering up at it from the bottom of an empty well. Her limbs are slack against the canvas even as the pain spreads its sulfurous wings above her. Voices are still speaking around her, but none of the syllables seem to add up to words anymore.

Agnes lolls as they load her stretcher into the back of a cart. She doesn't understand, doesn't know where they're taking her—until a woman in a starched apron leans over her and Agnes reads the words stitched across the breast in bold capitals: ST. CHARITY HOSPITAL.

Something is wrong and Juniper knows it. She can taste her sister's terror through the line between them, feel the tarry black of despair.

Juniper lets go of Bella's hand. She grabs a lead pitcher full of water and empties it onto the flagstone floor, ignoring Bella's squawk. She kneels, the water soaking through the loose weave of her skirt while she waits for it to go still.

She's supposed to have a possession of Agnes's to work the spell properly, but she doesn't care. Surely there's enough of Agnes in her all the time—in her blood and bones, in the stubborn streak they share, in all the hours of their sisterhood.

Mirror, mirror, on the wall.

Juniper feels Bella peering over her shoulder, sharing her will. A picture shimmers to the surface of the water: Agnes, lying slack against too-white sheets in a too-white room, her hair a black pool behind her head. Her skirts are rucked carelessly to the waist, her legs gelid and still, somehow indecent. Her face is perfectly serene, half drowsing; the only sign of distress is the occasional ripple of her belly, a tightness that shudders through limp limbs, and the clawing, terrible black of her half-lidded eyes.

There are other people in the room with her, their faces blurred, their motions shadowed. Juniper sees the shake of a head, a dismissive wave of a hand. One of them steps to the side and Juniper sees the shackles around her sister's wrists.

The water ripples as Bella takes a horrified step backward. She whispers *oh no, oh no* in a useless chant.

Juniper stands, shouldering past her. "I'm going."

"Then they'll have both of you!" Bella's voice is a wobbling wail. "What do you think will happen if you go charging into a hospital room?"

Juniper meets her sister's eyes and wavers. She doesn't want to go back down in the Deeps. She doesn't want to feel the unnatural cold of a witch-collar or the oily slide of shadows.

But she can't leave Agnes and her baby tied up and hurting. She can't even frame the choice properly in her head.

Neither can Bella, not really. Juniper sees it in the resigned droop of her head. "Let me gather a few spells, at least."

Juniper doesn't wait. She tugs the tower door open and presses her palm to the three woven-together circles. She says the words and thinks of the golden tree, as she has a dozen times before.

Nothing happens.

Nothing continues to happen.

"Bella," Juniper says, quite calmly. "How come I can't get out of this damn tower?"

Bella scurries nearer. "It can only mean the sign is gone. The circle back in New Salem must be broken."

They look at one another for a long moment, before Juniper says, "So you're saying we're—"

"Trapped. Yes." The Lost Way of Avalon is a ship cut loose from its anchor, drifting through nowhere, while Agnes is stuck back in somewhere.

There's a heavy silence, during which it becomes clear that Bella isn't about to leap to her feet and shout *aha!* and save them all.

Juniper limps back to the pool of water and crouches down beside it, looking down into the dark well of her sister's eyes. Juniper recognizes the thing she sees there: the despair of a woman trapped good and proper, who knows no one is coming to save her.

26

Dance, little baby, dance up high,
Never mind, baby, Mother is by.
Crow and caper, caper and crow,
Stay, little star, and don't let go.

A spell to steady a life, requiring hyacinth & a seven-
pointed star

Agnes Amaranth knows what childbirth is supposed to be like. She's heard the talk from young mothers working beside her in the mill, the girls back in Crow County who hadn't gone to Mama Mags for help. There's pain, they said, pain like cleaving open, like breaking in half, but there are other women there to help you bear it. Aunts and midwives, grannies and sisters, mothers to press cool palms against your forehead and hum half-forgotten lullabies in your ears.

You aren't supposed to be alone. You aren't supposed to be locked in a green-tiled room, chained and drugged, with nothing but the dull grate of men's voices for company. A doctor with his sleeves rolled to the wrist, his hands bare and pink and somehow repellent, grime crusted beneath his nails; an assistant or two with towels slung over their shoulders and nameless stains spattering their aprons; a pair of men in uniforms, who look down at her like she is a prize they intend to stuff and mount on their mantels. A nurse flits among them sometimes, young and sorry-looking as she sweeps and straightens.

The pain is still there, cutting like a clarion call through the fog, but Agnes can't answer it. She can only lie there with spittle trailing from the corner of her mouth, clawing like an animal inside the cage of her body. She counts ceiling tiles to distract herself. She prays. She tells herself witch-tales, but the missing mothers seem to taunt her, wailing from the margins while their daughters sleep in the cinders and flee into tangled woods and marry beastly husbands.

The pain comes again, urgent and vast, and Agnes feels her body straining and failing at some important task. Then the foreign scrape of fingers inside her, probing, pulling, conducting some secret evaluation and finding her wanting.

A sigh from the doctor, precisely like Mr. Malton sighing over a jammed loom. Agnes imagines her blood replaced with oil, her joints with gears; a misbehaving machine instead of a woman.

The doctor addresses the officers, rather than Agnes. "There's been no progression at all. We'll want to think about extraction, if you boys want her to survive to stand trial." One of the assistants rattles in a metal cart behind him and produces a long silver object. From the corner of her eye Agnes catches the ugly curve of a hook.

She thrashes against her shackles, her wild scream reduced to a choked moan. None of them look at her, except the nurse, whose eyes are huge and sad, her hands tight on the handle of her broom.

Agnes wants to bite her. She wants to claw and curse them all, to bring all the centuries of Avalon crashing down on their heads—but she walked away from all that, convinced the cost of power was too high, failing to calculate the cost of being without it.

She wonders if her sisters feel the echo of her toothless rage. She wonders if they would come to her, if they could.

Agnes feels her eyes widen, very slightly.

She finds that, if she focuses every ounce of fury into her left hand, she can curl her nails into her own flesh. She can drive them deep into her own palm until blood wells ruby-bright. She can unclench her hand and let the blood trickle to the point of her dangling finger and draw a blotched shape on the sheet beneath her: a red circle. She can even whisper the words, though her tongue is limp and wet in her mouth.

She can pray that her sisters are watching.

Juniper watches her sister's skin turn from ivory to alabaster to wax. Her features remain slack, but her fingers are curled into her own palm just above the ugly iron of her shackle. Agnes's fist clenches so tightly Juniper sees the dark gleam of blood gathering.

She flinches away. "We've got to get there somehow, Bell. Call the tower back into the square, if you have to. Undo the binding." But that would leave the library exposed and send every police officer and zealot into the streets to hunt witches. Would they even make it to Agnes before they were caught?

She expects Bella to object, to cling to her books like a mother protecting several thousand of her favorite children, but when she looks up she sees that Bella is, inexplicably, smiling. Her eyes are on the pool of water.

"I don't think that will be necessary. Look."

Juniper looks.

The red gleam beneath Agnes's fingernails has become a fistful of blood. One finger is extended, stretching at a painful angle, smearing the bed-sheet with shocking crimson. The finger moves slowly, as if it requires all Agnes's strength to keep it in motion, and it takes Juniper a startled moment to see what she has drawn.

A circle. A way where there was none.

"Hold on, Ag." Juniper whispers it to the water. Bella is already filling her arms with glass jars and paper bags, books and notes. Her owl swoops silently to her shoulder and she reaches a hand to stroke its onyx feathers. Juniper thinks she looks like a proper witch from one of Mags's stories, about to curse her enemies or ride a thundercloud into battle.

They return to the tower door and this time when they press their palms to the carved sign they think of Agnes and her circle of blood, the red path she drew them through the dark.

The tower vanishes.

Agnes is alone.

Until she isn't.

The air of the hospital skews sideways, a dizzy rushing, and afterward there are two hands pressed to the bloody circle on her bed-sheet. One of them is long and narrow, the fingertips stained with ink; the other is wide, sun-brown, marked with pale scars from thorns and thickets.

Her sisters.

Who were watching, who came when she called.

They stand above her like a matched pair of Old Testament angels, the kind with flaming swords and vengeful hearts. Stories spin through Agnes's head again, except this time she isn't thinking of the dead mothers or their lost daughters. She's thinking about the witches—the women who dispensed the glass slippers and curses and poison apples, who wreaked their wills on the world and damned the consequences.

There is a moment of crystalline silence while the gathered men stare at the three women and the black owl. Then comes Bella's voice, perfectly calm, and the sharp smell of herbs crushed between fingers. A wicked crack splits the air, very much like a small bone snapping.

The police officers fall sideways, clutching at their ribs and howling. The doctor lunges for Juniper, but she's already holding the hospital push broom in her hands. The handle cracks across his face with an unpleasant crunch. Bella whispers again and a heavy drowsiness descends on the room. The pair of assistants crumple to the floor and the howling officers fall silent.

The ward is quiet except for the heavy drag of bodies being hauled across the floor. The doctor rouses once, voice rising in a high whine. There are a few more thuds of broom-handle on flesh and he falls quiet.

Bella *tsk*s. "Honestly, Juniper. The sleeping spell would have done just as well."

"Sure." Agnes can hear Juniper's shrug in her voice, followed by a final, satisfied thwack of the broomstick.

Bella chants over Agnes's head—*Soundly she sleeps beneath bright skies, Agnes Amaranth awake, arise!*—and gives a sharp whistle.

The drug lifts from Agnes like a rising fog. She pants relief, limbs seizing against the chains. She cranes her neck upward and sees the sorry-eyed nurse holding open the narrow door of what looks like a supply closet while Juniper stuffs the limp bodies inside it. "Now go tell them the doctor doesn't want any interruptions—or better yet, take this." Juniper hands the nurse a small canvas sack. "You remember the words? Once you work it, hightail it home. With my thanks, Lacey."

Agnes wants to ask how they know one another and if every damn woman in this city is a witch, but another roll of pain sends her elsewhere, inward-facing, blind.

When it passes, her sisters are hovering above her. Their hands are gentle on hers, unbending her blood-gummed fingers, and their eyes are so full of love and worry that Agnes feels the pain receding a little. An owl calls from somewhere, a soft crooning that makes Agnes think of full-moon nights back home.

"We're here now." Juniper's voice is low and smoke-streaked, as soft as she can make it. "Bella's spelled the door and Lacey's sent half the hospital straight to sleep. It'll be all right."

"I shouldn't have—I should have—" Agnes's tongue is still slow, her speech slurred. "The doctor said the baby wasn't coming, that she would have to be *extracted*."

Bella tuts, setting glass jars in a neat line on the bedside table and clutching her black leather notebook. "I'm sure he did. But I remind you that he was merely a man. Whereas we"—she looks over her spectacles at Agnes and gives her a very small smile—"are witches."

Bella opens a heavy tome titled *Obstetrix Magna* and smooths the pages with a slightly shaking hand, wishing she felt as certain as she sounded. "Juniper, can you take care of these?" She gestures to Agnes's shackles, but Juniper is already chanting her rhyme, *Bend and break, bend and break*, and the chains are blushing red. The iron rusts and flakes, as if several decades of rain and weather have passed in a handful of seconds.

Juniper snaps the chains with vicious glee, the scar around her throat gleaming white.

Agnes pulls her arms inward, cradling her own belly. She doesn't scream or moan, but a low, animal growl leaves her lips. Juniper looks a little wildly at Bella. "Can't you do anything?"

Bella can. She claws through the *Obstetrix Magna*, past alarming illustrations of wombs and veins and infants with small ivory horns or flames for hair. Her fingers find the pages she marked back in the tower, where there are spells to draw fevers from the womb and persuade blood to remain in the body, to ease the pains of labor and steady the heart of the unborn.

"Juniper." Bella fumbles in her brown sack and finds a little tin of black-stained grease. "Draw a seven-pointed star around the bed, if you please."

Juniper daubs the unsteady shape of a star while Bella circles, whispering and chanting. She tucks jasmine flower beneath her tongue and hyacinth in her hair. She rings a silver bell seven times and watches Agnes's body unfurl a little further with each soft peal.

It's a strong working. Bella can tell by the scorch of power in her veins and the hot smell of witching in the air. Juniper's cheeks are flushed red from the effort of helping her, and Strix mantles on her shoulder.

Agnes sighs back down against the sheets, the trapped-animal terror receding from her face. Her gaze is unclouded, lucid for the first time since they arrived. "Thank you," she breathes. "I didn't know if you'd come."

"Jesus, Ag." Juniper shakes her head. "Have a little faith."

"I used to. Until..." Agnes slants a bitter look at Bella.

Juniper says, "That was a long time ago," just as Bella asks, "Until what?"

A contraction doubles Agnes around her belly, lips white, but her gaze stays clear and sharp as a bared blade. "Until—you—*betrayed* me," she pants.

"*I* betrayed *you*?"

"You were the only one I told about the baby. Because you were the only one I trusted." The words are spat poison, meant to wound, but Bella doesn't flinch.

Because they aren't true. Because she and her sister have wasted seven years hating one another for crimes neither one committed.

"Oh, Agnes." Bella's own voice sounds weary in her ears, worn thin by the weight of that single summer afternoon seven years ago. "I never told our daddy a damn thing."

Agnes's face makes Bella think of a ship in a dying wind, sails slack, as if the force that drove her has suddenly disappeared.

"Then how? How did he know?"

"The Adkins boy."

"I never told him shit—"

Bella shakes her head. "He saw you in the woods, afterward." Bella heard his *tap-tap* on their door, and her daddy's hollered answer. Then low voices rising quickly, and that butter-brained boy saying, *I'm sure, sir, I saw her bury it under a hornbeam.* "I think he was hoping if he told

Daddy you'd be cornered into a quick wedding." Bella's lip curls. "He didn't know our daddy. After he left, Daddy went looking for you. I followed."

She thought maybe she could help somehow, but she'd stood paralyzed as her daddy drew closer and closer to Agnes. As Agnes screamed that Bella was a liar, a sinner, an unnatural creature. Her story came out in jumbled sobs—going into the church cellar for fresh candles and finding Bella with the preacher's daughter, half-naked and ruby-lipped, reveling in sin—but even a poorly told story has power. Their father understood. He turned on her, too, and Bella begged—*Please, no, please*—

Bella had met her sister's eyes and seen nothing but a terrible, leaden cold. Hate, she thought then.

Now she thinks of the witch-queen who sent shards of ice into warm hearts and soft eyes, turning them against the ones they loved best. Now she thinks she isn't the only one familiar with betrayal.

"I never told, Agnes. I swear."

Agnes shuts her eyes. "I thought—I didn't—Saints, Bell." A ragged whisper. "What did I do to us?"

"You were just a child." Bella tries to sound measured and calm, as if it is a distant hurt long forgotten, rather than an ice-shard still buried in her breast.

"So were you." Agnes clutches at the hard ball of her belly, breath catching. "I shouldn't have said it. Even if you *had* told, I shouldn't have turned on you." There are tears mingling with the sweat on Agnes's face now, more dripping from the end of Bella's nose. She recalls dizzily that it was true love's tears that melted the ice in the story.

"I'm sorry," Agnes whispers.

"It's all right," Bella whispers back.

Another contraction wracks Agnes before she can answer. Bella can see the pain of it biting deep, even with the witching to ease it, and a tremor of fear moves through her. Perhaps even witching won't be enough.

She smooths sweaty tendrils of hair back from Agnes's brow.

Agnes looks up at her, pale and tired and scared. "Will you stay with me?"

"Yes," Bella answers. In her chest she feels that cold sliver of ice melt into blood-warm water. "Always."

Juniper doesn't know much about birthing, but she knows it shouldn't take this damn long.

She and Bella hover on either side of Agnes like a pair of black-cloaked gargoyles, standing vigil. It seems to go alright at first. Agnes pants and swears and strains against some invisible enemy, the veins blue and taut in her throat. But the baby doesn't come, and each contraction wrings her like a rag, twists something vital out of her. Bella flicks back through her books, hissing and muttering, tossing herbs in ever-wilder circles.

The baby doesn't come.

Agnes is supposed to be the strong one, but Juniper can see they're coming to the end of her strength. Bella is supposed to be the wise one, but she's running out of words. Juniper figures that leaves her, the wild one, with her wild will.

She casts around for anything that might help her sister cling to life, that might bind a woman to the world. The word *bind* rattles like a thrown pebble in her skull, rippling outward, and Juniper thinks: *Why the hell not?*

She plucks a single hair from her head. She tugs another one from Bella. ("Ow! What in the *world*—" "Hush.") The last hair she takes is from Agnes, who doesn't seem to notice.

Juniper twirls the strands in her fingers, three shades of shining black, and twists them into a slender wisp of braid. As she braids she sings the words to herself: *Ashes to ashes, dust to dust.* Little words, old words, to bind a split seam or a stray thread. Why not a life?

Beside her Bella gives a little gasp. "A *binding*? That's—what happens if s-she dies, and takes us with her—"

Juniper ignores her, and eventually Bella shuts the hell up and helps.

They speak the words together, circling round, rising and falling. The thing between them sings like a plucked string. and it's suddenly clear as daylight to Juniper that it's a binding, too, worn thin with time. She might wonder who worked it and why, except that she's busy pouring her whole heart into her witching.

Juniper sees the spell plucking at Agnes, reeling her back toward life, but Agnes doesn't want to come. Her head lolls against the sheets, sweat-sheened, and her eyes glitter from somewhere deep in her skull.

Juniper climbs carefully onto the bed beside her, fitting herself around the heat and hurt of her sister's body. She tucks her cheek in the hollow between Agnes's chin and collar, the way she did as a girl, and keeps speaking the words. *Yours to mine and mine to yours.*

"June. Baby." Agnes's voice is a hum against her cheek, a whisper in her ear. "Take care of her. Promise me you'll take care of her."

The words falter on Juniper's lips; the spell sags. "I promise," she says, and feels the promise weave a circle around her heart, a binding far older and stronger than any witchcraft.

Agnes softens after that, a final surrender.

Juniper thinks of the mornings when Mama Mags would come back from a hard birth with blood beneath her nails and heartache in her eyes. She would stare out at the white curls of mist rising like ghosts from the valley, rubbing her thumb across the brass shine of her locket. *It's just the way of things.*

Juniper is old enough by now to know that the way of things is, generally speaking, horseshit. It's cruelty and loss; locked doors and losing choices; sundered sisters and missing mothers.

What the hell good is witching, if it can't change the way of things?

Juniper puts her lips against the shining dark of her sister's hair and whispers, "Listen to me, Agnes. This isn't how it goes. This isn't how the story ends. All this—me and you and Bell—is just the beginning." A shudder moves through Agnes, a laugh or a sob, but her eyes are closed.

Juniper's arm tightens around Agnes's shoulders and her voice rasps low. "Don't leave me."

Agnes opens her eyes and Juniper sees a spark burning somewhere deep down in the dark of them. Her fingers find Juniper's on one side and Bella's on the other, so they form a circle between them.

Agnes's lips begin to move. *Ashes to ashes, dust to dust—*

Agnes speaks the words until they aren't words anymore. Until they become clasped hands and bound threads, a circle woven from sister to sister to sister. Until the rules of the world bend beneath the weight of their will.

Agnes feels that will thrumming beneath her breastbone, a rush of desire. She wants to live. She wants to stand shoulder-to-shoulder with her sisters and shout a new story into the dark. She wants to look into her daughter's eyes and see Juniper's wildness and Bella's wisdom, the wheel of stars and the snap of flames, all the everything she is and will be shining back at her.

Agnes is aware that she is crying, and that the tears are hissing against her skin. She is aware that the pain is an animal that has slipped its leash, biting and thrashing deep inside her, and that it carries her daughter closer.

That what they are doing—binding three lives together, holding a woman to life even while her pulse stutters and jolts—is an impossible reckless thing that only her dumbshit sister would think of, and that they are doing it anyway. Because she doesn't want to die and they refuse to let her.

That power fills her, scorching her veins and blackening her bones, and it is outside her, too, watching her. Weighing her, this not-yet-mother who will not die, who will break the laws of the universe rather than leave her daughter alone.

Somewhere in the blackness beyond her closed eyes, a hawk cries.

Then the silent rush of wings and the weightless bite of talons. Agnes opens her eyes to see the savage hook of a beak, the onyx shine of feathers. An eye like a comet, caught and polished.

In the brief lull before the pain and power surge again, it occurs to Agnes that Juniper will be insufferably, inconsolably jealous.

The pain crests. The hawk calls again, a wild shriek.

A final push, and Juniper is whooping and Bella is sobbing—"She's beautiful, Ag, she's perfect"—and someone, some new person who hadn't existed a moment before, is wailing.

Oh, baby girl.

Time skips forward again and Agnes is lying back against a soft mound of pillows with a precious, burning thing clutched against her chest. She stares down into a small, furrowed face, faintly imperious, like a tiny deity who hasn't seen much of the world yet but is already unimpressed. Her fists are two pink curls, and her eyes—open, staring solemnly back at Agnes, as if the two of them were instructed to memorize one another's faces—are a nameless color somewhere between midnight and ash.

"She—is she steaming?" Juniper sounds only mildly concerned, as if perhaps all babies steam for the first few days.

Bella is fussing with boiled water and clean linen, scrubbing away the streaks of red and gummy white. "She's just fine, I'm sure. It must be an effect of all that witching."

The baby's head is still glossy and wet, but already Agnes can see her hair is an unlikely shade of ruby red, like the deepest heart of a bonfire or the burning eye of a familiar.

Agnes glances sideways at the bird now perched on the bed rail. A river hawk, she thinks, all sharp angles and vicious curves, black as char. It looks down at the baby in her arms with the same fierce tenderness that Agnes feels, a love that has teeth and talons.

Agnes presses her lips to her daughter's fiery hair and feels her life cleaving, splitting cleanly into two pieces: the time before, and the time after.

The mattress shifts beside her. "What'll you name her?" Juniper's voice is reverent. Her hand hovers above the baby's head, not touching her, as if she isn't sure she ought to be near anything that fragile and precious.

Agnes has thought of many names—Calliope for her mother or Magdalena for her mother's mother, Ivy for power or Rose for beauty—but now a different name unfurls from her lips, snapping like a banner on the battlefield. "Eve."

A sinful name, a shocking name. A name that broke the first world and walked into the new one, unbound and unbowed.

Juniper laughs, a low rasp. "And her mother's-name?"

Agnes wants something deep-rooted and determined, something that grows in overturned earth and tumbled rocks. She thinks of the tough, silvery weed that was always threatening to overtake Mama Mags's herb-garden: cudweed, she called it, or—"Everlasting. Eve Everlasting."

Juniper dares to cup her palm around her niece's ruby head, to whisper, "Eve Everlasting. Give 'em hell, baby girl."

"She will," Agnes promises. She finds her fingers clutching the swaddled sheets. "And so will I, I swear. I'm sorry to you both for running away, for hiding. I thought..." She thought it was safer to creep and cower, to be no one rather than someone. Like her mother taught her. "I will not be a mother like ours was."

Bella settles on her other side. "Neither was she, once. You were five when she died, but I was seven." Agnes has always envied Bella those two extra years. "I remember her the way she used to be. I think she thought if she made herself small enough and quiet enough, she would be safe."

She was wrong. Bella doesn't need to say it.

Agnes swallows the salt in her throat and leans very carefully against her sister. A silence blooms between them, the gentle calm following a storm. Agnes is several steps past exhaustion but can't seem to close her eyes. She's mesmerized by the ammonite curl of her daughter's left ear, the delicate fall of her red lashes against the soft shape of her face.

She is studying the soft line of her cheek, wondering if she sees a hint of her sister's square jaw, when the hawk mantles beside her. Its wings snap wide, as if to defend itself against some invisible attack. The owl on Bella's shoulder does the same, eyes wide and round.

"Goodness!" Bella flinches from the slap of feathers, trying to stroke a calming finger down its breast, but it launches itself upward. The hawk joins it, circling near the ceiling on midnight wings. The pattern they draw is a warning, like vultures spiraling above some dying thing. A growing light gleams dull amber on their feathers, the rising sun, or the distant, electric glow of the Fair.

Agnes is looking up at them, clutching her daughter, when there's a loud bang against the ward door.

"Agnes! Are you in there?" More banging, a desperate fist. "*Hyssop*, for Chrissake!"

Bella looks at Agnes and Agnes nods. She unlocks the door and Mr. August Lee falls through it.

His hair is tangled and dark with rain, his eyes wild. There's a gray smear across one cheek and a smell rising from his clothes, trailing like a shadow behind him: acrid and sour, ugly in some way Agnes doesn't understand.

"Is she alive? Is the baby—" August's eyes rove between the three of them, fastening onto Agnes and the tight-wrapped bundle held to her breast. The relief in his face washes over her like daybreak.

Juniper says, sullenly, "They're just fine, thank you very much," but August doesn't seem to hear her. He moves to Agnes's bedside and kneels, still looking at her with that stripped-bare delight. Agnes turns her hand palm up on the sheet and he presses his forehead against it. "I'm sorry," he says into the mattress. "I got your message, but you weren't there. I looked and looked. Finally someone told me you'd been taken, but I didn't know where—"

"It's all right." She strokes her thumb across his brow, because she can, because she likes the weight of his head in her hand and the bent line of his neck. "I had my sisters." The binding thrums between them, a cat's purr, and it occurs to Agnes that she was dead wrong.

She thought survival was a selfish thing, a circle drawn tight around your heart. She thought the more people you let inside that circle the more ways the world had to hurt you, the more ways you could fail them and be failed in turn. But what if it's the opposite, and there are more people to catch you when you fall? What if there's an invisible tipping point somewhere along the way when one becomes three becomes infinite, when there are so many of you inside that circle that you become hydra-headed, invincible?

August is silent, head still pressed to her hand as if all he wants in the world is to feel the heat of her pulse.

"Well." Juniper clears her throat. "Not to interrupt, but it's time we get gone. Before somebody notices this whole hospital is asleep or follows this fool here." But she sounds less sullen, even faintly approving, as if she rather likes the sight of a man on his knees.

August looks up with a shadow looming in his face. "Where are you going? Is it that tower?"

Juniper shrugs at him, already turning to draw a circle on the white-tile wall. The birds still circle above her like some grave portent.

"You can't go back there."

"Excuse me?" Juniper wheels, chin thrust forward. "And why the hell not?"

But Agnes already knows why, because Agnes has finally recognized the smell rising from August's clothes: wild roses and fire.

"Because," August answers, "the tower is burning."

PART THREE

BURNED

&

BOUND

27

Wade in the water with me,
My daughter all dressed in red.
Wade in the water, and dress in white instead.

A song to stop bleeding after a hard birth, requiring twice-
blessed water & the Serpent-Bearer

James Juniper looks at the man kneeling beside her sister—at the gray smear on his cheekbone and the sorry angle of his shoulders—and tells him, very gently, "Bullshit."

"It isn't—"

"It is. Avalon would have to be somewhere in order for anybody to burn it, and I happen to know it's nowhere."

"It *isn't*. It's standing in the middle of St. George's Square and it's burning. Look out the window! You can see the light from here!"

Juniper doesn't want to look out the window, doesn't want to know the light glowing red on the underbellies of the clouds isn't coming from the rising sun.

"Listen, we bound that tower and buried the binding, and warded the place we buried it. So excuse me if I don't—"

"June." It's Agnes, her voice tired and cracked, pitched low so as not to wake the baby.

Juniper shoots August a *now look what you did* glare. "It's alright, Ag. I'm sure Mr. Lee is *mistaken*."

"June." And there's a sorriness in her voice that makes Juniper want to shout or stuff her fingers in her ears, anything so she doesn't hear what she says next. "There were men at the graveyard. The tree was uprooted. I think they must have found the binding."

Juniper doesn't say anything. She stares at her sister, and then at August, who is climbing wearily to his feet. "It's madness out there. I ran past people carrying torches, shouting about burning the witches out of their nest at last. They said the black tower had come back, and they said Gideon Hill was going to burn it."

"Bullshit," Juniper says again, but the word wobbles in her mouth. Agnes is looking up at her with a slick shine of tears in her eyes, and Bella has both hands pressed to her mouth.

Juniper looks away from them, anywhere else. Her eye catches on the bloody circle now dried and crusted on the bed-sheet beside her sister.

The trick to doing something stupid is to do it very quickly, before anyone can shout *wait!*

Juniper presses her palm to the circle and speaks the words, and then she is pulled sideways into the burning black.

Juniper hasn't yet been to Hell—although, according to her daddy, the preacher, Miss Hurston, and the New Salem Police Department, it's only a matter of time—but she figures when she gets there it'll look a lot like St. George's Square does now: fire and ash and ruination.

The door beneath her hand is burning, blue flames licking across charred wood, eating the inscription and sign both. She reels back, curling her hand to her chest, and stares up at the tower that was her hope and her home. Fire leaps from every window, fattened by the pages of

ten thousand books and scrolls, by all the words and ways of witches preserved for so many centuries. Ivy and rose-vines wither and blacken, peeling away from the stone in long twists of ash. The trees wear hungry red
crowns, like doomed queens, and birds caw and flap in frenzied circles.

Beneath the hungry roar of the flames Juniper thinks she hears a
keening sound, low and distant, like women's voices joined together in
some sad lamentation. Or maybe the sound comes from her own heart
as she watches the last hope of witches rising into the sky on wings of
ash and cinder.

Through the white haze of smoke and the hiss of rain Juniper sees
people ringing the square. Men and women stand with lit torches in
raised fists, Hill's symbol brought to hideous life. She can't tell through
the waver of heat and light if their shadows are their own. She isn't sure
she cares.

Behind the men and their torches—his eyes dancing with merry
flames, his pale skin flushed—stands Gideon Hill. A willowy blond
woman clutches his arm, looking up at him with such empty devotion
that Juniper shivers.

Hill's mouth is moving, issuing proclamations or commands or
spells. The crowd is too mesmerized by their violent delights to wonder why the flames burn so unnaturally hot, heedless of the rain, or to
notice the woman who now stands at the base of the tower, her hair
fire-whipped, her tears hissing to steam before they leave her eyes.

Only Hill sees her. His nostrils flare like a hound catching a long-
sought scent, and his eyes lift above the heads of his vicious, frothing
flock. Juniper feels them like hooks in her skin.

"You were cleverer than I thought, little witch." Hill is separated
from her by fifty men and a roaring blaze, but his voice is a whisper in
her ear. "But not clever enough."

The sound of his voice drags her back down into the Deeps, sends
shadow-fingers prying between her teeth. She spits. It sizzles where it
strikes.

She sees the white glimmer of Hill's smile through the haze. At his side Grace Wiggin frowns very faintly, as if she senses his attention wandering.

His laugh shivers in the air beside her. It's a relieved sound, almost giddy, and Juniper remembers the terrible fear that worked in his eyes. "I knew when you escaped that you must have found it, somehow. Dragged it back from wherever those hags took it. You hid it well, but anything lost can be found, can it not?"

Juniper thinks of the wards they'd set so carefully around the witch-yard, salt and thistle; she pictures shadow-hands plucking and pulling at them until they unraveled.

"You have given me the thing I have wanted above all others, James Juniper." The voice is passionless but sincere, and Juniper is struck by the certainty that he is telling the truth. "I am very grateful."

His laugh echoes across the square and she wants to charge through the crowd and wrap her hands around his throat, curse him eyeless and earless and tongueless—except there's a dark shimmer at her feet: shadows, many-armed, languorous as well-fed snakes, oozing across the scorched earth toward her. She whirls, presses her burned hand back to the hot ashes of the door, speaks the words a second time—

And she is on her knees in the stinking silence of the hospital ward, with hot tears tracking through the char on her cheeks.

Agnes knows from the broken slope of Juniper's shoulders, from the reek of ashes and roses she brings with her, that August was telling the truth.

A wail rises: Bella, keening as if her own flesh and blood is burning along with the library. Her hands scrabble for the drawn circle on the sheet.

Juniper catches her tight around the waist. "It's too late. It's gone, Bell. He's won." Her voice is even rougher than before, twice-burned by fire. Bella sags against her youngest sister, weeping, and Juniper shushes her. August looks at the floor, a stranger intruding on their mourning.

They stay like that, suspended in grief like gnats in amber. Agnes knows with cold clarity that soon someone will wake from their spell and raise the alarm. Rioters and officers will turn up looking for more witches to burn, and they'll find three sisters and a little witch-girl with hair the color of heart's blood. They'll rip her from Agnes's arms.

She looks down at her daughter—her hair drying in bright swirls of red, her cheeks round and slack in sleep—and thinks: *Let the bastards try.*

"We have to go," she says, very calmly. None of them move, mired in the selfishness of grief. Agnes raises her voice. "We have to go *right now*. Before they come for us, and for Eve."

At Eve's name Juniper looks up, blinking scorched eyes. "Where? They'll be watching the train station and the trolley lines, and I bet the streets are crawling. We might make it to Salem's Sin, maybe—"

Bella cuts her off, sounding surprisingly firm despite the snot and tears. "We can go to Cleo's in New Cairo. People are scared of the south side these days, and they have the means to hide us." Agnes suspects it isn't merely logic that drives Bella. Bella frowns at the clouds out the window and adds, inanely, "It's the full moon, too."

Juniper shakes her head. "We'll be moving slow, and they'll be looking for three women and a baby. It's too far."

Bella might have argued, but Agnes turns to August and says simply, "Help us. Please."

She knows from the warm twist of his smile that he hears it not as a command, but as an act of blind trust, the sort of thing one comrade might ask of another as they stand back-to-back, surrounded.

His eyes catch hers and hold steady. "It's far." He glances at the push broom propped against the wall, slightly splintered from Juniper's misuse. "Unless—can you—?"

Juniper's laugh is a bitter crack. "No."

"Well, I could get my boys to help." He trails off, worry creasing his face. "But it'll be rough going. Are you sure you ought to move, so soon after..." His eyes flick nervously to the bloodied sheets in the corner.

Agnes's voice goes very dry. "I'll manage, Mr. Lee."

"Are you sure? I always heard a woman shouldn't—"

A hawk's scream silences him. Agnes strokes the wing of her familiar. "Do you doubt me? Truly?"

Mr. Lee rocks back, like a man in a gust of fierce wind. He looks at her—at the black river hawk perched at her side and the redheaded baby clutched to her bare breast and the scorching heat of her eyes—and nods so deeply it's nearly a bow. "Never again," he breathes.

He turns to leave and calls over his shoulder, "Meet me behind the hospital in half an hour."

Bella has seen the undertakers' carriages before—black-painted wagons with ST. CHARITY HOSPITAL written in stark white capitals on the side—but she always imagined it would be several long decades before she rode in one herself.

She also imagined she would be alone, and dead, rather than pressed beside her sisters on the floorboards, very much alive and praying the baby won't cry as they clatter and jounce across the city.

Mr. Lee met them behind the hospital with several of his friends— scruffy, disreputable fellows who seemed well versed in mayhem—a cheap black suit, and a matched pair of carthorses that were persuaded to pull the carriage despite the smell of rot and arsenic. Mr. Lee helped them one after the other into the coach. His hand lingered around Agnes's, his mouth half-open, but the driver *hyah*ed and August vanished into the gloom.

Now the city passes in ghoulish flashes through the high windows: the flare of a lit torch in a bare hand; shouted curses and prayers; the stamp of feet marching in unnatural synchrony. The sour smell of wet smoke clings to her skin like grease, burying even the corpse-stink of the carriage.

A drifting flake of ash filters through the window and settles soft as snow on Bella's cheek. She wonders what mystery or magic it once held, now lost to the flames. Her tears slide silently to her temples and trickle through her hair.

The carriage rattles over trolley tracks and missing cobbles, the street roughening beneath them. The noise shifts from angry shouts to worried voices, pitched low. The clop of hooves falls quiet and the carriage sways to a stop.

Knuckles tap twice on the roof, and the three Eastwoods—four, Bella supposes, catching the delicate curve of her niece's cheek in the moonlight—stumble out into the night.

They're on a street she doesn't know, standing in the shadowed dark between two gas-lamps. Bodies move in the darkness around them, hurrying steps and hushed voices. Bella hears the snick of locks turning in latches, even the muffled thump of a hammer nailing shutters closed over a window, as New Cairo battens itself like a ship before a coming storm.

The driver tips his cap to them, addressing Agnes more than either of the others. "Mr. Lee begs you to send word to the Workingman, Misses Eastwood, once you're settled. He assures me you have your methods."

Agnes sweeps her stained cloak around herself and nods regally. "Thank you, sir." She falters, suddenly more woman than witch. "And thank him, for me? Tell him—" But she doesn't seem to know what she wants to tell him.

The driver grants her another grave tip of his hat. "I will, miss." Then, far less formally, "Trust August to fall for the most wanted woman in New Salem."

He flicks the reins and Juniper's affronted mutter ("I thought *I* was the most wanted woman in New Salem") is lost in the muffled clop of hooves.

Bella is blinking up at the stars, squinting through smudged spectacles at the distant street sign. "Ah—this way." Bella walks south and her sisters follow a half-step behind her, scuttling like field mice beneath a full moon.

No one sits on stoops or plays cards on street-corners. The barrooms are dark and vacant. The only people they pass are clusters of men carrying cudgels and hammers, and long-cloaked women with hard, fearless expressions that make Bella think there are reasons the police don't like to patrol Cairo after sundown.

She turns twice and doubles back once before she finds Nut Street. But the night market isn't what she remembers: the stalls and rugs are being rolled away, wares packed hastily into canvas sacks and crates, dark cloaks pulled over colorful skirts. Eyes turn and catch on Bella and her sisters—three white women and two black birds and one red-haired baby—but Bella ignores them.

She finds Araminta's shop and staggers through the door, weak-kneed and reeling. Araminta herself (Quinn's *mother*, Bella thinks with a small, internal wail) sits behind the counter. "Now what's going on—" she begins, but then she catches sight of Bella's face. Her eyes flick to Agnes, too pale and shivering in the warm evening. "I'll fetch her."

The three of them stand, swaying slightly, until Quinn appears wearing a half-buttoned gentleman's shirt over her nightdress. "Bella!" She reaches toward Bella as if she wants to hold her, but at that moment Agnes says *unff* and slumps sideways against a shelf of tiny wooden drawers.

Then the shop is full of low voices and reaching hands, the shuffle of feet as they hurry into the back room and make a pallet of pillows and spare quilts. They settle Agnes in the center while Araminta sings a spell against fever and another against blood loss, feet shuffling, a chalk map of stars drawn hastily on the floor. Juniper cradles Eve with her lower lip caught between her teeth, looking awkward and fierce and full of unwieldy, fresh-hatched love.

Araminta presses her palm to Agnes's forehead as the song ends and nods once. Juniper nests beside Agnes, the baby swaddled between them, and Araminta hauls herself upright and picks her way over to Quinn and Bella. "They'll keep for the night."

She looks at her daughter and the corner of her mouth twitches. "Get some sleep, you two."

Quinn ducks her head and heads up a narrow flight of stairs and Bella watches her go with a silent sinking in her heart.

Halfway up, Quinn turns. She meets Bella's eyes and extends her hand, palm up. An invitation, a question, a challenge. Bella hears Juniper's voice: *Are you such a coward?*

Bella isn't.

Quinn's hand is warm and dry. She leads Bella up the stairs to a room she recognizes. There's the bed with its saffron quilt, gone gray in the gloom. There's the pillow where Bella woke with the memory of warmth beside her.

Quinn sits on the foot of the bed and slides the gentleman's shirt from her shoulders. Her arms beneath it are bare and long, velveteen in the dark, her nightdress ghostly white. She looks like a living Saint, the street-lamp painting a glowing halo behind her head.

Bella thinks she should probably leave.

(Bella does not want to leave.)

Quinn smooths the quilt beneath her, a gentle invitation. Bella doesn't move or speak, as if her body is a fractious animal that will betray her given the slightest loosening of the reins.

"You can leave if you like." Quinn's voice is carefully neutral. "There's room beside your sisters."

"No, thank you," Bella breathes.

The white flash of Quinn's teeth in the dark. Her chin tilts in a *come here* flick, and this invitation is less gentle, warmer and sweeter and far more dangerous.

Bella makes an inarticulate sound, swallows, and tries again. "Mr. Quinn—"

"Does not live at this address, nor has he ever." Bella blinks several times and Quinn explains gently, "The two of us grew up together, and understood very young that neither of us was interested in...the usual arrangement. He lives in Baltimore with a very nice gentleman friend and a spoiled dog named Lord Byron."

"I...oh." Bella has not previously imagined any arrangements other than the usual one; she feels simultaneously too young and too old, terribly naive.

She looks again at the space beside Quinn. She sits.

"It's gone, you know." Bella's voice is hoarse from swallowed smoke. "All of it. The hoarded magic of witches, lost in a single night. It would have been safe if we'd just left it hidden where the Last Three put it, but we didn't. *I* didn't. And now it's gone and all our hope with it."

Bella thinks of all the women who followed them down this dangerous rabbit hole, all the Sisters hoping for the ways and words to change the bitter stories they were handed. "What have I done?" It comes out tear-thick, warbling.

"What have *we* done, I think you mean," Quinn says dryly. "Who found the spell in Old Salem, again?"

"You did, of course, I didn't mean—"

"So is it my fault, as well?"

"No!"

"And who got herself locked in jail and needed saving in the first place? And who had the baby early and kept you all distracted at the worst possible moment? Is it your sisters' fault, too?" Quinn shakes her head. "If you want to blame someone for a fire, look for the men holding matches."

"I...suppose."

Quinn turns sideways on the bed, facing Bella. "But let's look at what you've done, Belladonna Eastwood. You called back the Lost Way of Avalon and spread its secrets around half the city. You saved both your sisters' lives. You stood for something. You lost something. But…" Quinn's hands rise to either side of Bella's face to slide her spectacles from her temples. Bella finds it necessary to remind her heart to keep beating and her lungs to keep pumping. "You gained something, too, I think."

Quinn is close enough now that Bella can feel the heat of her skin, see the black swell of her pupils.

Bella wants very badly to kiss her.

The thought arrives without parentheses, a wild rush of wanting that Bella knows better than to give in to. She'll be punished, afterward, bruised or beaten or locked up until she learns to forget again. Except— and she doesn't know why this simple arithmetic has never occurred to her—isn't she already being punished, in her loneliness? And if it hurts either way, surely she should at least enjoy the sin for which she suffers.

Bella looks down at her own hands, steady as stones. She feels the even beat of her heart. They taught her to be afraid, but somewhere along the way she lost the trick of it.

She lifts her hand to Quinn's cheek, cups her palm around the curve of her jaw. Quinn holds very still, barely breathing.

"May I kiss you, Cleo?" She does not stutter.

Quinn exhales profanities.

"Is that a ye—" The end of Bella's question is lost, stolen along with her breath.

It isn't so much a kiss as a conflagration: of need and want long deferred, of lost hope and the wild abandon of two bodies colliding while the world burns around them.

Somewhere in the urgent fumble of buttons and clasps and the rushing rhythm of their breath, the touch of starlight on skin and the secret taste of salt, a treacherous thought occurs to Bella: that she would burn

Avalon seven times over as long as it led her here, to this room and this saffron-yellow bed.

Afterward, when they lie together like a pair of clasped hands, one fitted perfectly beside the other, Bella lies awake. She resists the soft tug of sleep for as long as she can, because the sooner she sleeps the sooner dawn will arrive with all its hard truths. Already she feels the weight of the world hovering above them, waiting to settle.

"Cleo?" Her name tastes like cloves on Bella's tongue. "Tell me a story?"

And Cleo does.

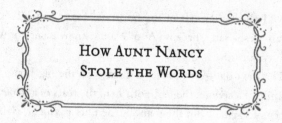

HOW AUNT NANCY
STOLE THE WORDS

This is the story of how Aunt Nancy stole all the words for her daughters and granddaughters and great-granddaughters. Aunt Nancy was an old, old woman—or perhaps she was a young woman, or a spider, or a hare, or all four at once—with clouds of cobweb for hair and shining black buttons for eyes, when her littlest great-granddaughter cried that she wanted to learn her letters.

Now Aunt Nancy would do anything for her grandchildren, so she went to the man in the big house and asked if he would please teach her to write. The man laughed at her, this little old woman with her cobwebbed hair. There was even a little black spider dangling beside her ear, watching him with tiny red eyes. In the end the man swore he would teach her to read and write if she brought him the smile of a coyote and the teeth of a hen, the tears of a snake and the cry of a spider.

Aunt Nancy smiled and thanked him very prettily and he laughed again, because she was so old and foolish that she didn't even know an impossible task when she heard one.

She hobbled back to her cabin in the woods. She sat on the porch and looked at the stars and sang a little song:

Cottontail and sly-fox
Terrapin and titmouse,
Come one, come all,
To your Aunt Nancy's house.

And all the animals of the farm and forest began to creep forward as she sang, because Aunt Nancy knew plenty of words and ways already.

The next day Aunt Nancy returned to the big house with the smile of a coyote, the teeth of a hen, the tears of a snake, and the cry of a spider. But the man spurned her payment, claiming it was a trick or a ploy, that she was a witch and he would see her burned at the stake before he taught her a single letter. He ordered her to leave, and Aunt Nancy left.

But every evening after that, when the man read books to his children before bed, there was a spider watching him from the window, black as night and cinder-eyed. And, in time, Aunt Nancy taught her great-granddaughter her letters.

28

Hide away, hide away, hide away with me,
Hide away, hide away home.

A song to avert an unwanted eye, requiring sympathy & the
Southern Crown

Beatrice Belladonna wakes just before dawn with her head pillowed on the soft meat of Cleo's shoulder. Cleo is still sleeping, her heart thudding slow and even in Bella's ear.

Bella pulls herself to one elbow and studies her, not counting the seconds: the clever arch of her brow, the polished shine of her skin, the hollow place where her collarbones meet. Bella thinks of all their long afternoons together at Avalon, annotating and translating, adrift in a private sea of words and ways.

Ashes, now, all of it. Men are probably wading through the wreckage at this very moment, smearing the remains beneath their boots. Laughing at the lost hope of witches.

The thought is a knife in her stomach.

She finds herself standing, slipping back into her stinking dress from the night before. She looks back once at the sleeping sprawl of Cleo's body, an offering at an undeserving altar, before tip-toeing down the narrow stairs.

Her sisters are still sleeping, nested close together. The binding between them seems to hum as Bella passes, and for a dizzy second she feels two hearts beating beside hers, two chests rising and falling, as if they are no longer entirely separate from one another. It ought to worry her, but there's a rightness to it, like three strands braiding together.

Bella catches the pale ghost of her own reflection in a hall mirror. Her face is subtly different, as if Cleo worked some arcane spell in the night: her hair is loose and long, her cheeks warm, her lips bitten pink. If this is the consequence of her sinfulness, perhaps she ought to sin more often.

Bella leaves her reflection behind and steps into the spice shop proper. She rattles briefly behind the counter, emerging with a pair of dull silver shears, and is inching toward the door when a voice stops her.

"Leaving already, Miss Belladonna?"

She wheels to find Quinn's mother perched on a stool with a steaming mug curled in one hand and a black silk wrap around her head. She clucks her tongue. "Without so much as a thank-you."

Bella tucks the shears behind her back, a guilty schoolgirl. "Thank you, Miss…"

"Miss Araminta Andromeda Wells. And just where were you going?"

"I—nowhere."

Miss Wells considers her for a second or possibly a century. She sighs. "Come here, girl." It does not occur to Bella to disobey. "I'd send you through the tunnels, but the doors only open for Daughters, and you don't have the mark." She taps Bella's wrist, right where Cleo bears her scarred pattern of stars. "This'll have to do."

Bella stands very still as Miss Wells hums a tune beneath her breath. She removes an ink-pen from her dressing gown pocket and draws a shape on the soft white of Bella's palm: a spiral of lines and diamonds, a starry crown. Bella thinks it's the same shape Cleo drew on the brick wall on St. Mary-of-Egypt Avenue when they ran from the rioters. She closes her hand tight around the marks, warm with witching.

"Thank you, Miss Wells."

"Cleo's a good girl," Araminta answers, somewhat obscurely. She amends, "Well, no, she isn't. She's always been curious as a cat and twice as sly. But she's mine, and she deserves…" She trails away, pursing and unpursing her lips, before finishing, "Make sure you come back."

Bella gives her a grave bow, hand over her heart.

The streets of New Cairo are still, the houses shut tight against the madness of men with lit torches. The stale, dead smell of smoke hangs thick in the air.

It grows stronger as Bella draws closer to the city's heart, muffling sound, obscuring the first gray streaks of dawn. There are people in the streets now—paper-boys and maids, workingmen heading west, street-cleaners and lamp-lighters—but they move with hunched shoulders and red eyes, as if the whole city is recovering from a night of drunken rage. Their eyes slide over Bella as if she is made of glass; none of them see the black-winged bird that keeps pace with her, high above.

A block south of the square she starts noticing white dust gathering in the cracks between cobblestones, clotting the gutters. There is a dizzy second when she mistakes it for snow before she recognizes it for what it is: ash.

At the final corner Bella ducks into the doorway of a closed shop. A gray drift of ash is gathered on the threshold, with a single rose petal lying atop it. The petal survived the fire with its edges only lightly charred, the center still soft pink. Bella bends and slips it into her skirt pocket.

She keeps her hand pressed over it as she peers around the edge of the shop and into the square.

The tower stands tall and terrible, strangely naked without its cloak of roses and ivy. The windows are desolate holes, revealing the hollow heart of the place that was once a library, a haven, a home. The woods around it are a smoking graveyard, the burnt stumps of trees leaning like headstones.

It seems to Bella she hears women weeping, softly and steadily, but the only people present are the men who pluck at the still-smoking ruins with shovels and rakes, sifting tentatively through the ash as if they are expecting vengeful witches to come soaring out of the coals on flaming broomsticks.

Someone stands among them, staring up at the corpse of the tower with a small, contented smile, like a man at the end of some long and arduous journey. He strokes the spine of the black dog beside him, who stands with her tail tucked between her legs.

Gideon Hill.

The last time Bella saw him he was ordering her sister's arrest. The sight of him now is another knife-twist in her belly, a hot rush of hate.

She withdraws the silver shears from her skirt and studies them. She isn't a librarian anymore and her library is nothing but ash, but surely she can still evict a misbehaving patron. Surely it's easier to lose something than to find it.

Bella glances up at Strix, circling so high above the square he could be mistaken for a crow unless you catch the hot gleam of his eyes.

Bella whispers her grandmother's words and snips the scissors once in the air. A simple charm for a hedge-witch hiding her potions or a child hiding her petty crimes, for secrets kept and truths untold.

The black tower and the gravestone-trees vanish in a fold of elsewhere. This time there is no binding to hold it close, no jar of earth and leaves, and the tower falls deeper and deeper, a coin dropped in a bottomless ocean.

Hill's men are left holding their rakes and shovels and blinking stupidly at one another, but Bella isn't watching them. She's watching Gideon Hill himself. His neck stiffens, the satisfied smile becomes a snarl. His colorless hair wisps into his face as he turns around. "Where is it? Who—"

Bella enjoys a second of savage satisfaction, but his expression is wrong somehow, unhinged in a way that makes Bella duck back behind her doorway. It reminds her of their daddy when one of them thwarted him: red fury stretched thinly over gray terror.

But Hill hasn't been thwarted. He's already won everything there is to win; what is there to fear in a vanishing ruin?

A dark twist of movement catches her eye. The shadow of the doorway is writhing as she watches it, sprouting hands and fingers, a malformed head. Bella doesn't move, doesn't breathe, as the shadow passes over her. It doesn't seem to see her, but the head rolls back and forth like a hound with a scent, searching.

Bella runs.

"Tonight, I think. As soon as it's good and dark. Are there tunnels that lead out of the city?"

Agnes wakes to the soft murmur of voices and the yellow slant of daylight. Through a doorway she sees Bella and Cleo sitting together at a scuffed kitchen table, their legs intermingled.

Cleo doesn't answer immediately, but lays her hand on the table, not quite touching Bella's. "Yes. But I'd rather you stayed." Her voice is soft but somehow urgent, intimate. It occurs to Agnes to wonder where her oldest sister slept last night.

"But we're putting you in danger just by being here." Agnes watches Bella's hand creep toward Cleo's, as if it possesses a mind of its own. "Someone is bound to notice three white women and a newborn living in your mother's spice shop, no matter how well we disguise ourselves or how thoroughly we hide. And we know now our wards won't hold against Hill forever."

"So we'll find other safe houses and move between them. Renew the wards twice a day. The Sisters will help, and maybe the Daughters—and what about Agnes's man, who delivered you to my doorstep so efficiently?" *Agnes's man.* What a novel, rather appealing arrangement, to own a man rather than being owned by him.

Bella huffs. "And who will feed and clothe us? Our savings burned along with everything else, and none of us have jobs anymore, you'll notice—"

"I do. And if they stop printing my stories we can steal or scavenge or beg. We'll find a way." Cleo pauses, eyes flicking across Bella's face, and her voice falls. "You're no coward."

Bella swallows, eyes falling to Cleo's hand still lying between them, then away. "It's not a question of cowardice or courage. It's just logic: We lost. He won. We thought we were the beginning of some grand new story, but we were wrong. It's the same old story, and if we keep telling it every one of us will burn. Witches always do."

There's an enormous, scathing *huh* from the opposite doorway. Agnes startles and the air above her twists. Dark wings, the gleam of talons: her hawk, returned from the other side of elsewhere to hover over Agnes and Eve.

He flutters to the back of a chair, glaring at the smallish, sharp-faced woman who stands in the doorway. Agnes's memory of the previous night is fragmented and feverish, but she thinks she recalls that face hovering above her, singing her well again.

Now her hands are on her hips, her face seamed and bitter. "I should have known. You spend all summer stirring up a hornet's nest worth of trouble, but as soon as trouble arrives you're heading for the hills."

Bella has her mouth open, but another voice shouts across her, "The *hell* we are." Juniper's objection is so loud and abrupt that Eve wakes with a startled snort. Agnes struggles upright—the entire middle of her is wrong-feeling, squashy and swollen and aching—and tries to wrap the swaddling back around her daughter before her wails wake the neighbors, or possibly the entire city. But Eve seems to have sprouted several extra arms and legs in the night, all flailing in separate directions.

Juniper scrambles upright, hair standing at wild angles. "It's all right, baby girl, Aunty June is here."

Aunty June proceeds to scoop Eve from Agnes's arms, swaying and patting. Eve's cries shrink to muttered complaints and Juniper beams down at her. It's a soft, half-sleeping smile that Agnes hasn't seen on her sister's face since they were girls.

"Sorry," Juniper whispers. "I only meant: I'm not going anywhere. I want to fight."

"We are aware, June." Bella scrubs a hand over her face. "But there's a time to fight, and there's a time to survive. If we leave now—"

"And let the bastards win? No, ma'am." Juniper's face isn't soft anymore.

But a faint frown crosses her sister's face as she looks down at the baby curled in her arms. Juniper looks burdened and a little bewildered by the burden, as if she's found herself hauling a heavy load entirely by accident. "And—it's going to get bad, isn't it? They're going to come for all of us, for every woman who knows more than she should, who doesn't smile when she's told to." Juniper sounds uncertain, feeling her way across unknown terrain. "It seems to me like Miss Araminta's right. We got them into this mess, and we can't walk out on them now."

A brief, slightly astonished silence follows. Agnes wonders when her wild baby sister started thinking about duty and debt, cause and consequence. Somewhere in the dark of the Deeps, maybe. Or right now, standing with the weight of her niece in her arms.

Bella is the first to collect herself. "That's very...laudable. But I went to St. George's this morning—"

"You *what* now?"

"—and saw Gideon Hill. There's something wrong about him, something sick—you were right. He was furious when I sent the tower away again, almost deranged. He'll keep coming after us. And what happens in November, if he's elected? What happens when he has more than just angry mobs and shadows?"

Agnes sees Bella glance down at Cleo's hand again, her eyes clouded with worry, and understands that it isn't herself she's afraid for.

Agnes thinks of August running through the rising riot, searching for her, and the relief on his face when he found her; of Eve staring up into her eyes, solemn as a Saint; of Juniper's voice breaking as she promised to take care of her. Of the terrible risk of loving someone more than yourself and the secret strength it grants you.

"Well," she says mildly, "I'm staying." Above her, the hawk croons.

Several sets of eyes swivel toward them. Bella adjusts her spectacles. "I thought you were done with all of this."

Agnes shrugs. That was before Eve, before her familiar flew out of the darkness to her, before her life cleaved into *before* and *after*.

"Aren't you worried for her?" Juniper tilts her chin at Eve, who is making a faint irritable-bee sound that might be a snore.

"Yes," Agnes answers, because she is. She lay awake half the night consumed by stray terrors and uncertainties, convinced the miraculous rise and fall of her daughter's ribs would cease the second she closed her eyes. But beneath the terror was something else, something clawed and fanged and ruthless that she doesn't know how to explain.

I am terrified and I am terrible. I am fearful and I am something to be feared. She meets Miss Araminta's eyes, dark and knowing, sharp and soft, and thinks maybe every mother is both things at once.

She gives her sisters another shrug. "Yes. But I'm still staying."

Juniper's face lights. Her eyes slide back to Bella. "Well?"

Bella lifts both hands in the air. "Well *what*? You two can make all the brave pronouncements you like, but what good are they? What good are *we*? Without Avalon—"

Araminta interrupts her. "You still have more words and ways than nine women out of ten. And"—her eyes slide to the hawk perched on her chair—"I know a familiar when I see one."

Bella opens her mouth and then closes it. "And how's that?"

Araminta smiles a sly, sidelong smile, and for the first time Agnes sees some of Cleo in her face. "Because I'm the tenth woman."

And as she says it an animal appears at her feet, coiling out of nothing: a black hare with ember eyes. Juniper whispers something profane and admiring. Agnes gasps. Bella merely looks intent.

"There's more witching left in the world than you think, girls," Araminta says, and her eyes are on Bella's. "The kind they can't burn because it was never written down."

Cleo speaks for the first time since her mother arrived. "And if they stay, will we help them? Will the Daughters stand beside their Sisters, Ohemaa?" Agnes frowns over the last word, but Araminta gives a little grunt, as if the title is an arrow aimed well.

She bows her head to her daughter and Cleo grins back. She turns to Bella. "What do you say?" Cleo's voice is low and too warm again, her eyes bright, burning gold. "All for one?"

Agnes almost feels sorry for her sister, subjected to the heat of that gaze. Bella's eyes search Cleo's face, and whatever she finds sends a flush tip-toeing up her neck. Her fingers creep those few final inches to curl tight around Cleo's.

"And one for all," she whispers.

29

What is now and ever and unto ages and ages,
may not always be

A spell for undoing, requiring a needle & a cracked egg

For three days, Beatrice Belladonna and her sisters remain in the dim back rooms of Araminta's Spices & Sundries. They're long, tiresome days: Agnes rests and wakes and rests again, her fever rising and falling like a stubborn tide; Eve alternates between cherubic contentment and fits of aggrieved screaming, as if she was promised some treat and then bitterly denied; Bella sits for hours with her black notebook on her knees, listening to Araminta Wells's lectures on constellations and sung-spells and the rhythm of witching. Juniper is mostly absent, arriving and departing at odd hours, filling her pockets with herbs and bones from the shop's stock.

The nights are long, too, but Bella does not find them tiresome. They are smothered laughter and lips, hands and hips hidden beneath the saffron quilt. They are hours stolen out of time, unburdened by the future and unsullied by the past.

(Though sometimes the past slithers in. Sometimes Bella wakes from dreams of cellars and burning barns. Sometimes she flinches from Cleo's touch as if it's hot wax, and Cleo lies very still until Bella's pulse steadies. Afterward she holds her carefully, like Bella has spun sugar for skin.)

By the afternoon of the fourth day Bella is beginning to hope they might be safe. That her sisters were not fools to stay in this vicious, hungry city. That she might wake up every morning with her cheek on Cleo's shoulder.

But then Juniper staggers into the shop with her mouth thin and her eyes hard. "Outside. The shadows are . . . gathering. Thickening. I don't know if they can smell us or track us or what, but I figure it's time to get gone."

They leave as the sun sets, drawing Nut Street in mauve and gray. They follow Cleo down into the tunnels: Bella, then Agnes with Eve wrapped tight to her chest in the manner Araminta taught her, then Juniper, swearing and shivering. Even before her time in the Deeps she didn't care much for being belowground. Now she detests it.

They emerge long after dusk, filing out of a tiny building that looks from the outside like a garden shed or a pigeon coop, then slipping through a hedge and onto a sedate east-side avenue.

"Is this close enough?" Cleo whispers.

"Yes," Bella answers.

"Send word once you're settled."

"I will."

Cleo runs out of things to say. She simply stares at Bella, tracing her face—and Bella has never liked her own features so much as she does in that moment, in the soft gold of Cleo's gaze—before touching the brim of her derby hat. "Three bless and keep you."

Bella and her sisters are left alone on the darkening street.

The east side is apparently untroubled by the riots and arrests plaguing the rest of New Salem. The houses have dignified gables and clipped lawns and the slightly burnished shine of old money. Their windows send soft lamp-light and the clink of crystal over the empty streets. A man's laugh floats from one of them, unworried, perfectly content.

Bella's sisters crowd close behind her in their borrowed clothes and black cloaks, like refugees from some darker, wilder world. An owl and a hawk wheel high above them.

She leads them to a red-brick house on St. Jerome Street, slightly shabbier and older than its neighbors. She knocks twice, and the silence that follows is sufficient for her to doubt every decision that brought her here.

Then the door swings inward and an elderly, sweatered gentleman is blinking up at her. "Miss Eastwood! Pardon me—*Misses* Eastwood." Mr. Henry Blackwell beams at the three of them as if they are unexpected guests to a dinner party rather than the most wanted criminals in the city. "And are those...my word."

Their familiars have swept to their shoulders in a rush of black feathers and hot eyes, talons curving like carved jet. Mr. Blackwell's genial smile shifts toward awe as he looks at them. He gathers himself. "I don't believe we have been introduced."

"This is *Strix varia*—Strix, I call him—and Pan." Bella gestures to the fisher-hawk on Agnes's shoulder. "For *Pandion haliaetus*, the western osprey, you know."

Behind her she hears Juniper mutter about the injustice of her sisters finding their familiars first if they were just going to give them such stupid long names.

Mr. Blackwell appears not to hear her. He gives each of them a small bow. "Do come in, all of you."

The hall is dark oak and dense carpet. As soon as the door clicks behind them Bella begins. "I'm so sorry to surprise you like this. It's an imposition, I know, and terribly dangerous, but my sisters and I need a place to—"

But Mr. Blackwell is waving a hand over his shoulder at her. "Oh, it's no trouble at all. I've been worried sick about you, to tell the truth."

Bella isn't at all convinced that amiable, bespectacled Mr. Blackwell understands the gravity of the risk. "If they find us here, you might well be arrested. Your property could be seized, your position terminated."

Mr. Blackwell reaches the end of the hall and bends to peruse a bookshelf, thumbing through clothbound spines until he reaches a little bronze statue of a dog, its head shined smooth with use. Blackwell gives a small *hah!* and tips the dog forward. Some unseen mechanism clicks and whirrs, and the entire bookcase glides smoothly away. Behind it lies a dim, windowless room with a slanting ceiling and several fat down mattresses.

Mr. Blackwell makes a polite throat-clearing noise. "I tidied up a bit last week, got the worst of the cobwebs out at least. I had a suspicion it might be needed." At Bella's wordless, openmouthed expression, he adds, "My grandfather built this house. He told me there would always be someone who needed to hide, and that there ought always be a Blackwell there to hide them."

Bella is searching for words that might adequately express her gratitude and relief when Juniper says, "Well hot *damn*, sir," in her burnt rasp of a voice, and Mr. Blackwell leads them into the kitchen, chuckling.

Much later that evening, after Bella and her sisters have consumed a frankly astonishing number of tiny crustless sandwiches and Agnes has retired to the secret room with Eve, her eyes bruised and sleepless, Bella and Mr. Blackwell sit in a matched pair of armchairs with a neglected checkerboard and an un-neglected bottle of chardonnay between them.

"Thank you. For letting us stay." It seems to require unusual effort to enunciate. "It's a lovely house."

Mr. Blackwell plucks an ebony checker from the board and studies it a little morosely. "I thought for a while it might be yours, if you would have me."

It takes several seconds for Bella to process this statement, and another several to respond. "You *what*?"

"Oh, merely as a matter of convenience! You had no family and I had no wife, and I thought we might be pleasant enough companions, despite the difference in our ages. Of course as soon as I saw you and Miss Quinn together several things became clear to me." Blackwell blinks at her, brow furrowed. "I hope I haven't caused you any distress."

"No, it's just...I never thought..."

Mr. Blackwell gives her another of his affable smiles, but the edges are turned downward. "Someone along the line misled you as to your worth, Miss Eastwood." Distantly, through the froth of chardonnay, Bella hears the word *nothing* in her daddy's voice. "I should quite like to give him a piece of my mind."

"I—thank you." She thinks of Juniper, the hiss of scales over straw, the sin she bore for all of them. "But it's no longer possible."

Mr. Blackwell nods, unsurprised. "Good."

She thinks of Cleo's eyes on her face before they parted, studying her as if she were precious, even vital. "Or necessary."

"Even better." Mr. Blackwell raises his glass. "Give Miss Quinn my warmest thanks."

They sip their wine. Bella imagines a version of her life where she never met Cleopatra Quinn, where she married Mr. Blackwell and lived in this pleasant red-brick house until she was a crone in truth, reading witch-tales by the fireside in winter and dreaming of better worlds. She thinks of the old story of the witch who buried her heart in a silver box beneath the snow so that she might never be hurt. A chill shivers up her spine.

Blackwell sets his glass among the checkers. "Did you truly find it?"

Bella knows from the soft reverence of his voice what he means. "We did." She can't help the note of pride in her voice.

"And is it truly gone?"

Her voice this time is a graveside whisper. "It is. Although—" She withdraws her little black notebook from her skirt pocket and runs her thumb across the cover. "It has been recently brought to my attention that not all witching was lost, that night."

"Oh?" It's the same *oh?* he used to give her over lunch in the College library, which granted her permission to lecture to her heart's content about the lives of Saints or the execrable handwriting of monks. Bella smiles a small, wistful smile for those quiet, safe days, and tells him more or less everything there is to tell.

She tells him about Old Salem and the sewing sampler and the owl winging toward her through the trees; living in the lost library of Avalon, outside of time and mind, and standing in its ashes; Araminta's spells, which rely on stars and songs rather than rhymes and herbs, and her growing suspicion that witchcraft isn't one thing but many things, all the ways and words women have found to wreak their wills on the world.

She tells him far more than she needs to, and he listens with considering nods and small smiles and a few *my words*.

"I was hoping to ask Araminta about the scarification process and their mother's-names, but then Hill's shadows turned up in New Cairo. Oh! The wards!"

Bella stands so abruptly that her blood thuds in her skull. She reels to the front door and pours a line of salt and thistle across the threshold. *Maiden, Mother, and Crone. Guard the bed that I lay on.*

She's on her sixth window before she notices the yellowing grains of salt already lying on the sills. "Did you ward your house already?"

Mr. Blackwell looks a little sheepish. "Not nearly so well as you are, I'm sure. It's just that fever—the Second Plague, some are calling it now—has been creeping north. It strikes me as uncanny, so I thought perhaps a little uncanniness might keep it at bay." He nudges his spectacles back up his nose. "My great-aunt taught me a few little charms here and there."

Bella would like to ask more about all this—a man working witchcraft, an uncanny sickness—but at that moment Juniper emerges from behind the bookshelf. She is wrapped in a dark cloak, limping badly without her red-cedar staff, her eyes the green-lit gray of the sea before a storm. She pauses to sweep the two of them a bow before slipping out the front door and vanishing into the deepening night.

"What *is* she doing, at this hour?"

"Whatever she can. Whatever might help." Bella sighs. "I imagine we'll read about it in tomorrow's papers."

Juniper has never cared much for reading (or any of the others of Miss Hurston's three R's), but over the next few weeks she acquires the habit of reading the paper over breakfast. Or at least the headlines: SISTERS EASTWOOD STILL AT LARGE; NEW SALEM CHIEF OF POLICE RESIGNS AMID RUMORS OF NERVOUS BREAKDOWN; HILL'S RALLY INTERRUPTED BY BAYING DOGS AND STRONG WINDS.

The other Sisters tell Juniper that Mayor Worthington is leaning on *The Post* not to print the most hysterical stories: that the Eastwoods can transform themselves into black birds or possibly bats; that the Crone herself is currently living on the south end, keeping company with colored women; that the Mother gave birth to a little devil-child with hair the color of Hell itself.

"Bet the bastards wish they'd just given us the vote when we asked nicely," says Electa Gage, with no small degree of satisfaction. "Too late now."

The previous week the City Council issued a statement that the suffrage question could not possibly be entertained in the current climate. "And frankly," Mr. Hill had told the papers, "if this is what happens when women gain some measure of power, we have grave doubts about the advisability of granting them more."

Following this announcement, several members of the New Salem Women's Association had found their way to the Sisters, their jaws gritted, looking for witch-ways and words.

The Sisters rarely congregate, these days. They speak instead by mockingbird and smoke-signal, by letters that can only be seen by friendly eyes and notes that ignite after reading. They meet only for furtive exchanges of spells and safe houses and disperse before they can be found by the things that hunt them: the mobs of men with brass badges and torches, the steel-jawed officers on white horses, the eyeless shadows that twist up from sewer grates and reach after them.

But they are prey with teeth and claws of their own, now. They have the spells they stole from Avalon before it burned, still stitched into hems or written in recipe-books; they have the words and ways taught to them by their grandmothers and aunts and neighbor-ladies, now shared between them; they have August's little boys' Latin and Araminta's songs, chanted prayers from a pair of dark-eyed Russian girls, and even a few shuffling dances from the Dakota woman. And Bella is still gathering more. Everywhere they stay she asks for their stories or spells or songs, whatever ways they've found to talk to the great red heartbeat on the other side, and adds them carefully to her collection. Her little black notebook has become a sort of patchworked grimoire, part spell-book and part diary. Juniper has seen Bella writing in it long into the evenings and suspects her of adding wholly unnecessary narrative; she figures it comes of reading too many novels as a girl.

So Juniper and her Sisters run, but they run with salt and snake's teeth in their pockets, ninebark and angelica root, honey-wax and black feathers and scraps of tanned hide. They tangle their pursuers in cobwebs and rose-vines, they slip into crowds and come out the other side wearing different faces. They vanish through ordinary-seeming doors and emerge hours later, smelling of roots and earth.

Not all of them get away. There are arrests and detentions, beatings and brutalities. A man in Bethlehem Heights finds witch-ways in his wife's sewing box and ties her to the bedpost until the authorities retrieve her; one of Pearl's girls is found bloodied and barely breathing with the witch-mark drawn on her back; an entire tenement on the west side is set ablaze by a gang of mean-eyed boys who claimed to have followed a black cat with red eyes.

It proves difficult to keep a witch behind bars. Workhouses suffer from rusted locks and shattered bars, missing shackles and stolen keys. Guards are discovered sleeping or missing or terribly confused, convinced they are lost in deep woods. Cells are found empty except for the wild smell of witching.

The smell is everywhere, now. The whole city reeks of wet earth and green things, char and crushed herbs and wild roses. It rises like steam from the alleys between tenements and the lawns of fashionable homes, as if some great dragon is rousing beneath the city, breathing smoke through the cracks. The streets heave over the bones of tree roots that grow faster than they should; thistle and pye weed sprout between bricks. Sometimes at night the stars shine more brightly than they have any right to, as if there aren't gas-lamps and bulbs buzzing beneath them, as if they're shining down on a black wood or an empty prairie. The wind is sharp and too cold for the final days of summer, as if the ghost of Avalon still lingers, haunting the city.

Almost, Juniper begins to believe it will be all right. That the women of the city will stand strong against mobs and shadows, that Gideon Hill will lose his election in November and slink back under whatever rock he came from. But their stores of witch-ways are running thin, and every midwife and herbalist has been driven out of town. The sickness is worsening, too—even *The Post* now calls it the Second Plague—and panic worsens with it. The shadows coil thicker and darker, like fattened flies, and Gideon Hill's face smiles down from every window and wall. *Our light against the darkness.*

Juniper and her sisters make it four nights at Mr. Blackwell's before Agnes spots a shadowless man standing on St. Jerome Street, staring blankly through the windows, waiting. That night they say farewell to Mr. Blackwell, who sends them with several bottles of wine and a hooked cane for Juniper. A Daughter escorts them north through the tunnels to stay with Inez and Jennie in the glamorous near-mansion Inez's deceased husband conveniently left behind.

They make it two days before fists thump on the door in the middle of the night. Bella whispers the words to tangle the halls and doors of the house in a winding labyrinth behind them—a spell taught to them by Inez's chatty Greek maid—while all five of them slip out the kitchen door.

They spend the following night beneath a bridge, huddled together with the heat of their spells warping the air around them, and another handful of days back in New Cairo, in the well-warded house of Cleo's aunt Vivica. But the shadows always find them eventually, and they always run.

By the end of August, Juniper can feel their list of willing hosts shrinking, doors slamming and locks clicking ahead of them. Partly it's the fear rising like sewer-stink through the city as Hill's mobs grow bolder and the plague worsens. Partly it's Eve, who screams at inconvenient hours of the night, and whose hair remains eye-catchingly red no matter how many spells or dyes they apply. Sometimes the problem is Miss Cleo Quinn; it turns out even the suffragists who seem sympathetic with the cause of colored women balk at the thought of welcoming one into their actual homes.

Another time they were asked to leave after the mistress of the house discovered Cleo and Bella in her washroom somewhat less than fully dressed. They behaved themselves better after that, but there was still an ardent, unsated thing between them. It unsettled people.

It unsettled Juniper, to own the truth. True, Bella's cheeks were flushed and her stutter was gone, but Juniper recalled the preacher's admonitions about man and wife and the natural order of things. She asked Agnes about it one evening and was told in no uncertain terms to mind her own damn business.

"What's wrong with loving somebody, anyhow?" Agnes hissed. "Doesn't she deserve a little happiness?" Juniper surrendered and resolved thereafter to mind her own damn business.

The morning after, she caught Agnes whispering to a mockingbird on the window ledge, watching it wing into the dawn as if half her heart was flying alongside it. The next time they have to run, Agnes says, quietly, "I know a place."

She leads them to one of the crookedy, higgledy-piggledy stacks of tenements in West Babel only a few blocks north of South Sybil. A thin, tired-looking woman opens the door, her hair brittle white. She flinches only briefly at the sight of three women, an infant, and a pair of uncanny birds standing in her hallway, before inviting them inside and introducing herself as Miss Florentine Lee.

Her apartment is a single cramped room, the walls stained with years of cooking-grease and close living. A small window provides a stingy square of summer-light, obscured by laundry-lines and balconies.

Mr. August Lee is waiting at the kitchen table. He stands as they enter and his face when he sees Agnes is—well. It's private, Juniper decides. She busies herself with her cane, wondering a little bitterly how her sisters found the time to pursue romance alongside all the witching and women's rights. She tries to imagine herself looking at someone like that, all soft and aching, but finds herself thinking instead of the mountainside back home, sweet and green.

That evening Miss Lee feeds them a cabbage-and-ham stew which Juniper doubts has done more than meet a ham once in passing. August's mother watches them eat with faded-cotton eyes, her gaze flicking from Agnes to Eve to August, not saying anything.

August clears the dishes from the table after supper and his mother fusses at him. "There's no need—"

"It's fine, Ma." She subsides with a fragile-looking smile. There's something strained and careful about the way Miss Lee and her son speak to one another, as if they're treading lightly over a fresh-mended wound.

Bella and June nest on the floor in a pile of tattered quilts and Agnes claims the rocking chair. But Eve refuses to settle, her usual whines escalating to ragged wails that burrow into Juniper's skull.

Agnes curses. "She won't eat. I don't understand—she's always had such an appetite."

Miss Lee leans over her, says, "May I?" and touches two fingers to Eve's forehead. "She's warm. A fever'll take the edge off an appetite."

The word *fever* drifts around the room like a stray cinder, too hot to touch. No one says anything for a long moment, while Agnes's face goes blotchy white and August watches her with a helpless expression. He takes a step toward her but Juniper beats him to it, scooping her niece into her arms and shooting a *get in line* glare at August.

Eve falls asleep that night with her cheek smeared against Juniper's breastbone, her cheeks blushing red. A product of the stuffy, too-small room, Juniper is certain.

In the morning Juniper wakes to see shadow-fingers sliding across the window, prying between the panes, trying to get in.

They run.

Agnes pretends to herself that her daughter isn't sick. That the rising bloom of red in her cheeks is the product of bad air in the tenements or too-tight swaddling, that the thin edge of her wail is just hunger or indigestion or exhaustion. But she sees the way her sisters look at Eve, feels their worry like a gathering cloud in the binding between them—and knows better.

Bella consults her little black notebook and produces long lists of rhymes and chants, poultices and cures. Juniper visits Araminta's spice shop and a few midwives in hiding and returns with feverfew and willowbark, silkweed and red thread. It seems to help, at first. Eve's eyes lose the dangerous, glassy sheen, and her usual imperious expression returns. But then her breath thickens again, her temperature rising as some unseen thing eats away at their spells. A cough emerges, wet and persistent, so that her breath rattles sometimes in her sleep.

"The plague, for certain," pronounces Yulia, a few days later.

They're staying with one of the several dozen Domontoviches scattered on the west side, stuffed in a warm loft above a barroom.

"You don't know that," Agnes snaps.

Yulia shrugs, unmoved. "Eh. This is how my cousin sounds, before they take her to St. Charity's."

"No one's taking Eve anywhere." There's a silent rushing in the air between them and Pan appears on her shoulder, a tangle of darkness that becomes a hawk. Yulia looks at the osprey—his vicious beak, his scalding glare—and subsides.

They sit with their Sisters at a round table in the middle of the loft, pocked and scarred from years in the bar below. It's a larger meeting than they've dared in weeks: Cleo sitting with her knee pressed against Bella's, Gertrude and Frankie sharing a long bench with the Hull sisters, Inez and Electa lost in a mob of Valkyrie-like women who can only be Yulia's relatives. Agnes can't help noticing that most of the women sit a little apart from the Eastwoods, as if they are either too dangerous or too revered to touch.

Juniper called them all by mockingbird after the most recent round of arrests, because the women are no longer being held in the work-houses. They've thrown them in the Deeps, with witch-collars and bridles around their throats, where their witching can't reach them. The shadows seem to fall more darkly around the Hall of Justice, sharp and black, like the jagged teeth of a trap.

The Sisters confer for hours, proposing spells and countermeasures and unlikely schemes. Some of them have daughters or sisters down in the Deeps, and their eyes burn like coals in their skulls. Agnes thinks of circles drawn wide, of bindings-between and one-for-all, and shivers a little at the strength of it.

Sometime past midnight Juniper stands. "Well, it's a start. Now, what witch-ways have you brought?" The women turn out pockets and empty brown paper sacks on the table. Agnes can tell from the worried bow of Juniper's shoulders that it isn't enough.

She's frowning and opening her mouth when Inez says, "Wait a moment."

Inez lays a long, thin object along the table, smiling at Juniper. Inez looks older and a little thinner than she did in the spring, her cheeks no longer merry and full. She and Jennie have been running, too.

Juniper frowns as her fingers peel away silk wrappings. Her mouth falls open as she sees what lies beneath. She stares down at the table for a while, looks up at Inez, then back down. "You did this?" Her voice is hoarse.

"Well, I provided the gems, being the only one of your dear Sisters with money to waste as I please. But Annie found the tree and Yulia found the woodworker. It was your sisters' idea..." She trails off. "You like it?"

Whatever Juniper is feeling right now, Agnes suspects *like* is too small a word for it. Her eyes are shimmering spring-green and her hands shake as she reaches for the thing on the table. As she lifts it to the light Agnes sees a long staff of polished yew, the grain knotted and stained black. A carved line spirals up the stick, ending in a bowed head: a snake with a pair of garnets for eyes.

Juniper swivels between Agnes and Bella, mute, reverent.

Bella shrugs. "Well, honestly, we couldn't have you running around with Mr. Blackwell's poor cane. This suits you much better."

The binding between them hums with fierce joy, enough to make Agnes forget for a moment that they are hunted and hounded by a city that hates them.

Until a small, tired voice calls, "*Hyssop.*"

Jennie Lind staggers into the room. The expression on her face sends a cold current through the gathered women. "Mayor Worthington is resigning tomorrow." She says it quick and sharp, a merciful blow. "The Council will call a special election by the end of the week."

All the glee drains from Juniper's face. "How do you know? Can you be sure?"

Jennie's mouth goes tight but Inez answers for her. "Mayor Worthington is her father," she says softly. "She's sure."

The burst of gasps and whispers that follow this is sufficient to wake Eve, who wails her thin, not-right wail while the Sisters of Avalon trade muttered fears and dark pronouncements. *He's ahead in the polls, I heard.*

The mutters trail into heavy silence as each woman feels the weight of an unseen boot pressing down on them.

"Well. There's nothing to be done tonight." Juniper lowers herself into a chair, staff across her knees. "Head home, girls. Get some sleep."

They leave in ones and twos, until only Yulia and her cousin remain with the Eastwoods. It's late, but no one seems to want to go to sleep; they sit around the table, silent and brooding, listening to the faint whistle of Eve's snores.

"Yulia?" Bella says, her head resting on Cleo's shoulder, her eyes sad and far away. "Why don't you tell us that story you mentioned?"

Yulia leans back in her chair, balancing on two legs, and begins.

Once upon a time a young maiden married a prince in a grand castle. She was very happy with her prince, who was young and handsome, until the day he went off to war and left her with nothing but a kiss and a command never to go down to the dungeons.

With time the kiss faded, and so did the command. One day the maiden went down to the dungeons, where she found an old, old woman languishing in iron chains. Her flesh was pale and drooping, hanging like loose cloth from her bones, and her moans were piteous. The old woman begged for saltwater and bread, and the maiden obliged because she could not stand to see such suffering. The old woman drank the water and then spat on her chains, which melted away.

The woman leapt from her cell, no longer a weak old crone but a wicked witch. She cackled her triumph and left the castle to seek vengeance on the prince that had kept her caged for so long. The maiden stole a horse from her husband's stable and took off after the witch, tears of remorse streaming down her cheeks.

But the maiden could not catch the witch, and she grew lost in the winter woods, her hoof-prints vanishing behind her. Eventually she took shelter in a little round house perched on long stilts, like the scrawny legs of a chicken.

Inside the house the maiden met another witch, who told her the name of the old woman she had freed from the dungeon:

Koschei the Deathless. A long time ago, Koschei bound her soul to a needle, and the needle to an egg, and the egg to a silver chest, which she buried deep beneath the snow. All the long years of living drove her mad, but also made her very powerful. Only by smashing the box, cracking the egg, and breaking the needle would her soul be sundered.

The maiden left the chicken-legged house with hope in her heart and a map in her hand. She faced many hardships on her journey, but eventually she found the silver box and the egg and the needle, and smote all three across the mountainside. Thus did the Deathless Witch meet her Death, and the maiden rescued her handsome prince.

30

The Queen of Spades
She made a blade
All on a winter's day.

A spell for sharp edges, requiring a crown of cold iron

On the first of September, James Juniper and her sisters are hidden in the velvet-and-silk halls of Salem's Sin.

The air is still summer-hot but there's a brittleness to it, a whisper like the shush of falling leaves or the burrowing of small creatures. Juniper wants to leave, to follow that whisper all the way back to the banks of the Big Sandy, but she stays shut inside the airless perfume of Salem's Sin.

Even Juniper doesn't dare go out on the day of the election.

Jennie Lind had been right: the mayor stepped down the previous week. *The Post* printed a cartoon of a saggy, weak-chinned fellow fleeing a burning building while innocent civilians wailed from the windows—Juniper wondered if it was accident or accuracy that led the artist to omit the mayor's shadow—and announced a special election on the first of September.

The number of speeches and rallies and door-to-door campaigners had tripled. New campaign posters papered the streets—*Clement Hughes for a Safer Salem! James Bright for a Brighter Future! Vote Gideon Hill—Our Light Against the Darkness!*—and every paper of record printed double-length issues full of editorials and interviews and the predictions of an elderly cat that had supposedly foreseen the results of the last four elections accurately. Even the news of fresh witchcraft was shoved to the second and third pages.

Juniper has felt the last week as a strange respite. The shadows seem to dog them less nimbly, as if they are distracted with some other business, and Hill's mobs seem more concerned with bullying votes than with witch-hunting. Even the Wiggin woman used her weekly column in *The Post* to advocate for Mr. Gideon Hill, "the noblest man I have ever had the privilege to meet, who brought me from darkness into light."

The Sisters and Daughters have done what they could, but none of them has a vote to cast. The Colored Women's League raised money to pay poll taxes for the husbands and sons and fathers; the New Salem Women's Association went door-to-door with little informative pamphlets until one of them had hot tea tossed in her face. Bella wrote a letter to the editor objecting to the "medieval attitudes held by Mr. Gideon Hill and his followers," and signed it *Outis*. One of the Hull sisters drew a rather gruesome but effective poster of Gideon Hill tormenting a young maiden in the cells of the Deeps, his cringing dog transformed into a snarling hound, his mild expression into a demented howl. The maiden swoons in her chains, innocent and soft-looking above the words A MODERN INQUISITION: VOTE AGAINST TORTURE!

"Is that supposed to be me?" Juniper asked, pointing to the maiden.

"I took certain artistic liberties," Victoria allowed.

Now there is nothing to do but wait. Juniper and her sisters sit in the comfortable, shabby back room of Salem's Sin, watching the sun fade from brass to copper to rose-gold. Strix and Pan rustle in the shadows or circle near the ceiling, restless and worried.

Pearl's girls rotate through at irregular intervals, rarely speaking. Juniper might have been puzzled by their odd hours and various states of undress, except that Frankie Black took her aside several weeks ago and explained in plain terms what sort of establishment Salem's Sin was, causing Juniper to snort coffee through her nose and reconsider several of her assumptions about decency, morality, and sin.

But there isn't much business this evening; most of the north end's wealthiest men are stuffed into boardrooms and elegant parlors, drinking champagne and waiting for the election results to come in like everyone else.

Juniper rises to renew the wards across the threshold and sills every so often, whispering the words like prayers. Bella sits with her notebook on her knees, not writing anything, and Agnes dozes with Eve in a puffy armchair. Eve's sleep is troubled, her face flushed and her brow wrinkled in angry furrows.

An angry woman is a smart woman, Mags used to say. Juniper feels a great swoop of sadness that Mags will never meet her great-granddaughter. She folds her fingers around the locket on her chest, flesh-warm.

She must fall asleep, because she wakes to find the room sunk into midnight-gloom, lit by a single candle. She sits with Bella for a while, feeling their breathing fall into perfect rhythm and knowing without looking that Agnes is breathing with them. Together they watch the subtle creep of shadows in the alley outside, looking for reaching fingers or sightless heads.

The next time Juniper wakes it's to the *tap-tap* of knuckles at the back door. The candle is a slumped puddle over-spilling its saucer, and the window is graying into morning.

Bella hurries to the door and Miss Cleopatra Quinn steps through it. All three sisters look up at her, a silent question hanging between them.

Cleo doesn't say anything. She merely looks at them, eyes somber and tired.

"Oh *fuck*," Juniper whispers.

Agnes shoots her one of her brand-new watch-your-mouth-there-are-children-present looks, but her face is pale. Pan alights on the arm of her chair, neck-feathers bristled.

"Was it close, at least?" Bella whispers. "Will there be a recount?"

Cleo slumps into an empty couch. "The *Post* headline this morning refers to it as a 'landslide,' I believe. *The Defender* prefers the term 'catastrophe.'"

Juniper feels a delicate snap in her chest, a final thread of hope breaking. She thinks of Hill's face—not his smiling, chinless mask, but the true face beneath it, all red gums and grubbing fear. He already possessed some dark, creeping power that lurked in alleys and stole souls; what would he do with the kind of power he could wield in broad daylight?

A voice swears softly in the doorway behind them: Miss Pearl stands there, clutching a slinky silk robe tight around her throat and staring at Cleo. Juniper notices the seams at the corners of her eyes for the first time, the soft folds of flesh at her throat.

Bella settles on the couch beside Cleo. "He won't take office for a while. We've still got time, we can prepare." She sounds like a woman trying to reason with a rifle or a bear trap. From the corner, Strix makes a soft, sorrowing sound.

Cleo shakes her head once. "In light of the city's great need—witches running loose, murderers not apprehended, recent evidence of black magic, et cetera—he's taking immediate control. The Fair is closing early, the police force is expanding. He spoke this morning from the steps of the capitol." She withdraws a flyer from her skirt pocket and passes it among them.

Bella gasps as she reads it. Agnes sighs. Juniper swears.

To protect our **BELOVED CITIZENS** against the ongoing scourge of **WITCHCRAFT**, the city of New Salem is obliged to adopt a new set of **ORDINANCES**:

For Immediate Effect

1. Any and all practitioners of **WITCHCRAFT** (including hedge-witches, street-witches, fortune-tellers, abortion-ists, midwives, suffragists, prostitutes, radicals, or other unnatural women) will be placed under immediate arrest and subject to **TRIAL BY FIRE**.

2. Any and all individuals harboring (offering aid to, sympathizing with, housing, feeding, or assisting) a known practitioner of **WITCHCRAFT** will be subject to arrest, imprisonment of up to ninety (90) days, and a fine of no less than $100.

3. Any individual or establishment selling materials known to be associated with the practice of **WITCHCRAFT**—herbs, potions, spells, bones, sacrificial animals, bodily substances, chalk, candles of particular colors, Satanic texts—will be subject to arrest, imprisonment of up to seven (7) years, and seizure of all assets.

4. The **GEORGIAN INQUISITORS** will be immediately reassembled and granted all former legal powers and privileges historically associated with their rank, with the sole purpose of enforcing the above ordinances, with special priority granted to the infamous **EASTWOOD SISTERS**.

The words *trial by fire* swim hideously in Juniper's vision. "They can't do this."

Cleo laughs. It isn't a very good laugh. "They already have."

"But it's not legal. It can't be. I wasn't the best student but Miss Hurston made us recite the Constitution in second grade."

"The *Constitution*? What, exactly, do you think the Constitution is? A magic spell? A dragon, perhaps, that will swoop down to defend you in your most desperate hour?" Cleo straightens in her seat. Juniper doesn't think she's ever seen a face so full of scorn. "I assure you it has only ever been a piece of paper, and it has only ever applied to a very few persons."

Juniper opens her mouth to argue or apologize, she doesn't know which, but Cleo is already standing, reaching for her derby hat. "I'm going home. I have to report to my mother, and help them prepare for . . . whatever comes."

"Cleo, wait—" Bella reaches for her hand but Cleo shifts slightly away. She reaches for the door, looking back at Bella with her face hard. "It will be worse for me and mine. It always is." She steps across their wards and out into the dull-iron dawn.

There is a brief, strained silence, broken by Miss Pearl. "I think you ought to leave, too." She holds the list of new ordinances in her lacquered nails. The whiteness of her face makes her mouth look like a wound, red and shining.

Juniper feels her eyebrows shoot high. "Excuse me?"

Pearl folds the page in neat quarters and tucks it down the front of her dress. Her fingers tremble very slightly. "Leave. Now. It just got a lot more dangerous to harbor witches or whores, and I can't risk both at once."

Juniper and her sisters stare at her, mute and accusing. The red slash of her lips thins. "I know it's not fair or right. But I owe my girls more than I owe you three. I want you gone before noon."

Her silk robe swishes as she turns to leave. "And take some tonic for the baby. Talk to Frankie before you go."

Agnes and her sisters have nowhere to go, so they go nowhere: the South Sybil boarding house.

They move across the city with their cloaks drawn high and their faces disguised by Miss Pearl's creams and potions, walking carefully apart from one another. They pass churches with their doors thrown wide, bells clanging in celebration; men with brass badges toasting one another in the streets; a knot of women with white sashes handing out wreaths and roses.

At the bridge they are forced to wait, standing among a cheering crowd as a procession of white horses passes. Gideon Hill himself rides in the center, looking stern and somehow noble, transformed by the glow of adulation into more than himself, more than a man: a painted icon or an angel. Agnes hunches to disguise the baby wrapped tight against her chest, watching Gideon through her lashes. She is almost surprised by how much she hates him, and how familiar the hate feels in her chest: the bitter, futile hatred of the weak for the powerful, the small for the strong.

They find South Sybil half-abandoned, strangely desolate. The landlady's door swings gently in the breeze, revealing a disheveled little room with no one inside it. In the halls every other door is marked with ashen Xs, whether for plague or for witchcraft they can't tell.

It's an absurd risk to return here, where Gideon and his shadows surely spied on them before, but Juniper argued that the sheer nerve of the thing would be some protection in itself. And neither Bella nor Agnes could think of anywhere else to run.

No. 7 is entirely empty. Agnes's few possessions have been tumbled and shaken from their places, as if some careless giant picked up her room and rattled it once or twice, and there's a sickly, rotten-food sweetness in the air, but it otherwise looks very much like the room where the Sisters of Avalon first signed their names in Bella's book.

Juniper wards the threshold and windowsills while Bella picks at piles of laundry and tangled sheets, trying to restore some sense of order. "Well. It's only for a night or two." Bella is clearly trying for a hearty, bracing tone, but landing closer to bleak. "Perhaps tomorrow we can reach out to the Sisters. Discuss our strategy."

Maybe Juniper or Agnes would have answered her, but Eve coughs in her sleep and begins to wail, fists clenched, tiny tears pearling at the corners of her eyes.

As if she knows what's coming, as if she knows there's no such thing as the Sisters of Avalon any longer.

31

There is a balm in Gilead
To make the wounded whole.

A song to cure a stubborn sickness, requiring feverfew & the Big
Dipper

Three days later, Agnes Amaranth is alone at South Sybil.

She's thinking back over the summer and trying to pinpoint the moment they should have stopped, given up, run away. Perhaps after Avalon burned, or after Juniper's arrest. Perhaps even before all that, as soon as they saw the shape of the tower in the sky and felt the wild wind of elsewhere on their cheeks.

All she knows for certain is that they should have left before the election. Now there are Inquisitors patrolling the streets every dusk and dawn, armed officers at every trolley stop and train station. Now women are arrested and dragged past jeering crowds, their dresses torn and their throats collared, and the Deeps echo with the wails of caged women. Now Hill's purge has begun, and it's too late to run.

Agnes's sisters are both off doing what they can, which isn't enough. Juniper left at dusk to hassle the patrols of Inquisitors, leading them on a merry chase and granting their targets time to run. She kissed Eve's cheek and strode into the hall with her black-yew staff gripped tight and her jaw set.

Bella left even before that, escorted by an impassive, oak-skinned woman into the tunnels to confer with Cleo and the other Daughters. The papers reported that Mayor Hill was recruiting "concerned citizens" to help settle the unsettled south side, massing a small army of men and torches at the edge of New Cairo. Cleo and her mother were trying to ward what could be warded and funnel the young and old out of harm's way.

"I'll ask Araminta if she has any feverfew left. Or anything else that might..." Bella didn't seem to know how to finish the sentence, but merely cast a worried look at Eve.

Agnes and her sisters had cast every spell and charm they could find to drive back the fever, to soothe her racking cough. Agnes fell asleep each night chanting spells like prayers, stroking the bloody red of her daughter's curls, but none of it seemed to last.

Now their witch-ways have run out. Now her daughter's every breath rattles like dead leaves across pavement, as if autumn itself slunk down her throat and burrowed in her small chest. Now Agnes curls around her body on the narrow bed, willing her skin to cool.

She thinks a little sunlight might help, a little clean September air in her lungs, but she keeps the doors and windows shut tight and draws a salt-circle around their bed. A new wanted poster appeared on the streets the previous day, offering a generous reward for "an infant with red curls, cruelly stolen from her rightful mother; Eastwoods suspected." Juniper brought it home crumpled in her fist.

So Agnes stays hidden, waiting.

Sometime after dawn Eve falls into a deeper sleep. At first Agnes is grateful, after a long night of coughing and fussing. But the longer she sleeps the less grateful Agnes becomes. Eve's arms lie limp on the quilt, chest flushed pink, tiny fists unclenched. Even the frown-lines on her brow have unfolded.

Agnes strokes her bare skin with one knuckle. Eve doesn't move.

Terror jolts through her, spine to skull. Pan appears at her shoulder, voicing a piercing hawk's cry. Eve's eyelids give the barest flutter.

Agnes says, firmly and calmly, "*No.*"

This isn't how the story goes; she doesn't cower in the dark while her daughter dies. She doesn't lie back and let the tide of the world have its way with her, like her mother did.

She stands and paces, rustling through empty jars and turning out every pocket. A handful of thorns, black-pearl seeds, a few twists of herbs, curled and brittle. Not enough. There has to be someone in this city with the witch-ways or words she needs, or someone who will find them for her. She thinks of circles and bindings and joined hands. Of Mr. August Lee, who came when she called him.

She fumbles in her skirt pocket for her last mockingbird feather, raggedy and crimped. She pricks her palm with the hollow point and whispers the words. *Hush little baby, don't say a word.*

Heat snakes through her veins. Agnes unlatches the window and sends the feather into the sky along with a whispered name. "Tell him to meet me"—she hesitates, unwilling to say the words *South Sybil* out loud in case some unfriendly shadow is listening in the alley—"at the corner of Lamentation and Sixteenth," she finishes.

Agnes rubs pale dye into her hair and ties a maid's apron around her waist. She wraps her daughter in gray wool—her head lolls, a thin line of white gleaming beneath the red of her lashes—and steps across their wards and into the hall. For a long moment she stands there, warring with herself, before lifting her hand to knock at the door to No. 12.

A pair of blondish, round-cheeked girls answer the door, so similar they can only be twins. All their hearty Kansas aunts and cousins must be at work. They blink up at Agnes, neither one recognizing the gray-haired maid standing in the hall as their former neighbor.

"I need someone to watch my baby girl while I run to the grocer's. Please, just for a minute. She's sick."

The girls look at one another, communicating in the same silent language Agnes once shared with her sisters. They nod, and Agnes sets Eve in their arms with shaking hands. Better to keep her hidden away than risk someone on the street spotting a red curl.

Agnes hurries up the street with her head bent and her shoulders hunched, trying to look harmless and timid and forgettable. Every now and then her gaze crosses another woman's and she sees the same desperate innocence in their faces. It sends a shiver of fury through her.

She arrives at the corner of St. Lamentation and Sixteenth before August. She circles the block rather than lingering, ducking her head politely at a pair of patrolling Inquisitors.

He still isn't there when she returns. Fearful questions clamor in her skull—was he detained or delayed? Was he already in the Deeps, outed as a witch-sympathizer?—but she keeps her feet shuffling and her face slack. A flash of shadow tells her Pan is hovering somewhere high above her.

She circles the block again. This time August's absence is a bell tolling in her chest, a low warning. If he could have come to her, he would have: it was written in the tilt of his smile, the shine of his eyes when he looked at her.

Had her mockingbird failed somehow? Had it gotten lost or eaten or—her heart vanishes mid-beat, a breathless silence—intercepted?

Agnes feels something falling inside her from a very great height, a silent rushing.

She runs. She runs as if there are wolves or shadows at her heels. Her body jars with the running, her breasts tender, her belly weak, but she doesn't stop.

Eve, Eve, EveEveEve.

She crashes through the boarding-house door, heaving up the steps. She doesn't bother to knock at No. 12. The door bangs against the cracked plaster. "Where is she? Is she safe?"

The blond girls are holding one another on the floor, shoulders shivering with sobs. One of them looks up at Agnes with the shine of tears on her cheeks, one eye puffing with the promise of a bruise. "They c-came knocking right after you left. They said—"

But Agnes can't hear her because she's listening to the silence running beneath her, the terrible absence of the sound she's heard every second for seven days: the dry, desperate rattle of her daughter's breath.

The silence swells inside her. It presses against her ribs and pops in her ears, until Agnes is nothing but pale skin wrapped around a sound-less scream.

Her own voice has a distant, underwater warble. "Who?"

The other girl answers this time, reaching an arm around her sister. "Inquisitors. A pair of them, wearing those red-cross uniforms. They knocked and Clara answered, and they said they were looking for a baby girl." Her eyes shift a little, uncertain. "They said a w-witch had snatched her straight from her mother's arms and run off with her." Her arm tightens around her sister, as if she thinks Agnes might snatch one of them next.

"And where"—her voice is still perfectly calm; only the very tips of her fingers tremble—"did they take her?"

"Don't know," says the girl. "They—they said if you had any questions you could take them up with the mayor."

The mayor. The girl sounds doubtful as she says it, because even a little girl knows mayors don't meet with witches. But Agnes recognizes it for what it is: an invitation.

A trap, into which she would walk willingly and open-eyed, because he has stolen her daughter away from her and there is nothing she would not do to get her back.

The girls gasp and clutch at one another. It's only when one of them pants, "What—what is that?" that Agnes becomes aware that Pan has materialized on her shoulder, talons biting through her blouse. "You *are* a witch!"

"Yes," Agnes answers distantly. "And they should have thought of that before they took what was mine."

And then she's back in the street, stumbling over cobblestones and shoving past strangers. She's crossing the Thorn, heading for St. George's Square, before it occurs to her, with a faraway flick of annoyance, that her sisters will follow her into the trap. That they will feel her fear through the binding between them and come running, and then Gideon Hill will have all three—*four*, Agnes thinks, with a swallowed scream—Eastwoods in his palm.

She thinks how very tiresome it is to love and be loved. She can't even risk her life properly, because it no longer belongs solely to her.

A feathered shadow sweeps across her. *Pan.* What is he, really? A piece of magic itself, flown through from the other side and tethered to her soul. An else-wise, otherworldly creature that doesn't particularly care what is and isn't possible.

Agnes cranes her neck upward. "Warn them for me, Pan. Tell them to stay away." She feels the hot spark of his eyes on her. "Please." He shrieks back to her, a shivering, wild sound entirely out of place in the civilized sprawl of New Salem.

Agnes runs.

Bella thinks at first it's a roll of thunder cracking over the city, out of season, or perhaps a distant earthquake. Some vast, shattering thing, blind and angry.

Then she realizes it's her sister's heart splitting in two.

The spell of warding dies on her lips. "Three bless and keep me," she whispers.

Miss Araminta Wells and another pair of women look over at her, harassed. "Thought we were working these wards together," Araminta drawls.

They're standing at the north end of Nut Street, their fingers crusted with salt, their pockets weighted with thistle and chalk. The canniest and cleverest members of the Daughters of Tituba have gathered to work what wards they can while others ferry the youngest and oldest occupants of New Cairo into the tunnels, blindfolded. Bella provided them with all the words and ways she could and a list of addresses and households willing to shelter them until Hill's raid was over.

Araminta held the list, running her thumb over the names in tidy writing: *Miss Florentine Lee, 201 Spinner's Row, Room No. 44 (3 persons). Mr. Henry Blackwell, 186 St. Jerome St. (15 persons).*

"I keep waiting for you to disappoint me," she said querulously, before bustling off to gather supplies from her cellar.

"That's more or less a declaration of love, from my mother," Cleo sighed at her elbow.

Now Araminta glowers as she watches Bella. "What is it? Who is it?" She bites hard into the words, like a woman used to bad news and dark portents.

"It's Agnes." But Bella thinks: *It's Eve.* Surely nothing else could crack her sister's heart like that. Bella catches the worried O of Cleo's mouth, but she can't seem to focus on anything except the splitting of her sister's heart. "I'm sorry. I said I would stay but I have to go."

"Go, child," Araminta tells her. "We'll finish without you." Her mouth works for another second, as if there's something unpleasant caught in her teeth. "And call on the Daughters, if you have need of us." She touches her breast pocket and Bella hears the crinkle of folded paper.

She wheels to Cleo and presses her hand once, too hard. "Meet me tonight. Back at South Sybil."

If Cleo answers, it's lost in the frantic thump of her feet and the mutter of spells as Bella runs.

She follows the echo of Agnes's fury north out of New Cairo. At Second Street she grabs the rail of a passing trolley and steps aboard, glaring with such ferocity that the conductor elects to look the other way.

The city whitens around her. Police stroll past, batons swinging jauntily, and Inquisitors strut in their still-fresh uniforms. None of them notice a hunched, white-haired woman clinging to the trolley as it jangles past, or the flitting shadow of an owl's wing above them.

Bella sees the dome of City Hall ahead and tastes the sour bite of fear in her throat. Why would Agnes be at the square? Why would she leave the safety of their circled wards?

She hops down from the trolley and stumbles against a plain-looking woman pushing a frilly pram, limping on every other step. It's only after the woman hisses in her ear, "Saints, Bell, you look older than Mags," that she realizes the pram is empty.

"June! Did you feel it? Do you know what's happening?"

Juniper's face is blotched and pale beneath her disguise. "Something bad. She's running this way, seems like, but Lord knows why."

A bird swoops suddenly between them, a ragged snatch of midnight. Bella lifts her arm and feels the bite of talons before she realizes the bird does not belong to her. "*Pan?* What are you doing here? Where's Agnes? Someone will see!"

He ignores her, eyes red and reproachful. He opens his beak and a human voice echoes out of it. "*Stay away. Please. Stay away.*"

The voice belongs, quite unmistakably and impossibly, to their sister.

Pan closes his beak and vanishes in a swirl of ash and smoke, leaving the two of them surrounded by mutters and staring eyes. Bella wipes a smudge of char from her spectacles. "I didn't know they could do that."

Voices and running steps rise around them. Juniper grabs her sleeve and hauls her into an alley. "What do we do?"

Bella snorts, half-hysterical. "Didn't you listen to any of my witch-tales?" Juniper marches her onward, whispering words and spitting over her shoulder. It hisses on the cobblestones and rises like steam behind them, obscuring their escape.

"In the stories, it's generally best to do whatever the hell the talking animal tells you."

32

May the Devil take you down
And break your golden crown.

A mortal curse, requiring hemlock & hate

The mayor's office is all oiled leather and oak paneling. The walls are lined with paintings in gilt frames, displaying the usual association of horses and Saints and men in powdered wigs. An especially noble-looking Saint George of Hyll does battle with a dragon the color of hellfire, hounds baying at his side.

A dark-stained desk hulks in the middle of the room. On its surface, between neat stacks of papers and the dark shine of an inkwell, lies a mockingbird. A clawed shadow is cast across it, pinning its wings at precise and hideous angles. Its ribcage throbs in panic.

Agnes Amaranth looks away, swallowing hard. Pan croons on her shoulder.

Mr. Gideon Hill stands at the tall window, watching the scurry and bustle of the street below with his hand resting on the iron collar of the dog at his side. The five o'clock slant of the light draws deep shadows behind them.

The dog faces Agnes first, its tail giving the faintest, cowardly wave. Mr. Hill turns to Agnes with a mannered smile, as if she is a necessary but tiresome guest. "Ah, Miss Agnes Eastwood, I presume." Agnes's disguise is a careless one: the windswept braid over her shoulder is already threaded with sleek black and her eyes are boiling back to silver. "But surely Miss Tattershall ought to have shown you in?"

"The receptionist?"

"Yes."

Agnes shrugs without looking away from him. "She's sleeping." Her head had knocked against her desk with a hollow, split-melon sound, but her eyes remained peacefully closed. Agnes supposes it was possible that she overdid it—Bella mentioned princesses who slept for centuries and dozing gentlemen who missed entire wars—but she finds she doesn't much care.

"How generous of you." Hill does not appear in the least relieved about Miss Tattershall's fate. His gaze on her is—strange. Almost wary, as if he is waiting for her to produce a pistol or a spell from her skirt pockets.

Her pockets are empty except for the weak remnants of her witching: the crumbled dust of herbs, a few sweat-damp matches, the waxen stub of a candle.

"My daughter, Mr. Hill. Where is she?" She wonders if he hears the shake in her voice, and whether he mistakes it for fear.

Hill strolls to the dark island of his desk and sits, dog padding meekly behind him. It folds itself beneath his chair, looking at her with sorry black eyes, while its master steeples his hands above the mockingbird. It writhes, desperate, trapped.

"If you read the new city ordinances closely, you will find they specifically revoke the parental rights of known witches or witch-sympathizers," he observes.

"She's mine. She belongs to *me*." Every ruby-red curl of her hair, every soft fingernail. Agnes feels the absence of her weight like a spreading bruise on her arms.

Hill's eyes are still watchful, calculating, as if he is prodding a caged creature to see what it might do. "She belongs to the city of New Salem, Miss Eastwood. She will be—"

Agnes snaps the match in her pocket and hisses the words August taught her months before, when the city still hummed with springtime and she still thought spells and sisterhood could alter the cruel workings of the world.

She doesn't need to borrow her sisters' will this time, does not even need the familiar perched like a red-eyed gargoyle on her shoulder; her own will might level cities.

The room shatters. Bright shards zing through the air as every pane of glass in Hill's office fractures and bursts.

In the silence that follows, the September breeze sings through the jagged holes of the windows, tossing glittering specks of glass-dust into the air. Ink spreads from the cracked inkwell and pools like black blood over his desk.

Agnes feels a damp trickle down her jaw, a stinging line across her cheekbone. Hill appears entirely untouched.

He brushes a splinter of glass from his shirtsleeve and continues speaking, perfectly even. "—taken in by the New Salem Home for Lost Angels until such time as a more fit mother may be found. Or"—and in the sliver of space following that word she feels the jaws of his trap closing around her—"until I grant you a pardon for your past crimes and restore her legal custody to you."

Agnes goes very still. Pan's talons curl into her shoulder.

Hill's smile is a marionette's cheery lie, red and white painted over dead wood. "But first, tell me: do you and your sisters still visit the tower?"

"Do we—why would we?"

"Well, Miss Eastwood, I've been looking for the three of you for weeks now."

"You and everybody else in this damn city." A summer with Juniper has put a little bit of Crow County back in her voice. She almost wishes Juniper were here now, half-full of horseshit and brave as brass, before remembering she wants her to remain far away.

"When I look for a thing I find it." Hill flicks his chin and the shadows in the room roil, sprouting wriggling fingers and reaching hands. "But I didn't find you. I caught glimpses—Miss James running about, a few houses warded better than they ought to be—but nothing certain. If the child hadn't fallen ill, if your messenger hadn't flown into my hands...who knows?" The mockingbird pants on the desk, open-beaked. "I wondered if perhaps you'd called their tower back again and hidden your binding better this time."

Agnes almost laughs at him. It isn't some ancient witchcraft that's kept them hidden—it's merely the ordinary women of New Salem, the laundresses and maids and housewives who opened their doors despite the risk.

"Well, we haven't." And why would he care if they had? What is it to him if they crouch in the burnt ruins of a tower that was once a library?

"I wonder if you are telling me the truth." His marionette-smile has worn thin; rotted wood is showing through the paint. "The three of you have become very adept at witching, very quickly." His eyes flick to Pan and away. "Did you, perhaps, receive instruction?"

"No." Their teachers were desperate need and decades of rage; the hoarded words of their mothers and grandmothers; one another.

"Don't *lie* to me." Agnes hears the lick of fear in his voice and sweat pricks her palms. Her daddy was never more dangerous than when he was afraid, and he was always afraid: that they might wriggle out of his grasp, that he was weak, that someone somewhere was laughing at him.

"If you love your daughter, you will tell me now: have you spoken to them?" *There's something broken about him*, Juniper told them. *Something sick*. It's only now that Agnes can see it, the terror and madness seeping through the cracks. "Are they still there? Still hiding from me?"

His shadow lengthens behind him, creeping up the wood-paneled wall. It boils with heads and limbs, arms extending at warped, unnatural angles. On the desk the mockingbird writhes and flutters more desperately, wingtips drawing mad patterns through spilled ink, fragile ribs flattening as a shadow-hand presses downward. The dog whines, high and mournful.

"Stop! I don't know what you mean, I swear I don't."

There's a terrible crunch, like china crushed beneath a boot, then silence. The mockingbird is very still.

Hill watches her face for another pressing second before his shoulders unwind. His shadow shrinks back to more plausible dimensions; he stitches the split seams of his mask.

"Very good. Of course I didn't really think—but one never knows. Now, Miss Eastwood." He prods the mockingbird into a wastebasket with a jagged shard of glass and lays the glass neatly back on the desk, like a man arranging his pens. "I called you here to make an offer. I am willing to pardon your crimes and grant you custody of Miss"—he refers to a typewritten page—"Eve Everlasting Eastwood—my, what a mouthful—if you are willing to assist me in locating and apprehending your sisters. This witch-hunt has gone on long enough, I think. People will grow discontented soon, perhaps doubtful, if I don't produce the witches."

Of course this is the choice. It's always this choice, in the end—sacrifice someone else, trade one heart for another, buy your survival at the price of someone else's. Save yourself but leave your sister behind. *Don't leave me.*

Agnes feels cold water pooling around her ankles, rising fast. "And what... what will happen to my sisters?"

"That's for the courts to decide."

The water is belly-deep now. "And what happens if I say no?"

"Then your daughter remains deathly ill, in the dubious care of the Lost Angels. You will wait in the Deeps until I catch your sisters—which

I will, sooner or later—and they will burn just the same. Except you will burn beside them."

The water laps at her neck, icy and black. Hadn't they drowned witches sometimes, in the way-back days? "What if—what if I convinced them to leave the city, instead? We'll disappear. You'll never hear our names again. We won't work another spell as long as we live."

His smile reminds her of Mr. Malton's when he told them their shifts were cut or their pay was docked, soothing and false. "I'm afraid that wouldn't satisfy my constituents. I'm sure you understand." His tone turns musing. "It's just the way people work. You tell them a story, and they require an ending. Would anyone know Snow White's name if her Mother never wore hot iron shoes? Or Gretel's, if her Crone never climbed in the oven?"

Hill's smile now is sincere. "The witches always burn, in the end. You see?"

Agnes does. The cold water closes high above her head.

"Please." She hates the taste of the word in her mouth, but she says it anyway. Sometimes begging was enough to turn her daddy's fist into an open palm, a slap into a shout. "Please just give her back. She's sick." Tears gather and fall.

"I know, dear." His smile is venom and honey. "Wouldn't you like me to make her well again?"

Could he? Clearly he knows witching she and her sisters don't; who's to say what powers he possesses?

Her answer feels inevitable, a choice made in the moment she first looked down into Eve's midnight eyes. There is nothing she wouldn't do for her daughter.

"What will it be, Miss Eastwood?"

Agnes tries to picture her life after the choosing: gray and listless, alone except for the bitter taste of her own betrayal, the frayed ends of a broken binding. The summer of ninety-three would blur and fade, a little girl's dream of a time when the three of them were one thing, whole and inviolate.

But she would have Eve. She would whisper the words and ways to her daughter, disguised as songs and stories, in the secret hope that the next generation could take up their fallen swords and carry on the battle. It was what Mama Mags had done, and her mother before her: sacrifice in order to survive, and hand their sacrifice down to their daughters.

Now Agnes will choose the same. Gideon Hill's smile gleams at her in the shard of windowpane still lying on his desk. The point shines crystal-white, sharp as shattered bone.

A very foolish idea occurs to Agnes. A bolder trade, a third choice.

They would catch her, of course, and there would be no fire hot enough for the witch who murdered the mayor of New Salem, their Light Against the Darkness. But without Hill and his shadows surely her sisters could save Eve, could flee the city and raise her in secret, surrounded by wild roses and stone.

She will need to be very fast. She falls to her knees as if overcome with grief, and Pan startles from her shoulder. Hill says something insincere about understanding the difficulty of her position, but she can't hear it over the thud of blood in her ears. She fumbles a stub of candle wax from her pocket and draws an X on the polished parquet.

She covers her face with her hands and whispers the words to her palms, a hard line of Latin. Heat billows in her chest, burning back the cold water. Her hair drifts gently upward, as if gravity is an absent-minded god who has forgotten her for this single, desperate second. Beneath his chair, Hill's dog whines.

She thinks of her sisters: Juniper who would not hesitate, Bella who would not miss. She thinks of her daughter.

She leaps. The glass is in her hand and driving toward Hill's left eye before he can flinch, almost before he can blink. The point parts the fine gold of his lashes. She braces for the wet puncture of his eye, the scrape of bone against glass—

But it doesn't come. The shard *skrees* off Hill's face and bites into the desktop instead, slicing Agnes's palm. There is an airless moment while both of them look down at the red-slicked glass, before a dozen shadow-hands claw toward her. They wrap around her wrists and ankles, slick and cold, and force her backward across his desk, limbs wrenched and splayed. She thinks of the mockingbird, twisting and twisting.

Gideon Hill looks down at her with a pair of watery, pink-rimmed eyes, entirely unhurt.

He gives her a pitying shake of his head. "I admire your spirit, Miss Eastwood. Truly I do. But please understand that I am not going to be harmed by nursery rhymes or bits of glass. I am going to ask you a final time—"

A black shape dives between them, talons outstretched. The claws rake. Blood blooms. Then the dog is barking hysterically and Hill is screaming and another shadow-hand is rising into the air, reaching for her hawk.

Pan is already gone, vanished back into elsewhere. Hill is left panting and powerless, blinking blood from his eyes and touching the ragged edges of three deep furrows Pan scored across his face.

He reels, his painted mask split. Beneath it Agnes sees raw, wild terror. "No! *No!* How dare you touch me! How dare you—shut *up*, *Cane!*" The black dog ceases her yelping.

Red drips from Hill's chin. His face is someplace beyond fear, beyond fury, gray and still. Agnes realizes distantly that she knows that face, has seen it reflected back at her from her sisters: the terrible resignation of someone who is accustomed to pain. Who suffered too many blows, too young, and is always waiting for the next to fall.

Hill meets her eyes and she wonders if he will kill her now. If he will crush her like a bird in his fist for the crime of seeing him bleed.

The shadows tighten around her ankles, press against her ribs. She feels the scrape and pop of cartilage, the grind of bone against bone—before he flicks a finger in dismissal and sends her skidding backward off the desk.

He reaches into his breast pocket and Agnes flinches, thinking of pistols or knives or magic wands, but the thing he withdraws is small and soft, perfectly innocent: a tiny curl of hair. Agnes thinks it's brown or maybe chestnut until the light catches it. The curl shines a deep, bonfire red.

She would prefer a knife.

"If you ever want to see your daughter again—if you want her to recover from the fever—you and your sisters will be in St. George's Square tomorrow before sundown."

Agnes looks at the blood still weeping from his wounds. It's ordinary blood, red and wet. "Yes," she whispers. "Alright."

"Good. Now *get out*."

Agnes does as she is told.

She does not run, this time. She walks, steady and upright, following the lines that lead back to her sisters, hardly noticing when passersby scurry out of her way. She should be despairing, regretting every choice that had led her here to this last and worst one, but she isn't.

Instead she is merely thinking. Turning pieces over and over in her mind like stones: the fear in his face, ancient and terrible; a children's story about witches who did not die when they should have; the bite of glass in her palm and the shine of Hill's blood.

A thought is forming, surfacing like a leviathan from the black:

You are not invincible, Gideon Hill.

And if he is not invincible—if he can bleed and break and die like any other man—then he should never have touched a single hair on her daughter's head.

Juniper feels her sister drawing closer like a gathering storm. Bella and Cleo wait with her, huddled together in the half-dark of the South Sybil boarding house, their eyes meeting sometimes then falling away. The room is silent except for the occasional rustle of skirts, the brush of feathers in the shadows.

Footsteps ring like mallets on the stairs. The door scrapes.

Agnes steps into the room looking fifty years older and a hundred years meaner. Blood crusts her fingertips and bruises shadow her wrists. Milk weeps down her blouse, and the sight of those stains is a knife between Juniper's ribs.

Pan trills on Agnes's shoulder, low and mournful, and Strix answers.

"What happened? Where's Eve?" Juniper's voice cracks over the name: Eve, who is ruby-red innocence, who is tiny and furious and perfect in some way that Juniper doesn't understand but wants fiercely to protect. Who might still be safe with her mother if it wasn't for Juniper and her troublemaking.

Agnes doesn't appear to have heard her. "We'll need more candles. I have three, I think. Maybe matches will do. And maiden's blood, crone's tears—Lord knows I've got the milk." She scurries around the room as she speaks, rattling through drawers.

Juniper's eyes meet Bella's. Cleo asks, gently, "Agnes? Why do you need candles?"

Agnes finds a handful of candle-stubs in a crate beneath her bed and arranges them in a hurried circle, muttering to herself. She looks perfectly deranged.

"Agnes." Bella's voice is even gentler than Cleo's. "What are you doing?"

But Juniper already knows. So does Bella, judging by the tremble of her fingers. "She's calling back the Lost Way of Avalon. Again."

Agnes doesn't pause, doesn't even look up.

"But *why*?" Bella sounds very close to tears.

"Because I'd like to talk with the Last Three."

A small silence follows this announcement. Even Cleo's mouth hangs open, her journalist's composure overcome at last. Juniper says, as casually as she can, "Sure. The thing is, though—and I don't want to upset you—the Last Three are dead."

Agnes makes a faint noise of irritation at such nitpicking.

"*Real* dead. Exceptionally dead. There are legends and stories about how dead they are. You might've heard some of them."

"I have, yes," Agnes acknowledges. "Still."

This is apparently too much for Bella, who wails, "What's wrong with you, Agnes? There's nothing left."

Agnes still doesn't look up. "What about Yulia's story? What about the witch who bound her heart to a needle or an egg or whatever it was, and lived forever?"

"A fable. A *myth*."

"And how many of our spells came from fables? What if it's more than a myth?"

Bella looks as if she's considered actually tearing her hair in frustration. "It isn't possible."

Agnes raises her head from her candle-circle and meets their eyes. She should look like a grief-struck madwoman, broken and hopeless, but instead she looks like an angel cast down from Heaven struggling back to her feet with blood on her teeth, ready to make war with God himself.

"I do not," she says, very clearly, "give a shit."

She withdraws a rust-smeared shard of glass from her pocket and hands it to Juniper. Her eyes say *please* and Juniper can't refuse her. She slices the glass across her open palm, cutting deep, and opens her hand to let her blood drip onto the warped floorboards of South Sybil.

33

Red sky at night, witch's delight.
Red sky at morning, witch's warning.

A spell for storms, requiring red cloth & wet earth

Beatrice Belladonna catches her sister's hand in hers before her blood falls. "Saints, *think*," she hisses. "What happens if you materialize a tower on top of a boarding house?"

Neither Agnes nor Juniper seem overly concerned. Juniper even looks slightly eager, like a child anticipating fireworks.

Bella suppresses an urge to shake the pair of them until their teeth rattle. "People live here! Lots of them! You can't just drop a library on top of them! The Mother only knows what it would do to our wards. And I still don't understand why we'd want to call Avalon in the first place—"

"He took her." Agnes's voice is quiet but ragged-edged, like a distant scream.

"Who did?" But Bella knows who.

"Gideon Hill. And he's scared, Bell. He has his shadows and his city and my daughter, but he's still frightened of something." Agnes looks up at her. "Of *Avalon*. Even though all the books are burned." Bella presses her fingertips to the paper-dry petal of the rose in her pocket, the only thing she saved from the ashes. "He asked me if they were still there. And I thought—who is *they*?"

"Sometimes when it was real quiet at Avalon I heard voices. Or thought I did." Juniper speaks slowly, feeling her way toward the edge of the impossible. "And down in the Deeps I heard...somebody."

She doesn't look at Bella, as if she expects scorn or pity, but Bella is quiet. She's remembering the times when she was alone in the rose-scented silence of the tower, when her attention wandered and she heard whispers murmuring and scuttling in the shadows. Words spoken in voices of dust and ivy, there and gone again.

There's a rustle of wool as Cleo shifts on the bed. "Do you mean... ghosts?" Bella feels a rush of relief that Cleo seems willing to entertain the possibility rather than edging quietly out of the room.

"I don't think they could be. What ghost could last four hundred years?" Ghosts were lingering specters, especially tenacious souls that clung to life a few hours beyond death. They didn't haunt towers or castles for centuries, except in wives' tales and rumors.

Cleo shrugs. "Some kind of spirit or memory, then? Perhaps preserved by—"

"I don't care what they are or aren't. I'm going to find them." Agnes touches her damp dress-front and reaches for the floor with fingers slick with milk.

"*Wait!* Please." Bella catches Agnes's hand in her free one, so that she stands between her sisters with their fists tight in hers. "I'll help you. But not here."

"Where, then?" Agnes's voice suggests she ought to decide quickly.

Where can they call a burned black tower back into existence without being seen and caught? Where in New Salem is free of both Inquisitors and innocents?

Then Bella remembers fleeing from the north side just the previous week, pausing at the padlocked gates of the Centennial Fair. It had closed after the election, but deconstruction was delayed in the name of the city's crisis. The sight of that long boulevard, empty except for crows and scattered puddles reflecting the blind gray of the September sky, had sent a shiver of melancholy down Bella's spine.

"The Fair," she breathes.

Her eyes cross Cleo's and for a moment the memory of that June afternoon blooms between them, shimmering and sweet, when they swayed together in the glass cage of the Ferris wheel. Bella feels a surge of regret that she wasted those precious minutes on worry, rather than wringing every ounce of joy from the world while she could.

Bella sees some of her own wistful hunger reflected in Cleo's face before she stands and places her derby hat neatly on her head. Her chin lifts. "Shall we, Misses Eastwood?"

Bella tries to tell Cleo she ought to run, that she doesn't have to follow them this far into madness, but the words lodge like swallowed stones in her throat. Instead she finds herself reaching for Cleo's hand as the four of them sweep down the steps of South Sybil and out into the dying day.

The nearest entrance to the railroad is two blocks east, down a set of stone steps and through a door reading *Miss Judy's Tea Shop: CLOSED*. Cleo shows the door her patterned scar and it opens into cool darkness.

They follow the tiger's-eye of Cleo's witch-light in silence. Bella thinks about the hands that carved the tunnels like veins beneath the city, the bodies laboring unseen and unfree; she thinks of the ways people make for themselves when there are none, the impossible things they render possible. She looks at the white of Agnes's knuckles and begins, just a little, to believe.

They emerge from an outhouse door on the north side. It's after curfew, and every door is locked tight, every curtain drawn. There's no one to notice four women filing through the alleys with familiars winging behind them. No one to hear the steady clack of a black-yew staff across the cobbles.

No one to see them pause beneath the high arch of the fairground entrance, or to wonder how they open the gate despite the stout iron padlock and the heavy chain around the bars.

They could hardly have chosen a better setting for the summoning of undead spirits. The bones of the Fair hulk around them like the remains of some prehistoric creature: the Ferris wheel, skeletal and dark; the sagging strings of light bulbs; the empty stands and tents, canvas flapping in the wind. The only sound is the dry capering of old ticket stubs across the boulevard and the cawing of crows.

The sun seems to be graying rather than setting, as if someone is wrapping stained gauze around it, but the tower would still be far too visible. "We should wait for full dark." Bella's voice echoes eerily.

"Why not make our own?" Juniper withdraws a red-dyed handkerchief from her skirt pocket. She spits into the dirt at her feet and whispers to the wet earth. *Red skies at night, witch's delight.*

She calls, and the storm answers. Above them the clouds darken like bruises. The watching crows go silent, vanishing into the blackening sky behind them. Strix and Pan circle, visible only by the firelight of their eyes.

"How's that?" Juniper's face is flushed with the heat of witching, eyes shining.

"Good enough." Agnes kneels on the cold stone and lays her candle-stubs and matchsticks in a circle a second time. Bella and Juniper kneel beside her. Agnes lets three drops of thin milk fall into the circle. Juniper scrapes her bloodied palm on the ground.

The wind rises. It lifts their hair from their shoulders, three shades of black tangling together, and buffets the wings of the owl and hawk high above them.

The first time Bella worked this spell she was in her office in the Salem College Library, foolish and alone. The second time she was with

Cleo in the wild ruins of Old Salem, full of desperate hope. Now she is here in the empty fairgrounds with her sisters and her lover and her familiar, and they have whatever is left behind when hope fades—a scorched, enduring thing, like the earth after a wildfire.

It will have to be enough.

Bella holds out her hands to her sisters.

Juniper frowns. "Is this part of the spell?"

"No," Bella admits. Juniper's hand closes tight around hers and the lines between them seem to sing, like a string finally in tune. Bella's tear slides cinder-hot down her cheek and splashes silently into the circle.

They speak the words together, a children's song about wayward sisters and lost crowns. A rhyme too dangerous to be written down, which was whispered and sung and stitched in secret, passed in pieces through the centuries. Bella thinks of the faint verse she found written in the back of *Children and Household Witch-Tales*, placed there by a different pair of sisters. She wishes she could thank them.

The heat strikes and catches behind their ribs as the Eastwoods speak the words. They draw three circles with their edges overlapping, and the heat becomes a flame that becomes a blaze.

Agnes's will is an anvil, an avalanche, cold and inevitable. Her fisher-hawk screeches a war-cry and Strix echoes him, their eyes scorching the sky. Just at the moment Bella thinks her skin will split and crack with the heat, it is done.

The tower stands in the unnatural dark of the New Salem fairgrounds. Gray curls of ash drift and shush around their skirts and burnt branches crisscross above them. On the ground between them three circles glow white.

Bella bends, scooping ash and earth into a glass jar. She works the binding and Cleo works the banishing, and then—with the faint snick of silver shears cutting the air—the tower vanishes again, tucked neatly into nowhere like a handkerchief folded back into a pocket.

Cleo slides the scissors back into her pocket. "There. Now hurry.

I'm sure someone saw something, even with the clouds, and I don't intend to be here when they come looking."

Agnes and Juniper are already crouched again above their drawn circles, their faces white and ghoulish in the eerie light, like a penny-paper illustration of wicked witches leering above a bubbling cauldron.

Bella hesitates, looking at Cleo with her cloak rippling in the autumn wind and her hand tight around the glass jar. "Thank you," Bella says softly, inadequately.

"I'll wait for you back at South Sybil." Cleo attempts one of her brash smiles, but it warps beneath the weight of worry. Her lips are warm against Bella's wind-chilled cheek, and then she is gone.

A few moments later, after a whispered rhyme and a twist in the air, the fairgrounds are entirely empty. A passerby, had there been one, might peer through the iron gate and notice nothing but an unusual number of crows gathered on the electric lines and rooftops, and the faint, wild smell of ash and rose on the wind.

Agnes didn't see Avalon after the fire, but she saw the bloody color of the sky as it burned and breathed the smoke of a thousand burning books. She isn't surprised to find herself standing in a ruin, a charred door beneath her hand, a desolate tower looming above her.

Yet, beneath the dead smell of ash and fire, there's a wetter, greener scent. She steps back from the door and sees tendrils of green snaking up the smoke-blackened stones: rose-vines, sprouting tiny buds and pale thorns. Grass reaches tender fingers up through the ash, and moss creeps like green velvet over the scorched roots of trees.

The only sounds are the rustle of wings and the pant of their breath and—is Agnes imagining it? Is her heart conjuring hope out of nothing?—the soft, secret murmur of women's voices.

Juniper stomps her foot on the ground as if she is knocking on a door. "Hey, ghosts! Wake up!"

Bella makes a strangled sound. "They aren't ghosts, June, I already said. And even if they were I hardly think shouting at them would be an effective—"

"Well, what's your plan, then?"

Agnes answers, "Little Girl Blue."

There's a short silence, until Bella says tentatively, "I'm not sure—that's a spell for rousing the sick or sleeping. I'm not sure it has the strength to wake lost souls from the dead, even if such souls *do* exist. Perhaps if we modified it somehow, added certain words or stronger ways—"

But Agnes is already bending to the earth, laying her palm among the soft green shoots of grass. "I don't know that the words and ways matter all that much, Bell." She hears Bella make a small, librarianish sound of objection. "Or maybe they matter, but not as much as will." Agnes swallows once, hard. "And I promise you I don't lack the will."

Her sisters speak the spell with her. *Little Girl Blue, come blow your horn.*

There's a little of Mama Mags lingering in the words, her sparrow-bright eyes and her tobacco-stained teeth. Agnes wishes she could call her spirit up from wherever it sleeps or drifts, just to cry once more against her breast.

Her sisters stumble at the final line, uncertain who they are waking, but Agnes fills in the gap. "Maiden, Mother, and Crone, awake, arise!" and whistles, sharp and high.

It's a small spell, like Bella said, a hedge-witch's cure for a drowsy babe or a touch of Devil's-fever. But Agnes feeds her will into it until her skin burns and her blood boils, until the magic sinks down into the black earth of nowhere and finds—a silent pulse. A secret, a whisper.

The sisters fall silent. The heat wicks away from Agnes's flesh.

"Did it work?" Juniper's voice rings too loud in the hush of nowhere.

Agnes ignores her, still reaching after that secret whisper in the dark, but it's gone. Vanished. Tears slick her eyes, blurring the gray-green earth before her.

But then: "Gone, all of it gone, after all that work—"

"—disgraceful, what they've done to the place—"

Voices, querulous and strange, their accents lilting and lisping. Just on the other side of the tower door.

One of them shushes the others, and then—"In our day eavesdropping could get your ears turned into parsnips and your lips sewn shut. Come in, if you're coming."

James Juniper is the wild sister, fearless as a fox and curious as a crow; she goes first into the tower.

Inside she finds a ruin: snowdrifts of ash and char, the skeleton of the staircase still clinging to the walls, greasy soot blackening every stone.

And three women.

There is a strangeness to them, a blurred shine like moonlight on moving water, but it seems to fade even as Juniper watches, until they are as real and solid as the stone beneath their feet.

The first thing Juniper thinks is that none of them look like their storybook illustrations. They're either uglier or more beautiful, she can't tell which, riddled with scars and specks and the small imperfections that divide the real from the make-believe. And in the drawings the Three are always a matched set, like a single woman caught and preserved at three different ages. Sometimes they're sisters; sometimes they're grandmother and mother and daughter.

Juniper thinks the women standing in the tower are unlikely to share any ancestor besides the first witch herself.

One of them is gnarled and golden, with white-streaked hair and delicate lines of script tattooed across the veined backs of her hands. Her robes are wide-sleeved and monkish, black as ink.

One of them is beautiful and brown, with scars stippling her cheeks and a sword strapped crosswise over one shoulder. Her armor is overlapping scales, shining black as old blood.

400 ALIX E. HARROW

One of them is pale and fey, with ivory antlers sprouting from matted dark hair and yellowed teeth strung in a necklace around her throat. Her dress is ragged and torn, black as a moonless night.

She meets Juniper's eyes and Juniper feels a thrill of recognition.

Juniper always loved maiden-stories best. Maidens are supposed to be sweet, soft creatures who braid daisy-crowns and turn themselves into laurel trees rather than suffer the loss of their innocence, but the Maiden is none of those things. She's the fierce one, the feral one, the witch who lives free in the wild woods. She's the siren and the selkie, the virgin and the valkyrie; Artemis and Athena. She's the little girl in the red cloak who doesn't run from the wolf but walks arm in arm with him deeper into the woods.

Juniper knows her by the savage green of her eyes, the vicious curve of her smile. An adder drapes over her shoulders like a strip of dark velvet, like the carved-yew snake of Juniper's staff come to life. Juniper's smile could be the Maiden's own, sharp and white, mirrored back across the centuries.

Agnes Amaranth is the strong sister, steady as a stone and twice as hard; she walks second into the tower.

She's never liked mother-stories much. They make her think of her own mother and wish she'd been someone else, someone who would've sent their daddy running for the hills the first time he raised a hand against her. Someone like the Mother herself.

Mothers are supposed to be weak, weepy creatures, women who give birth to their children and drift peacefully into death, but the Mother is none of those things. She's the brave one, the ruthless one, the witch who traded the birthing-chamber for the battlefield, the kitchen for the knife. She is bloody Boadicea and heartless Hera, the mother who became a monster.

None of the stories mention the oiled brown of her skin or the smooth lines of scars along her cheeks, but Agnes knows her by the iron set of her jaw, the unyielding line of her spine. A black python wraps around one arm, heavy-bodied and red-eyed.

Agnes bows her head and the Mother bows back to her, like two soldiers meeting in battle.

Beatrice Belladonna is the wise sister, quiet and clever as an owl in the rafters; she walks last into the tower.

She never believed in crone-stories, even as a girl. She determined long ago that the Crone was an amalgamation of myths and fables, an expression of collective fear rather than an actual old woman.

Old women are supposed to be doting and addled, absent-minded grandmothers who spoil their sons and keep soup bubbling on the stove-top, but the Crone is none of those things. She's the canny one, the knowing one, the too-wise witch who knows the words to every curse and the ingredients for every poison. She is Baba Yaga and Black Anna; she is the wicked fairy who hands out curses rather than christening-gifts.

Bella knows her by her fingertips: ink-stained, tattooed with words in a dozen dead languages. A delicate asp coils around one wrist.

"Well met, Misses Eastwood." Her voice is dust and honey, her accent patchworked together from a hundred languages living and dead.

"Took you long enough." That's the antlered woman, with a voice like snake teeth and briars.

"Well." Juniper shrugs. "We were busy. And you were dead."

The Maiden makes a hissing sound, as if this complaint is a very foolish one.

The Mother intercedes in a voice like iron. "Why have you woken us? What is it that you need?" She looks at Agnes as she asks, her eyes tracing the milk-stains down her blouse. There's a darkness in her face that makes Bella think of sharpened blades.

"Help," breathes Agnes, before she buries her face in both hands and begins to sob.

34

Maleficae quondam,
maleficaeque futurae

Purpose unknown

James Juniper catches her sister around the shoulders and eases her
down to the black-scorched stones. Agnes is trying to explain between
gulps and shudders, about Gideon Hill and the election, about Eve and
votes for women and the burning of the library, but Juniper isn't sure how
much sense she's making.

The Three watch her with concern in their mismatched eyes. The
Three who shouldn't have eyes at all, who should be dead but aren't.
Juniper watches the Maiden, all deerskin and white flesh, and resists the
urge to touch her, to see if her hand passes through her skin.

Eventually the Mother says, "Hush, child," and Agnes hiccups to
a stop. The Mother stamps her foot once and a sudden wind whips
through the tower, scouring away the heaped ashes and the stink of
smoke. The Maiden flicks her hand and moss wriggles up between the
seams of the flagstone floor, green and soft as spring. The Crone settles
herself with a huff that makes Juniper think of Mama Mags.

"Start at the beginning," she orders, and Juniper wonders which beginning she means. The day they called the tower into St. George's Square and found one another again? Or seven years before, when she ran down the rutted road after her sisters, begging them not to leave her? Or maybe the beginning of their story is the same as the middle and the end: *Once there were three sisters.*

Agnes starts with Eve, which Juniper figures is the beginning of a different story. She tells the Three about the fever they couldn't cure and the mockingbird message she shouldn't have sent. She tells them about Hill holding the red curl of her daughter's hair, and Juniper feels the pain of it in the binding between them, an open wound sown with salt.

"And even if we could find Eve I don't think we can save her. Hill is powerful, and not just in the usual way. He has followers, and these shadows that creep around the city—"

A stillness falls over the Three as she says the word *shadows*. Even their serpents stop coiling and twining, their hot-coal eyes fixed on Agnes. The Mother swears in a language Juniper thinks might be a dialect of Hell.

"Almost sounds like you've met him," Juniper drawls.

The Maiden bares her teeth in an expression that bears no relation at all to a smile. "Oh, I've met him," she hisses.

"He's the man who bested us at Avalon," the Mother growls.

"And he's the man who burned us, after. Heard he got a sainthood out of it," the Crone finishes. "Bastard," she adds, reflectively.

Juniper thinks she's never heard a silence quite like the one that follows: there's a depth and coldness to it, a thoroughness that could only exist after sundown on the other side of nowhere, when six witches and their familiars have just learned they have an enemy in common.

"Shit," she says. And then, more emphatically, "*Shit*."

Bella rallies first, clinging to the last fraying threads of reason. "But how? There's no such thing at the Fountain of Youth or the Philosopher's Stone. How is he still alive? How are *you* alive?"

"We're not, strictly speaking." The Maiden strokes her adder with one white finger. "Alive, I mean."

"I never liked being called the Crone. I've forgotten the name my mother gave me, but I'm sure it wasn't that. And she's no maiden." The Crone points her chin at the Maiden, who smiles in a distinctly unmaidenly fashion.

"I am a Mother," muses the armored woman. "But more, too."

Bella resettles her spectacles. "But the spell to call back the Lost Way of Avalon. It required a maiden, a mother, and a crone, did it not?"

The Crone shrugs. "Every woman is usually at least one of those. Sometimes all three and a few others besides."

Bella blinks several times. "So we weren't called, then. Or—chosen." Juniper figures she's remembering the thing that drew them together that day, the tugging of the line between them.

The Crone makes a sound that can only be described as a cackle. She catches her breath, tries to answer, then breaks into another fit of cackles. "*Chosen?* If you three were chosen, it was by circumstance. By your own need. That's all magic is, really: the space between what you have and what you need."

Bella looks like a woman shuffling through the several dozen questions that occurred to her, but Agnes beats her to it. "What do you know about Gideon Hill?"

The Three look at one another, stillness settling back over them.

The Maiden lifts her chin, hair sliding back over pale shoulders. "More than anyone alive."

The Mother's eyes flick again to the milk-trails on Agnes's blouse. "Enough to help you, I hope."

The Crone heaves a long, humorless sigh. "Let us start from the beginning."

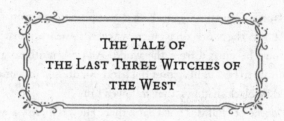

THE TALE OF
THE LAST THREE WITCHES OF
THE WEST

nce upon a time there were three witches.

The first witch was a scholar of Samarkand who dedicated her life to the study of words and witchcraft, who mastered a hundred languages and a thousand potions, who consulted with princes and khans on two continents.

The second witch was a slave from the Zanj sold in Constantinople who used the witching of her ancestors and her captors to free herself and her daughters, who made her bloody way through the world as the commander of a band of mercenaries.

The third witch was a peasant girl from the Blackdown Hills, abandoned with her brother in the deep dark of the trees. The boy returned to his village some years later; his sister was never seen or heard from again, except as a green-eyed shadow, a rumor with white teeth.

They were, in short, three ordinary witches of their times. Perhaps a shade more desperate and a half-step more learned, but certainly not legends.

None of them would have been remembered at all if it wasn't for the plague. A ghastly, uncanny illness that crept into every village and down every city street and left bloated bodies behind it.

Most witches helped where they could, but the sickness came quickly and killed quicker, and even the cleverest witch couldn't save them all. This failure—all the people they couldn't save and the husbands and aunts and neighbors they left behind, grief-crazed—became their undoing.

Rumors began to spread: that the plague was unnatural; that it was the work of women-witches, somehow; that such evil must be purged from the world. And when a hero arose, promising to be a light against the darkness, dressed in white but trailed by black shadows, they followed him.

George of Hyll was not a Saint then. He was merely a witch, no different than the witches he hunted—except that he was a man, and man's power was God-given.

"But—how could a man work witchcraft?" Bella interrupts. The Maiden laughs at her. "You think magic cares what's between your legs? Or how you do your hair?" Bella does not interrupt again.

His followers burned the books first, swallowing centuries of learning in seconds. Then George asked: What of the women who carry the words and ways in their skulls? Who will surely teach them to their daughters and sisters?

They came for the witches then. The hedge-witches in their caves and hollow trees, the midwives and soothsayers, the sybils and scholars. The witches fought them with every curse and jinx they knew. But the harder they fought the more frightened the people became, and the larger George's armies grew. The witches burned beside their books.

What words and ways were preserved were slipped into songs and rhymes, folded into fables. Women sang them to their children and taught them to their sisters, and even the watchful neighbors and listening shadows thought nothing of it.

The purge continued. The world changed. The weeds and herbs grew wild on the hillsides, with no one to tend them; the trees and animals fell silent, with no one to speak with them; there were no more dragons seen on the winds of morning.

It wasn't long until witches retreated to a few last strongholds:

the Black Forest in Saxony, the drifting isle of Lemuria, a certain haunted fen in the south of England, sometimes called Avalon.

One night the Mother and the Crone staggered into that misty moor, battle-worn and hopeless, and met the Maiden. They knew by their familiars that they shared some kinship, by soul if not by blood, and they shared a meal around a fire that night.

And there in the wild woods, at the bitter end of the age of witching, the three of them began to plan.

The Maiden had a place: the deep woods, where the remains of a tower stood, well hidden.

The Mother had the strength to defend it, at least for a while.

The Crone had something worth defending: all her decades of study, all her words and ways. She wrote down every spell she remembered or even half remembered, and then slipped out into the world to gather every unburned book or surviving scroll she could find.

Word spread among the remaining witches, and women arrived every day with scraps of spells and charred recipes. In return the Three taught them as much witchcraft as they could: for hiding and hurting, for birthing and breaking, for surviving. Some of them stayed—to defend the tor, to ward the tower, to patrol the fragile borders of their half-secret kingdom—but more often they fled back into the countryside.

The Three had the help of their own familiars, too, as if magic itself did not want to be forgotten. When the tower was complete their snakes twined their bodies together into three circles and burned the mark into the tower door. The Three found afterward that they had a way back to the tower no matter how far they traveled.

They traveled very far indeed. The Crone spent weeks in the baked-earth halls of the mosque at Djenné. The Mother completed the three tasks set by the librarians at Constantinople. The

Maiden visited Cambridge and contrived to steal an entire room of their library, which she affixed to the tower.

But fewer witches found them over the years. The Three tasted ash on the wind and knew George of Hyll was coming.

Later, the storytellers would say the Three lost the battle at Avalon. That Hyll and his Inquisitors dragged them screaming to the stake and broke the power of witching forever after.

But if the Three—the cleverest witches of their age, battle-tested and canny—had wanted to escape, they would have. Instead, they waited.

They waited with their familiars at their feet and words on their lips. They fought George of Hyll for three days and three nights, while their daughters and sisters and friends vanished into the hills. And when they came to the end of their strength they carved their promise on the tower door—*Maleficae quondam, maleficaeque futurae*—and knelt before Hyll with bent necks.

He burned them the next day, back-to-back, the flames dancing yellow and white in his eyes. They did not scream as they burned: they sang. About roses and ashes and falling together, hand in hand.

Because those words had never been spoken before and were no spell he knew, and because men are fools when they think they've won, George of Hyll ignored them. He didn't understand that the Three had spent years wading deeper and deeper into witchcraft, studying spells from every nook and cranny of the world. That they had begun to wonder where the words and ways came from in the first place, and write their own.

The spell they sang that night was a binding, far stranger and bolder than any worked before. They bound their souls one to the other and then to their beloved library. As their bodies burned, their souls fled to the other side of elsewhere—and took

Avalon with them. They took the tower and the books, the trees and stars, even the tricksome autumn wind.

George raged at their escape. For years and years he scoured the earth for any sign of the Last Three Witches of the West or the Lost Way of Avalon. He found rumors and songs, bits of rhyme, but he never saw that black tower again.

The Three waited. They studied and argued and wept, despaired and dreamed, undying, and eventually they lay themselves down to sleep. They let the shape of themselves coil down among the black roots and dark earth, slipping between stones and the brittle pages of books. Souls were never meant to linger for centuries.

But they did not let themselves fade entirely. They waited, still clinging to the slimmest thread of themselves, for the day when they would be called back to the world. When what was lost would be found again, and witching would return.

It never came.

35

Lady bird, lady bird, fly away home.

A spell for flight, requiring rowan & starlight

If James Juniper closes her eyes she can pretend she is a little girl again, curled with her sisters on the rag rug beside the stove while Mama Mags tells them tales. She can pretend it's all make-believe and myth.

Until Bella says, tentatively, "But that isn't so. Avalon was called back, wasn't it? Before us?"

The Crone almost smiles at her. "Well, it wasn't much use to hide the library if no one could ever find it again. We left the words with our daughters before they fled, so they could call us back when the world was safe again. It never was, but still they called us from time to time."

"Old Salem," Bella whispered.

"And Wiesensteig in the fifteen-sixties, before that, and the Auld Kirk Green at the end of the century. Navarre in the early sixteen-hundreds. Anyplace there were at least three witches with the will. But over the centuries there were fewer and fewer women who remembered the words and ways. The age of witches was nothing but stories now, and we listened to those stories twist and darken over the years, until every witch was a wicked one."

The Crone's smile is still in place, but the corners are twisted and mournful. "He nearly got us in Salem. Tituba and her coven banished us back to nowhere just before the flames took us."

Bella presses her hand to her skirt pocket, where Juniper can see the square shape of her little black notebook. "I found the words written in the Sisters Grimm, half-faded..."

"The Grimms were clever girls," says the Mother, fondly. "Jacobine and Willa called the tower and roused us from our sleep long after Old Salem, but they weren't interested in powerful words or ways—perhaps they knew the trouble it would bring, by then. They just wanted our stories. Made a nice profit for themselves, I heard."

"No one has called us since then." The Maiden sighs. "We thought perhaps no one ever would. We contented ourselves with the thought that at least *he* never found us." The Maiden's eyes flick up to the charred shelves and sagging stairs, then back to the Eastwoods. Her voice cools considerably. "Until recently, that is."

A small, sorry silence follows, while they listen to the susurrations of ash, the hollow howl of wind through the windows.

Agnes breaks it. "Gideon Hill." She says his name carefully, the way a woman might stroke the edge of a fresh-sharpened blade. "And Saint George of Hyll. They're the same man?"

"The same soul, at least," the Crone allows.

"How?"

The Three exchange a look that Juniper recognizes: it's the way three sisters look at one another when they've caused a great deal of trouble.

"We should have known," says the Crone. "He watched us work our final spell. When the tower followed us into the dark he understood what we'd done. He was a formidable witch himself, by then, enough to try a binding of his own."

The Maiden's lip slides out from beneath her teeth. "But we weren't thinking about immortality! We were just trying to survive, we never meant—"

"It doesn't matter what we meant." The Mother's eyes are on the clenched-fist shape of Agnes's face. "The first time we were called back into the world they told us George of Hyll had died a decade before and been sainted shortly after. But then we saw him. He wore a different face and a different name—Glennwald Hale, an Inquisitor and a churchman—but still we knew him."

"We'd shown him the secret of bound souls. And he'd realized he could tether his soul to anything he liked, not just stones or roses or books." The Crone's snake slithers from her wrist to her throat, sliding its obsidian cheek against hers in a gesture that looks almost like comfort. "He bound himself to living bodies, one after the other. All he needed was the ashes of the body he was leaving and something from the body he was stealing. And enough will to stamp out the soul still living in it, I suppose." She touches her familiar's head. "I imagine he preys most often on the young and defenseless, to ease the binding."

Juniper feels abruptly sick, like she's turned over a log and found something foul and dead beneath it. She remembers the stories she heard about the dreamy, bookish boy whose favorite uncle died when he was young. How he changed after that, grew less dreamy and more calculating. How he asked his teachers to call him by his middle name: Gideon.

Juniper wonders how it felt, to have an ancient spirit steal your will, colonize your body and march it around like a wooden puppet. She pictures the long line of bodies stretching behind him, plucked like ripe fruit and hollowed out from the inside, discarded as easily as apple peels. And what happened to the souls he stamped out? Did they fade when their bodies died, or were they dragged along from corpse to corpse, trapped in a hell of his making?

"*Bastard*." Her voice is a rasp, twice-burned. "So he's just been hopping from kid to kid, getting a little smarter and a little meaner every time—"

"Gaining power, gaining witchcraft, and..." Bella gives a little gasp. "Covering his own tracks. Stealing records and burning books, fading whatever words and ways still remain." Her tone makes it clear that she includes this among his most insidious crimes.

Agnes hasn't blinked or flinched. She remains stone-faced, implacable. "Yet he's still scared. What is he afraid of?"

"Same thing every powerful man is afraid of." The Crone shrugs. "The day the truth comes out."

"The day he gets what's coming," says the Maiden.

The Mother meets Agnes's eyes and Juniper sees something pass between them, the gleam of a tossed blade. "Us."

Agnes feels her lips curving for the first time since her daughter was stolen. It isn't her usual smile—her mouth feels over-supplied with teeth and her jaw aches—but there's a furious glee filling the hollow place her heart left behind it.

"And why's that?" It's nearly a purr.

"Because he burned us but our souls rose from the ashes, and he knows it. Because we know exactly what he is, and how to end him." The Crone's smile is subtle poison, the kind that has no taste or smell. "Because any binding may be broken."

"Tell me how."

"Same way you'd break any other binding: break the ways. Kill whatever body he's wearing these days—"

Juniper makes a rasping sound in her throat. "If you're telling us the secret to killing him is to *kill* him, I swear by Saint Hilda I'll hex you."

Bella and the Crone swat her simultaneously.

"—then banish his soul," the Crone continues frostily. "I imagine it will want to linger even without the binding, out of habit and spite."

"And how do we banish a soul?"

"We wrote the words especially for him," says the Maiden. "After we saw what he'd become. But he was strong by then, wrapped in stolen shadows, and no witch ever got near enough to work the spell."

"I will," Agnes says. "Teach them to me."

The Maiden does. Agnes is surprised to find that these words, too, are familiar, a children's rhyme made eerie by the burned tower and slanting moonlight. *All the king's horses and all the king's men couldn't put Georgie together again.*

Agnes repeats the words to herself, rolling them over her tongue. They taste like grave-dirt and vengeance, like death long overdue. Pan's claws flex around her shoulder, pricking her flesh.

You are not invincible, Gideon Hill.

Bella pushes her spectacles up her nose. "What about the three of you? If you bound yourselves to Avalon, and Avalon was burned, why haven't your souls been sundered?"

The Crone's eyes don't twinkle—twinkling eyes are for soft, grand-motherly women who bake gingerbread and crochet scarves—but they glint. "Did you think I bound my everlasting soul to *books*? To paper and ink?" The glint sharpens. "We bound ourselves to the words them-selves, Belladonna. We won't fade until children forget their rhymes and mothers lose their lullabies, until the last witch forgets the last word."

"Oh." Bella's face lights with a fervent, librarianish glow. "So the words survived. They're still out there somewhere. They could be col-lected again, preserved."

"Or written anew. Every spell that exists was once spoken for the first time, by a witch who needed it."

Bella actually claps her hands together. "Then the library could be...oh, but it would take so much work."

The Crone huffs. "It always does."

"Always?"

"Avalon wasn't the first library. Alexandria, Antioch, Avicenna... They keep burning us. We keep rising again."

Bella opens her mouth again, but Agnes stands, dusting the ashes of the library from her skirts. "Thank you all." She bows her head to the Maiden, the Crone, especially the Mother. "But I have to go now."

Agnes looks down at her sisters. It occurs to her that they might stay in this place, if they liked, hidden safe on the other side of somewhere. Eve isn't their daughter, after all.

But Bella and Juniper are already standing, their shoulders warm on either side of hers. Juniper looks a little wistfully at the tower, at the deepening night of nowhere around them, free of the stink and noise of New Salem. Agnes wonders if she's thinking of her nights back in Crow County, moon-bright and alive, of the time when she had a place to call home.

Juniper scuffs her shoe in the ash. "Maybe we'll talk again someday. Once Hill gets what's coming to him."

The Maiden looks up at Juniper in a manner that causes Agnes to recall that she has lived and listened to the world for centuries. She is still the wild Maiden of the woods, but there's a certain wisdom in her eyes, too. "He wasn't always... what he is now," she says softly.

"A monster," Juniper supplies. "And a real bastard."

The Maiden flinches but doesn't disagree. "He didn't use to be. I am not so foolish as to think he could be redeemed, but I wish..." She chews at her lip with those sharp teeth. "I wish he might die with his true name in his ears. Tell him, before the end?"

Her antlers brush the tangled black of Juniper's hair as she whispers into her ear. Juniper frowns, then nods, solemn as a Saint.

They are nearly to the door, their palms reaching for the charred remains of the Sign of the Three, when Juniper turns back. "Could you really fly? On broomsticks, like the stories said?"

The Three smile at her in perfect unison, and in their eyes Agnes sees the silver shine of starlight, the damp silk of clouds, the memory of a thousand windswept nights spent soaring above the slow turning of the world.

The stars twist away above them, and then Bella and her sisters are crouched together on the floor of an unfamiliar room. Their palms are pressed to a ragged circle carved into the floorboards, and the ceilings vault high above them. There are rows of wooden benches alongside them, slicked smooth from years of use. It's been a long time since Bella set foot in a church, but she remembers the quiet of the air, the warm smell of candles and wine.

A voice mutters a soft rhyme and a hot, golden light fills the room. Bella blinks against the sting of tears and follows the light back to its source: Miss Cleopatra Quinn, sitting cross-legged against the pulpit with her wand glowing like the orange eye of a cat.

"Took your time, didn't you, ladies," she says tartly. But Bella hears the warm relief behind the words.

Bella doesn't bother to look anywhere else, or even to stand. She crawls down the aisle and wraps both arms around Cleo's legs. She lays her cheek against her knees.

"Get a hold of yourself, woman." Cleo's voice is rough but her fingers on Bella's face are soft. "Did you find what you needed?"

"Oh, Cleo, we saw them. We *spoke* to them! The Three themselves! I need a pen." Bella's fingertips fizz with the need to write it all down, to decant the marvels and curiosities of the last hour into the safety of ink and paper. She looks a little wildly into the shadows, as if an ink-pen might materialize. "Where are we?"

"The Mother Bethel Church in New Cairo. We warded it as best we could, but we shouldn't linger."

"We?"

Quinn lifts her wand-light and other faces swim out of the darkness, lining the pews: the Hull sisters with their hoods pulled high; Jennie

Lind looking grim, one eye blacked; Yulia and her daughters sitting next to Annie Flynn; a scrawny, raw-boned girl who stares at Agnes with some combination of resentment and gratitude; a half-dozen others, their shoulders squared and their eyes steady.

The Sisters of Avalon. Their sisters, still.

Juniper is grinning, hard and fierce. Agnes is staring around at them, white-faced. "What are you all doing here?"

Yulia ticks her chin at Cleo. "She called. Said you three were doing something very stupid." Yulia's voice goes gruff. "Said they took your baby girl."

Agnes swallows several times.

"You will get her back now?"

Agnes nods once, her eyes like hot steel.

Yulia grunts. Bella waits for the Sisters to ask questions, like *how?* or *with what army?* But they merely sit and wait. Bella fights an embarrassing impulse to cry.

She is rescued by Cleo tapping her gently on the shoulder. "You spoke to them?"

"Yes. That is, their spirits. They invented a binding that breached the usual corporeal bounds of the soul. They tied themselves to the library— or to witchcraft itself, I suppose. And I was right about rhymes as vehicles for the preservation of spells during the purge. They told us—"

"They told us Gideon Hill is an immortal and a witch," Juniper interrupts, perhaps wisely. "In addition to being a pain in our asses. And they told us how to kill him." She slouches into a pew across from Yulia, crossing her staff over her lap. "The only trouble will be catching him with his guard down and getting rid of those damn shadows of his." Her gaze lands on the burning light at the end of Cleo's wand. Her eyes narrow in speculation. "Huh."

Bella shakes her head. "That's just a housewife's spell to shed light. I'm not sure it could do anything but annoy him."

"But what if there were more of us? And what if he didn't see it coming? If we could catch him at some kind of public speech, maybe, or a parade. He's bound to hold one eventually, man like him."

Agnes's voice slides across Juniper's, thin and tired. "We have until tomorrow at sundown."

Bella and Juniper stare at her.

"Hill made a deal with me." Agnes swallows. "I'm supposed to betray you to him by tomorrow at sundown if I want Eve back alive and well." She speaks her daughter's name carefully, as if it's broken glass or bent nails in her mouth, likely to cut her.

"Oh." Juniper scrubs her palms over her face. "And what did you say?"

Agnes swallows, throat tensing in the long shadows of the wand-light. "I said yes."

Juniper nods, unbothered. "Good girl. Doesn't give us long to plan, though. Any of you know a way to get the mayor out in public, surrounded by our people? Jennie? Inez?" A pair of lines appear between her brows. "Where's Inez?"

Jennie answers her, voice shaking very slightly. "They got her yesterday. Electa, too. We were trying to get food to the girls in the Deeps, but the shadows held them fast. I tried to stay with them, to help, but Inez told me to run. She was...forceful." Jennie touches the swollen edge of the bruise around her eye.

Juniper doesn't say anything, but the lines between her brows deepen. Her shoulders bow, as if a heavy weight has settled over them. It occurs to Bella that she doesn't look much like the wounded, wild seventeen-year-old who came staggering into the city six months ago; there's a gravity to her features, a weight to her limbs. As if she has seen the price of her wildness and is no longer certain she wants to pay it.

Bella feels the heat of Cleo's fingers on her shoulder and wishes for a wild second the two of them could run. Could leave the city, the country, the world itself.

From the corner of her eye, Bella sees Juniper's shoulders unbow. Her eyes kindle. It's an unsettling expression, familiar to Bella as the light that generally precedes something dangerous or illegal.

"You know," Juniper observes to the gathered women, "there's nothing more public than a good old-fashioned witch-burning. And it's nearly the equinox."

Her tone is conversational, almost airy, but Bella feels the cold slither of premonition in her stomach. She can sense the edges of Juniper's idea through the thing between them, formless but terrifying.

Agnes gives their sister a quelling, don't-even-think-about-it frown that tells Bella she feels it, too. "So?"

"So." Juniper stands and strolls down the aisle, staff clacking. She spins on her heels to face them and spreads her arms wide, like some ancient priestess offering a bloody-handed blessing. "Let's give this city what it wants."

PART
FOUR

WHAT
IS
LOST

36

Rain, rain go away
Come again another day.

A spell to delay a coming storm, requiring mere luck

Beatrice Belladonna never understood how brief a single day could be until it was her last. It's as if the hours sprouted wings in the night.

She is crouched in the dim, dust-specked attic of an abandoned house on Sixth Street, surrounded by a small ocean of books and papers, hastily scrawled notes and half-written spells for rust and sleep and sunlight, for changeling children and flying brooms. Candle-stubs puddle precariously close to piles of poorly folded cloaks in a dozen shades of charcoal and ink, still smelling of summer. In the middle of this mess Bella sits in a ring of salt, fingers cramped around a pen and sleeves rolled to the wrist, trying to ignore the feathered passing of the hours.

Her battered black-leather notebook is propped against a mug of cold coffee, the pages dog-eared and marked. It occurs to Bella that if their plans go awry, it might be the only surviving record of events that isn't skewed by Gideon Hill's propagandizing. It isn't much—part memoir, part grimoire, interspersed with rhymes and witch-tales, a scrapbooked record of their summer—but her fingers trail lovingly over the cover.

She flips to the first page, where a nameplate is pasted neatly in the center:

> *Beatrice Belladonna Eastwood*
> *Assistant Librarian*
> *Salem College Library*

She blots out two-thirds of the nameplate and adds four lines above it:

> *Our Own Stories*
> *Being the Entirely True Tale of the Sisters Eastwood in*
> *the Summer of 1893*
> *By*
> ~~*Beatrice*~~ *Belladonna Eastwood*
> ~~*Assistant*~~ *Librarian*
> ~~*Salem College Library*~~
> *Avalon*

She can't quite bring herself to cross out the word *librarian*. It was her home and refuge, the thing she became once she was no longer her father's daughter or her sisters' keeper. She thinks of herself now as a librarian awkwardly bereft of a library, obliged to build her own.

Except she can't build her own. It would take years and decades—a lifetime of research and collecting, of following every hummed lullaby and half-forgotten rhyme—and she doesn't have decades. She has a few final hours to scrape together the words they need most.

Her sisters have gone out to assemble the ways and wills, spinning through the city like spiders weaving mad webs, but the sun is already slanting toward afternoon. The shadows rise like cold water up the walls, smelling of first frosts and last chances.

Bella wonders if the cells of the Deep are smaller than her room at St. Hale's. She wonders if despair is waiting for her down in the darkness, ready to swallow her whole. She flexes her hands, remembering the deep bite of bound thread around them.

The trapdoor creaks upward and the smell of cloves and ink wafts into the room.

"Cleo!" Bella sits straighter in her paper-nest and pats ineffectually at her hair.

Cleo tosses a bulging brown paper sack onto the bed beside her. Bones clack as it lands. "It's thin pickings now. The shop is practically empty. I bought what I could and bartered or begged for the rest. Tell Juniper she owes me—I bought those snake teeth from a little witch up from Orleans who gave me the honest-to-God *chills*." Cleo is fidgeting distractedly in her skirt pockets as she speaks, as if her mind is elsewhere. "I spoke with the Daughters, too. My mother says to tell you this entire plan is, quote, 'dumber than a bucket of bricks,' and 'doomed to fail'—"

"If only she felt she could be honest with me," Bella murmurs.

"—and that she'll be there. Along with any Daughters who volunteer." Cleo smiles a little crookedly. "Although none of them like it much."

"What don't they like about it?"

"The part where three white ladies who know all their secrets wind up in the claws of Gideon Hill. You could betray us all."

"Oh." Bella finds her own fingers fidgeting now. She tries very hard not to think of witch-trials and tortured confessions. "Well. We won't. I won't."

"So I told them." Cleo says it lightly, but there's so much trust in her voice that Bella finds her eyes stinging.

After a slight pause Cleo asks, "How are things here?"

Bella flaps her hands at the crumpled pages. "A mess. I've done the best I could without the library, but I don't know if it will be enough. I don't know if *we're* enough. This is by far the worst idea Juniper has ever had, and let me tell you that's saying something. When I was nine she tried to sneak a fox kit into the house as a pet. One time she jumped off the roof with our kitchen broom in one hand because she wanted to fly. Mags had to stitch her up." Bella is aware that she is babbling, saying everything but the thing she ought to say.

She stops herself with considerable effort. "You and I need to talk, Cleo."

"We do, yes." Cleo is smiling, hands now back in her pockets.

"I—I'd like you to leave New Salem." Bella's tongue feels wrong-sized, reluctant to form the words.

Cleo's eyebrows form a matched pair of arches. "It's a little late for that, don't you think?"

"Quit smiling, I'm serious. You've already risked more than any sane woman would for us—for me—and this plan of June's—"

"The plan in which I play an extremely daring and heroic part? Without which the entire thing collapses?"

"We could find someone else!"

"You really couldn't."

"Cleo, please. Eve isn't your niece, Agnes and June aren't your sisters, I'm not your—anything."

"Bella." Cleo's voice softens, the smile replaced by a dangerous sincerity.

Bella looks away, knotting her fingers together to keep from reaching out. "I can't stand to think of you captured or hurt, for my sake."

The soft shush of skirts, the creak of a floorboard. "Beatrice Belladonna Eastwood. Look at me."

Bella looks. Cleo is crouched on one knee inside the ring of salt, her eyes blazing and her lip caught between her teeth. She has something held carefully in her palm, fingers bent around it in a cage that quivers very slightly.

Bella feels dizzy, delirious, as if she's back on the Ferris wheel, swinging through sky. "What are you—"

Cleo opens her hand. A ring lies in the precise center of her palm, tarnished and battered. The cut-glass gem is fractured and badly chipped, very much as if it was dropped from a great height and spent a summer abandoned on the weedy cement, until a clever-fingered witch found it again.

"I believe this is yours, if you'll have it." Cleo's voice is less sure now, higher than usual. "As am I."

Bella finds her fingers extending of their own accord, trembling over Cleo's open palm. "I thought one marriage was enough for you. I thought you didn't make the same mistake twice."

Cleo gives a one-shouldered shrug. "It's possible I was mistaken."

"A novelty for you, I'm sure." Bella is breathless, swaying high above the city.

"It won't happen again."

Bella's hand hovers above Cleo's, hesitant. She closes her eyes against the sudden pulse of memories: *Thud.* Her daddy looking at her with death in his eyes. *Thud.* The suffocating silence of St. Hale's, her hands bound together in forced prayer. *Thud.* Cleo's voice advising her to trust less easily. *Thud.* The ashes of Avalon around her ankles, the taste of failure in her mouth.

Thud. Her mother. Who chose only what was good and proper, who tucked away every piece of herself that was wayward or unruly until she was a pale imitation of herself.

Bella opens her eyes. She looks down at Cleopatra Quinn: baresouled and brave, entirely herself.

Bella cradles her head with ink-smeared hands and draws her upward. Their lips meet in a rush of heat and salt.

Cleo pulls away, panting slightly. Her thumb brushes the trail of tears on Bella's cheek: "Is that a yes, Miss Eastwood?"

Bella nods once and Cleo slides the battered, broken, perfect ring onto her finger.

Bella laughs a little hysterically. "Don't you need one, too?" She pats her pockets and finds nothing but a few snapped matchsticks, a candlewick—and a single rose petal, plucked from the ashes of the library. It smells faintly of witchcraft and smoke.

Bella draws it out and wraps it gently around Cleo's finger, tucking it between her knuckles. "There. I've made an honest woman of you."

The rest of the conversation is silent, conducted in the wordless language of skin and heartbeat.

Later—either several days or merely an hour; Bella has lost track of the winged passage of time—the trapdoor squeals again and Juniper's voice rasps into the room.

"You about ready, Bell? Agnes should be back any—Saints save us." Her sister's footsteps pause on the ladder. "Is now really the time, ladies?" When neither Cleo nor Bella answer her, being otherwise occupied, Juniper gives an irritated huff.

They hear the clatter of feet on the ladder and a carrying shout: "I'll be back in half an hour, and I want everybody's clothes back where they belong. We've got hell to raise."

The last time Agnes visited the Workingman it was early summer. She was giddy and coy, half-drunk with hope. Eve still slept safe beneath her ribs; Agnes wore a cloak to match her eyes.

This time it's early autumn, and Agnes wears a pair of men's pants and a tattered cloak the color of mud, with her hair tucked beneath a cap and her features dulled by magic. This time she feels like a lightning-struck tree or a pitted peach, hollowed out, empty; this time Eve is gone.

The first time she met him, Mr. August Lee was feckless and fearless, with a gambler's grin and nothing to lose. This time his face is creased with fresh-made lines and his eyes are sober, almost frightened, as if he's found something he doesn't want to lose.

He sits across from Agnes with his haystack hair and his gray wool vest, a scrap of paper held tight in his hands. A covered basket sits on the table between them, smelling of clay and river-water.

Agnes nods to the list in his hand. "Well?" Her voice is cold and flat.

He scrubs his hand over his beard, brow knit. "Saints, Agnes. I haven't seen you in over a week. No messages, no mockingbirds"— Agnes flinches, hearing the echo of small bones breaking—"and now you turn up with the Devil's own groceries and a list of demands, looking like—" But he declines to say what she looks like. Agnes has avoided her own eyes in mirrors and windows, unwilling to look at the open wound of her face.

"Where's Eve?" August asks. Agnes knows his voice is gentle, but her ears ache as if he screamed the name. "Here. Look." From his breast pocket he withdraws a small, smooth-polished thing and sets it upright on the table between them: dark wood, carved into the wary shape of a perched hawk. Agnes can tell from the curve of beak and the sleek taper of wings that it's an osprey, and from the watchful angle of its body that it's her hawk, meant to watch over her daughter.

She pictures August worrying over it in the lengthening evenings, looking out into the lamp-lit dark of the city and hoping that she and Eve are safe. She pictures him turning the wood in his palm and choosing to carve the shape of her soul, dangerous and dark; rendering each talon without flinching from it.

"My dad would've been a wood-carver, if he could. He taught me some." His voice is still gentle. Her skull still pounds as if he shouted.

Agnes reaches toward the little hawk without meaning to, fingers trembling, before closing her eyes and pressing her palm flat to the table. "I—I can't—" She takes a long, steadying breath. "I need to know if you are able to work the spells we have supplied, Mr. Lee."

She hears the long sigh of his breath, the sag of his shoulders. "I'm no witch."

"I have it on good authority that everyone is a witch, given the proper words and ways." Agnes tilts her head at the covered basket. "I've supplied you with both."

August's eyes flick to the basket and back to her face. Agnes wishes, stupidly, that she could abandon her glamor and let his eyes rest on her true features, feel the warmth of his care on her skin. Perhaps she will find him again after it's over, if she's lucky enough to have an after. The future has narrowed in her mind, vanishing toward the moment she holds her daughter again.

August's brows knit tighter as he watches her. "Agnes, won't you tell me what's going on? Why you need me to do all this?" He eyes the list, lips shaping the words *fire* and *changeling*. "Why can't you just work the spells yourselves?"

"We will be otherwise occupied."

"Doing what?"

"Burning, I expect."

"*Excuse* me?"

On previous occasions Agnes has enjoyed rendering Mr. Lee speechless, but now her lips barely twitch. Now the sun is swinging low and they are running out of time. "Because there's no other way. Because the witches always burn in the end. Because *I want my daughter back.*" The last sentence is a strangled growl. The barman casts an admonitory take-it-outside-boys look at their booth.

Everything leaches away from August's face, the hurt and irritation and puzzlement. He stares at her for a long, searing second. "When? Who?"

But it doesn't matter when and he already knows who. "I'll kill him." His voice is casual but perfectly sincere. The scar shines white along his jaw.

"No," Agnes answers, just as evenly. "You won't." She looks at the carved statue of the hawk between them, the killing curve of its beak, and knows she does not need to tell him who will.

She takes another breath, less steady. "I'm not asking for your outrage

or your concern or your advice. I'm asking for your help. Do I have it?"
She is distantly surprised by how easily the word *help* slips between her
lips. Is this what it is to draw your circle wide, to need and be needed in
turn?

August studies her, from the black-snake coils of hair slipping out
from under her cap to the hard line of her mouth to the steel of her eyes,
not looking away. Who does he see? A helpless girl, a hysterical woman?
A mother gone mad with grief?

But it isn't pity she sees in his eyes. It's something several degrees
warmer, far more dangerous. "You have it." His voice is too low, rough
with unsaid things. "I am yours to command, Agnes Amaranth."

Agnes feels a heady heat through her, like summer wine. Men really
ought to try offers of fealty rather than flowers.

She lets her fingers rest on the back of his hand. The hand turns palm up
and their calluses slide against one another, fit smoothly into place. His fingers close around hers very carefully, as if her hand is a bird likely to startle.

Agnes thinks she should leave. She thinks about circles and costs,
weakness and wants. Then she thinks these hours might be her last as a
free woman and figures she can linger in this beery basement just a little
longer, with the heat of his hand around hers.

She feels their bodies tilting toward one another, pulled by some
secret gravity.

"It's going to be dangerous." The words come out crowded, slightly
breathless. "If it goes wrong, if we fail—you could lose everything."

August makes a considering *hmmm* in his throat. "And what do I get
if I win?"

Still a man who can't back down from a bet, still a man who likes
his odds long. Agnes feels a helpless smile curling the corners of her lips,
despite everything. "A kiss."

She finds the distance between them closing, the careless blue of his
eyes fragmenting into a hundred shades of slate and lapis, his lips parting
in wild hope—

She stops a bare inch from his face. "Be at the Home for Lost Angels by dusk today. When you see Pan, it's time."

August exhales a soft but heartfelt string of curses as she pulls away, running his fingers through the bright gold of his hair.

Agnes stands, straightening her cap, and tucks the wooden hawk into her skirt pocket. It knocks softly against her hip.

"Oh, and we'll need three branches. Good stout rowan-wood, if you please."

The last time Juniper visited Inez Gillmore's house it was glowing and gilded. Her Sisters were with her, laughing at their own daring, at the pop of champagne on their tongues.

Now the house is dark, quiet except for the tapping of Juniper's black-yew staff across the tiles. She wades through drifts of shattered crystal, torn pages from books, tangles of drapes; the house has been searched at least twice since Inez's arrest. It isn't safe to linger, but Juniper won't be waiting long.

She isn't alone. Miss Jennie Lind sits at the polished dining room table, staring at nothing, her face framed in long chestnut curls. The bruise around her eye has mottled to yellow and gray, like bad fruit.

"You don't have to come, you know." Juniper doesn't mean it to come out so hard. She starts again. "I only mean..." But she doesn't know how to say what she means. That Jennie doesn't have to keep following her deeper and deeper into trouble, like that Italian witch who walked through nine circles of Hell; that she is the first friend Juniper made in her life, and the thought of her harmed on their behalf takes all the air from Juniper's lungs.

Instead, she says, "I only mean this isn't your fight. You're not like us. You have a home to run to—a rich daddy, a place to weather the storm—"

"I really don't." Jennie's smile is brief and bitter.

"Why's that?"

"Because." Jennie pauses here for so long that Juniper doesn't think she intends to go on. Then she heaves a hard sigh and meets Juniper's eyes. "Because my father and mother are adamant in their belief that they raised a son, instead of a daughter." She lets the statement stand for a moment before adding, gently, "I never had a brother, Juniper."

Juniper feels her head tilting. "But why—oh." *Oh.* She feels simultaneously very stupid, mildly aggrieved, baffled, curious, and shocked. She recalls the delight on Jennie's face the first time she worked women's witching and the silent clench of her jaw when they accused her of men's magic, the entire summer she spent shoulder-to-shoulder with Sisters she couldn't quite trust with her secret. Juniper adds shame to her list.

Before she can express any of these things, Jennie lifts her chestnut wig from her head. Beneath it Juniper sees her cornsilk-colored hair has been cut brutally short. It stands in shocked tufts, as if refusing to take such abuse quietly. "When I was arrested they threw me in the men's workhouse, burned my skirts, and did this." She gestures to her hair. Juniper imagines shadowy figures holding her down, the silver gleam of shears, soft coils of cornsilk drifting to the prison floor. And then Juniper doesn't feel anything except sorry, and mad as hell.

"Does anyone else know?"

"Inez." Jennie says her name with such care that Juniper thinks there are one or two other things she didn't know about Jennie Lind. "And Miss Cady Stone, of course."

"*That* old—"

"Yes. She knew my father. She hired me as a secretary for the Women's Association after he turned me out. She's not…She's better than you think she is."

There's a brief silence, while Juniper works to revise another half-dozen or so of her assumptions. "Jennie, I—"

"This fight." Jennie rubs the broken bridge of her nose. "To just—live, to be—is one that I was signed up for before I was even born. I don't get to walk away."

Her eyes flick up to Juniper's and away. "And they have Inez." Another pause. "Who I love."

Juniper stops her pacing after that. She sits at the other end of the polished dining table, staff across her knees, thinking about bindings and blood and the sideways logic of love: all for one and one for all, a dead-even trade that adds up to infinity. She thinks how upside-down it is that she started this fight out of rage—spite and fury and sour hate— and that she'll finish it for something else entirely.

It's full dusk by the time it appears, folding out of darkness: a black owl with burning eyes that speaks in her sister's voice.

"It's time."

37

Now I lay thee down to sleep,
I pray the Lord your soul to keep.

A spell for sleep, requiring crushed lavender & a whisper

If it was one of Mama Mags's stories, James Juniper thinks it would go like this:

Once upon a time there were three sisters.

They were born in a forgotten kingdom that smelled of honey-suckle and mud, where the Big Sandy ran wide and the sycamores shone white as knuckle-bones on the banks. The sisters had no mother and a no-good father, but they had each other; it might have been enough.

But the sisters were banished from their kingdom, broken and scattered.

(In stories, things come in threes: riddles and chances, wrongs and wishes. Juniper figures that day in the barn was the first great wrong in their story. She whispers it to herself as she runs through the streets of New Salem this evening, the September shadows long and cold, the leaf-rot smell of fall hidden beneath the coal-smoke and piss of the city: *One.*)

The sisters survived their breaking. They learned to swallow their rage and their loneliness, their heartbreak and their hate, until one day they found one another again in a faraway city. Together they dared to dream of a better world, where women weren't broken and sisters weren't sundered and rage wasn't swallowed, over and over again. They began to build a new kingdom from rhymes and rumors, witch-tales and will. It might have been enough.

But their new kingdom was stolen from them, burned to rubble and ash. (*Two*, Juniper whispers.)

The three sisters survived the fire. They hid in attics and cellars, flitting like secrets through the streets, chased by shadows and torches. Perhaps they should have disappeared entirely—swallowed their rage and faded from the city like a bad dream, crept into some hillside town in need of a witch to cure their coughs and charm their crops, and been forgotten. It might have been enough.

But their baby girl was stolen from them. (*Three*, Juniper hisses into the half-light. Anybody who knows stories knows that after *three* comes the ending, the comeuppance. The reckoning.)

Now the three sisters run toward their reckoning with the setting sun at their backs and whispers and curses at their heels. They wear no disguises, have indeed dressed the part: their cloaks are ragged and dark, their skirts black velvet and obsidian silk. *Witchy as hell.* Juniper wonders if anyone sees them and wonders at the absence of pointed black hats.

They toss salt and poppy-flowers as they run, tangling the alleys and blurring the street signs behind them, so that their pursuers will find themselves circling the same block several times without knowing why, or discovering dead-ends that were through-ways the day before. The sisters know it won't save them, but they don't intend to be saved.

It seems to Juniper the city itself does its best to help them. The branches of linden trees duck low behind them, and roots leave the sidewalks humped and treacherous in their wake. Crows watch them with too-bright eyes, swooping in front of trolleys and passersby at just the right moment to distract them as three witches run past. Juniper thinks it might be her imagination or the spirits of the Last Three or the red heart of witching itself, helping them, whispering at their heels, *yesyesyes*.

The three of them converge on the bridge, cross the Thorn, and step into St. George's Square together. It's empty in the deepening dusk, except for the soft burbling of the pigeons and the whisper of September wind.

They walk to the precise center of the square, where Saint George of Hyll himself once stood. There's nothing there now but a marble plinth, quite empty. Juniper scrambles atop it and reaches down for her sisters' hands.

Her vision doubles as they look back at her, so that she sees her sisters, but also two strangers who have stepped out of a winter's night witch-tale.

One of them wise and wary, with her red-eyed owl perched on her shoulder like a demon escaped from Hell. Her hair straggles loose from its bun and her cloak pools like ink around her feet. A broken-glass ring glints on one finger. She doesn't look like a librarian anymore.

One of them strong and seething, with her osprey on her arm and death in her eyes. Her braid flows like velvet over one shoulder; her dress is stitched together in a dozen shades of funeral-black. She doesn't look like a mill-girl anymore.

And Juniper herself, wild and wicked. Her hair swings ragged just above her shoulders and her arms are bare and white. A silver scar climbs her left leg and another wraps around her throat, newly healed, from the two fires she's survived so far. She wonders distantly what the third one will cost her.

She wishes she had a familiar. She wishes she were back home, wading through the cudweed and nettles around Mama Mags's hut. She wishes Mr. Gideon Hill would choke on a chicken bone and save them all a world of trouble.

She smiles instead, looking between her sisters. "Ready?"

But she doesn't need to ask. She can feel their wills burning through the binding between them, their hearts racing in perfect synchrony, their throats full of the same words.

"Thank you," Agnes says, softly.

They work two spells that evening. The first smells of lavender and midnight-dreaming. They pour their wills into it, their skins feverish, their lips chanting—*Now I lay thee down to sleep*—and Juniper feels the spell pool and rise like deep water around them. The square grows eerily silent as every rat and roach and scuttling creature falls into an unnatural sleep.

But the spell is not for them. The owl and the osprey rise into the air. Their talons clench as if they are grasping an invisible ribbon in the air, and they vanish into the cooling blue of the sky, carrying their mistresses' spell with them.

The owl, Juniper knows, will appear on the ledge of a window at the Hall of Justice. The shadows that writhe thick around the Deeps will not wait on that particular window ledge, because someone—one of the maids who scrubs the cells, perhaps—has left the sill strewn with salt, the window half-open.

The owl will wing through it, their words pouring from his open beak, soaring past the startled evening-shift of officers and guards and secretaries. Before they can shout the alarm, before they can do more than blink in confusion at the coal-colored owl flying through their offices—they will fall into a deep and boneless sleep, from which they will not wake for several hours, or possibly days. The prisoners locked in the Deeps beneath them—the city's malcontents and drunks, its radicals and rabble-rousers and especially its witches—will hear nothing but the silent rush of wings and the hollow thuds of skulls against desks.

The osprey will not follow the owl to the Hall of Justice. His mistress has other business in the city. Juniper glances sideways at Agnes's face and wonders if she can see through her familiar's eyes: the grimy cinder blocks of the Home for Lost Angels, the cold swirl of Hill's shadows around it. Mr. August Lee climbing through a window with a scrap of witchspeak in his pocket and a lump of clay that looks—if you squint in poor light, with bewitched eyes—like a baby girl.

Juniper begins the second spell when her sisters' familiars return.

London Bridge is falling down, falling down.

She drinks saltwater from a flask in her pocket, whiskey-tainted and bitter, and spits it onto the cobbles. Her sisters reach for her hands and they chant the words with her until they see red rust climbing the lamp-posts along the edges of the square, until the air tastes of old blood and passing years.

The owl and the osprey carry that spell, too. Back to the Hall of Justice, past the slumped bodies of guards, down the steps to the crowded cells of the Deeps.

Juniper imagines how it might feel to wake in that fetid dark and see ember eyes watching you. To see the black iron bars of your cage—so real, so absolute a moment before—rusting away, leaving nothing but orange flakes floating on the scummed surface of the water.

The owl will open its beak, afterward, and speak with a woman's voice. "*Run, sisters,*" it will say, "*You have nothing to lose but your chains.*" Some of the women in the cells will recognize that voice, smoke-eaten and rasping. One of them—a ruddy-cheeked woman whose fashionable furs have been replaced with a dingy white shift—will cackle aloud and crash through the weakened bars of her cell.

Before she can reach the steps, the owl will speak again. It will ask a favor of them.

Some of them will ignore it, Juniper knows: the women with hungry children or pining lovers, the women who want only to run and keep running. But some of them want something else, something that tastes of pitch and blood and rage unswallowed. Those women will linger and listen and—perhaps—do what Juniper asks of them.

In the square Juniper hears the sharp singing of iron-shod hooves, sees the angry glow of torchlight rising up the white walls of City Hall, and knows their time is up. She holds her sisters' hands tight in hers and stands tall, waiting for the end of their story to come riding to meet them.

Agnes sees two men when she looks at Gideon Hill. Maybe three.

The first one is the one the rest of the city saw: the watery, weak-chinned mayor who now sits astride his white horse, loyal hound trotting at his side, red cross painted on the bright silver of his shield. He should look absurd, like a bank teller playing dress-up, but somehow his features are made grander in the reflected glow of his shield. He looks like a painting come to life, like a Saint come to save their souls.

The second man she sees is the one her sisters see: an ancient, unnatural creature who speaks with shadows and feasts on souls. A monster who murders women and steals children, who cut a red curl of hair from her daughter's head to taunt her.

The third man she sees is her daddy: a monster. A coward. A man whose comeuppance is coming.

A dozen ranks of Inquisitors march behind him into the square, their eyes zealous and their uniforms starched white beneath silver armor. Hill pulls his horse to a showy halt before the plinth, his dog standing stiff-legged beside him, too-tight collar biting into its neck.

Hill looks just slightly down his nose at the three sisters still standing back-to-back. Three red lines run across his face, pulling and twisting the soft flesh of his lips.

Agnes isn't aware that she's thrown herself toward his throat, lips peeled in an animal snarl, fingers bent into claws, until she feels her sisters holding her back. She screams and Pan screams with her somewhere high above them, a hawk's shriek echoing over the square. Some of the Inquisitors flinch.

Hill lifts his chin. "Inquisitors—arrest these women. For murder! For malice! For witchcraft most wicked."

The scrape and clank of armored men shifting behind him, the heavy drag of chains. Gloved hands reach for their ankles, a little hesitant, as if even plate armor and fifty friends might not be enough to keep them safe from the most wanted witches of New Salem.

One of them catches the trailing edge of Juniper's cloak and she kicks her leg without looking down. Agnes hears a muted crunch that might be a human nose.

"Where is she, Hill?" Agnes's voice is flat and low.

The corner of Hill's mouth twitches, as if it wants very much to smile but knows it would be off-script. "Silence, witch!" he screeches instead.

There are many hands on their skirts now, hauling them down. Juniper is swearing and kicking. Bella is whispering *oh dear, oh dear* in a desperate circle. Agnes pitches her voice far louder. "Where is she? You promised me my daughter back!"

This time the smile escapes, a cruel curl of lips puckered by Pan's claw-marks. "Witches don't have daughters, Miss Eastwood."

Agnes isn't surprised, not really. She knows powerful men only keep their promises when they have to, and they never have to. But she's surprised how angry it makes her to be told she has no daughter—when her belly is still slack and empty from carrying her, when her breasts still ache with the certainty of her motherhood. She's surprised, too, by the sound she makes, a keening howl.

Juniper flings herself down onto the Inquisitors, fists bruising against armor, and Agnes lunges for Hill a second time. Hands intercept her, tangle in her cloak and skirts, drag her to the cobbles. Pan's claws *skree* against helmets and shields and men's voices swear. Beside her Bella's chant has escalated to *oh hell, oh hell*, interspersed with the hiss of spells. Several Inquisitors collapse, bee-stung or sleeping or clawing at their own sewn-shut mouths.

But there are so many of them, and so few Eastwoods.

Soon Agnes is kneeling beside her sisters with a mailed fist snarled in her braid and iron cuffs around her wrists. Collars creak and snap around their throats, frost-cold, and Agnes feels the great red heartbeat of magic go gray and distant. Pan and Strix vanish. The lines that lead to Juniper and Bella go slack, replaced by the heavy pull of chains leading from collar to collar. Agnes hears the ragged pant of Juniper's breathing, feels the shiver in her chain, and wishes she could hold her hand.

Hill dismounts in a fluid sweep. His shield reflects the last yellow edge of the dying day; his face is stern, like Old Testament God descended from Heaven to visit some calamity on sinning mortals, but Agnes sees the strut in his stride. Behind him, his dog licks her teeth nervously, not looking at them.

Agnes closes her eyes. "P-please, sir," she begs him, because he expects her to beg, because men are stupid when they think they've won. Because it might work. "Please."

He doesn't bother even to answer her, but merely turns his back to the three witches and speaks to his men. "Bind their tongues, that they may not work their devilry, and follow me."

He doesn't watch as his Inquisitors approach the sisters with jangling metal bridles, as thumbs bruise their jaws and force their mouths open, as Juniper curses and spits until she's silenced by the bit between her teeth. The cage locks around Agnes's skull, the bit pressing into her mouth like a metal tongue.

Hill doesn't watch as they are half dragged, half marched down Third Street to the Hall of Justice, as the evening crowd swells around them and rumors swoop like cruel-beaked birds through the air—*I heard they put half the city into an enchanted sleep; I heard Mr. Hill banished the Devil himself from the square; why not burn them now, before their master returns?*—and the crowd's murmurs turn to mockery and then malice. They throw spoiled fruit and insults at first, then bottles and stones. Juniper swears around her bridle and Bella clenches her hand tight around her battered brass ring, and still Hill does not look back.

If he had, he might have seen the promise seething in Agnes's eyes: *That is the last time you will ever hear me beg, you bastard.*

The three sisters are not locked in the seeping dark of the Deeps, as Mr. Hill intended, because upon arriving at the Hall of Justice they found no single piece of iron or steel unrusted. The bars of the cells stood like rows of snapped teeth; doors hung at mad angles from rotten hinges; rings of keys were nothing but circles of red-orange rust on the floor.

Instead the Inquisitors locked the sisters on the highest floors, generally reserved for the drunk sons of City Council members or businessmen whose lawyers were sure to raise a fuss about unsanitary conditions. The cells are dry and clean-swept, with chamber pots and barred windows that divide the moonlight into clean silver stripes.

Agnes lets the moon touch the bruised flesh of her face with cool fingers. It trails over the ugly iron of her witch's bridle and collar, down the bare white of her shift. She misses the weight of her cloak and skirts; she misses her sisters locked in their separate cells. But mostly she feels nothing at all.

Mags used to tell a story about a witch who cut out her own heart and buried it deep. Agnes knows precisely how she must have felt, walking around with nothing in her chest but an absence.

The moonlight vanishes, replaced by scorched black wings.

Agnes opens her eyes to see Pan perched on the narrow window ledge. He looks somehow translucent, barely there, as if she isn't really seeing him but merely his reflection in a smudged and dim mirror. The collar burns dully against her throat, a rising warning.

Agnes crawls as close to him as she can before her chain draws short. Pan opens his beak and a voice issues from it, a faint echo: "*I have her. She's safe.*" A man's voice, low and steady, that tugs at the absent place in her chest.

Pan wisps into smoke and vapor. Her collar cools. The moonlight shines clear once more.

Agnes collapses on the dry stone, trembling with relief and exhaustion and wild laughter, because she knows the same thing the heartless witch knew: without your heart, they cannot hurt you.

38

Roses are red,
Violets are blue,
The Devil will pay,
And so will you.

A spell for vengeance, requiring thorns & blood

The Salem College archives include several hundred trunks full of records relating to the witch-trials of the purges, and Beatrice Belladonna has read most of them. She knows what's coming better than her sisters. She knows that history digs a shallow grave, and that the past is always waiting to rise again.

First: the convening of the court.

They gather in a small, lightless chamber in the Hall of Justice: the judge, pale and lipless, like a large mushroom forced into a starched white collar; a panel of milky men in pressed suits; a reporter and a sketch-artist from *The Post*. Gideon Hill himself, standing with his hound beneath the bench, smiling faintly.

Three chairs wait in the center of the room, stained and old, with iron bands waiting like open hands. The Eastwoods are chained to their seats by a pair of Inquisitors who must have been selected for their sober expressions and clean-parted hair, the perfect human opposites to the bedraggled witches between them.

Already Bella can hear the excited scritching of the artist's pen, see the cartoons that will run in *The Post* for weeks: three women bound and bowed, their limbs bare and indecent, their hair poking at wild angles through their bridles. Most people will unfold their papers and *tsk* their tongues at the sight of such wicked witches.

A few of them, though, will see the fury in their eyes, blazing even through the callous caricature, and suspect that behind every witch is a woman wronged.

Second: the evidence against them.

Gideon begins with a sanctimonious little speech about sin and sedition and the propensity of evil to flourish where good men do nothing. Then comes a parade of witnesses, ranging from the purely fanciful—a red-nosed barkeep who claims to have seen Agnes cavorting "in a most unseemly manner" with a fork-tailed gentleman; a housewife who was supposedly seduced by Bella's "foul glamors" into visiting a house of prostitution on the south end—to the uncomfortably plausible.

There's a series of disgruntled fairgoers who saw Juniper's hat-trick; a handful of doctors from St. Charity Hospital, one of whom watches Juniper with an anxious expression, rubbing a pink scar on his forehead; a paper-boy who claims to have seen Bella riding a broomstick while kissing a colored woman, which is at least half-true; a handsome, earnest young man named Floyd-something who testifies that Agnes is a seductress and a snake, and that the infant taken into custody might belong to half the gentlemen in New Salem for all he knows. He looks at Agnes as he says it, with a kind of bruised, vicious meanness; Agnes looks mildly back, unmoved, even bored.

Madame Zina Card limps to the stand next, looking thin and hollow. Yes, she says, Agnes Amaranth sought her services as an abortionist. Yes, she repents her own part in such wickedness.

Miss Munley from the Salem College Library testifies that Bella abused her position to gain knowledge of the occult, and notes that all such materials have been submitted to the mayor's office for destruction. Bella waits to feel the numbness of betrayal, but all she feels is sorry and sad and weary.

Miss Grace Wiggin is the final witness.

"You spoke to one of these women on the night of the solstice, is that correct?"

"Yes, sir."

"And what did you speak about?"

"She asked me if I would join them in their dark purposes." Wiggin looks up at Hill through her lashes, a child eager to please.

He gives her a stern, bracing smile. "And what purposes were those, my dear? Be strong now, and tell us."

Grace brushes a lace handkerchief across her forehead. "To end the rule of man," she answers, tremulously. "To bring about a second plague."

The courtroom dissolves into gasps and whispers. Hill smiles. "The city thanks you for your bravery, Miss Wiggin."

There is no cross-examination, no defense. This is a witch-trial, after all, and witches have even fewer rights than women. Bella can do nothing but sweat and stand on aching legs, listening to her own damnation with the taste of iron on her tongue.

Third: the confession.

Bella doesn't know why Hill bothers, really. Whether they repent or plead innocence or keep their silence, they'll burn just the same. She supposes it's merely the proper end to the story he's telling.

An Inquisitor fiddles with the clasps of their bridles. The mask falls away and Bella retches as the metal tongue slides from her mouth.

Then Gideon Hill asks them a series of questions: Will they repent before God? Will they provide the names of their companions in sin? Will they spend their eternity in Hell?

At this Juniper laughs, a sound like a rusted hinge creaking in the wind. She grins up at him through swollen lips. "Ask for me when you get there, Hill. I'll be waiting."

Hill watches her for a long, watery second before nodding to one of his Inquisitors.

After that he asks all his questions again, but they're harder to hear. It's the screaming, Bella thinks.

She wonders if Hill expects the pain to break them, and some delirious part of her wants to laugh. They know pain too well. It dined with them at their table, slept beside them, grew with them like a fourth sister. What are hot needles and cold mallets to the Sisters Eastwood?

Over the iron smell of her own blood, Bella thinks that Araminta Wells will have to keep waiting to be disappointed.

After that Bella goes away for a while. (St. Hale's taught her that trick.)

When she returns, Gideon Hill is at the judge's bench, whispering. The judge stands, flushed and blinking, his white collar wilting.

"This court, convened on September the twenty-first in the year eighteen-hundred and ninety-three, finds the Eastwood sisters guilty on all charges." He clacks his hammer once. "They will burn at dusk tomorrow."

Over the sudden noise—the murmurs and *hear-hears*, the curses of the officers now wrestling Juniper back into her iron mask—Bella hopes no one notices that Agnes is smiling.

The first time Gideon Hill visited Juniper in her prison cell she was reeling and wounded, stunned to meet a witch in the Deeps beneath New Salem.

This time, she's the witch. This time, she's waiting for him.

The moon has already risen and ripened by the time she hears the soft tap of boots, the click of claws. The steps pause outside her door.

She thinks of beasts who came for maidens in the night, of knights who plucked princesses from their towers like fruit from the branch.

A hissed exhalation, a twist of shadow, and Gideon Hill and his dog are standing in her cell. He's not himself, she sees, or maybe more himself: his features are the same, but the muscles beneath them are arranged differently. His shoulders are no longer stooped, his spine no longer furled.

Juniper looks at him through the iron bars of her bridle, waiting.

He flicks his hands and a pair of five-fingered shadows peel lazily away from the window and inch toward Juniper. She doesn't recoil when they slide over her bare ankles, crawl like hands up the thin cotton of her shift. Her collar flares hot beneath their touch and her breath hitches in her throat—but the shadows pass on, coiling like snakes around her bridle.

The bit slides from Juniper's mouth. She rolls her jaw and listens to the wet pop of tendons and bones. "Still paying house calls before sunrise, I see. Guess you can't teach an old dog new tricks, can you?"

Hill's eyes sharpen at the word *old*, searching her face for hidden messages or veiled threats. *Keep him stupid*, Agnes warned her.

"I'm still not in the mood for a confession, if that's what you came for." Juniper knows it isn't.

The sharpness leaves his features. He gives her a strange, angled smile, almost wry. "No, I thought not. May I sit?"

Juniper makes a grand gesture to the bench opposite her, shackles clanking. She tries to keep her face scornful, but there's a tenseness in her stomach, a whisper of uncertainty. She expected Gideon to gloat or sneer or possibly rave, to torment her like a cat with cornered prey. It's what her daddy did as he dragged them to the cellar, drunk with his own power.

Gideon's face doesn't look much like her daddy's. It's watchful in the moonlight, hungry in some way that Juniper doesn't understand. "You must hate me," he observes.

Juniper feels her eyebrows rise. "You make it pretty damn easy."

A soft laugh from the shadows. "Yes, well. One does what one must to survive, and not all of it is pleasant. I thought you might understand that better than anyone."

Juniper doesn't say anything. She thinks of the slide of snake scales, the addled terror in her daddy's face at the very end.

"I was wondering, Miss Eastwood, if I might tell you a story. And then ask you a question, after."

Juniper thinks about telling him precisely where he can shove his story. Thinks about showing him the swollen red places where the needles burrowed deep, the blackening bruises along her knees and knuckles, and telling him he already asked enough damn questions.

He seems to see her answer in her face, because he withdraws something from his breast-pocket: a battered brass locket. "Here. A trade in good faith."

He places Mama Mags's locket on the bench beside her. Juniper tries hard not to scrabble for it too eagerly, to press it too hard against her breastbone. "I only ask a little of your time, in exchange."

The locket is warm against her skin, despite their hours apart. She leans back against the wall, and listens.

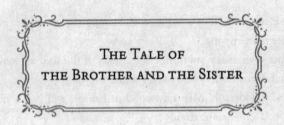

THE TALE OF
THE BROTHER AND THE SISTER

Once upon a time there were a brother and a sister who loved each other very much because they had no one else to love them.

The sister told the brother it wasn't always so—she remembered the warmth of their mother's arms, the boom of their father's laughter—but the little boy never knew their parents as anything but hungry and hateful, with bitter coals for hearts.

In time they grew hungrier and more hateful, until one day their mother led them into the deepest dark of the woods. She gave them a single loaf of bread, more sawdust than wheat, and told them to wait for her return. They waited, as the owls swooped and the badgers burrowed, as the woods turned from blue to black and the tears froze on their cheeks, but their mother never came back. The little boy found that he, too, had a bitter coal burning in his heart.

The boy and his sister wandered farther into the woods. They ate their meager loaf of bread and shared the last crumbs with a black raven who watched them from the trees. The raven gave them a long, red stare, then led them along a twisting path until they found a little house tucked beneath the roots of an ancient oak.

Juniper thinks she knows this tale. In the version her sister told her, the house is made of gingerbread.

The house was crooked and wild-looking, and so was the woman who lived inside it. "A witch," the boy whispered to his sister, but she didn't seem to mind.

The witch sat them at her table and wrapped her fingers around their wrists. She *tsk*ed at the grate of their bones beneath their skins and fed them sweetmeats. When they were both reeling and drunk with the fullness of their bellies, she told them they could stay if they liked.

The boy's sister agreed readily. For the next seven years she studied with the witch in the woods and grew wilder and stranger, until she was nearly a forest creature herself, until she seemed not to remember the mother and father who left them in the woods.

The boy studied, too, but he did not forget their mother or father, and looked always for the words and ways that would let him return to them. For that he required more than the witch's old books and rhymes; he needed spells that could break wills and command hearts, that could change the nature of a soul.

One winter's day the witch found the boy, who was no longer a boy, in a grove of rowan trees. The trees were full of starlings, but they were strangely silent. None of them cast a shadow on the ground. The witch watched while the boy commanded them to sing, and then to fly, and then to hurl themselves to the frozen earth, their necks twisted and bent at wrong angles.

The witch asked the boy to leave then, because she feared him, and feared the cost of his ways. The boy agreed without complaint, not because she asked him to but because he had learned what he needed. He asked his sister to come with him, but she refused. She chose to remain in the woods without him. He left with the coal burning bright in his chest.

The boy who was no longer a boy returned to his village. He found his mother and father still living, less hungry now without two more mouths to feed. His mother cried out when she saw him. Before she could curse him as a ghost or banish him a second time, the boy stole her shadow and her will. Her eyes turned empty and faraway, and she smiled as she held out her arms to him. "Welcome home, my son."

The boy and his mother and father lived happily ever after. For a time.

39

Remember, remember till the fifth of December!
I know no reason why a single season
Should ever be forgot.

A spell to recall what is forgotten, requiring saltpeter &
a single tear

James Juniper thought Gideon Hill was just like her daddy: a cowardly shit of a man who only felt whole when he was breaking something.

Now she thinks he's more like her. Or what she might have been if she never found Agnes and Bella again, never stood arm in arm with her Sisters or held Eve tight in her arms: a vicious, broken creature who knew how to survive and nothing more.

Gideon Hill is staring at the ceiling, his hands clasped loosely in his lap. His dog is staring straight at Juniper with those mournful black eyes. Juniper doesn't figure that's their natural color.

"No one's ever guessed what she is." Juniper says it softly into the cell, the air still rich and thick with storytelling.

"I hide her well." Hill's fingers stroke the iron collar at his dog's throat and the dog flinches.

"I thought witches were friendly with their familiars."

Hill shakes his head at the ceiling. "That's what the stories say, isn't it? But if you want real power you must abandon sentiment. You must learn to think of your familiar not as a pet or a companion, but as a tool. And if a tool fails to do what is necessary, if it resists its master's hand—" He shrugs in a manner that's supposed to look careless but doesn't.

Juniper tries to imagine what kind of devilry you'd have to wreak before witching itself resisted you, before your own familiar bared its teeth at you. Was it when he first bound his soul to someone else, and stole their body for himself? Or was it even earlier, when he drove a grove full of starlings to their deaths?

Her eyes fall to the rubbed-raw skin beneath the dog's collar, and she wonders if it's more than it seems. The first witch-collar, perhaps, crafted by some way-back incarnation of Gideon Hill to control his wayward hound. Then she wonders what would happen if it were free.

Gideon is still looking upward, waiting patiently for her next question. Juniper asks it. "What happened? After the happily-ever-after?"

Gideon sighs. He lifts one hand and its shadow stretches and roils across the cell floor, digits and joints bending in unnatural shapes. "The words and ways this requires are...potent. They come at a price—power always does. This isn't a matter of wrong or right, you understand, but merely the working of the world. If you want strength, if you want to survive, there must be sacrifice."

That's not what Mags taught them. *You can tell the wickedness of a witch by the wickedness of her ways.* "So who paid your price?"

He bends his neck to look directly at her, weighing something. "A fever spread through my parents' village that first winter."

The word *fever* rings in Juniper's ears, a distant bell tolling.

"It was nothing too remarkable, except the midwives and wise women couldn't cure it. One of them came sniffing around, made certain deductions...I took her shadow, too. And the sickness spread further. The villagers grew unruly. Hysterical. I did what I had to do in order to protect myself." That line has a smoothed-over feel, like a polished pebble, as if he's said it many times to himself. "But then of course the fever spread even further...I didn't know how to control it, yet. Which kinds of people were expendable and which weren't. I'm more careful these days."

The ringing in Juniper's ears is louder now, deafening.

An *uncanny illness*, the Three had called it. Juniper remembers the illustrations in Miss Hurston's moldy schoolbooks, showing abandoned villages and overfull graveyards, carts piled high with bloated bodies. Was that Gideon's price? Had the entire world paid for the sins of one broken, bitter boy?

And—were they paying again? *I'm more careful these days.* Juniper thinks of Eve's labored breathing, the endless rows of cots at Charity Hospital, the fever that raged through the city's tenements and row houses and dim alleys, preying on the poor and brown and foreign—the expendable. *Oh, you bastard.*

But Hill doesn't seem to hear the hitch in her breathing. "People grew frightened, angry. They marched on my village with torches, looking for a villain. So I gave them one." Hill lifts both hands, palm up: *What would you have of me?* "I told them a story about an old witch woman who lived in a hut in the roots of an old oak. I told them she spoke with devils and brewed pestilence and death in her cauldron. They believed me." His voice is perfectly dispassionate, neither guilty nor grieving. "They burned her books and then her. When they left my village I left with them, riding at their head."

So: the young George of Hyll had broken the world, then pointed his finger at his fellow witches like a little boy caught making a mess. He had survived, at any cost, at every cost. *Oh, you absolute damn bastard.*

"And your sister? Did they catch her, too?" But Juniper doesn't think they did. Juniper thinks his sister escaped, retreated to the lonely tor of Avalon, and wrote herself into a dozen new stories. Until the day her brother came with an army at his back and burned her for the crime of not loving him enough.

"No."

"Did you ever see her again?"

"Once. I asked her again if she would come with me, stand at my side—I could have protected her—but she refused me. Again."

Juniper has always thought of the final days at Avalon as a grand battle, a clash between the forces of good and evil, Saint against sinners. Now she pictures instead a brother and a sister looking at one another through the flames, both haunted by the same hateful story. The Maiden, who found her way into a better one, who made a way for herself among the crows and foxes and wild things. The Saint, who never found any ways except cruel ones.

Juniper wonders what it cost the Maiden to refuse the brother she loved. She wonders what it cost the Saint to burn the only person who ever loved him.

Gideon Hill is watching her again, and she imagines she sees something of that cost in the hollow blue of his eyes. "You remind me of her," he says, very softly. Juniper looks away.

He straightens on the bench, voice clipped and quick again. "Which brings me to my question, James Juniper: Will you stay with me? Or will you, too, burn?"

Her neck snaps back toward him. She feels her jaw dangling and closes it carefully. "Come again?"

"I've been alone for—a very long time. I grow weary of it. I have no wife, no family, no lovers."

"What about Miss Wiggin? Isn't she your daughter?"

Hill makes a soft, derisive noise in his throat. "She's useful to me, in her way. A pliable will, a pretty face. Excellent for politics. I've met a dozen women like her in my time." Juniper is willing to bet he's met hundreds, maybe thousands. How dull the world must look after centuries of soul-eating, slinking from body to body like a disease. How many wives has he buried? How many children has he outlived? Grace Wiggin must seem to him nothing but a mayfly, another collared creature under his sway.

"But you are a rarer species. Free, feral, forceful. And such a will—didn't you wonder why I never stole your shadow?" His smile is warm, almost admiring. "What a witch I could make of you."

"And my sisters?"

The smile dims slightly. "The people need a villain again. Someone has to burn." Beneath the watery red of the eyes he stole, Juniper thinks she sees a glimmer of his true self: a little boy lost in the woods who doesn't want to be alone. "But not you."

Juniper can tell by the curl of Gideon's smile that he's confident in her answer, certain she'll forsake her sisters and survive. It's what he did, after all.

It's what Juniper herself might have done, back when she was a heartless, hurting thing. Now she wants so much more than merely to survive.

She pretends to consider it, catching her lip between her teeth and making worried eyes. Hill stands slowly and steps closer, hungry-eyed, hopeful, hands lifting as if he wants to take her in his arms. She waits until he's close enough that she can see his pulse jack-rabbiting in his throat.

"I told you before, Hill." Her whisper is soft, sincere. "*Go fuck yourself.*"

Shadow-hands slam her spine against the stone wall. The collar burns at the touch of his witching, but Juniper's throat is knotted and scarred now, half-numbed to the pain. Distantly it occurs to her that men like Gideon ought to stop breaking people, because sometimes they mend twice as strong.

Hill's face swims dizzily before her: chalk-white and mad as a spring starling, the lost little boy replaced by the ancient, addled soul.

"She refused me and she burned for it," he hisses into her face. "And so will you, James Juniper."

He vanishes in a swirl of shadow, and she is alone.

Juniper sits for a long while after, not sleeping. She touches the brass locket lying warm against her breast, thinking of all those long hours lying on Mama Mags's grave waiting for a ghost that never came, thinking of the voice she heard the last time she was locked up. Wishing she could hear it again.

Then she thinks: *Why not?*

She draws the chain over her head and cracks open the locket. Half of it is occupied by a face that Juniper never lets her eyes linger on for long.

She lingers now. The photograph is blurred and silvered, the face blooming out of shadows. She's beautiful, like Agnes. Freckled, like Bella. Juniper has never found much of herself in her mother, but she supposes they share a certain tilt in their chins, a wildness in their eyes. A heavy hand rests on her shoulder. The picture is too small to show its owner, but Juniper knows every scar and knob of her daddy's knuckles.

The other half of the locket holds a single curl of thistledown hair, tufted and white. Juniper strokes it once.

She knows it's madness. She knows it's the foolish dream of a frightened girl. But she whispers the words anyway: *Little Girl Blue, come blow your horn.*

She hesitates when she comes to the place where a name should be. She figures a person should be respectful when summoning the dead, so she calls her grandmother by her true name: *Magdalena Cole awake, arise!*

Nothing happens except that the collar sears white-hot and Juniper swears.

And the wind rushes through the cell window, smelling of tobacco and earth and midnight. Of home.

Juniper swallows very hard. "Mama Mags?"

No one answers her. But a cool touch trails over her brow—the wind over her skin or the brush of ghostly lips.

"I'll be twice-damned." Juniper's voice is hoarse, tear-thick. "You did it, didn't you? Bound yourself to this locket?"

Ashes to ashes, dust to dust. The words are the creak of floorboards, the whisper of moonlight.

It's nothing but a hedge-witch's spell to mend split seams, but maybe it isn't the words that matter, really. Maybe magic is just the space between what you have and what you need, and Mama Mags needed to leave some pale scrap of herself to watch over her granddaughters.

A suspicion occurs to Juniper then, about what else Mama Mags might have bound. About the invisible force that pulled Juniper and her sisters to St. George's Square that day in March, the lines that still stretch between them. Not fate, not destiny or blood-right, but merely the faded remains of their grandmother's gift.

Juniper rests her head in her palms and feels the tears sliding down her wrists. *Shh, shh*, whispers the wind. *It's alright, baby girl.*

Juniper cries until the breeze dies and the smell of tobacco fades from the room, until her collar cools around her neck and the bitter coal in her heart finally burns itself to cold ash and blows away.

40

When she got to the top of the hill,
She blew her trumpet both loud and shrill.

A spell to shout, requiring daring & day-old meadowsweet

The sky is the milky blue of old china and the wind whips from everywhere at once, as if the ceiling has been lifted off the world to let in a draft. The city feels brand-new, scoured clean.

If Agnes Amaranth must burn, at least this is a good day for it.

Her feet are bare and cold on the cobbled streets and her hair flies long and loose around her face. Her sisters walk one behind and one ahead of her. She can almost pretend they're girls again clambering up the mountainside, following the crow-feather tangle of Juniper's hair.

Except instead of calico and cotton they wear rough-woven wool with ashen Xs painted across their chests. Instead of laughing and shrieking they are silent, their jaws locked tight in their iron cages. Instead of the soft shush of leaves and the sing-songing of creek-water, they're surrounded by the clank and grate of their own chains, and the fevered hissing of a crowd.

Agnes has never seen such a large crowd; it's as if every building in New Salem has been upended and shaken until its occupants fell out and swarmed into the streets. There are workingmen with their sleeves rolled high and clerks with their derby hats tilted back. High-society ladies in fur-lined cloaks beside leering drunks with split-veined noses, entire families sprawled on checkered picnic blankets. All of them come to watch the witches burn.

Their eyes are bright and empty, shining like wet stones in their skulls; their shadows pool like oil behind them, viscous and misshapen.

But not every eye is empty, and not every shadow is twisted. Scattered through the crowd Agnes finds other faces: the Domontovich girls standing with their mother, vast and blond; Annie, standing in a cluster of girls from the mill; Ona, the raw-boned girl, glaring among them; Frankie Black and Florence Pearl and six other women from Salem's Sin; Rose Winslow beside the Hull sisters; Gertrude the Dakota girl and Lacey the nurse from Charity Hospital; Inez, disguised by a heavy cloak and a white wig, holding so tight to Jennie Lind that the two of them look like a single creature; a dozen other women freed from the Deeps, their eyes dark and their lips curled, waiting.

The Sisters of Avalon, who were not their sisters in truth but who still came when they were called.

And so had others. Agnes sees ranks of disreputable-looking young men she remembers from the Workingman, looking entirely too eager for mayhem. There are knots of brown-skinned women standing together, wearing long cloaks and grim expressions—Cleopatra Quinn is beside her mother, her eyes like a pair of lit torches as she looks at Bella—and even a few ladies from the Women's Association. Miss Cady Stone stands behind Jennie Lind, her jaw lifted.

More—far more—than Agnes dared to hope, all here for Eve. And here for more than Eve: here because they are tired of stolen children and missing women, of creeping and hiding, of raids and arrests. Because none of them is strong enough to face Gideon Hill alone, so they did not come alone.

Annie Flynn catches Agnes's eye and bows her head once, a soldier to her general, one witch to another. She slants her eyes sideways at someone else and Agnes sees him: Mr. August Lee.

He wears a cap pulled low over the blond bird's-nest of his hair and a red scarf wrapped under his chin. His eyes blaze at her, as if he can't see the witch-mark daubed on her chest or the iron muzzle over her face, as if she is a queen ascending her throne rather than a convict marching to her death. He holds a silver flask in one hand and something bundled tight in the crook of his arm. The bundle squirms very slightly.

Agnes stops walking, ignoring the yank of the collar around her throat, the curse as Juniper stumbles on her bad leg. The crowd shifts, someone steps aside, and she sees a ruby glint of hair, a tiny pink fist raised high. Her heart, held safe.

Eve. The nurses and nuns at the Home for Lost Angels must not have noticed yet that they're tending a lump of clay. The spell will crack and fade in another few hours, but by then it will be too late. She and Eve will be free among the stars.

Someone hauls their chain forward. The collar feels light as lace around her neck now.

St. George's Square has been transformed into a scene from a cheap play. A scaffold stands over George's plinth, built from wood so green it weeps around every nail-head. A stake points up from it like an accusing finger, piled deep with pine and white oak, glistening with lamp-oil.

A second scaffold stands upwind of the first, filled with ranks of grave-faced men in judges' robes and Inquisitors' armor. Grace Wiggin is the only woman among them, her white sash crossed neatly between her breasts, her expression fixed and vacant. Agnes stares up at Wiggin as they pass, willing her to look down and see her own dark reflection there: a woman bound and bridled, stripped of her words and ways. Wiggin doesn't look down, but a thin line appears between her brows.

A man in a stained gray suit stands at the base of the steps with a lit torch held high. The sight of it—the greasy coil of smoke, the aged iron—makes Agnes feel unmoored in time. As if she's drifted out of the world of trolleys and elections and into some murkier era of castles and knights and midnight bonfires.

Her feet are numb on the steps. The stake nestles between the winged bones of her back. A pair of men wrap cold chains around their waists, pinching tight, while another unlocks their bridles and shackles, leaving only their collars. Witches always went to God with their tongues free to repent and their hands free to pray. Agnes doesn't intend to do either.

It seems to her as she stands beside her sisters that it was always going to end like this: the three of them back-to-back, besieged on all sides. The wayward sisters, burned and bound. It seems to her it has happened this way before and will happen again, until there are no witches left to burn or no men left to burn them.

The crowd blurs and sways before her. She catches ripples of motion—the scarlet flash of August's scarf as he shoulders through the tight-pressed watchers, circling the scaffold, the dark flutter of Cleo's skirts as she edges closer—but then everything is obscured by a man in a suit the color of old honeysuckle.

Gideon Hill's shadow oozes two steps behind him, lazy and full-bellied. It stretches its arms high and spills over the platform's edge, down into the crowd, twisting around ankles and slinking up skirts. His dog trembles beside him, eyes huge in its thin skull.

"Last chance for a confession, ladies." He addresses all three of them but his eyes linger on Juniper.

None of them answer. Agnes can't sense her sisters through the cold iron around her throat, but she feels the wound-tight tension in the press of their shoulders against hers.

Hill steps closer to Juniper and says quietly, "Repent. Forgiveness is still possible." His voice is urgent, almost desperate.

Juniper smiles at him. "No," she says. "It isn't."

His jaw tightens. He turns away in a swirl of cream cloak. His dog lingers a step behind him, looking mournfully at the Eastwoods, until Juniper rasps, "S'alright, girl. Just a little longer." It creeps after its master.

Agnes feels the dull thud of boots and paws down the scaffold steps, the sawblade buzz of the crowd. Stars appear overhead, dim and distant through the blaze of torchlight.

Hill takes his place in the balcony across from them. He tucks Miss Wiggin's hand beneath his arm and she gazes up at him with such vacuous rapture that Agnes's stomach turns. At least their daddy never forced them to love him; at least he never took their selves or souls away. She wonders if Grace hates him, somewhere deep down in her china-doll body.

Hill surveys the gathered citizens, face severe and mournful. Agnes thinks he might make another speech about morality and Satan and modernity, but he doesn't. Instead he lets his gaze rest on the torchbearer below him. He nods once and a hideous hush falls over the square.

The torch hisses and snaps. A baby wails somewhere in the crowd. Agnes's thoughts run in dizzy circles—*a wise woman keeps her burning on the inside—sorry, Mags—hurry, August—*

Bella's voice comes soft and calm from the other side of the stake, as if she is sitting behind a collections desk rather than staked in the city square. "I translated that inscription, by the way. The one on the door: *Maleficae quondam, maleficaeque futurae.*" She ignores Juniper's softly muttered, *Jesus, Bell.* "In English it's 'witches once and witches in the future.'"

"And what does that mean?" Agnes asks.

"I think it means witches will return, one day, no matter how many of us they burn." Agnes can hear the smile in Bella's voice, sharp and secret. "I think it means—us. All of us."

Then the torch touches the pyre and flames lick like tiger claws into the sky, and the Eastwood sisters are burning.

Agnes Amaranth has burned once before. She's familiar with the glass-shard sting of smoke in her eyes, the way the heat rolls up her body in waves, lifting her hair from her shoulders and singeing the ends. The way her own tears whisper into steam on her cheeks.

The first time, Agnes saved herself. She poured a circle of creek-water around her sisters and said the words and the heat vanished. She and her sisters stood perfectly still as the fire licked and twined around them, as if it was a newly tamed wolf that might still bite.

This time it's August Lee who saves them. She sees his face through the honeyed glaze of the flames: eyes fixed, lips moving, arm still tight around Eve. The silver flask lies dripping on the cobbles, its contents scattered in a wide circle around the scaffold.

Agnes can see the shine of sweat slicking August's forehead and the tense set of his shoulders, as if he's braced beneath some immense weight. All witching takes is will, really, and he will not let her burn.

The scaffold hisses and pops beneath her feet and the flames snap high into the night, but they don't seem to touch her, as if her skin is coated in armor made of running water. Only her collar feels hot, warming at the presence of magic. It throbs against her throat.

The crowd howls and moans and cheers around August, their cheeks flushed and their eyes glowing red. Their shadows have merged into a single creature behind them, hydra-headed and many-limbed, exultant. Hill looks down on them with no expression at all, as if they are nothing to him but hollow puppets.

When he looks back up at the Eastwoods there are flames dancing red in his eyes, perhaps a trace of grief—but also vast relief, that this threat to his endless, weary life is finally laid to rest.

But soon his relief will flicker. Soon his brow will furrow. He has burned many, many women over the centuries, and surely all of them have screamed.

The Eastwoods are not screaming. The flames are wrapped like hands around them, tearing at their white wool dresses. Their chains are glowing red-hot—but their skin is whole and smooth, unblistered. Soon Gideon Hill will notice that his witches are not burning.

But they aren't ready. They need just a little more time.

Agnes takes a deep breath that should sear her lungs, but doesn't. She tastes cinders and ash and August's witching on her tongue. She thinks of Eve bundled tight in his arms, bathed in the light of her mother's burning, and thinks: *Listen close, baby girl.*

She shouts into the night, clear and taunting and fearless. "Is it a confession you want?"

Bella hears her sister's voice but hardly recognizes it. It booms and cracks, unrestrained, raw with rage. The sound of it thrums somewhere in Bella's bones, a plucked string too low to hear.

"I confess it freely, Mr. Hill: I am a witch."

The jeering crowd falls still at the sound of her voice. They stare up at the flames with wary faces, like hunters who hear their prey thrashing in the bracken, wounded but still dangerous. Gideon Hill stands very still on the balcony.

Bella feels the scaffold shudder beneath her feet as if someone is climbing it, as if they're attempting something very daring and heroic without which their entire plan would collapse. *Three bless and keep her.*

"I am a witch." Agnes shouts it a second time, louder, flinging her voice into the night. "And so are my sisters, and so will be my daughter and my daughter's daughter." Her voice roughens at the mention of Eve, as if the collar around her throat has constricted.

Behind them comes the sound of footsteps, then the whisper of words and the sizzle of saltwater spat on hot iron. Their chains crackle with unnatural rust. Their collars boil at the touch of witchcraft.

Bella bites her cheek until she tastes blood, but Agnes doesn't seem to feel her collar at all. Her head is tilted back against the stake, her eyes closed, her voice strong. "And so is every woman who says what she shouldn't or wants what she can't have, who fights for her fair share."

Every eye is on Agnes, transfixed. No one notices the fourth witch standing on the scaffold, singing her song to avert unwanted eyes. No one notices their chains and collars thinning and flaking, turning brittle as old bone.

Agnes gives a contemptuous twist of her shoulders, like a woman shrugging off an unwelcome touch, and the chain snaps. She steps forward, feet bare and unburnt on the blackened wood, hair dancing in the flames, and Bella hears the rushing sound of several hundred people drawing breath together.

She's surprised to feel a pang of pity for them: they thought they were in the kind of story where the wicked witches were caught and burned at the end, where all the little children were tucked safely into bed with the smell of smoke in their hair. It must be upsetting to discover themselves in the kind of story where the witches make friends with the flames instead, where they snap their chains and laugh up at the stars with sharp teeth.

Agnes lifts her arm and the fire wraps around her naked flesh like golden armor. She points at Gideon Hill where he watches from the balcony, his face twisted, his mouth half-open to snarl orders to his Inquisitors over the wild barking of his dog. Grace Wiggin still clings to his arm, looking at Agnes with horror. But there's a sliver of brightness in her eyes, as if a small, treacherous part of her is glad to see a witch walk out of the flames.

Bella's throat is blistering beneath the thinning collar, each rust-flake searing her skin where it falls. She can't see Cleo standing beside her, but she hears her voice whispering in her ear. "Hold on, love, it's almost done—*London Bridge is falling down, falling down*—"

Agnes is still pointing at Hill. Bella can only see the back of her head, but she can sense the vicious, delirious grin on her face. "I am a witch, Gideon Hill." Her voice is low, dangerous, the twitch of a cat's tail before it pounces, the final circle of an osprey before the plunge. "*And so are you!*"

As she says it, several things happen one after the other, like playing cards in a collapsing house.

Their witch-collars fall away from their necks, reduced to nothing but rust and malice. Bella can sense her sisters' souls singing loud through the binding between them and magic seething again on the other side of everything.

An owl and an osprey appear in the smoke-hung sky, black as spades or hearts, and the first true screams ring through the square.

Gideon Hill shouts orders. White-and-red Inquisitors surge toward the scaffold just as most of the crowd scrabbles away. They clash into one another without noticing the knots of people who aren't moving at all. Who are standing like stones or sentinels, watching the fire. Waiting.

Bella stumbles away from the stake and sags into Miss Cleo Quinn's arms.

"What happened to your ring, woman?" Cleo murmurs into Bella's hair. "I let you out of my sight for ten minutes."

"It's your fault, really, for letting me out of your sight."

"I don't make the same mistake twice." Cleo's hand finds hers and holds it so tightly her knuckle-bones creak.

Juniper limps free of the fire, raises her arms high, and laughs. It's a raucous, devilish laugh, the laugh of the crow as it raids the cornfield, the trickster as she weaves her web. Bella catches the wild edge of her smile as she looks out at the crowd

"I believe my cue is coming, love," Bella whispers. "Did you bring the wandwood?"

Cleo presses a thin strip of holly into her palm just as Juniper shouts a single word.

"*Hemlock!*"

Bella steps forward between her sisters as the crowd answers Juniper's command.

She watches a hundred women reach into a hundred pockets and satchels and baskets to withdraw a hundred hats in black muslin and gray velvet, dark silk and ragged lace. Their arms arc upward as every witch in the city of New Salem dons a tall, pointed hat, and whispers the words.

Skirts and cloaks cascade over their bodies from nowhere. Fine gowns of draping chiffon and cotton day-dresses with their sleeves ripped away, black cloaks with long trains of feathers and evening gowns trimmed in dark mink. Some of them were sewn by the Sisters of Avalon and some of them were dug out of cedar chests and wardrobes for the occasion. Some of them aren't true black but navy blue or lake-bottom green, but in the fickle light of stars and flames it hardly matters. The crowd sees women in tall hats and dark dresses and knows exactly what they are.

One witch you can laugh at. Three you can burn. But what do you do with a hundred?

Most people run, it turns out.

Hill isn't running. He's standing on the balcony shouting orders to his Inquisitors. He gathers fistfuls of shadow and tugs them like puppet-strings or fishing lines. Half the crowd lurches to a halt, swaying and blinking, too weak to wrest free of his will.

Perhaps his puppets might have stood their ground and overcome the witches of New Salem, but Bella touches her holly wand to the torch and lifts it high above her. The crowd below does the same, withdrawing thin strips of oak and applewood, birch and blackthorn. The women who have no matches borrow heat from the ones who do, touching their wand-tips one to another.

Bella speaks the spell without a trace of a stutter. A hundred voices echo her: *Queen Anne, Queen Anne, you sit in the sun—*

Simple, small words a woman might sing as she peered into her sewing box on a winter's night. Words about driving back the darkness, about sunlight piercing shadows.

As fair as a lily as white as a wand.

Each wand below her casts its own particular light, from palest dawn to bloody sunset, silver moon-shine to golden candleflame. The lights meet and merge, joining to form a wave of noon-bright sun.

The shadows flee before the witch-light, unwinding from ankles and tearing free from skirt-hems to run like unclean water over the cobblestones. They pool around Hill, a writhing darkness that hisses and spits like oil in the pan.

The spell grows brighter. The shadows shrink until they're the size of a single person standing tall, then a wizened old man, then a child, then nothing at all.

Gideon Hill stands shadowless and exposed, bathed in sunlight, his dog baring its teeth at the sky in a snarl or a smile.

A ripple moves through the crowd. Bella sees faces upturned, squinting at the witch-light with watering eyes and half-open mouths. Their shadows curl meekly beneath them once more, tame and ordinary. If the spell ends now she thinks most of them would be happy to stumble home, haunted by the memory of hate that wasn't their own. But the spell doesn't end.

Queen Anne, Queen Anne—

The witches didn't stop chanting when Hill's shadow vanished. The sunlight now is blinding, hot, boiling down on black wool and autumn cloaks, and the spell itself is becoming something more that itself, something that swallows lies and sheds truth.

Gideon Hill begins to change. The flat blond of his hair darkens to matted black. The chin sharpens, the flesh recedes to reveal a thin, hungry frame. This must be his true soul showing through his stolen body; Bella is surprised by how young and desperate it seems.

The dog beside him changes, too, her master's illusion burning away. Her legs and jaw lengthen, her fur roughens, her ears stand up: a lean wolf with black fur and boiling red eyes.

The crowd is frozen, staring up at the savior. Their light against the darkness, their would-be Saint. The word *witch* rustles through them.

Bella lowers her wand with a dizzy, savage glee pulsing in her temples. At least if they fail now the truth will still be told. The man who spent centuries twisting history and telling false tales will still be laid bare for everyone to see.

Their daddy died a good man, in the eyes of the world; Gideon Hill will die a villain.

Bella turns to Juniper, who is watching Gideon Hill with a strange expression on her face, nearly mournful. "Your turn, June."

Juniper is watching the boy on the balcony—the vicious, frightened boy who should have died a very long time ago—when her sister tells her it's her turn.

Cleopatra Quinn presses two things into her hands: a black-yew staff and a long, curved pair of teeth.

Juniper leaps from the scaffold with her scorched and tattered dress flapping like burnt wings behind her. She lands barefoot on the cobbles, bad foot curling beneath her, knee cracking against stone. The teeth bite deep into her palm and blood pools in her hand.

She remains crouched, buffeted by the panicked crowd. She slicks her blood along the black-yew staff and whispers the words for the third time in her life.

May sticks and stones break your bones, and serpents stop your heart.

Vicious, venomous words that burn her throat and scorch her tongue. Words that require a furious will behind them. Juniper has always had a brimming cup of hate inside her, a well of rage that never runs dry, but it seems to her now that she has to reach deeper to find what she needs, that perhaps her well is not so bottomless after all.

Still: she thinks of Eve, of the Three, of all those poor people dying in the cots of Charity Hospital, and she finds the will she requires.

The staff twists in her hand, the wood grain replaced with smooth scales, the carved snake suddenly warm against her palm. It looks back at her once with its glass eyes, and she nods to it. *Go.*

Juniper struggles to her feet as the snake slides unseen through the trampling feet. Gideon Hill is leaning over the platform railing, glaring into the crowd below, searching. His eyes find her and a stillness falls over him.

His face is familiar to her. It's the face she saw in every mirror and windowpane she passed for years. It's the face of a broken, betrayed child, holding on to hate because they have nothing else.

What would it be like to remain that broken child for centuries, all alone?

The black-yew snake is coiling up the platform timbers now, sliding nearer. Gideon is too busy staring at Juniper to see his own death creeping closer.

But Juniper's will is wavering. The snake is near enough to strike but it coils around itself, poised. Waiting.

Saints know he deserves it. So did her daddy, twice over, but she spared his life that day in the barn. She let him live seven years more, until he wore away every ounce of grace and goodness she had left. She didn't hesitate the second time.

She's spent the summer running, hunted and haunted, looking for someplace to put all the leftover hate in her heart. Maybe she's come to the end of it, finally. Maybe she's weary of vengeance earned and struck, of sacrifice and sin and too-high prices.

She feels the serpent hardening back to black wood, its venom seeping away.

Above her Gideon sees the weakness in her face. His eyes glitter in triumph. Juniper knows with cold certainty that he won't hesitate, that he will pay any price merely to live and keep living.

Gideon sees her, and smiles at what he sees.

What he doesn't see is the woman standing beside him on the balcony, her shadow lying at her feet where it belongs, her will finally her own once more: Miss Grace Wiggin.

41

As I lay dying upon the earth,
I raised my hands to her,
But she would not even close my lips nor my eyes.

A spell for a final regret, requiring a betrayal most bitter

Agnes Amaranth sees her.

Agnes stands at the edge of the scaffold with her back turned to her own pyre. She sees Gideon's shadows banished, his power broken. She sees Miss Grace Wiggin slip away from him like a kite with a cut string.

At first her face remains cool and empty, but then the truth comes boiling to the surface. Confusion first, then revulsion, as if she wants to peel her own flesh from her body. Then rage: pure and white-hot, toothed and fanged, entirely foreign on Miss Wiggin's docile features.

She turns to face the man who took her in then took her will, the father who cursed his own daughter. She looks in that moment less like a woman and more like a harpy. Like an ending long overdue, like a reckoning in a white dress.

Agnes figures Gideon Hill has always chosen his victims with care:

the small and strange, the lonely and weak. Old women who lived in the woods and young women with wayward hearts. His own dreamy, bookish nephew. He burned them and blamed them, ate them whole and spat out the seeds and never once worried that one of them would sprout behind him and bear poison fruit. That even the weak can make powerful enemies, if there are enough of them.

A red light is glowing now in Wiggin's eyes. Her fingers clutch at her skirts, searching for some weapon or way and finding none. Then her hands land on the pale sash that runs from hip to shoulder. She strokes the neat-stitched lettering slowly, almost wonderingly, before pulling the sash over her head. She holds the white silk like a sword laid flat across her palms. Women are good at making their own ways when they have none.

Hill doesn't see it coming. And even if he had—if he turned and saw the sash between Wiggin's hands and the rage in her face—Agnes doubts he would have believed it until it was too late.

Wiggin throws the sash over Hill's head and it settles gently across his throat. Before he can tear it away, before he can even cast an irritable glance downward, it twists tight around his neck.

"Saints save us." It's Bella, staring at Hill with her hands covering her mouth.

Cleo draws air through her teeth. "But not him."

Below them Juniper is looking up at Hill and Wiggin with her mouth open. Her black-yew staff is gone but Agnes doesn't see a serpent anywhere.

One of the Inquisitors on the balcony has noticed that the head of the Women's Christian Union is strangling the mayor. He apparently objects, even if the mayor no longer looks quite as he should, and strides forward.

"*No!*" Agnes shouts it uselessly, hopelessly,

Gideon's dog—now tall and red-eyed, no longer a dog at all but a wolf with an iron collar around her throat—turns on the Inquisitor. Her teeth snap inches from his flesh, hackles high. Her collar glows a punishing orange, but she does not back down.

More Inquisitors join the first. Before they can knock the wolf aside, a dark streak of feathers strikes, talons first. Pan joins the wolf, followed by Strix. The three familiars keep the shouting men at bay with teeth and claws and burning eyes. Behind them, Wiggin's sash tightens across Gideon Hill's throat. The wolf howls in agony or triumph.

Hill's face goes from white to red to mauve, darkening to a bruised, bloated color like meat gone bad. His lips are foam-specked and bitten, still moving in some final, futile spell. His legs kick weaker and weaker, his honeysuckle suit stained with spittle and piss. His wolf staggers.

All his malice and might, all his centuries of learning, and death came for him just the same. Agnes intends to watch until the very end, until his legs quit kicking and his heart quits beating, but someone shouts her name.

"Agnes Amaranth!" She ignores it.

But a baby cries, and Agnes knows that cry. It's written on her heart and carved into her bones. It echoes in her dreams, haunting her.

She turns away from her cold triumph to see August Lee climbing the scaffold steps with her name on his lips and her daughter cradled against his chest.

Agnes isn't aware of reaching for her until she feels the rightness of Eve's weight against her arms and hears the endless nonsense-stream of her own voice (*Baby girl, little love, it's alright, Mama's here, I've got you*). Her ribs ache as if something feathered is trying to escape them, like vast wings.

She smells sawdust and feels the careful weight of arms around her. She leans her cheek against August's chest and the arms settle. His skin is still warm with witching.

In the hollow between them she looks down into her daughter's solemn eyes, shining with stars and flames and the beginnings of ten thousand stories. Once there was a girl who was stolen and won back.

Once there was a girl who was raised by three witches. Once there was a girl who rose like a phoenix from her mother's ashes and winged into the light of a new world.

August releases her and presses a smooth branch into her palm. "Rowan-wood, just like you asked." It smells raw and green, cool against the burning air.

"Me and my boys will keep the crowd back."

Agnes looks up at him, this man who loves all of her, this knight who has gotten his tales crossed and fallen in love with the witch instead of the princess. Here he stands with her at the end, ash-streaked and sweating, and it seems perfectly clear to her what comes next in the story.

She kisses him. Despite the screaming crowd and the too-close lick of flames, despite the bruised sting of her lips and the startled blue of his eyes. His palm rises uncertainly, hovering above the line of her jaw. His lips are hesitant against hers. Agnes presses harder, teeth against skin, reminding him what she is. He burns back at her, all want and heat, fingers tangling in her hair.

It ends too soon, not a kiss so much as a promise, hope translated into flesh.

She releases his collar and August touches his bitten lips with the expression of a person who has suffered a religious revelation or a recent head injury.

"Agnes—" His voice is pleasingly hoarse.

She meets his eyes and lifts her chin in challenge. "Come find me, Mr. Lee. When it's over."

He touches his hand to his heart and she knows he will. Trusts it, body and blood.

Agnes grips her rowan-wood broomstick in one hand and reaches for her sister with the other. Bella's fingers catch tight around hers. "Where's June? There's still the banishing to work."

Agnes sees her. Juniper is still standing in the crowd below, looking up at Grace Wiggin as she's finally dragged away by bitten and bleeding Inquisitors. At her feet, Gideon Hill lies dead. His wolf has curled beside him, her slender nose on his chest, her eyes closed.

Juniper should be triumphant or gleeful or at least grimly satisfied— but instead she is perfectly still, staring. There's a bloodless terror in her face that makes the hair on Agnes's arms prickle. She has seen her sister raging and weeping, laughing and lying and a hundred other things; she has never seen her afraid.

Juniper knows what a man looks like when he dies. He looks sick and scared and finally sorry, like a skinflint villager when the Piper comes to collect. He looks impotent, weak, unlikely ever to hurt you again.

Gideon Hill doesn't look like that.

His face is bruised-black and his eyes are wet rubies, blood-streaked, but his expression at the very end is placid, almost bored. Just before the end he meets Juniper's eyes—as the crowd wails and panics around them, as Wiggin's fingers go white around the sash, her face lit with that wild, killing hate—and smiles.

His fist dangles over the raw-wood edge of the balcony. His fingers slacken as he dies and a bright ribbon flutters free: a single curl of hair, soft as feather-down.

Red as blood.

42

All the king's horses and all the king's men
couldn't put Georgie together again.

A spell to sunder a soul, requiring a death long overdue

O f all the souls James Juniper has seen this summer—four, by her accounting—Gideon Hill's is the foulest.

It leaks like hot tar from his open mouth and pools on the balcony beneath him, wet and black. Juniper figures that's what happens to a soul when it lingers too long, feeding on stolen shadows: it goes to rot, like a diseased organ.

His soul leaks away from his body, away from the wolf who lies with him—shouldn't a familiar vanish, when its master dies?—and drips between the boards.

It splashes to the cobbles and runs like black water along the cracks. It's hard to be sure through the trampling feet of the crowd, but Juniper thinks it's heading dead north. Toward her.

She looks back to the scaffold behind her, where her sisters are silhouetted by flames. Bella and Cleo are shoulder-to-shoulder, rowan branches in their hands. August is shouting to his men, guarding the platform against the rioting crowd.

Agnes is looking down into the face of her daughter, smiling with such love that Juniper's throat seizes. She thinks all of it—the Deeps and Avalon, the scar around her neck and the coals in her heart—might be worth it, if only Agnes and Eve make it out of this twice-damned city together.

Then Juniper thinks of the ruby curl of hair falling from the balcony. The smile on Hill's lips as he died. The Crone's voice saying *something from the body he was stealing.*

She understands that Gideon's soul isn't headed for her, after all. It's headed for the scaffold, for the only truly pure thing Juniper has ever seen in the world, the only thing neither she nor her sisters could ever bring themselves to harm.

Eve.

And she understands that she only has one choice, and that it's a losing one.

First she curses—Gideon Hill and his damn shadows, herself and her terrible choices, the world that demands such a steep price just for living—then she says the words.

Ashes to ashes, dust to dust, mine to yours and yours to mine.

The words Mama Mags used to bind split seams, then sisters, then her own soul. Surely they would work now, for Juniper.

Bindings usually involve ways and means, objects and complicated affinities, but Juniper has nothing but the taste of Gideon Hill's bridle between her teeth, the scars of his collar around her throat, and her own will, which does not waver.

She reaches for his soul as it runs past her, curls her fingers into it. It twists in her hands, fighting to escape, but her will is a hammer and anvil, a stone and a sledge. She doesn't let go. She says the words again and the shadow goes limp and cold in her hands.

Juniper fights the urge to toss it to the ground and stamp it like a roach. But she couldn't even if she wanted to: it's streaking up her arms, twining upward. She feels it climb her collarbone and writhe up her neck, pressing like a cold finger between her lips and pouring itself down her throat. It's like drinking pond-slime or January mud, thick and foul and unnatural. She retches at the oily touch of his soul inside her.

A laugh rings from somewhere inside her skull, sickly familiar, and a voice whispers: *I wanted you to stay with me, James Juniper, and now you always will.*

He swallows her whole. The world goes black as the belly of a whale.

Bella sees the shadow reaching toward the scaffold.

She sees her sister step—stupidly, bravely, perfectly predictably—into its path. The darkness flows up her arms and slips into her mouth, stretching black tendrils up her cheeks and filling her eyes with shadows. Bella feels it through the thing between them, a suffocating, poisonous cold.

Juniper stiffens, her mouth open in a silent howl, her fingers clawing at her own chest as if a weed has taken root inside her. Bella's scream is lost in the howling chaos of the crowd.

Only Cleo hears her. "What is it? Oh, Saints." She sees Juniper, her spine bent in an unnatural arc, her nails digging into her own skin. Her eyes are black as graves.

Bella is aware that her own lips are moving, a breathless chant of *oh no, oh no, oh no.* "He's taking her, just like he took the others."

"She's got a strong will, your sister. Maybe she can stop him."

"No, she can't." Bella knows it, feels it through the binding between them. Her breath catches. *The binding.* "Not alone."

She shoves her will toward Juniper, every scrap of fear and fury and desperate love she possesses, and prays it's enough.

Juniper flinches. Her neck snaps toward the scaffold and her lips peel back from her teeth in a snarl that doesn't belong to her—then it passes.

Her spine unbends. Her shoulders square, familiar and stubborn. The blackness recedes from her eyes and leaves them clear silver, entirely her own.

She meets Bella's worried gaze and gives her a tired half-smile. Bella feels a giddy rush of relief.

Until she sees movement at Juniper's side. The black wolf—the one that lay beside its master's body on the balcony—is standing now beside her sister, looking up at her with red, red eyes.

Juniper figures a few hundred years of always getting his own way has spoiled Mr. Gideon Hill. He's grown used to weak wills and whispered words, to women bound and burning.

But Juniper learned spite in the cradle. She knows all about long odds and losing choices, about grit and spine. She plants her feet and holds fast.

He might still have won, in the end—Gideon Hill who was once George of Hyll, who has been stealing souls for centuries before Juniper or her mother or her mother's mother were even born—except that Juniper is not alone.

Bella's will floods her heart like the first warm wind of spring. It drives the chill back, presses Hill down inside her until he's nothing but a shard of ice between her ribs.

A mocking voice hisses in her head. *How long do you think you can keep this up? How long can you resist me?*

Not forever, she knows—he's a tumor in her breast, waiting for the moment her attention slips or her will flags—but she doesn't need forever.

Long enough, you bastard, she thinks, and takes a single step. It's harder than it ought to be, like there's a weight pulling hard against her, like her muscles aren't quite her own. A warm weight leans against her leg and she looks down to meet a pair of mournful red eyes: Gideon Hill's familiar, still wearing her iron collar. Still bound to her master, following him loyally to his next body.

For the last time.

Juniper digs her fingers into her dark ruff and the two of them walk back to the scaffold, to her sisters and the stake, to the flames that curl like fingers into the sky, beckoning.

Bella watches her sister walk back to the scaffold as if she's wading through knee-deep water. As if each step costs her dearly but she is bound to take it anyway.

There are people running and shoving around her—well-dressed gentlemen fleeing in terror, shouting Inquisitors with blood smeared on their white tunics, mad-eyed men clutching stones and broken bottles, looking for wicked witches to kill—but none of them seem willing to touch the young woman and the black wolf.

Bella reaches for her hands as she climbs the steps, but Juniper flinches away from her touch. Her hands curl back on themselves as if they're smeared with something foul. She buries one of them in the black fur of the wolf at her side.

"June! What happened? Did he bind himself to you somehow?"

Juniper shrugs one shoulder and doesn't meet her eyes. "No."

"Then how—what—"

"I bound him to me."

Bella considers bursting into tears. "Oh June, *why*?"

Juniper still isn't looking at her. Bella follows the line of her gaze and sees Agnes shushing a wailing Eve. Juniper shrugs again. "Had to."

"Well, we can fix it somehow. We can find a way to banish him, or contain him. A warding spell, maybe, or a healing—"

"There's no time, Bell." Juniper says it very gently, like a doctor telling a patient some unfortunate news. She tilts her chin at Agnes and Eve. "Take care of her, won't you? She's got to have it better than we

did. A mama that sticks around, maybe even a daddy worth a damn."
Juniper squints speculatively at August, who is standing guard at the
scaffold steps with an iron bar in his hand and the frenzied expression of
someone fully prepared to lay down his life.

"She'll need you and Cleo, too, to teach her the words and ways.
Mags would like that, I figure." Juniper smiles at her oldest sister. It's the
kind of smile that has farewells and regrets tucked in the corners. Bella
doesn't like it in the least.

"June, what exactly—"

Juniper limps closer and kisses Bella once on the cheek, her lips
cracked and hot. Bella falls silent.

Juniper steps around her and pauses in front of Agnes. Agnes frowns at
the wolf padding beside her, points up at the stars with the rowan branch in
her hand. But Juniper shakes her head. Her hand hovers above the feather-
down curl of Eve's head, not quite touching her, trembling very slightly.

Agnes asks her a question and Juniper answers, still wearing that
smile shaped like a goodbye. She kisses Agnes's cheek, too.

It's only as she turns away and stands staring into the flames—her
hair fluttering in the heat, her eyes steady—that Bella understands what
she's going to do.

Juniper doesn't have much time, but she has time enough to say goodbye to her sisters.

Agnes is clutching Eve in one arm and her rowan bough in the
other, scowling at Juniper. "Where's Gideon? Why is that thing following you?" Her eyes flick to the wolf still walking patiently at her side.
"It's time to go, June." Agnes points up at the sky.

Juniper remembers lying in bed between her sisters when she was
young, listening to the slur and stomp of their daddy downstairs. Agnes
would stroke the hair back from Juniper's forehead and whisper, *It'll be
alright.*

Even as a child Juniper knew it was a lie. But it was the kind of lie that became true in the telling, because at least there was someone in the world who loved her enough to lie.

Agnes is frowning so fiercely at her that Juniper thinks she must know what's coming, must see it in the tremble of Juniper's hand over her daughter.

"What's going on?"

Juniper leans down to kiss her cheek. "It'll be alright."

She turns to face the flames.

She hesitates. Partly because Gideon Hill is railing and screaming inside her, straining against her will like a mad dog against the leash, but mostly because she likes being alive and wants to keep doing it.

She wishes she could stay right where she is, with the frost-bitten edge of the wind in her hair and the wild wheel of stars above her and the beat of her sisters' hearts beside her.

She wishes she could run away. Mount her rowan branch and disappear with her sisters, never to be seen or heard from again. They might go back home, to the mist-hung mountains and the cold creeks, and build their tower deep in the green woods. They might let the blackberry vines grow high as a rose-thorn hedge around them and raise Eve together in the leaf-dappled dark, safe and secret.

She wishes she were one of those firebirds from Mags's stories, that something might rise from her ashes.

She can't hold out much longer. Gideon Hill's soul seeps like venom through her veins, settling into her bones. It seems like a fitting end, at least: her mother died for her and now Juniper will die for Eve. Maybe Eve will be the one to finally redeem all those generations of debt, all the sacrifices of the women who came before her.

Juniper draws a last breath. Pats the black wolf once on the head, like a loyal hound.

Hill twists like a knife inside her but she still feels some reserve in him, a calculating calm. Maybe he can't quite believe she'll do it, even now, because he can't quite imagine loving anything more than he loves himself.

Or maybe he thinks he'll survive it. Maybe he plans to slither away from her burning body the way he left his last one, clinging to the world until he finds some weak-willed creature to bind himself to.

He doesn't know the Eastwoods have spoken to the Last Three, that they have the secret to his unmaking. That all his sins have finally come home to roost.

Juniper licks cracked lips. "You've had a lot of names, Gideon Hill." She feels him cease his struggling, listening. "Gabriel Hill. Glennwald Hale. George of Hyll. Always Gs and Hs, so I guess you must have missed her." He coils tighter inside her, cold and terrible and just beginning to be afraid. "Your sister sends her love, Hansel."

Juniper feels a tremor move through his soul, a wave of confusion and longing and finally terror, as he understands that this death will be his true and final one, that all his scheming and stealing will end here, tonight, in the fire he lit himself.

Juniper steps into the flames and they close their waiting arms around her, hot and close. She hears Agnes screaming, Bella wailing, "June, no! Stop her!"

Then there's nothing but the sound of burning and the words in her own mouth.

All the king's horses and all the king's men—

43

Ring around the roses,
A pocket full of posies,
Ashes, ashes,
We all rise up.

A spell to bind a soul, requiring an untimely death & a
destination

Agnes Amaranth screams. The wolf howls. The crowd roars. And beneath all that desperate noise Agnes hears the soft, inevitable sound of her own heart breaking.

She should have known better than to draw that circle wide. Should have known what it would cost her.

Agnes rushes toward the flames but reels back at the snap of black teeth. Gideon's wolf is standing between her and the fire. There is no wrath in the deep red of her eyes, but merely a weary duty.

Agnes curls her spine around Eve to protect her from the hiss of cinders. "August!"

He's already beside her, drawn by her scream. She knows by the sound of his swearing that he's seen Juniper standing in the white heart of the fire, her hair floating in a dark halo around her head, her woolen shift burned black.

"Help me—the damn wolf—" Agnes can't seem to string her words into sentences—Juniper's pain is echoing through the binding between them, vast and hot—but August understands her. Agnes feints left and the wolf follows her while August leaps behind it.

He dives into the flames without hesitation or second-guessing, as if it's his own sister burning, and Agnes has the fleeting, mad desire for her daddy to appear beside her so she could show him what love ought to look like.

The wolf snarls and follows him into the flames, jaws reaching for a boot or a leg. A too-long second follows, while the wolf pulls August backward and August refuses to be pulled. Both of them tumble out of the fire, smoking faintly, coughing and retching—

Without Juniper.

"She won't let go of the post!" August's voice is raw and smoke-laden, his face smeared with soot.

Agnes looks back into the fire, squinting against the rising heat. Her sister's arms are wrapped tight around the stake. Agnes can feel the grit of her will through the binding, running like steel beneath the pain. Her mouth is open, lips forming words that Agnes recognizes even through the bright lick of flames and the haze of smoke. *All the king's horses and all the king's men—*

The words to sunder a soul. The words the Last Three had written for Gideon Hill, centuries ago.

Agnes understands what Juniper must have done, and what she is doing now, and why she will not permit herself to be saved.

Agnes feels the broken edges of her heart grate against one another. Here she thought she had escaped Hill's trap, refused his too-high price, but in the end she'd merely delayed it. In the end it's still your life or your freedom, your sister or your daughter, and someone still has to pay.

August is beating uselessly at the flames with his shirt now, his chest smeared with char and ash. He calls to his men down in the square, begging for water, but they're busy holding back the maddened crowd. There will be no circle of cold water and no whispered words to save Juniper this time.

Pan and Strix are circling the fire, crisscrossing above Juniper. Other birds have joined them—the ordinary pigeons and common crows of the city, come to witness this last great act of witching, eerily silent.

Agnes hears the wolf give a low, mournful howl, like a bell tolling in the distance, and knows it's too late. Juniper's hair has caught fire, a bloody crown, and her dress is flaking away from her body in gray sheets of ash. Smoke boils thick and greasy from her skin.

Agnes is the strong sister, the steady sister who stands unflinching, but now she looks away. She cannot bear to watch her sister burn.

Juniper is unraveling. Her soul is unspooling from her body, slipping like smoke through the cracks of a burning building. She wants to follow it, to drift into the sweet dark while her flesh spits and sizzles, but she stays. She speaks the words.

All the king's horses and all the king's men couldn't put Georgie together again.

The words are like fingers picking at a knot, patient and persistent. They burrow between her ribs and find the black tangle of Hill's soul and prise it away from the world, pulling it toward the vast silence of the hereafter. He resists, naturally—Juniper feels him clawing and screaming and generally kicking up three kinds of fuss, reduced to nothing but the wordless will to keep existing—but Juniper's lips keep moving, the spell steady as a heartbeat and hot as hellfire. Maybe it's her sisters' wills added to her own.

Maybe it's Mama Mags whispering in her ear. *Keep going, honey-child.*

Or maybe dying for someone else is just worth more than living for yourself.

Her dress burns first. Then her hair. She'd hoped maybe she wouldn't feel it—her daddy always said the healing hurt worse than the burning, that he'd prayed for life during the fire and prayed for death afterward—but pain licks like a barbed tongue over every inch of her skin. It nibbles and bites, sinking its teeth bone-deep.

It occurs to her that she won't be able to speak the words, soon. Already her tongue is cracked and swollen and the smoke is ground glass in her throat, but Hill still clings to her like clay on a boot-heel. She feels him stirring with the malicious hope that she might die before his soul is entirely sundered.

She might have. Except sometimes, if you reach deep enough into the red heart of magic, some little scrap of magic reaches back out to you. Sometimes if you bend the rules long enough, they break.

Juniper's eyes are closed, but she feels it arrive: a winged darkness. A shape that smells like witching and wild places. It perches on her shoulder and brushes hot feathers against her cheek.

It occurs to her that it's exactly her kind of bullshit luck that she'd finally get her familiar but die before she laid eyes on him.

She tries to touch his claws with her hand, but there's something wrong with her arms, her hands, the skin and sinews between them. All she can do is send him the words and hope, somehow, that it will be enough.

"All the king's horses and all the king's men—" It's her own voice singing strong and clear through the flames, but it doesn't come from her cracked and boiling lips. It's her familiar carrying the words for her, singing them loud and clear even as her throat closes and her lips burn.

There's a loosening in her chest, a knot unbinding. Hill's scream sounds very far away, as if he's on a train heading into a long tunnel. The only thing holding him to the world now is Juniper's own life, and that won't last long.

The heat of the flames fades. So does the crackle of burning wood, the hiss of her own skin. Even the pain fades, and she knows then that she is dying.

Juniper is the wild sister, the sly sister, never caught, always running, but she can't run from this.

She hears singing as she dies, distant and familiar. A children's rhyme she used to chant with her sisters on summer evenings when they were young and whole, when the world was soft and green and small, when they thought they could hold hands forever, unbroken.

Bella feels her sister dying but doesn't believe it. How can Juniper die? Juniper who is so young and so bold, who seems twice as alive as everyone around her? And if she can die—if that's truly her body burning on the pyre, her pain ringing loud in the line between them—then the world is a far crueler place than even Bella imagined, and she wants nothing more to do with it.

She knows precisely how the Last Three must have felt at the end of the age of witches, knowing that something fierce and beautiful was leaving the world, so desperate to preserve even some small piece of it that they let their bodies burn around them.

But not—Bella draws a sharp breath—their souls.

The Three stole Saint George's victory from him at the last second. They bound their souls to a tower of words and disappeared into nowhere to wait, undying, for the next age of witches to begin. What is magic, anyway, if not a way when there is none?

Cleo has her arm tight around Bella's shoulders, holding her steady. Bella breaks free and spins to face her. "The rose petal I gave you, the one I put around your finger—do you still have it?"

Cleo's face says this is a very odd thing to ask while your sister burns and the city riots, but she reaches into her skirt pocket and produces the petal, even more crumpled and dry, but still whole. "Having second thoughts, love?"

"Never." Bella cups the petal in her palm. Such a small, fragile thing on which to rest her sister's soul. "Agnes!"

492 ALIX E. HARROW

Agnes is swaying and pale, too tear-blinded to see the rose in Bella's hand, too grief-struck to understand the eager intent in her eyes. Then Bella says the words, and hope rises like the sun in Agnes's face.

They're the words the three of them had sung as little girls, dancing beneath the fireflies. They're the words the Three wrote to bind their souls to witchcraft itself, which have filtered down through the ages as a children's rhyme, not quite forgotten.

Ring around the roses, pocket full of posies, ashes, ashes, we all rise up.

Cleo joins Bella's chant, then Agnes. August comes next, his voice low and unsteady, and Strix and Pan high above them. More voices follow, too many to count, singing up from the crowd below—the Sisters of Avalon and the Daughters of Tituba, the Women's Association and the workers' unions, the maids and mill-girls, all the witches of New Salem who came when the Eastwoods called.

Together they call the magic and the magic answers, boiling through their veins. Bella waits until it crests like a wave in her chest before she curls her fist around the petal, crushing it. She tosses the remains into the night.

The sky does not split open. No black tower appears. But a sudden wind rises, sharp and green and rose-sweet. The wind tangles Bella's skirts and whips the flames high. It hovers above the pyre, waiting.

Bella knows the precise moment Juniper dies.

The line that leads to her youngest sister goes slack; Agnes screams; the wolf's howl goes abruptly quiet. Bella sees a pale shadow rise from the fire, like mist, before the witch-wind carries it away.

For a moment she thinks she hears voices calling, almost like three women welcoming a fourth, or maybe she merely hopes she does. The spell ends and the wind dies and a strange silence falls over the square, as if even the most foolish of them know something grave and grand has happened.

Bella feels her knees crack against the scaffold, then the sting of tears and the warmth of Cleo's arms around her.

Bella is the wise sister, the bookish one, the knowing one, but she doesn't know whether it was enough.

Agnes wants to climb into the fire and burn alongside her sister. She wants to scream until her throat is flayed raw from screaming, until the whole city has to stop and look and see what they have wrought. She wants to step into nowhere and call Juniper's name.

But there are people swarming up the steps now. Some of the most devout Inquisitors and their followers have rallied and fought past August's men. August rushes to meet them, iron bar whipping back and forth, but Agnes knows he can't hold them for long. She looks down at Eve—awake now and frowning fiercely—then reaches for the rowan-wood branches and climbs to her feet.

She tries to think of nothing but the cool strength of the wood in her hand and the sharp scent of sap. Not the third bough she leaves lying on the scaffold, riderless. Not Juniper's face when the Crone told them the spell for flight. Not the way she looked up at the sky as they were bound to the stake, sly and knowing, as if the moon was a long-lost lover she would soon meet again.

The scaffold blurs before her, fractured by tears. She stumbles to Bella, who leans half-collapsed in Cleo's arms, and presses a branch into her hand.

"Come on, Bell. It's time to go."

Bella looks as if she, too, would like to lie down and let the flames wash over her, but she doesn't. She stands slowly, as if she's aged several decades, and offers her hand down to Cleo. She pulls her to her feet but does not release her hand. "You could still come with us."

Cleo shakes her head once. "I'm needed here. The Daughters have work to do, and a chance to move in the open, without Hill." But she touches Bella's face, thumb brushing over her cheekbone. "I'll come when I can." Then she draws a stub of chalk from her pocket and marks a shape on the scaffold, singing a song. Cleo blurs around the edges, not quite invisible.

"Don't keep me waiting, Miss Quinn," Bella says, and the heat of it makes Agnes look away. Her eyes find August, forced to the top of the stairs now, iron bar still swinging. His mouth is red and swelling. A bright line of blood runs from a cut at his temple. He throws a wild look back to Agnes and she knows he intends to stand there until she is safely gone or until he can stand no longer. This last look is the closest they can come to goodbye.

Agnes reaches for Bella's hand and whispers the words. *Lady bird, lady bird, fly away home.*

An airy, weightless feeling spreads from Agnes's fingertips to her ribs, as if her blood has been replaced with rising mist.

She and her sister (she stumbles over the singular word, the absence of that soft *s* at the end) mount their rowan branches and feel their bare feet lift from the scaffold. They rise into the air like smoke. Or like witches, in the way-back days when they flew with clouds as their cloaks and stars in their eyes.

They follow the spirals of cinder and ash with their familiars winging alongside them, leaving behind the city that hates them and the people who love them and their sister who died for them. It's only in Agnes's head that she hears a small, wild girl begging her: *Don't leave me.*

The air grows clean and cold as they fly higher, smokeless, moonlit. The world feels vast and boundless around Agnes, like a house with all its walls and windows thrown down, and she clutches her daughter tighter to her chest. She thinks she hears a muffled gurgle from the wrapped bundle, almost like a laugh.

The sound outweighs the grief in Agnes's chest, like a brass scale tipping. They had lost too much—a library called back and then burned; a sister found and then lost forever—but not everything. Not the sound of her daughter flying with moon-shine on her skin, laughing.

Beneath them the city square looks small and dim. Agnes sees upturned faces, feels the tug of hundreds of watching eyes. She can almost see the new stories cast like dandelion-seeds behind them, taking root in the city below. Stories about shadows stolen and then set free, about villains and wolves and young women who walk willingly into the fire. About two witches flying where there should have been three.

An owl and an osprey fly beside them. Agnes wonders if any of them notice a third creature winging with them, black as sin, nearly invisible against the night. Or perhaps they see it and think nothing of it. Every crow is black, after all.

Perhaps, from so far below, they can't see the way the crow's eyes burn like the last stubborn coals of a dying fire, or the way they stare at some distant point in the sky, as if he's flying to meet someone just on the other side of nowhere.

PART FIVE

WHAT
IS
FOUND

44

How many miles to Babylon?
Threescore miles and ten.
Can I get there by candlelight?
There and back again.

A spell for safe travel, requiring a lit candle & seventy steps

On the spring equinox of 1894 there is still snow lingering on the streets of Chicago. It gathers along curbs, sooty and sullen, waiting to crumble over boot-tops and soak the trailing hems of cloaks, while the wind sneaks down collars and beneath the brims of hats.

Agnes Amaranth doesn't mind it; she will be leaving soon.

She steps into the early evening alley with her cloak pulled tight around her neck and her ears full of the hum and song of women's voices. Agnes came to Chicago following a story she read on the second and third pages of the papers, well below all the hysterical headlines about witches and burnings (CHAOS REIGNS IN NEW SALEM; VOODOO REVOLT SHAKES RICHMOND; COVEN DISCOVERED IN ST. LOUIS—WILL YOUR CITY BE NEXT?). It's a story about a lowly button-sewer at Hart & Shaffner Garment Factory who

took issue with her employer's decision to cut women's wages and insti-
gated a strike. The strike was met with brutal beatings and the illegal-
but-unpunished burning of at least one accused witch. Agnes suspected
such brutality wouldn't break the garment-workers' rebelliousness at
all, but merely harden it, like beaten steel.

She wasn't mistaken. In the dim basement of a settlement house,
Agnes met a collection of women with clenched jaws and iron spines,
their eyes bruised with too many long shifts, their knuckles swollen
with too many hours bent around a needle. Their English was sparse
and shifting, interspersed with lilting strings of foreign words and unfamiliar vowels, but they brought their daughters to translate for them,
and both women and children looked at Agnes with a mix of skepticism
and hope.

One of the older women asked, in a voice like pipe smoke and lead,
"And who are you, exactly?"

Agnes's arms were bare beneath her cloak, and she spread them
wide. "A sister. A friend. A woman in want of a better world." She
smiled her witchiest smile. "I have in my possession certain ways and
words you might find useful—from what I've read, you already have the
will."

There were whispers and glances. Some women shuffled out,
unwilling to add witchcraft to the list of their crimes, but some edged
nearer. Some remembered the words their mothers sang to them on
winter nights and the spells their aunts chanted on the solstice; some of
them had tasted power, and wanted more.

Agnes gave them the words on thin slips of paper, rolled tight. There
were words for binding tongues and breaking machines, for healing
hurts and causing them, for setting fires and walking through them
unscathed. The papers disappeared up sleeves and beneath aprons and
waited, like hidden knives, for their moment.

One of the girls—young and fierce-looking, with the wary black
eyes of a winter fox—stared at the paper in her hands with such intensity

Agnes thought it might burst into spontaneous flame. Her fingertips were pressed white where she held the paper.

Agnes is not, therefore, entirely surprised to hear soft footsteps padding after her down the snow-spotted alley. She does not look behind her. She turns down an even narrower lane, crisscrossed with drooping laundry and lined with dim doorways, before turning around.

"Bessie, wasn't it?"

The girl flinches, eyes huge and feral, but tosses her head in denial. "They call me Bessie when I get here. Bas Sheva is my name." Her accent makes Agnes think of hip-deep snow and rich furs, and a little of Yulia. The Domontoviches stayed in New Salem, living in the west wing of Inez and Jennie's well-warded house. Agnes visited once over the winter, and found the manor transformed into a sunny, sprawling safe house. A place to run, for any woman who wants it.

"How may I help you, Bas Sheva?"

She doesn't answer, but her eyes skitter hungrily over every inch of Agnes, from the sleek silk of her hair to the ragged black of her cloak. They linger on her face, as if mentally comparing it to the etchings on wanted posters and cartoons in the papers. "You're one of them, aren't you?"

Agnes has found it unwise to advertise her identity. Witch-hunters have sprouted like thistles across the country, along with wanted posters listing rather gratifying sums of money in reward for information leading to her arrest. She travels in disguise, under false names and befuddling magics, and never lingers long in one place. Although she's found herself in Chicago several times over the winter.

So when Bas Sheva asks her name Agnes widens her eyes and says, "One of who?"

The girl glares before she says, low and quick, "The First Three."

Agnes should deny it. But there's something about this girl—the desperation or the fury or the fingerprint bruises circling her wrist—that makes Agnes nod her head once.

Bas Sheva's face ignites. She licks her lips. "Then I wonder if—I want—" Agnes suspects she struggles less with her English and more with the immensity of her desire, the hollow shape of her hunger. The light in her eyes reminds Agnes strongly of her youngest sister.

"Here, girl. Speak these words and draw a circle, and you'll find the place you need to go." Agnes steps closer and sings her a rhyme about wayward sisters and stolen crowns. She doesn't write them down—these words are too precious, too dangerous to risk anything more than a whisper—but she doesn't have to. The girl's lips move over the syllables like hands running over a key. "Not tonight, though. It's the equinox. We'll be busy."

The girl bows her head, hesitates, and withdraws a small pewter charm from her skirt: a delicate case bearing a series of branched and rooted symbols that might be letters. She presses it into Agnes's hand. "My great-grandmother knew certain words she should not. Hang these at your daughter's door. For protection."

Agnes slips it into her pocket and presses her palm over it. "Thank you."

Agnes watches Bas Sheva leave—shoulders braced, hair dark and wind-tangled—and allows herself to pretend for a moment that she is a different young woman in a different city. The wind whips her tears dry before they fall.

She is several strides farther down the alley when a low, teasing voice speaks behind her. "Evening, miss."

She squints into a nearby doorway but can't seem to make her eyes focus on the shape inside it. The voice whispers again and two figures come into sudden focus: a bearded man with a gambler's grin and a red scarf, and a rosy-cheeked baby girl perched in the crook of his arm. Curls spill like flames from beneath her woolen cap.

The girl raises both arms to Agnes and demands, in the tone of a monarch who has been kept waiting longer than she is accustomed to by her underlings, "Ma*ma*!"

"Hello, loves." Eve falls into her arms with a satisfied *oomph* and immediately grabs two fistfuls of Agnes's hair.

Mr. August Lee watches them with his smile pulled crooked and wry. August returned to Chicago six weeks previously along with a smallish gang of men from New Salem, with the intention of spreading women's witching among his old friends and malcontents, and seeing if perhaps certain concessions couldn't be won from the Pullman Palace Car Company after all. He claims his work will be done before summer, when he will join Agnes with whatever fight she's found for them next.

"Weren't you two supposed to be lying low at the Everly Club?" Miss Pearl had provided Agnes with the name and address of a madam sympathetic to the cause of witches and working-women, who was willing to trade certain words and ways and hard-to-come-by herbs in exchange for safe harbor.

August shrugs. "Inquisitors showed up asking questions, looking for trouble."

"And did they find any?"

August's eyes spark like flint against hers. "A bit, yes. More than they bargained for, in fact." He touches his jaw, where a bruise is beginning to bloom beneath his beard. "I took care of them, but I thought it best to leave the Club, so as not to draw more unwelcome attention. Besides"—he grabs Eve's toe and wiggles it—"her Ladyship wanted her mama."

Agnes kisses her daughter's cap and breathes the summery smell of her, all sunshine and sweat despite the icy chill of the wind. She glances up at the sky, dimming quickly into darkness. "Perhaps I ought to stay tonight, if—"

August brushes this away. "No, you two go on. I'll find us a place to stay and draw a circle for your return." He chucks Eve under the chin and she burbles pleasantly at him. "Give them my regards."

Agnes kisses him once—and if she lingers longer than is strictly decent, if his hand is lower and warmer on her waist than it ought to be, she finds she doesn't care.

She turns away and draws a stick of white chalk from her pocket. She sketches a neat design on the wall: three white circles, interwoven. Her daughter's small fingers splay beside hers on the soot-stained brick for a half-second before the two of them are pulled into elsewhere, or perhaps nowhere.

45

There is a house down in Orleans they call the Rising Sun.
It's been the ruin of many a woman,
By God I won't be one.

A spell against conception, requiring a red dawn & a drawn star

By the spring equinox of 1894, the city of New Orleans has slid past spring and is flirting shamelessly with summer. The air is soft and heavy, magnolia-sweet, and the sun drapes itself like a warm cat around bare shoulders.

Beatrice Belladonna has been in the city for three weeks now, staying in a rented room in the Upper Ninth Ward, and hopes to stay longer.

She is sitting now at a broad desk with the breeze plucking at her endless stacks and piles of notes. More than half of them are written in Miss Quinn's careless, slanting handwriting, dashed off during her many meetings and interviews—which always seem to occur in midnight graveyards or abandoned bell-towers and involve a great deal of danger—and then jammed haphazardly in a pocket or purse when the authorities arrived.

Cleo dismisses Bella's concerns with airy waves of her long fingers. "Writing a book is dangerous business, if done correctly."

Over the winter Cleo received a not-insubstantial contract from John Wiley & Sons to write a book chronicling the sudden upsetting rise of witchcraft among the sharecroppers and freed-women of the South. Her editor desired a lurid account of cannibal-witches and voodoo queens, a book so scandalous it would provoke fainting spells and lengthy speeches about the moral decay of the nation, and which would sell like ice cream on the fourth of July.

Cleo intends to oblige him, to a certain degree; her working title is *Southern Horrors*, and it so far contains many hair-raising tales of hexed landlords and haunted sheriffs, of boo-hags and haints and courtesans with poison smiles, although it is conspicuously free of specific names or locations.

It also contains a number of engraved illustrations. Above the depictions of mayhem and murder there are inky black skies pricked with white stars in very particular patterns. If a person happens to know their constellations, and if they bear no ill intent toward witches or women, they might reveal certain words and ways that John Wiley & Sons never intended to publish.

Bella serves mostly as her typist and assistant, assembling notes and organizing chapters, but she also devotes considerable hours to their other, much more ambitious and secret undertaking: to restore what has been burned, to find again what has been lost. To rebuild the Library of Avalon.

Bella and Cleo collect spells wherever they go, hidden in rumors and stories, preserved in rhymes and hymns and sewing samplers, and record them as accurately as they can. Already Bella has begun a dozen new spell-books: grimoires and guides, books of weather and medicine and beauty and death. She's written the words and ways from the smallest household spells—charms to sort bad eggs from good or remove stubborn stains from white sheets—to curses that will stop hearts or poison wells or heal bones.

Many of the spells sound strange to Bella's ear, nothing like Mama Mags's rhymes. They come in odd forms and unlikely languages—Spanish prayers and Creole songs and Choctaw stories, star-patterns and dances and drum-beats—and not all of them are easily translated to ink and paper. Bella begins to believe that the Library of Avalon was only ever a sliver of witchcraft in the first place. She begins to believe that the words and ways are whichever ones a woman has, and that a witch is merely a woman who needs more than she has.

Mr. Blackwell agrees. Bella sends him pages of notes and ideas every other week and he returns long missives stained with tea and wine, dotted with helpful questions and possibilities. He also includes regular updates on the state of New Salem and the Sisters of Avalon. Bella is amused by the frequency with which Miss Electa Gage's name recurs; she will not be surprised to hear news of their engagement soon.

Most days Bella is hopeful, proud of the work they've accomplished in a mere six months—but sometimes a certain melancholy takes her. Some days when she steps back into the tower she is overwhelmed by the scent of ash and grief, haunted by its hollow heart. On those days what they have gained seems to pall before the immensity of what they have lost.

But the tower is no longer lost, nor is it a ruin. The trees surrounding it are flecked with green-furred buds and the rose-vines have crept up to the first window. There aren't any blooms yet, but Bella has seen tight curls of red hidden among the thorns, waiting.

Bella and Agnes swept out the ashes and hauled burned scraps from the tower. They scrubbed the scorch marks with lye and hung twists of lavender and cat-mint in the windows. Mr. August Lee turned up with a number of useful tools—many of which were stamped with company names and certainly did not belong to him—and helped the sisters fell and cure the timber they needed. It sits now in neat stacks, drying. By summer perhaps they will have a staircase again, and the beginnings of bookshelves. All they have now is a rope ladder leading up to the little round room at the top of the tower, where three beds still stand in a neat circle.

Bella and Cleo have spent many nights in the tower—when Cleo provokes some particular outrage, or when Eve goes through one of her long phases of refusing to sleep except when held in someone's arms, and that someone is walking beneath the trees, humming *Greensleeves*. Bella likes it there. Although sometimes after a visit to Avalon she finds corrections and additions to her notes, written in a querulous hand and signed with three circles intertwined.

This evening Bella is not working on spells or stories; she's typing out the final pages of her first and most precious book. All winter she's been transcribing and editing her little black notebook, making additions and subtractions, badgering Agnes and Cleo where her own memory fails her, sometimes despairing of ever weaving the thing into anything believably book-shaped.

It will never find a publisher—what publisher would risk moral and legal condemnation from the Church, most major political parties, the government, and every law enforcement organization?—and even if it did, most readers wouldn't believe half of it. But it will be the first book she gives to the Library of Avalon: part story and part grimoire, part history and part myth. A new witch-tale, for a new world.

It's the title that's taken her longest. Cleo suggested gently that *Our Own Stories* was a little vague, and Bella spent the next month moaning and dithering. "*A Vindication of the Rights of Witches*? *The Everywoman's Guide to Modern Witchcraft*? *A Memoir of the First Three*—"

"You are certainly *not* the First Three Witches of the West, no matter what they're calling you."

"No, of course, I just—"

"Nor were the Last Three truly the last anything, as it turns out," Cleo added, musingly. "History is a circle, and you people are always looking for the beginnings and ends of it."

She swept out and left Bella to think about endings and beginnings and circles. She thought of the Sign of the Three burned into the door of Avalon and the phrase inscribed above it, and found that—if she took certain liberties with the Latin—it made a perfectly serviceable title.

The light is fading as Bella tears the final page from the typewriter and lays it neatly on the stack. There's still one last chapter to be added, but her part is done.

The moon rises like a silver dollar in the window and the church bells ring in the equinox-eve service. Cleo will be out late, attending a gathering of the Orleans chapter of her organization, the Daughters of Laveau. Bella will be spending the equinox elsewhere.

She tidies her papers and clears a small space on her desk. She lays a single rose on the bare wood, and beside it a smooth golden ring.

The ring isn't much to look at—without diamonds or engravings— but the metal is warm to the touch even days after the casting. Bella found a goldsmith in the Garden Quarter who permitted her to inspect the gold before casting. Bella smiled and thanked him, and then bound spells to every gram of metal. The ring ought to offer some protection from unfriendly eyes and ill wishes, from cold iron and hot coals, bad dreams and mean dogs and broken bones.

She tucks a scrap of paper beneath the ring: *Yours, if you will have it. As am I.*

Bella dons a half-cloak and a historically inaccurate hat, black and pointed, and draws a charcoal circle on the floorboards. She whispers the words and steps into elsewhere.

Epilogue

I figure since I'm the one who started the story, I should be the one to finish it.

It's the spring equinox of 1894 and I'm sitting with my back against the sun-warmed wood of the tower door, rose-vines pricking the soft meat of my arms and meadow-grass shushing against the bare soles of my feet. A crow perches on my knee, watching me write with a cocked head and a candleflame eye.

The farm hasn't changed much in the year I was away: the mountains still stand like green gods on all sides and the Big Sandy River still coils like a king snake through the heart of it. Owls still call three times at moonrise and dogwoods still bloom in the deep blue shadows. Mama Mags's house has sunk a little farther into the earth, like an old woman settling deeper into a rocking chair, and her herb-garden has run wild and weedy, but otherwise I can almost believe no time has passed at all. That I'm still seventeen and all alone, living for the day my daddy would finally die.

Except I'm not alone, now. Neither am I living: I died on the fall equinox in St. George's Square, and death doesn't brook any back-talk or take-backs.

But witching is nothing if not a way to bend the rules, to make a way when there is none. My soul lingers, bound alongside the Last Three to the Lost Way of Avalon, to the rose-covered stones and the burned books and to witching itself. It isn't the same as being alive—I don't eat or drink except to remind myself that I can, and I don't sleep now so much as come undone. As soon as my attention wavers I unravel like a dropped bobbin, losing myself among the roots and stone. But it's a damn sight better than being dead, I figure.

On bad days I have Corvus. My familiar is a creature of the margins and in-betweens, being half-magic and half-bird and three-quarters mischief, and he laughs his crow-laugh at me when I fret about whether I'm dead or alive, sundered or saved. Just looking at him reminds me that I can still feel the sunlight on my skin and breathe the rich wet smell of spring and if that isn't enough, well, it's all I've got.

I wasted time brooding, in the early days after my death. I dreamed about stepping into the flames, smoke filling my mouth, my throat, my lungs. About all the sights I'd never see and the hell I'd never raise. But then Bella and Agnes called the tower back out of nowhere, and I held my baby niece in my arms, and all those regrets faded like cheap newsprint in the rain.

The farm still isn't mine, legally speaking; it's still my dumbshit cousin's name on the deed. But he isn't around much these days.

At first he thought to rebuild Daddy's house and rent it out, or at least lease the fields, but nothing ever came of his plans. Carpenters found their survey stakes missing and their tools rusted overnight; planted seed went bad and crops wilted without reason. Briars grew twice as tall and three times as thick as they did elsewhere in the county, obscuring the clay drive and rising like thorned walls along the borders, and in the end my cousin threw up his hands and left my land alone.

So there was no one around to notice three women and three black birds slinking through the woods. No one to see the tower appear on the back acres, lit by stars from another time and place, covered in the burnt bones of rose-vines. (Bella fretted sometimes about leaving Avalon in Crow County, and suggested they find a place even more remote and defensible, but I wanted to stay home, and my sisters don't deny me much of anything these days.)

I rarely wander far from the tower. I can, but I feel thin and anxious when I'm away too long, like a poorly knit shawl that might unravel at any moment. And I never lack for company. Bella and Cleo visit to help Agnes or bring supplies, sitting side by side to write by the fire, their silence interspersed with heartfelt swearing and the scratching out of unsatisfactory lines.

Agnes and August stay with me when they aren't out teaching witchcraft to women and workingmen. Sometimes they leave Eve behind them, who generally leaves me feeling outnumbered and surrounded, although there's only one of her.

Then there are the others my sisters bring with them. Stragglers and lost girls, outcasts and outlaws. Girls running from their suitors or fathers or uncles or neighbors; from weddings and boarding schools and convents; from desperation and despair and the siren call of wading into rivers with stones in their pockets.

I give them a place to hide and to rest, to gather the frayed ends of themselves. And sometimes, if they ask, I give them more. I teach them which herbs to pick and which words to say, which spells work best on the Milk Moon and which require the heat of summer. I teach them every bit of witching Mags taught me and every spell Bella and Cleo drag back, and send them out into the world like thistleseeds tossed into the wind. I hope they might take root and grow tall, thorned and beautiful.

I suspect they will. Already I can feel the world shifting around me, changing like a riverbank beneath rising water. The papers Bella brings home talk about burning factories and brutal men found dead, about a sewing circle caught spreading seditious spells and a Colorado mining town where no man dared to tread. Out west the Indian Wars are going poorly—or well, according to my line of thinking—and there are rumors of rebellion in Old Cairo.

I guess something rose from my ashes, after all. Makes me wonder if maybe those phoenix stories were never really about birds in the first place.

The backlash will come one day, the way it always does. I know the world won't change easy, that more women will burn before it does, but at least I got to see the beginning. Bella says I could linger as long as I liked, being dead and all.

I don't figure I'll stay longer than is natural. One day when Eve is long grown and my sisters grown old, when perhaps the lost girls come less often to visit me because the world is less cruel, I'll just lay myself down to rest beside the Maiden and Mother and Crone. The Three will become Four and the Eastwoods will fade into myth and rumor and fire-lit witch-tale.

It's dusk now. Very soon the air will twist and two women will appear on either side of me. Their cheeks will be flushed with the heat of witching and their cloaks will twist in the autumn wind that still blows in Avalon, even in springtime. One of them will be tall and narrow and clever-looking, eyes bright behind her spectacles; one of them will be sweet-faced and sturdy, a baby clinging tight to her chest.

I will smile up at them and see for a moment not my sisters but as the first notes of a half-familiar song, the first lines of a story that has been told before and will be told again:

Once upon a time there were three witches.

Acknowledgments

If I were to tell you the tale of writing this book, it would go like this: Once there was a girl with a story she wanted to tell. She'd told stories before, so she set sail boldly. Very soon she found herself lost at sea, besieged by plot twists and broken arcs, murky metaphors and shifting themes. She had the words, but she lost her way and her will.

Fortunately, she wasn't alone. She had her agent, Kate McKean, to answer even the most dramatic late-night emails with common sense and comfort. Nivia Evans, her editor, to see the story she was trying to tell and help her chart a course toward it. Lisa Marie Pompilio to make it beautiful; Roland Ottewell and Andy Ball to make it right; Ellen Wright and the rest of the Orbit/Redhook team to share it with the world.

She had Andy Ball, Edward James, and Niels Grotum to provide last-second Latin consultations; the courtyard of the Madison County Public Library to provide sunshine and silence; the Moonscribers to provide wit and wine.

She had the most generous and insightful early readers anyone could ask for: Laura Blackwell, E. Catherine Tobler, Lee Mandelo, and Ziv Wities. Without them she would have surely sunk, all souls feared lost.

She had babysitting and brunch from Taye and Camille; a constant supply of love and puns from her brothers; bottomless faith from her parents even when she lost all faith in herself.

She had Finn and Felix, who were far too busy writing their own stories to worry much about their mother's.

And she had Nick. Her north star, her compass, her lighthouse, her once-upon-a-time and her happily-ever-after. Who sailed beside her through every storm and never once doubted she would bring them safely into harbor.

After a year at sea—after a hundred dark nights beneath nameless constellations, after missed deadlines and scrapped chapters—she did. The girl stood on the shore, under-slept and over-caffeinated, her story told.

She thought she might tell another.

extras

orbitbooks.net

about the author

Alix E. Harrow is an ex-historian with lots of opinions and excessive library fines, currently living in Kentucky with her husband and their semi-feral children. Her short fiction has been nominated for the Hugo, Nebula and Locus awards. *The Ten Thousand Doors of January* was her debut novel. Find her on Twitter at @AlixEHarrow.

Find out more about Alix E. Harrow and other Orbit authors by registering for the free monthly newsletter at orbitbooks.net.

reading group guide

1. Throughout the book there are references to feminized versions of real literary and historical figures (the Sisters Grimm, Andrea Lang, Alexandra Pope, etc.). What does this say about the world of New Salem? How does it speak to the broader themes of the book?

2. The main events of the text happen in 1893, but there are references to many real-world events that occurred earlier or later, including the Pullman Strike and the Triangle Shirtwaist Factory fire. Why? Why not adhere to a more accurate historical timeline?

3. The Maiden, Mother, and Crone are traditional figures in Western folklore and mythology. In what ways do Juniper, Agnes, and Bella fulfill or subvert their archetypal roles? What about the Last Three?

4. The return of magic is a classic trope in fantasy fiction, usually accomplished by a prophesized hero or a grand spell; restoring witchcraft is a little more difficult for the Sisters of Avalon. What setbacks do they encounter? Why are those challenges significant, in a thematic sense?

5. There are seven retold fairy tales in this book, all of them significantly altered from their familiar versions. How were they altered, and why? How do they complement the central story?

6. In *The Once and Future Witches*, witchcraft requires particular words and ways, but women from different cultural backgrounds use very different spells. Why isn't witchcraft universal? Why are there so many different languages and approaches?

7. The American suffrage movement was successful and admirable, but it was also riddled with racism, classism, and division. How does this story grapple with both the heroism and villainy of the suffrage movement?

8. The Sisters of Avalon find many of their spells hidden in nursery rhymes and children's songs. Why would such important words be found in such seemingly frivolous sources?

if you enjoyed
THE ONCE AND FUTURE WITCHES

look out for

THE MIDNIGHT BARGAIN

by

C. L. Polk

Beatrice Clayborn is a sorceress who practises magic in secret, terrified of the day she will be locked into a marital collar to cut off her powers. She dreams of becoming a full-fledged mage, but her family are in severe debt, and only her marriage can save them.

Beatrice finds a grimoire with the key to becoming a mage, but a rival sorceress swindles the book right out of her hands. Beatrice summons a spirit to help, but her new ally exacts a price: Beatrice's first kiss . . . with the sorceress's brother: the handsome, compassionate and fabulously wealthy Ianthe Lavan.

CHAPTER I

The carriage drew closer to Booksellers' Row, and Beatrice Clayborn drew in a hopeful breath before she cast her spell. Head high, spine straight, she hid her hands in her pockets and curled her fingers into mystic signs as the fiacre jostled over green cobblestones. She had been in Bendleton three days, and while its elegant buildings and clean streets were the prettiest trap anyone could step into, Beatrice would have given anything to be somewhere else—anywhere but here, at the beginning of bargaining season.

She breathed out the seeking tendrils of her spell, touching each of the shop fronts. If a miracle rushed over her skin and prickled at her ears—

But there was nothing. Not a glimmer; not even an itch. They passed The Rook's Tower Books, P. T. Williams and Sons, and the celebrated House of Verdeu, which filled a full third of a block with all its volumes.

Beatrice let out a sigh. No miracle. No freedom. No hope. But when they rounded the corner from Booksellers' Row to a narrow gray lane with no name, Beatrice's spell bloomed in response. There. A grimoire! There was no way to know what it contained, but she smiled up at the sky as she pulled on the bell next to her seat.

"Driver, stop." She slid forward on the fiacre's padded seat, ready to jump into the street by herself. "Clara, can you complete the fitting for me?"

"Miss Beatrice, you mustn't." Clara clutched at Beatrice's wrist. "It should be you."

"You're exactly my size. It won't matter," Beatrice said. "Besides, you're better at the color and trimmings and such. I'll just be a few minutes, I promise."

Her maid-companion shook her head. "You mustn't miss your appointment at the chapterhouse. I cannot stand in for you when you meet Danton Maisonette the way I can at the dressmakers."

Beatrice was not going to let that book slip out of her grasp. She patted Clara's hand and wriggled loose. "I'll be there in time, Clara. I promise I won't miss it. I just need to buy a book."

Clara tilted her head. "Why this place?"

"I wrote to them," Beatrice lied. "Finding it is a stroke of luck. I won't be ten minutes."

Clara sighed and loosed her grip on Beatrice's wrist. "Very well."

The driver moved to assist, but Beatrice vaulted to the street, tight-laced stays and all, and waved them off. "Thank you. Go!"

She pivoted on one delicate pillar-heeled shoe and regarded the storefront. Harriman's was precisely the kind of bookstore Beatrice sought every time she was in a new town: the ones run by people who couldn't bear to throw books away no matter what was inside the covers, so long as they could be stacked and shelved and housed. Beatrice peered through the windows, reveling at the pang within her senses that set her ears alert and tingling, her spell signaling that a grimoire awaited amid the clutter. She hadn't found a new one in months.

The doorbell jingled as Beatrice crossed into the bookkeeper's domain. Harriman's! O dust and ink and leather binding, O map-scrolls and star-prints and poetry chapbooks—

and the grimoire, somewhere within! She directed her smile at the clerk in shirtsleeves and weskit waiting at the front counter.

"Just having a browse," she said, and moved past without inviting further conversation. Beatrice followed her prickling thumbs between stacks of books and laden shelves. She breathed in old paper and the thin rain-on-green-stones scent of magic, looking not for respectable novels or seemly poetry, but for the authors certain young women never even dared whisper to each other in the powder rooms and parlors of society—the writers of the secret grimoires.

It was here! But it wouldn't do to be too hasty, to follow the pull of her senses toward the stack where the volume rested, its spine bearing an author name like John Estlin Churchman, or J. C. Everworth, or perhaps E. James Curtfield. The authors always bore those initials on all of the books in her modest collection, stored away from curious eyes. The clerk might wonder at how she knew exactly where to find the book she wanted in all this jumble. She browsed through literature, in history, and even in the occult sections where other patrons would eye her with disapproval, because the realm of magic was not suitable territory for a woman of a certain youth.

Just thinking of her exclusion made Beatrice's scalp heat. For women, magic was the solitary pursuit of widows and crones, not for the woman whose most noble usefulness was still intact. The inner doors of the chapterhouse were barred to her, while a man with the right connections could elevate himself through admittance and education among his fellow magicians. Anyone with the talent could see the aura of sorcery shining from Beatrice's head, all the better to produce more magicians for the next generation.

Oh, how she hated it! To be reduced to such a common capability, her magic untrained until some year in her twilight, finally allowed to pursue the only path she cared for? She would not! And so, she sought out the works of J. E. C., who was not a man at all, but a sorceress just like her, who had published a multitude of volumes critics dismissed as incomprehensible.

And they were, to anyone who didn't know the key. But Beatrice had it by heart. When she lifted a dusty edition of *Remembrance of the Jyish Coast of Llanandras* from the shelf, she opened the cover and whispered the spell that filtered away anything that wasn't the truth hidden amid the typesetting, and read:

> To Summon a Greater Spirit and Propose the Pact of the Great Bargain

She snapped the book shut and fought the joyful squeak that threatened to escape her. She stood very still and let her heart soar in silence with the book pressed to her chest, breathing in its ink and magic.

This was the grimoire she had needed, after years of searching and secret study. If she summoned the spirit and made an alliance, she would have done what every male initiate from the chapterhouses of sorcery aspired to do. She would be a fully initiated magician.

This was everything she needed. No man would have a woman with such an alliance. Her father would see the benefit of keeping her secret, to use her greater spirit to aid him in his business speculations. She would be free. A Mage. This was her miracle.

She'd never leave her family home, but that didn't matter. She could be the son Father never had, while her younger sister Harriet could have the bargaining season Beatrice didn't want. Harriet would have the husband she daydreamed about, while Beatrice would continue her studies uninterrupted by marriage.

She stepped back and pivoted away from the shelf, and nearly collided with another customer of Harriman's. They jumped back from each other, exclaiming in surprise, then stared at each other in consternation.

Beatrice beheld a Llanandari woman who stood tall and slim in a saffron satin-woven cotton mantua, the under-gown scattered all over with vibrant tropical flowers, the elbow-length sleeves erupting in delicate, hand-hooked lace. Hooked lace, on a day gown! She was beautiful, surpassing even the famous reputation of the women of Llanandras. She was blessed with wide brown eyes and deep brown skin, a cloud of tight black curls studded with golden beads, matching a fortune in gold piercing the young woman's ears and even the side of her nose. But what was she doing here? She couldn't be in this affluent seaside retreat away from the capital to hunt a husband just as Beatrice was supposed to be doing. Could she?

She stared at Beatrice with an ever-growing perplexity. Beatrice knew what the young lady found so arresting—the crown of sorcery around Beatrice's head, even brighter than the veil of shimmering light around the woman's. Another sorceress attracted to the call of the grimoire Beatrice clutched to her chest.

"Ysbeta? What has your back like a rod?"

He spoke Llanandari, of course, and Beatrice's tongue stuck to the roof of her mouth. She knew the language, but she had never spoken it to an actual Llanandari. Her accent would be atrocious; her grammar, clumsy. But she plastered a smile on her face and turned to face the newcomer.

Beatrice beheld the same features as the lady, but in a man's face, and—oh, his eyes were so dark, his hair a tightly curled crown below the radiant aura of a sorcerer, his flawless skin darker than the girl's—Ysbeta, her name was Ysbeta. He was clad in the same gleaming saffron Llanandari cotton, the needlework on his weskit a tribute to spring, a froth of matching lace at his throat. Now both these wealthy, glamorous Llanandari stared at her with the same puzzlement, until the young man's brow cleared and he slapped the woman on the back with a laugh like a chuckling stream.

"Relax, Ysy," he said. "She's in the ingenue's gallery at the chapterhouse. Miss . . ."

"Beatrice Clayborn. I am pleased to make your acquaintance," Beatrice said, and hardly stumbled at all. This young man, achingly beautiful as he was, had seen her portrait hanging in the ingenue's gallery at the Bendleton chapterhouse. Had studied it long enough to recognize her. He had looked at it long enough to know the angle of her nose, the shape and color of her eyes, the peculiar, perpetually autumn-red tint of her frowzy, unruly hair.

Ysbeta eyed the book in Beatrice's grip, her stare as intense as a shout. "I'm Ysbeta Lavan. This is my brother, Ianthe. I see you admire the travelogues of J. E. Churchman." She spoke carefully, a little slowly for the sake of Beatrice's home-taught Llanandari.

"His telling of faraway places enchants me," Beatrice said. "I am sorry for my Llanandari."

"You're doing fine. I'm homesick for Llanandras," Ysbeta said. "That's a rare account of Churchman's, talking about the magical coast where Ianthe and I spent a happy childhood. It would do my understanding of your language some good to read books in your tongue."

"You speak Chasand."

She tilted her head. "A little. You are better at my language than I am at yours."

Flattery, from a woman who knew exactly what Churchman's book was. Beatrice's middle trembled. Ysbeta and her brother walked in the highest circles in the world, accustomed to wealth and power. And Ysbeta's simple statement betraying a feeling of loneliness or nostalgia confessed to an assumed peer were the opening steps of a courteous dance. The next step, the proper, graceful step would be for Beatrice to offer the book to soothe that longing.

Ysbeta expected Beatrice to hand over her salvation. The book carried her chance at freedom from the bargaining of fathers to bind her into matrimony and warding. To hand it over was giving her chance away. To keep it—

To keep it would be to cross one of the most powerful families in the trading world. If Beatrice's father did not have the acquaintance of the Lavans, he surely wanted it. If she made an enemy of a powerful daughter of Llanandras, it would reflect on every association and partnership the Clayborn fortunes relied on. Weigh on them. Sever them. And without the good opinion of the families that mattered, the Clayborn name would tumble to the earth.

Beatrice couldn't do that to her family. But the book! Her fingers squeezed down on the cover. She breathed its scent of good paper and old glue and the mossy stone note of magic hidden inside it. How could she just give it away?

"It hurts me to hear of your longing for your home. I have never seen the coast of Jy, but I have heard that it is a wonderful place. You are lucky to live in such a place as your childhood's world. I wish I knew more about it."

Her own desires presented as simple sentiment. A counterstep in the dance—proper, polite, passively resisting. She had found the book first. Let Ysbeta try to charm her way past that! Frustration shone in her rival's night-dark eyes, but whatever she would say in reply was cut off by the intrusion of a shop clerk.

He bowed to Ysbeta and Ianthe, touching his forehead as he cast his gaze down. "Welcome to Harriman's. May I be of assistance?"

His Llanandari was very good, probably supported by reading untranslated novels. He smiled at the important couple gracing his shop, then flicked a glance at Beatrice, his lips thin and his nostrils flared.

"Yes," Ysbeta said. "I would like—"

"Thank you for your offer," Ianthe cut in, smiling at the clerk. "Everyone here is so helpful. We are browsing, for the moment."

The clerk clasped his hands in front of him. "Harriman's is committed to quality service, sir. We do not wish you to be troubled by this—person, if she is causing you any discomfort."

"Thank you for your offer," Ianthe said, a little more firmly. "We are quite well, and the lady is not disturbing us."

Ysbeta scowled at Ianthe, but she kept her silence. The clerk gave Beatrice one more forbidding look before moving away.

"I'm sorry about that," Ianthe said, and his smile should not make her heart stutter. "It's clear you both want this book. I propose a solution."

"There is only one copy." Ysbeta raised her delicately pointed chin. "What solution could there be?"

"You could read it together," Ianthe said, clapping his hands together. "Ysbeta can tell you all about the tea-gardens on the mountains and the pearl bay."

Beatrice fought the relieved drop of her shoulders. People would notice Beatrice's friendship with such a powerful family. And to make friends with another sorceress, another woman like her? Beatrice smiled, grateful for Ianthe's suggestion. "I would love to hear about that. Is it true that Jy is home to some of the most beautiful animals in the world?"

"It is true. Have you been away from Chasland, Miss Clayborn?" Ysbeta asked. "Or do you simply dream of travel?"

"I dream to—I dream of travel, but I haven't left my country," Beatrice said. "There are so many wonders—who would not long to float through the water city of Orbos for themselves, to stroll the ivory city of Masillia, or contemplate the garden city of An?"

"An is beautiful," Ianthe said. "Sanchi is a long way from here. You must call on my sister. She was born in the middle of the sea. The horizon has captured her soul. You should be friends. Nothing else will do."

On a ship, he meant, and that last bit made her blink before she realized it was poetic. Beatrice gazed at Ysbeta, who didn't look like she wanted to be Beatrice's friend. "I would like that."

Ysbeta's lips thinned, but her nod set her curls bouncing. "I would too."

"Tomorrow!" Ianthe exclaimed. "Midday repast, and then an afternoon—it's the ideal time for correspondence. Bring your copy book, Miss Clayborn, and we shall have the pleasure of your company."

Access to the book. Friendship with the Lavans. All she had to do was extend her hands to let Ysbeta take the volume from her grasp and watch her grimoire walk away, tucked into the crook of a stranger's elbow, taken from this unordered heap of insignificant novels, saccharine verse, and outdated texts.

She glanced from Ysbeta's dark gaze to Ianthe's merry-eyed humor—he meant for his compromise to be fulfilled. Beatrice sorted through a mental selection of her day gowns. Would they suffice for such company?

This was no time to worry about gowns. She had to tread this situation carefully. She offered the volume to Ysbeta. Once in her hands, Ysbeta offered her only smile, betraying slightly crooked lower front teeth.

"Thank you," she said. "Excuse me for a moment."

They left her standing in the stacks. Ianthe left for the carriage as Ysbeta signed a chit guaranteeing payment on billing, then marched straight for the exit. The bell rang behind her.

Ysbeta had no intention of giving Beatrice an invitation card.

Beatrice had been robbed.

Off in the distance a turquoise enameled landau turned a corner, and as it vanished from sight, the rippling sense of the grimoire faded.

Lost. Stolen! Oh, she would never trust the word of a gentleman again! She had found her chance to be free—drat politeness! She should have refused. She should have said no!

A pair of women stepped around her with clucking tongues. Beatrice hastily moved to the edge of the promenade. She couldn't have said no. That would have gone badly for her family. She was already planning to tarnish the respectable name of the Clayborns with her plans to remain unmarried. That was trouble enough. She couldn't bring more—there was Harriet to think of, after all.

Beatrice's younger sister drew pictures of herself in the green gowns of wedding ceremonies. She read all the novels of women navigating the bargaining season, set in a world that was positively overrun by ministers and earls who fell in love with merchants' daughters—Harriet wanted her fate. Beatrice couldn't destroy her sister's chances.

But the book! How would she find another?

She waited at a street corner for the signal-boy to stop carriage traffic and joined the throng of pedestrians crossing to Silk Row. Large shopwindows featured gowns mounted on dress dummies, wigs on painted wooden heads. Heeled slippers suspended on wires mimicked dancing. She walked past displays and stopped at Tarden and Wallace Modiste.

Tarden and Wallace was the most fashionable modiste in Bendleton, led by its Llanandari proprietress. Its design magazines were printed, bound, and sold to young women who sighed over illustrations of gowns that maximized the beauty of the wearer, with nipped-in waists, low, curving necklines, and luxurious imported fabrics. This shop was the most expensive, and Father had paid for her wardrobe without a murmur.

Beatrice caught herself chewing on her lip. Father would have chosen another modiste if he couldn't pay for this one. He would have.

She pushed open the door and stepped inside.

Everyone turned their attention to her entrance, took in her windblown hair, her dusty hems, and her gloveless hands. Two women, sisters by their identical floral-printed cotton gowns, glanced at each other and covered their mouths, giggling.

Beatrice's face went hot. She hadn't stayed in the carriage, and now she showed the signs of walking along the common promenades. The weight of *A Lady's Book of Manners and Style* balanced invisibly on her head, correcting her posture. She fought the urge to bat dust off her plain tea-dyed skirts.

Clara emerged from a dressing room and smiled. "You'll love everything, Miss Beatrice. Tonight's gown is ready, and I have ordered four more—"

An assistant followed Clara out of the dressing room, carrying a half-finished green gown in her arms, and Beatrice swallowed. That was meant to be her wedding dress. She was supposed to wear it to a temple and be bound in marriage to a moneyed young sorcerer, losing her magic for decades. She averted her gaze and caught Miss Tarden herself staring at the same garment with a sour pinch to her full mouth.

"Miss Beatrice? Did you want to try on your gown?" Miss Tarden asked, her accent rich with cultured Llanandari.

Beatrice stared at the wedding gown with her heart in her throat. "I have another engagement, I'm afraid."

Clara gestured toward the fitting room. "We'll be cutting it close, but we can take a few minutes to—"

"No, that's all right," Beatrice said. "Tell me all about the new gowns on the way to the chapterhouse tearoom."

The sisters glanced at each other in surprise. Beatrice ignored them.

Clara bobbed her knees, hoisting the case in one hand. "It wouldn't do to be late."

Beatrice led the way out of the shop. Clara swung the case as she boarded the fiacre Father had hired for Beatrice. "You didn't buy any books."

Beatrice watched a herd of gentlemen on leggy, long-maned horses ride past, laughing and shouting at one another. They wore embroidery and fine leather riding boots, but no aura shone from their heads. Just young men, then, and not magicians. "The volume I wished to purchase was taken by someone else."

"Oh, Miss Beatrice. I am sorry. I know how you love old books," Clara touched Beatrice's arm, a delicate gesture of comfort. "It'll turn up again. We can write to all the booksellers asking after it, if you like."

Clara didn't understand, of course. Beatrice couldn't tell her maid the truth, no matter how much she liked the slightly older woman. She couldn't tell anyone the truth. Drat Ysbeta Lavan! Couldn't she have turned up just five minutes later?

She had to get that book back in her hands. She had to!

"But now you have tea with your father to look forward to," Clara offered, "and meeting your first young man. Do you suppose Danton Maisonette is handsome?"

Beatrice shrugged. "With a title and the controlling interest in Valserre's biggest capital investment firm, he doesn't have to be."

"Oh, Miss Beatrice. I know you're not concerned with the weight of his pockets! Leave that to Mr. Clayborn. It's his worry, after all. Now, what do you hope? That he's handsome? That he's intelligent?"

"That he's honest."

Clara considered this with a thoughtful frown. "Sometimes honesty is a knife, Miss Beatrice. But here we are!"

Beatrice had been trying to ignore their approach to the chapterhouse. The carriage stopped in front of the building that dominated the south end of the square it presided over, its shadow cast over the street.

The Bendleton chapterhouse was the newest one built in Chasland, with a soaring bell tower and matching spires. Its face was polished gray stone. The windows sparkled with colored glass. Beatrice stood on the promenade, glaring at the building as if it were her nemesis.

She glared at the heart of social life and education for mages all over the world, the exclusive center of men's power and men's influence denied to women like her. Even when she was finally permitted to practice magic in her advanced years, the chapterhouse had no place for her. She was permitted—when escorted by a man who was a member—to enter the gallery and the teahouse, and no farther.

Boys aged ten to eighteen sheltered within, learning mathematics and history alongside ritual procedure and sorcerous technique. Full members shared trade secrets with their brothers, decided laws before they even reached the Ministry, and improved their lot through their magical skill and fraternal vows.

The chapterhouse held facilities for crafting and artificing, suitably appointed ritual rooms, even apartments where brothers of the chapter could claim hospitality. Thousands of books of magic rested in the scriptorium, written in Mizunh, the secret language of spirits. Centuries of tradition, of restriction, of exclusion were built into the very stones of this building—Beatrice stared at her nemesis, indeed.

"Don't scowl so, Miss Beatrice. You can't ruin this with every feeling that flits across your face," Clara urged. "Smile."

Beatrice stretched her lips and made her cheeks plump.

"With feeling. Think of something pleasant. Imagine doing something wonderful."

Beatrice imagined that she had a right to every inch of the chapterhouse, that she and her greater spirit would be known scholars of the mysteries. That gentlemen smiled at her not because she was beautiful, but because she was respected, and girls hurried from one lecture hall to another, openly studying the art and science of high magic. She thought of the world she wanted and remembered her posture.

She smiled as if the chapterhouse were her friend.

"That's much better!" Clara praised. "I'll take these gowns home, as you will be returning with your father. Good luck!"

"Thank you," Beatrice said, and set her path for the tall double doors.

Cool and dim, the arched ceiling of the grand foyer picked up her footsteps and flung the sound across the room purposed as the display of the ingenue's gallery. Vases of costly flowers stood next to fourteen painted canvases, their scents mingling with the clean, cool stone of the hall. Beatrice walked toward the portrait of Ysbeta Lavan, stunning and vibrant in a gown of deep turquoise, her hand outstretched to catch a topaz blue butterfly attracted to the lush, drooping blooms of the perfume tree in the background. A jeweled diadem held back her light-as-air crown of tightly curled hair. She dominated the room with her splendor and beauty; her portrait hung in the principal position in the center of the room. Empty spaces flanked her image as if nothing and no one could compare.

Beatrice's own painting was in a dim corner next to a couple of girls who were plain-faced, but still obviously wealthy. She had sat in velvet, and the painter had captured both the soft glow of the fabric and the unfashionable puffed sleeves on her gown. She held her violon across her lap.

She barely remembered the smell of linseed oil and the cursed dust in the air making her want to sneeze. Or the incredible boredom of having to sit very still with nothing to occupy her mind but the desperate desire to scratch an itch. But most of all Beatrice remembered the peculiar feeling of being so thoroughly examined while the truth of her remained invisible as the artist from Gravesford painted her.

It could have been interesting. He had been on fire to paint Beatrice with a rifle after he met her carrying one tucked in the crook of her elbow after a morning ride through the wood. Beatrice tried to explain she only had the rifle due to the dangers of encountering wild boar, forest manxes, and even the occasional bear, but the painter was too enamored with his vision. Father ended the painter's inspiration by threatening to send him home without pay.

If only he'd gotten his way. The canvas Beatrice was exactly what a viewer would expect. She ought to have carried a rifle under her arm—or a pistol, dangled from one hand while she slouched in her seat like a gentleman at ease. Something to show that she was a person, anything to show that she was something more than what people expected of a woman: ornament, and trained silence.

"Starborn gods, what an aura. You must be Beatrice," a voice in accented Llanandari said.

She turned and regarded a young man who must have been—"Danton Maisonette. Good afternoon. Have you seen the new chapterhouse?"

"They're all new, in Chasland," Danton said with a dismissive little sniff. "Valserre's been part of the brotherhood for seven hundred years. Chasland is running itself to tatters, trying to keep up with the better nations."

Beatrice pressed her lips together at the string of slights and insults. "It's not to your standard, then?"

He glanced up to the stone, laid with all the skill of Chasland's masons, and dismissed it with a shrug. "It's the latest style. Chaslanders are all gold and no taste."

Beatrice had to search for a hold on her temper and the right words. "Then what would you have done? Valserrans are known for their—knowledge of beauty."

"Aesthetics," Danton corrected. "Building in an earlier style would have been pretending to a legacy that doesn't exist here, come to think of it. But chapterhouses ought to have gravity. They should be timeless, rather than fashionable."

Beatrice searched for the right words, but Danton filled the silence for her. "Though the quality of the sound in the working rooms is startlingly good."

"That would be thanks to the builders," Beatrice said. "The designer was a Hadfield, the family who build holy sanctums for generations."

"Built," Danton corrected her Llanandari once more. "You all sing to the gods for worship. It must sound impressive at Long Night. Can you sing, then?"

"I have trained," Beatrice began, "like any Chaslander lady."

Danton's mouth turned impatient. "But are you any

good?"

This rude . . . oaf! The arrogance! Beatrice lifted her chin. "Yes."

"You're rather sure of yourself." He contemplated her for a moment. "But I believe you."

He turned his head, taking in the sight of Ysbeta Lavan's portrait, then back to her.

Danton Maisonette was scarcely taller than her, but his brown coat and buff-colored weskit were satin-woven Llanandras cotton, well made and embroidered in tasteful geometric patterns. He was handsome enough, but his thin little mouth clamped up so tight Beatrice couldn't imagine a kind word escaping it. He stood with an upright, chest-forward posture, his bearing reminding Beatrice of a soldier—which made sense. As a Valserran heir to a marquessate, he was expected to take a high position in that nation's army. His hooded eyes were a watery blue, and he had a direct, pointed stare.

Or perhaps it was just that he was staring at her. He examined her so completely it made Beatrice's stomach shiver. When he turned his chin to compare what he'd seen to the portrait Beatrice on the wall, Beatrice seethed behind a smile that matched the demure curve depicted on the canvas.

"You really are pretty," he said. "Too many redheads look like they're made of spotty chalk."

"Thank you." That wasn't what she wanted to say at all, but she promised Father she'd be kind. If only someone had made Danton promise the same. Her wish for honesty had been answered. She hadn't expected to be treated like a clockwork figurine, incapable of being insulted by whatever thought flitted from Danton Maisonette's mind to his lips.

"This meeting's going to be boring talk. Trade and investment. Did you bring handwork to amuse yourself?"

If only she could widen her eyes. If only she could drop

her jaw. But she smiled, smiled, smiled at this rude, demanding man. "I'm afraid I don't have anything with me."

One side of his mouth turned down as he said, "I had an interest in joining the conversation."

Instead of the labor of keeping her amused, since she hadn't brought a lace hook, Beatrice kept her smile up and asked, "Have you seen the chapterhouse gallery?"

"The only thing that's new is the ingenues," he said, leaving the hint to escort her through the gallery gasping on the floor. "Only fourteen of you this year. Private negotiations are becoming too popular."

Beatrice blinked and cocked her head, and Danton knew an opportunity to explain when he saw one. "People are arranging marriages outside of bargaining season. Ha! Chasland's number one export, since you all have children by the bushel. Most of the best-bred ladies are already bound. Where are you from, that you don't know this?"

Ladies do not strike people. Even rude, insufferable churls. "Mayhurst."

His eyebrows went up. "The north country," he said in titillated horror. "That's practically the hinterlands. Have you ever been to Gravesford?"

No. Not this man. It didn't matter that he was heir to a marquis. She would not marry him and travel to distant Valserre, far from her family, to become his wife—indeed, she would not spend an unnecessary minute in his presence. "We traveled there before coming to Bendleton."

"For your wardrobe, I imagine." He took in her walking suit and shrugged. "I don't think you have much need for fine-woven Llanandras cotton when you're outrunning boars."

"Oh, we have rifles." Beatrice realized what she'd said, but too late.

He stared at her, aghast. "You shoot?"

"I am good at it," Beatrice said, and at last her smile had some real feeling in it.

"I see," Danton said. "How perfectly ferocious of you. We should have tea. Do you have tea, in the country?"

Beatrice coated her grin with sugar and arsenic. "When it comes to us. By dogsled, one hundred miles in the snow."

"Really?"

Beatrice's smile widened. "No. There's at least six ports up north."

Now he didn't like her at all. Perfect.

Beatrice glided beside him as he took her to the tearoom. She smiled prettily at the marquis and took her seat, ignoring the hired musician toiling over a piano sonata to pay attention to the talk of trade and investment Danton had promised would bore her. She asked questions and ruined her genteel display of curiosity with remarks of her own. Father bore it well, but he frowned at her once they bid the Marquis and his son farewell and boarded the landau hired to take them back to Triumph Street.

Father settled on the bench across from her and sighed. Beatrice's heart sank as Father, handsome in brown cotton, even if the jacket and weskit bore a minimum of adorning needlework, gave her a look that deepened the worry lines across his forehead, his mouth open as if he were about to say something. But he glanced away, shaking his head sadly.

"Father, I'm sorry."

Beatrice had a decent guess what she was supposed to be sorry for, but Father would fully inform her soon enough. She waited for the inevitable response, and Father gave it with a pained expression. "Beatrice, do you realize how important it is for you to be agreeable to the young men you meet while we're here?"

"Father, he was awful. Snobbish and arrogant. If I had to marry that man we'd square off from morning 'til night."

Father ran a hand over his sandy, silver-shot curls, and they tumbled back in place, framing his fine features, lined by experience and too many burdens, including her willful self. "That perfectly awful young man will be a marquis."

"Marquis de Awful, then. I couldn't be happy with him, not for a minute."

"I had hoped you would be less difficult," Father said. "This meeting was a special arrangement. And you told him you knew how to shoot? What possessed you?"

"It just slipped out. And I apologize. But he laughed at me for being from the country, and assumed me an ignorant fool, as if Chaslanders didn't have an education of any kind."

"I probably should have sent you to a ladies' academy abroad," Father sighed. "Too late now, though perhaps Harriet could enter a finishing school."

Paid for with the financial support of Beatrice's husband. "Harriet would adore that."

"If we can manage it, she will go. But there are only fourteen of you." He brightened at the notion of a brides' market, and the number of young men who would crowd around Beatrice simply because she was one of only a few ingenues left to woo. "But if you'd kept him on your string . . ."

"There are more young men where he came from," Beatrice said. With luck, she'd alienate them all. And then she needed more luck, to get the grimoire in her hands once more—

The thought clanged in her mind like a bell. She could get the book back. She knew exactly how. Excitement surged in her, filling her with the urge to leap from the landau and run faster than the showy black horses could trot. She clasped her hands and fought to appear attentive as Father chided her.

"It's not that I want you to marry a man you can't abide,

Beatrice. Just—try, will you? Try not to judge them hastily."

Beatrice nodded, but her mind was already consumed by her plan. "Yes, Father. I will try harder next time."

She watched the tree-lined streets of Bendleton, hazed green with new spring buds and heavy with sweet blooming flowers, and couldn't wait to get home.